Praise for Kristin Hannah

BETWEEN SISTERS

"Enormously entertaining . . . Hannah has a nice ear for dialogue and a knack for getting the reader inside the characters' heads."

—*The Seattle Times*

DISTANT SHORES

"In fast-moving prose punctuated by snappy asides, Hannah examines whether love and commitment are enough to sustain a marriage."

—*People*

SUMMER ISLAND

"An emotionally intense exploration of mothers and daughters."

—*Houston Chronicle*

ANGEL FALLS

"An all-night-reading affair—you won't be able to put it down."

—*The New York Post*

By Kristin Hannah
Published by Ballantine Books

KRISTIN HANNAH

IF YOU BELIEVE

BALLANTINE BOOKS • NEW YORK

A Ballantine Book
Published by The Random House Publishing Group

Copyright © 1993 by Kristin Hannah

All rights reserved under International and Pan-American Copyright Conventions. Published in the United States by The Random House Publishing Group, a division of Random House, Inc., New York, and simultaneously in Canada by Random House of Canada Limited, Toronto.

www.ballantinebooks.com

Ballantine and colophon are registered trademarks of Random House, Inc.

ISBN 0-345-46710-8

Manufactured in the United States of America

First Edition: January 1994

OPM 10 9 8 7 6 5 4 3 2 1

To Elisa Wares, Rob Cohen, and Megan Chance, who always believe in me.

Special thanks . . .

 Lori Adams, for a truly great idea. Maybe next time . . .
Vicki McClellan and the fabulous Seven Hills Winery.
Jill Marie Landis, and Jill Barnett for knowing just what
to say. Always.

Prologue

JULY 1894
SOMEWHERE IN TEXAS

Mad Dog took the first punch. A hard-knuckled right to the chin that sent him stumbling back against the ropes. The sharp, metallic taste of blood filled his mouth.

A roar of approval swept through the crowd.

He shook his head and blinked. His vision cleared. The crowd stared back at him. Hundreds of upturned faces, circlets of pale pink against a sea of drab, dark clothing.

They whispered in anticipation. He closed his eyes, listening, knowing what would follow. Waiting for it, needing it.

It started slowly, tentatively, a single voice, a single pair of clapping hands. One person joined in, then another and another, until the hot, dry Texas air became a living, breathing monster of enthusiastic sound. A pulsing chant of voices raised in unison. *"Mad Dog, Mad Dog, Mad Dog . . ."*

Adrenaline coursed through his body, made his breathing quicken. God, he loved this.

He pushed himself away from the ropes and sauntered toward the center of the makeshift ring. An expectant hush fell over the fairgrounds.

He backhanded the trickle of blood from his mouth and gave his opponent a slow, lazy grin. The same devil-may-care, you-haven't-hurt-me smile he'd given a thousand times before. "That the best you got, Sue?"

The huge, hairy man glared at him. His ham-sized hands balled into dangerous fists. "Name's Stew, you two-bit piece o' shit."

"Stew? As in Stewart?" Mad Dog glanced at the spectators. As if on cue, they leaned slightly toward him, waiting . . . waiting.

"Well, hell," he drawled, "with that punch, I figured your name was Susan for sure."

The crowd burst into laughter.

"You arrogant bastard—" Stew lunged forward.

Mad Dog skipped to the left, ducked, and spun back.

Stew stumbled to a stop and looked around, confusion wrinkling his heavy face.

"Oh, Stew . . ." Mad Dog taunted.

Stew turned toward the sound.

Mad Dog punched him. Hard.

Stew staggered back against the ropes, clutching them for support.

Mad Dog glanced down at his fist and shook his head. "Damn, that hurts, don't it, Sue?"

A ripple of laughter, punctuated by applause, worked through the crowd.

"Why, you . . ." Stew launched himself off the ropes and barreled toward Mad Dog.

Mad Dog braced himself, his lazy grin faded. He

waited a tense second, then slammed his fist into Stew's jaw. Bone hit bone in a grinding, crunching *smack*.

Stew exhaled in a booze-scented grunt of pain. A look of almost comical disbelief crossed his fleshy features before he pitched, face-first, into the dirt.

The mob roared with approval.

Mad Dog looked up from Stew's prone body and grinned at the swarm of sweaty humanity gathered around the ropes. He raised his right hand and made a fist in the air. Then he grabbed a towel and wiped his face.

He felt an arm curl around him, yanking him close. "You done good, kid. Like always," said a gravelly, tobacco-fed voice.

Mad Dog slowly lowered the towel from his face. Sneaky Joe, the fight's promoter, grinned up at him through watery gray eyes.

"Thanks, Joe." Mad Dog tossed his towel into the corner and patted Joe's humped back. "Where's my cut?"

"Right here." Joe dug deep in his ratty pocket and pulled out a wad of bills. "One hundred and fifty-two dollars. Should last you till next season. If you're careful."

Mad Dog pocketed the money without bothering to count it. "When have you ever known me to be careful?"

Joe laughed. "Never."

Mad Dog went to the corner of the ring and picked up his Stetson, clothes bag, boots, and a bottle of tequila. Everything he owned in the world.

Tearing off the cork, he took a long, satisfying gulp

of tequila and wiped the dribble from his unshaven chin and drooping mustache.

Joe scurried up behind him, moving as quickly as his misshapen body would allow. "See you at Rochester in May?"

Mad Dog took another long, slow swallow and smiled. Rochester was the first fight of the season—and his favorite. There was a particularly pretty widow in town. He'd been in Rochester every May for sixteen years. It was as close to a commitment as he'd ever made. "What'd stop me?"

Joe glanced back at the still unconscious, spread-eagle body of Stewart Redman. "Not him for damn sure."

Mad Dog slowed. "That reminds me, Joe. About the talent you been finding to fight me . . ."

Joe winced. "Yeah?"

"They're perfect. Keep it up."

Joe grinned. "I'll check the veteran's home in Rochester."

"You do that." Mad Dog's gaze strayed to the thinning crowd. Paper and debris littered the brown, scorched grass. The yellow-hot sun streamed through the fairgrounds, silhouetting the retreating crowd. Multicolored tents dotted the field. From somewhere came the musical sound of laughter.

It took him only a second to find her. She stood apart from the rest of the spectators, facing the ring instead of turned away from it. Long, curly blond hair framed her pale face and veiled her arms, its outline gilded by the sunshine. A scandalously low neckline showcased her considerable charms—charms Mad Dog remembered from his last time through town.

A smile curved his mouth. He loved to have a pretty woman waiting for him after a fight—even if he couldn't remember her name. He waved at her. She waved back, and started walking toward him, her movements slow and seductive.

Mad Dog slung the clothes bag over his shoulder and put on his hat and boots. "Gotta run, Joe. See ya next year."

Joe chuckled. "You're gonna spend all that money tonight, ain't ya?"

Mad Dog vaulted over the ropes and dropped onto the crisp grass. The woman ran over and threw her arms around him, hugging him with abandon.

He closed his eyes. God, she smelled good. Like hot, sexy nights in a featherbed. Like passion.

He loved women, all women, but especially the easy, alley-cat types who showed up for his fights. They cost him, but it was worth it. They laughed with him, kissed him, and undressed for him with ease—his money ensured it. And when he left, they waved good-bye with a smile. Just the way he liked it.

He grinned down into her beguiling, promise-laden blue eyes. Suddenly, fleetingly, he wished he remembered her name—it was Susannah or Sunshine . . . something that started with an *S*, but he couldn't for the life of him recall what. Not that it mattered, of course. She didn't expect him to remember it. That was the beauty of women like her. They didn't expect anything except gold coins and heavy breathing.

"Mad Dog?" She purred his name in a practiced, seductive voice that stirred all the hard, wet memories it was intended to. "You going to stand around here all day?"

He glanced down at the creamy swell of cleavage and pulled her even closer. "Not a chance, darlin'," he whispered against her small, soft ear. "Not a chance."

Chapter One

**WASHINGTON STATE
SEPTEMBER 1894**

Mad Dog leaned back against the shuddering wall of the box car. The article he was writing about homelessness lay beside him, forgotten for the moment. Wind clawed his face and raked his hair, curling the papery edges of his notebook. The metallic clackety-clack of the iron wheels vibrated up and down his spine.

Two short blasts of sound rose above the clattering of the train. The piercing wail hovered momentarily in the air, then melted into the puffing chugs of steam and disappeared. Wheels locked with a clanging screech.

Another town. The words carried with them the familiar magic, the seductive allure of unopened gifts.

He reached for his clothes bag. It was slumped in the corner of the boxcar, the patched, grayed fabric caved in on itself. There was next to nothing inside—just a faded change of clothes, a bedroll, and a few notebooks—but it was everything Mad Dog had. Everything he needed.

Except food and money.

He shook his head. It was too bad he hadn't saved

something from that last fight. Just enough to get him a place in Mexico, a few bottles of tequila, and a willing woman to keep him warm through the winter . . .

Winter.

He thumped his head back against the corrugated metal wall and closed his eyes. Christ, he hated that word. It was one of the few things that actually depressed him.

It was still autumn; almost an Indian summer, in fact. But yesterday's warm sun didn't fool him. He'd been drifting across this country for too long to be fooled by Mother Nature.

Winter was coming. Winter, when the world was cold, the fields were fallow, and work was impossible to find. Winter. The season when homeless, unemployed vagrants like Mad Dog were found dead by the side of the road and thrown in markerless paupers' graves by lawmen who didn't know what it felt like to be footloose and carefree . . . or alone and hungry and filled with despair.

He had to find work now, during harvest, while there was work to be found. There would be no more fairs until late spring, no way for his fists to earn the money he needed. He had no choice but to get a real job.

Shit . . .

The train whistle blew again, three short, sharp blasts.

Mad Dog stuffed a half-finished editorial into his canvas bag and staggered to his feet. Standing in the open doorway, he stared at the blurred brown landscape. Particles of wind-driven dirt stung his eyes, turned into a gritty paste on his tongue. He rammed his battered Stetson on his head and jumped.

He landed hard. Pain ricocheted up his legs and throbbed in his knees. He groaned and staggered to his feet, brushing the dust from his Levi's.

Goddamn, sometimes it hurt to be free.

He walked to the fringe of a town called Lonesome Creek and stopped. Green fields fanned toward the horizon like a huge patchwork quilt, the color grafted by irrigation to a brown prairie that rolled into forever. In the distance, bluish gray hills rose into a sky so blue, it hurt the eyes.

A cold, early morning draft buffeted his stubbly cheeks and pulled at his long, unkempt mustache. He crammed his hands in his pockets, trying to find some meager warmth in the holey interiors.

The town was practically empty this early in the morning, which was just as well. He'd learned long ago that respectable citizens didn't cotton to vagrants like him. They didn't understand a man who didn't want a white picket fence to trap him in or a steady job to pay his bills.

They wanted the world to be clean, respectable, predictable.

He didn't blame them or judge them. Fact was, he didn't even think about them. He just walked past them, saying nothing, and slipped into the rum-soaked, lively part of town they denied existed. The part wreathed in shadows, punctuated by laughter and drowned in rotgut whiskey. The part where people had fun.

He tucked his chin into the fraying collar of his oilskin coat and strolled casually toward town. The wide dirt road rolled over a tiny rise, then melted into Main

Street. Rows of false-fronted clapboard buildings lined the street on either side, their doorways linked by a wide wooden boardwalk. A few well-dressed people strolled from store to store, talking quietly among themselves.

A sign stood out from all the rest, grabbing Mad Dog's attention. MA'S DINER.

Smiling, he reslung the pack over his shoulder and stepped up onto the boardwalk, pushing through the diner's slatted wooden doors. The mouth-watering aroma of baking cinnamon buns and frying bacon greeted him, made his stomach grumble loudly.

He moved cautiously forward, eyeing the place. The tablecloths were clean and pressed, a bright red and white check that bespoke Sunday suppers and family gatherings. Dust-free globed lamps hung at regular intervals from the dark wooden beams, casting pockets of light along the oak floorboards.

Ma's place was neat, respectable, and profitable. In short, a disaster. Odds were equal or better that he'd be thrown out within moments. He had to get to the job board fast.

Mad Dog hurried toward the corner of the restaurant and squinted up at the weathered scraps of paper that were tacked to the wood-planked wall. The ads were just what he expected; the sort of ads he'd been reading and answering for fifteen years. *Apple picker wanted, work hard but steady; Hay baler needs part-time help, no drinkers, no women; Sutton ranch needs general hand to dig irrigation ditches—top dollar paid.*

He scanned the words without much interest. He was just about to close his eyes and pick one when a phrase caught his attention. His gaze ricocheted back to the ad at the far right. The paper was curled and yellowed by the sun, as if it had been there a long time. Cautiously, almost afraid that it would vanish at his touch, he smoothed the paper and began to read.

General handyman needed for small orchard. Room, board, and minimal wages provided in exchange for manual labor. Good food and clean sheets available. Inquiries should be directed to Professor Erasmus Throckmorton, Epoch Farm, corner of Palouse and Mesozoic streets. P.S. Good conversation skills a plus.

He grinned just thinking about clean sheets. And if there was one thing he could do, it was talk.

Hell, it was a job made in heaven.

He plucked the scrap of paper off the job board and crammed it in his pocket, then headed out of the diner. It was a long, hot walk out of town, but Mad Dog hardly noticed.

All he could think about were those damn clean sheets.

Jacob Vanderstay saw Mad Dog coming and he panicked. He'd followed too closely this time, he knew it. *Darn!*

He slammed his rail-thin, adolescent body against the splintery side of Harriman's Mercantile and jerked the hat down over his eyes, trying desperately to be invisible. Blood pounded in his ears like an oncoming train. He held his breath and prayed like crazy. *Please don't let him catch me. Please ...*

Mad Dog strode past him without so much as a glance.

Jake sagged against the wall, feeling equal measures of relief and disappointment.

Mad Dog hadn't seen him . . . again.

With a sigh, he pushed away from the wall and shoved the hat back on his head. He scratched his sweaty forehead with dirt-caked fingernails and shoved a hank of coppery hair out of his eyes. Gosh, he was tired of this. Tired of skulking around in the shadows, eating disgusting food, sleeping on the cold, hard ground. He just wanted it to be over.

But it wouldn't be over until he confronted Mad Dog. And he was no closer to doing that than he had been four months ago when he'd first started trailing the man.

He waited awhile, let Mad Dog get a good distance ahead, then Jake flung his sack over his shoulder and followed him out of town.

Mariah Throckmorton stood back from her work, studying it critically. The shelves above her father's oak desk glistened with beeswax. Stark, white piles of paper created a perfectly ordered checkerboard atop the dark wood. In the exact center of the desk sat a crystal ink-stand and pen rack and the Eureka Ink Eradicator. Fossils lined the shelves, their sharpest points peering over the edge like a hundred tiny noses. Everything was perfectly in order.

But somehow she was certain she could do it better, do *something* to make her father actually notice what she'd done. . . .

She sighed. It would never happen. Her father wouldn't care, of course, wouldn't even notice how hard she'd worked to keep his collection dusted, cleaned, and in perfect array. But it was something her mother had done for him, and now that she was gone, the task of keeping Rass organized fell to Mariah. And with her father's whimsical, impractical nature, it was a considerable task indeed.

She tried to tell herself it didn't matter that Rass wouldn't notice her efforts. It shouldn't. She was thirty-four years old. How could she *still* be trying to impress a father who clearly didn't care to be impressed?

She moved back to the desk and pulled out the long drawer. Dozens of ragged erasers lay in a clumped heap. She removed each one and carefully began restacking them in the front left corner.

As she was setting the final eraser in place, she heard a faint, faraway rasping sound, like the creaking of an old man's joints. It came from the open window.

The eraser slipped from her fingers and landed with a muffled *thwop*. She closed the drawer with her hip and walked over to the window, pushing the white eyelet curtains aside.

At first glance, everything looked exactly as it should. The vegetable garden was a patch of green-studded brown earth alongside the springhouse. Fruit trees marched across the pasture in a dozen perfect rows toward the barbed-wire fence line, their symmetry broken only by a weathered wooden barn and a few outbuildings. A neat, white picket fence outlined the well-tended perimeter of the grassy, flower-edged yard. Just inside the gate, her father was crouched in the dirt, digging for fossils.

Suddenly a man emerged from the leafy umbrella of an apple tree and moved toward her father.

Mariah gasped. Her hands came up and pressed against the glass. A strangled sound escaped her throat.

She spun away from the window and did what any self-respecting spinster would do when confronted with a strange man on her property. She went for her shotgun.

Mad Dog stood beneath the fragrant canopy of an apple tree, shrouded by low-hanging boughs. Every now and then a breeze came through, rustling the leaves and releasing the delicate scent of fruit. He pushed the battered Stetson higher on his forehead and peered through the leaves.

It was a quiet, well-tended little farm. In the exact center, at the end of a flower-trimmed gravel path, sat a boxy, two-story white farmhouse with a curlicued overhang that shaded a homey porch. Evenly spaced pillars, twined with dead vines, connected the roof to the porch floor, and bunches of drying flowers hung from the white railing. A swing creaked slowly back and forth, touched by the invisible hand of a late afternoon breeze. Everything about the house declared itself a home.

He felt a stirring of discomfort. This wasn't his kind of place at all. Somewhere in this dusty little town was the sort of place Mad Dog belonged. A room filled with the same hard-drinking, hard-hitting, homeless men he met on the line. He could always find that room, no matter what town he crawled into. A broken-down farm on the edge of town, a crew of losers digging ditches, an itinerant group of shearers. Somehow they all found one another in the dark underside of small-town life, all congregated in the dirty gutters.

That's the kind of place he felt comfortable, the kind of job he usually took.

But they didn't have clean sheets.

Just the thought made him smile again.

"What did you say, Greta?"

Mad Dog peered through the leaves again. This time he noticed an old man, digging in the dirt not more than forty feet away. The man was hunched over, his clawlike, big-knuckled hands wrapped around a small spade. Thin strands of cottony hair curled along his liver-spotted scalp. A ratty muslin shirt hung from his small shoulders and hugged his sunken chest. Sweat glistened on the sparce white hairs that stuck up from his open collar.

"Rather birdlike," the old man muttered. "What do you think, Greta?"

Mad Dog glanced around. The meticulously tended yard was empty except for the old man. "Are you looking for someone?" he asked.

The old man's head came up with a snap. He saw Mad Dog and blinked in surprise. "Who are you?"

He moved toward the old man, his hand outstretched in greeting. "Folks call me Mad Dog."

The man squinted up at him. "Injun?"

Mad Dog bit back a smile. *Yeah, I'm a blond-haired, gray-eyed Indian. There's a million of us.* "Fighter."

The man nodded as if he understood, which Mad Dog was certain he didn't. He set down his spade and got to his feet. His tired joints creaked in protest. "I'm Professor Erasmus Throckmorton." He shook Mad

Dog's hand. "You can call me Rass. What can I do for you?"

"I'm here for the handyman position."

Rass frowned. Thick white eyebrows veed owl-like above startlingly blue eyes. "Really? You want the job?"

Mad Dog shrugged. "I'd take it for a while."

Rass nodded slowly, eyeing Mad Dog with an unnerving intensity. "This is a surprise. . . . I'm not quite sure . . ."

"You did place an ad, didn't you?"

"Uh-hummm," he answered, blinking up at Mad Dog.

Mad Dog didn't feel a stitch of discomfort. He was used to being sized up by employers. How he fared usually depended on how desperate they were. Only desperate men hired Mad Dog Stone.

"You got a wife?"

Mad Dog laughed. "Nope."

Rass was still frowning. "The job pays eight dollars a week plus room and board. That's probably not enough. . . ."

Mad Dog grinned. "That'll be just fine."

"Oh." Almost reluctantly, Rass turned toward the house. "Follow me."

They walked side by side down the manicured path. When they were almost at the house, Rass dropped his spade in the dirt.

Mad Dog reached down for it.

Rass stopped him. "Don't bother. I leave my stuff laying around. It gives my daughter something to do."

Mad Dog paused. "Your daughter?"

From somewhere inside the house came a shrieking *"Rass!"* and then thundering footsteps.

Rass sighed. "That'll be her, coming to save me."

"Why—"

The front door swung open and slammed against the wall. Something tall and brown hurtled through the open door. There was a high-pitched scream, a glint of silver.

Mad Dog reached for Rass to protect him.

"Don't you touch him!" the brown thing screeched.

Before Mad Dog could answer, something cracked into the side of his head. It was the hardest damn punch he'd ever taken. Pain exploded behind his eyes. He weaved unsteadily for a moment, then pitched to the ground.

He lay sprawled in the damp grass. There was a moment of excruciating pain and then an envelope of soothing darkness.

When he came to, he was alone.

Chapter Two

"Are you *mad*?"

Rass held up his gnarled hands. "Now, Mariah—"

She whirled on him. "You walk in here, calm as can be, and tell me you hired that . . ." She glanced through the open door and saw the man, still sprawled in her prized purple dahlias. He was up on his elbows now, brushing a greasy lock of hair from his eyes. His gaze was glassy and unfocused, but soon that would change, and he would look this way. Mariah shuddered at the thought.

She fought to remain calm. "You hire that . . . person to help me out around the farm, and I'm supposed to be *happy* about it?"

Rass sighed tiredly. "It's been a long time since I expected you to be happy, Mariah."

Mariah felt a tiny catch in her heart, a snag of sadness. Why? she wondered for the millionth time. Why did everything her father say to her have to hurt so badly?

She'd worked hard to run this farm, damn it. Worked as hard as any man, and she'd done a good job. But even that wasn't good enough for Rass. He'd gone behind her back and hired someone to replace her.

It was all she had to offer her father, all she did well. And now he was taking it away, telling her again that she wasn't good enough. . . .

"I won't let him stay," she said.

Rass shuffled toward her, his blue eyes swimming in sadness. "We've been alone here too long, Mariah."

She backed away from him, afraid suddenly to meet his gaze. She knew what he was going to say next and she didn't want to hear it. "It hasn't been that long. . . ."

"Mama's gone. You've got to get on with your life."

His words hit her like a slap. "I won't have it," she said, curling her hands into fists. "I won't let you bring that stranger into my home."

"It's my home."

Mariah flinched at the quietly spoken words. She'd lost. Her father had hired the man, and Rass wouldn't change his mind. Sometime, somehow, she'd done something wrong, something to make Rass think she was incapable of caring for their home. The realization filled her with a familiar, sinking feeling in the pit of her stomach.

God, she tried so hard to be perfect, to make Rass proud of her and atone for the shame of her past. Why didn't it ever work?

"Look at him."

She stiffened. "Absolutely not."

"Look at him. Please," Rass pleaded.

Reluctantly she turned toward the open kitchen door and looked at the man outside. The stranger was sitting up now, apparently trying to focus. His clothes were old and ragged and filthy. She could smell him from here.

He was younger than she'd first thought—perhaps

thirty-five or six. But worn for his years. There was a sinewy leanness to his face that bespoke long, lonely roads and too much alcohol. A bushy, drooping brown mustache obscured his mouth and blended into a fuzzy stubble of new beard that fanned down his neck. He obviously hadn't shaved in days.

His hair was ragged and too long, streaked by a hot sun to the color of wheat. The frayed, once white collar of his shirt hung open to reveal a dark, hairy chest.

The sight of it resurrected a hundred forbidden images, a thousand buried longings. Mariah's mouth went dry. A tiny pulse at the base of her throat throbbed.

"Like what you see, lady?"

Mariah's gaze jerked back to his face, and she found herself plunged into a pair of pewter gray eyes. His gaze locked with hers, dared her to look away. His eyes were focused and hard, with a bone-rattling intensity that cut through her self-control. He had Stephen's eyes.

Her breath caught. She wanted to look away, ached to look away. But his gaze held her in a perverse, velvet grip. Fear pressed in on her.

Calm down, Mariah. Don't let him do this to you.

She let her breath out in a steady stream and closed her eyes, silently counting to five. When she felt better, she let herself look at him again.

She was wrong. His eyes weren't familiar. Stephen's had been warm and brown and filled with easy laughter; the stranger's were cold and gray. It was simply the *look* in the eyes that was familiar.

Uncommitted. Alone. The eyes of a man who never stayed in one place too long.

Her irrational fear turned to disgust. He was everything she despised in a man. A shiftless, lazy loser. The kind who'd attracted her once—when she was a starry-eyed girl—but never would again.

"Trust me," Rass said quietly.

"Fine, Rass. I'll trust you." She spat the words out, then shot a last glance at the stranger. "But I won't trust him."

Mad Dog touched the bruise that was already forming at his jaw. *Christ, what had the schoolmarm hit him with? A pickax?* Then he remembered. The brown blur had smashed the butt of her shotgun into his jaw.

Shaking his head to clear it, he tried to get to his feet. His first effort was a wobbly failure. He sank back into the plants, smashing another row of purple blossoms. The sickly-sweet scent of the flowers clogged his nostrils and brought a burst of nausea.

He was gonna puke. Shit . . .

Squeezing his eyes shut, he clutched his gut and tried to will the nausea to pass.

"You all right?"

Mad Dog opened his eyes. Rass was standing close, peering down with a fatherly smile on his wrinkled face.

He forced a smile. "Never better."

Rass kneeled and held out a handkerchief. "Here."

Mad Dog eyed the embroidered scrap of linen. It was the size of a postcard. Rass had obviously never been coldcocked. "That should help."

Rass frowned for a moment, then brightened as if at a sudden inspiration. "Get the man a steak, Mariah."

"I will not. He can wait until supper to eat."

"It's not to eat," the old man answered. "It's for the swelling."

The woman in the doorway didn't move. Mad Dog pushed himself up on his elbows to see her better. His vision was still slightly blurry, but what he could see was discouraging. She looked like a tall, disapproving owl. From the tip of her carefully coiled hair to the pointed toes of her sensible shoes, she was entirely brown. Brown hair, brown eyes, brown dress, brown apron.

She stood as stiff and unforgiving as a statue. Head held high, arms crossed, mouth pinched, she watched him study her. She had a face that looked as if it had been carved from stone. No laugh lines pleated the flesh around her eyes or bracketed her pursed lips. When his gaze finally reached her eyes, he was surprised by the hot emotion in her gaze. "It's not polite to stare," she said curtly. "I see your manners are as exemplary as your dress."

Mad Dog shrugged. "As are yours."

"Mariah," Rass said sharply. "Get the man a steak. It's the least you can do after you knocked him out."

The woman called Mariah snorted. For a second Mad Dog thought she was going to ignore her father. Then, with a defiant snap of her dull brown skirts, she turned and went into the house.

Rass gave Mad Dog an apologetic shrug. "She's rather . . ."

Rude? Dim-witted? Battle-trained?

"Headstrong," Rass finished. Then, slowly, he got to his feet. "I'll go get you some Purola Sizz. You're going to have a hell of a headache later on."

Mad Dog nodded. "Thanks, Rass."

"No thanks needed, son. I'll be right back." With a wave, the old man wandered into the house and disappeared.

Mariah emerged a moment later, holding a tiny scrap of beef between her thumb and forefinger, as if it were a dead rat to be offered to a cur dog. Lifting her skirt a fraction of an inch, she descended the porch steps and came to a stop at Mad Dog's feet.

Her gaze swept his outstretched body in a single condemning glance and stopped at the holey soles of his cowboy boots. She grimaced and held out the meat. "Here."

Her obvious disapproval struck Mad Dog as funny. It was as if she actually expected him to care what she thought. One thing he didn't care much about were judgmental, narrow-minded spinsters. He sat up and offered her a cocky grin. "It's an awfully small piece of meat."

"It's an awfully small bruise."

Mad Dog burst out laughing. "So the wren has a temper."

Slowly he got to his feet.

She started to back up, then stopped. The porch's bottom step pinned her in place. She squared her shoulders and met his gaze head-on.

She was tall for a woman, with a straight-backed stance that made her seem even taller. The top of her head came almost to his jaw, and he was six feet tall. Fuzzy, curly strands of hair tickled his chin, and he knew instinctively that she hated the defiant curliness of her hair.

Up close, he could tell he'd been wrong to dismiss her as a brown wren. She was . . . more.

Everything about her bespoke grit, from the strong set of her delicately pointed jaw to the defiant tilt of her chin. Her face was chisled and sharp, without a hint of softness. Strong, prominent cheekbones slashed above hollow cheeks; pale, colorless lips spread in a thin, unforgiving line. She wasn't beautiful by any means, barely even pretty. But there was something interesting about her face, something that made her seem almost attractive in spite of her austere, freckled features. If she'd smile, she might actually be pretty.

It was the eyes. At first glance he'd thought they were brown, like everything else about her, but on closer examination, he saw that they were the extraordinary hue of maple syrup, and fringed by thick, dark lashes. Against the milky paleness of her skin, they seemed huge and vibrant.

"Are you going to stare at me all day?"

He shrugged easily. "I've been known to stare at a pretty woman for that long."

She stiffened even more——if that was possible. "No doubt you have. Why don't you go find one? Sapphire Lil's in Walla Walla probably has just your sort of woman."

Grinning, he extended a hand. "They call me Mad Dog."

She looked at his grubby hand as if it were a garden slug. "And you let them?"

He laughed. "Worse. I *like* it."

"And what's your last name? Bite?"

"Stone."

Somehow, she made *that* seem unacceptable, too. She sniffed and tilted her chin. "What did the advertisement say?"

"Handyman wanted. Room and board in exchange for *light* manual labor."

"Obviously my father placed the ad without my knowledge or consent. However, since you've answered it, I have no choice but to put you to work."

"Gee, thanks."

"You may keep your sarcastic comments to yourself, Mr. Stone."

He grinned. "I will if you will."

She looked at him then, took in everything about him in a single, disapproving glance. "The bunkhouse is a mess, but I don't imagine cleanliness matters much to you."

He gave her an exaggerated frown. "Is that an . . . insult? And from an obviously Christian woman such as yourself?"

She ignored his remark completely. "The bunkhouse will be cleaned, and the linen changed on Saturday. As usual."

He shrugged, feeling no more than a moment's disappointment. "I can use my bedroll till then."

For the first time, she smiled. It was a grim tightening of her lips that made her look even colder. "Somehow, I don't think you'll last until then, Mr. Stone."

"You mean you hope I won't."

"That's exactly what I mean." She nodded toward the building beside the front gate. "That's the bunkhouse. You may put your things away and report back here in ten minutes for work."

He frowned. "You want me to start now?"

"Oh, yes, Mr. Stone. You wanted to work—" she paused for effect "—and you will."

Mad Dog eyed the small whitewashed bunkhouse. A slow, appreciative smile curved his lips. He tripped the latch, swung the narrow door open, and went inside. The door creaked loudly and thumped against the wall, rattling the whole building. Dirt showered down from the open rafters. A wedge of filtered sunlight dove into the room, its golden glow marred by dancing motes of dust.

He coughed, blinked.

The small, cramped room was a scratchy blur that reeked of disuse and darkness, with just a hint of old beeswax. A narrow cot jutted from the center wall, its mattress covered by a thick, blue woolen blanket that draped almost to the floor. Two graying pillows huddled against the metal headboard. The bedside table was an upended packing crate that held a dusty lantern and a tin matchbox.

Against the left wall, an old oak dresser leaned awkwardly to one side, its oval mirror hung on the peeling wall above. There was one window. Tired gingham curtains let in faint rays of sun. The floor was thick-planked wood, scarred and stained from years of use. A squat, potbellied stove occupied the corner.

Shit, it was nice. Private.

No prying eyes would bother him here, no conductor would rouse him in the middle of the night and throw him off, no innkeeper would demand payment. He could put his bag on the floor and be sure it would be there in the morning, the contents undisturbed.

He tossed his bag in the corner of the room and sat down on the bed. It squeaked and groaned beneath his weight. Wishboning his arms behind his head, he flopped backward and stared up at the pitched wooden ceiling.

For no reason whatsoever, his thoughts drifted to Mariah Throckmorton.

Prim, proper, look-down-her-nose-at-you Mariah.

She was exactly the kind of woman he shied away from. Not that they usually wanted anything to do with a man named Mad Dog anyway. She was the sort of woman who hurriedly crossed the boardwalk in front of him, the kind who never glanced at a dirty drifter.

He could tell that by the tidy little bun she wore at the back of her neck—and the stiff, unapproachable way she carried herself. And the brown . . . God, didn't she look in the mirror? That god-awful color made her look like a corpse.

He pitied the woman. Her hair was so damn tight, she probably suffered a perennial headache. Life was too short to spend it all tied up in knots.

And too short to spend it working.

He sighed and pushed up to his elbows. Shaking the dirt off his boots, he got slowly to his feet and headed toward the door.

Christ, he hated farm work.

Chapter Three

Mariah stood on the porch, watching that man swagger toward her. Her mouth tightened into a disapproving pinch.

Everything about him screamed shiftless, from the scruffy tips of his cowboy boots to the battered tilt of his black hat. He moved slowly, casually, with his hands thrust in his pockets. As if he didn't care if he arrived someplace on time, or, and this was probably more accurate, as if he didn't care if he arrived at all. And he was staring at her, rudely. She could feel his gaze like a prickling heat across her face.

He was an affront to hardworking people everywhere.

She crossed her arms and glared at him, willing him to pick up speed.

He slowed down. In the shadow of his hat, his mouth was a white curve. "You're lookin' mighty tense, Miss Throckmorton," he drawled, coming to a stop directly in front of the house. Casually he rested his boot on the bottom step. It landed with a *thunk* that reverberated up Mariah's spine and lodged as a migraine at the base of her skull.

She clenched her jaw and glared down at him. "I'm surprised you even know the word *tense*, Mr. Stone."

He tilted his hat back and grinned up at her. "Ain't that what Indians live in?"

She let out her breath in a disgusted sigh. She deserved that for even speaking to the man. With a sniff, she bent and picked up her basket and hammer. Then, tilting her chin up, she marched down the steps and sailed past him without so much as a sideways glance. "Follow me."

He waited a full ten seconds, then followed.

She could hear him behind her, his bootheels crunching through the carpet of crispy autumn leaves. Every snap of a twig or crinkle of a dead leaf hit her like a slap.

She couldn't believe her father had invited that . . . that vagabond into their lives. Their home.

She gritted her teeth. *Damn, damn, damn.* The silent curses matched her every step, echoed the quickened pounding of her heart.

She had to get rid of him. Now. And she had the perfect plan to do it. He was obviously a man who made no commitments, a man who never stayed too long in one place. A man who didn't like hard work.

All she had to do was work him hard—brutally hard—and he'd be gone by sunup.

At the huge walnut tree behind the washhouse, she came to a stop and spun around, prepared for battle.

Mr. Stone ran right into her.

Mariah grunted in surprise and dropped her basket. Her arms flailed backward. She started to fall.

His arms were around her in an instant, holding her

tight. He drew her toward him. "Steady there," he murmured.

His gaze snagged Mariah's, held it. Her breath caught. She blinked at him. Up close, he had a face that was full of laughter and warmth. The kind of face that drew a woman in, the kind of eyes that quietly lured confidences. The kind of eyes she'd fallen for once before.

She jerked backward, stumbling in her haste to be away from him. "Don't ever touch me again."

"Then keep your distance. When a woman throws herself at me, I tend to catch."

Heat crawled up Mariah's throat. "I did *not* throw myself at you."

"All right, hurl."

Mariah felt her self-control start to slip. A tiny, niggling thread of fear uncoiled in her stomach. She was reacting to Mr. Stone in entirely the wrong way. She wanted to ignore him, not banter with him.

She bit down on her lower lip and turned away, focusing instead on the green orbs that dotted the brown grass at her feet. Then, when she felt stronger, she bent down and picked up one of the walnuts from the ground. Slowly, breathing steadily, she turned around. "These are walnuts."

"Now, ain't that fascinatin'."

She ignored him. "I want you to shake the branches and dislodge as many of the nuts as you can. Then you crack the soft husk, extract the nuts, and put them in that basket."

He shrugged. "Sounds easy enough."

"For a man as . . . *handy* as you, no doubt it will be."

With a curt nod in his direction, she plucked up her skirts and headed for the house. At every step, she resisted the urge to turn back around and see how he was doing.

There, she thought, *crack walnuts for ten hours and tell me you'll be here in the morning.*

"Sleep well, Mr. Stone?"

The sharp-edged words pierced the comforting darkness of his sleep.

Mad Dog winced. *Shit.*

He cracked one eyelid open. Old button-up brown eyes peered down at him. And she did not look pleased. But then, he wasn't entirely convinced it was possible for her.

"Hey, Miz Throckmorton." He straightened, came more fully awake.

She went to the basket in a swish of drab skirting and plucked up a handful of shelled walnuts. Then she turned to him, a look of incredulous disapproval stamped on her pale face. "You call these shelled?"

He shrugged. "I don't call 'em squat."

She thrust her hand toward him. A lone walnut sat huddled on her flat palm, its brown meat flecked with remnants of green shell. "There's green on this nut."

He looked up, met her gaze. "What am I supposed to do—suck it off?"

She bristled and snapped her palm shut. "Don't use that kind of language around me."

He laughed. "I said suck, not fu—"

"*Mister* Stone!"

He couldn't help laughing. "I did the best I could. I

didn't fall asleep for hours." He held up his bruised, stained hands. "And I got the injuries to prove it."

Her gaze flicked uncaringly across his hand, then returned to his face. "I suppose that means you'll be leaving. . . ."

His lips twitched. Suddenly he understood this afternoon. Old button-up had done this to him on purpose. She'd known cracking walnuts was hard work, and somehow she'd surmised that he wasn't a man who liked hard work.

He should have been angry, but instead he felt a grudging respect for her. It was a damn good idea, and it had worked like a charm. After today, he couldn't wait to take a few bucks from the professor and get the hell out of here.

Even clean sheets wasn't worth this shit. His thumb felt like an oxcart had run over it, and his arm ached from shoulder to wrist. Yeah, he was leaving, all right.

But first he was gonna have a little fun with the schoolmarm. "Naw. Where would I go?"

"Anywhere."

Casually he got to his feet and walked toward her. She didn't move, didn't back away, but she wanted to. He could see it in the fearful flaring of her nostrils and the way she leaned slightly backward.

He smelled her fear and it challenged him; it was just like when he was in the ring. All of a sudden he felt less tired. "What if I like it here?"

"I'll . . . pay you."

He tilted his hat back and gave her a slow, pointed once-over. His gaze started at her pale, severe face and leisurely moved down, over the curves she tried to hide beneath a baggy brown dress. But if there was one thing Mad Dog could find, it was a woman's curves, and the wren wasn't built too badly. Biting back a smile, he let his gaze wander once again to her face. "With what?"

She gave him a look of pure, red-hot hatred. "Money."

He cocked an eyebrow. "A little egg money you've saved to ward off prowlers?"

"Sixteen dollars," she said. "Cash."

Mad Dog grinned. Now, *that* was an unexpected bonus. Sixteen dollars was damn good money for doing next to nothing. He could hole up for a long while on that.

She saw his interest and gave him a gloating smile. "I knew that'd get your interest."

Ah, damn, he thought, *don't do that. Don't gloat.*

"A man like you couldn't last on a farm."

He rolled his eyes. *Oh, that's it. Add a challenge.* "Shit." He said the word on a sharp exhalation of breath. He wanted to leave, really wanted to. But now she'd made it impossible.

There were only two things Mad Dog prided himself on: He never walked away from a fight, and no one ever told him where to go. And now Miss High and Mighty had just started a fight and told him where to go in a single breath.

"Naw," he said softly, "I think I'll just earn my keep."

Her smile crashed. "But—"

"But nothing. I'm staying."

"Just my luck. You choose *here* to make an honest wage."

"Gotta do it somewhere."

She bent down and picked up the basket. Ramming the hammer in with the nuts, she gave him a look sour enough to curdle milk. "Supper's in one hour. I'll leave yours on the porch."

"What? I'm not invited to the table?"

She frowned at him. "Hardly."

"Now, that's not too neighborly of you, darlin'. I'm beginnin' to feel downright unwelcome."

She gripped the basket and held it tight against her body. Thrusting her chin up, she marched past him and headed for the house. "And I thought you were stupid."

Her words floated back to him in a rustle of swishing skirts. He burst out laughing.

Mariah stared down at the *Knoigsberger Klops* and had an almost overwhelming urge to grab the cast-iron skillet and throw the whole mess across the kitchen.

With exaggerated calm she picked up the slotted spoon and began removing the meatballs from their broth. When she finished, she poured a flour-and-water mixture into the bubbling liquid and stirred the thickening gravy.

She heard the slow, steady thump-thump-thump of Rass coming down the stairs, and she straightened.

"Evening, Mariah."

She spooned the meatballs back into the gravy and dished up supper. Then, two plates in hand, she turned to face her father. "Hi, Rass."

He went to the head of the table and sat down. "Something smells mighty good."

"*Knoigsberger Klops.*"

He grinned. "Ah, no wonder." He glanced around the

table and frowned. "There isn't a place for young Mr. Stone."

She wanted to say, *Mr. Stone's as young as I am*, but she bit her tongue and forced a smile. "He's not eating with us. I put a cold chicken supper in a basket for him. It's on the porch."

"Why should he want to eat alone?"

Mariah scooted up to the table and poured two glasses of milk. "Probably wants to practice with a fork."

Rass made a soft, clucking sound. "Now, Mariah, that's not very charitable of you."

She stabbed a meatball with her fork. "You have enough charity for both of us."

Rass put down his utensils. They hit with a tinny little clang that seemed loud in the quiet room.

Mariah tensed, feeling her father's gaze on her face. *No emotion, Mariah. None.*

"Change is part of life, Mariah."

"So are natural disasters."

Rass snorted. "Mad Dog is hardly a natural disaster."

"You haven't seen him crack walnuts."

"Give the man a chance, Mariah," he said softly.

She turned to him then. Anger narrowed her eyes. "You should know better than to even suggest such a thing. I did that once."

Rass's wrinkled old face fell. Sorrow magnified his rheumy eyes. "Ah, Mariah . . ."

For a heartbeat, Mariah felt herself weaken. She looked away. "Don't look at me that way."

"You're not sixteen anymore."

Panic uncoiled inside her, chewed at her self-control.

She lurched to her feet, clenching her hands to quell the shaking. "I don't want to talk about this now."

"Of course you don't. You never have."

She faced the six-hole Windsor stove that had been her mother's pride and joy. "And I never will." She tried to make the words sound strong and defiant, but the best she could manage was a watery plea.

"Okay, come on back to the table."

She composed herself, then turned around and went to her seat. "Just don't mention Mr. Stone again. I'd like to keep my supper down."

They lapsed into a familiar silence, punctuated by the gentle wheezing of Rass's breath and the tinny echo of their silverware on the crockery plates.

Finally she pushed her half-empty plate away and leaned back in her chair.

"Good supper," Rass said quietly.

She glanced at her father, surprised by the depressed sound of his voice. And immediately wished she hadn't.

He looked inestimably sad tonight; his once bright eyes were rheumy and dull. And he hadn't eaten much of his supper. He was thinking about Mama again.

She wished she could touch him right now, tell him she understood his sorrow. But it had been years since she'd done something like that. She didn't even know what to say to him anymore. And somehow, every time she tried to reach out to him, she did the wrong thing, or said the wrong thing, or kept silent when she should have spoken. She'd never really noticed how bad it was until her mother died. After that, Mariah and Rass sort of drifted apart.

She didn't want it that way. She wanted . . . more.

He eased back from the table. "Well, I think I'll go up and read. I'm halfway through that treatise by Professor Mittlebaum."

"Really? Is it any good?"

He smiled, but even that was a poor imitation of the old days. "His evidence seems to bolster my theory that Pike's Peak is the place to start digging."

Sadness tried to creep in on her, but she pushed it away. "That's wonderful."

"Yeah." He sighed wistfully. "Maybe someday we'll go there together." He said the words softly, and Mariah could tell that he tried to sound hopeful. Tried and failed. And no wonder. It was a sentence he'd said before, too often. The words sliced past her brittle armor and pierced her heart. It was another disappointment, another little way she'd let her father down.

They both knew she wouldn't be trekking to Colorado with him. It had been years since she'd even left the farm.

He pushed slowly to his feet. "Well, I'll see you in the morning."

Mariah forced a smile. "Good. I've a long list of chores for Mr. Stone. If he's still here."

"He will be."

"I doubt it, but if he is, we might as well get our money's worth. No telling how long he'll stay."

"Where were you thinking of starting him tomorrow?"

"I don't know. The porch needs whitening . . . and the apples might be ready."

"The apples . . . your way?"

She stiffened, stung by his criticism. "There's nothing wrong with the way I harvest the apples."

"Course not." He smiled tiredly down at her. "Night."

"Night, Rass. See you at five-twenty."

"Five-twenty." He shuddered. "God, I hate farmers' hours."

Mariah smiled at the familiar complaint and got to her feet. As soon as her father left the room, she started clearing the table and stacking the dirty dishes on the slopstone.

Maybe someday we'll go there together.

She gazed out the window, trying to banish the hurt. Through the shadowy, moonlit darkness of the farm, she saw it, marching across the property in a straight, arrow-tipped line. The fence.

She closed her eyes, unable to look at it. But the darkness didn't help, didn't take away the shameful sting of her past. Or the irrationality of her fear.

Once, long ago, she hadn't been afraid to leave the farm. She'd run through that gate with ease, laughing all the way to the train. Sixteen years old, she'd been, full of life and fire and dreams. Unafraid.

Her smile faded. Now, what had made her think of that? It had been years since she'd thought about those days, those memories. Why would they come back to her now?

But she knew. It was because of *him*. He was reminding her of a past she wanted to forget.

She curled her hands around the cool porcelain of the sink and stared out the window. He was making her feel things she didn't want to feel, think about things she wanted to forget.

"Damn him," she whispered. She'd spent fifteen years making her life safe and secure, making her heart and soul untouchable. And now Mr. Shiftless sauntered in here and wanted to change all that.

She wouldn't have it. She'd worked too hard to forget to let some no-account drifter make her remember.

Somehow, she had to get rid of him.

Mad Dog set his plate down and stood up, stretching his arms. The cool autumn night wrapped around him, wreathed him in the tangy scents of ripening fruit and dying leaves. A million stars twinkled in the velvet sky.

God, he felt good. He had a place to sleep, clean hair, and a full stomach. He couldn't ask for more.

Out of the corner of his eye, he saw something move. He slowly brought his arms down to his sides. In the distance, the barn was a sharp-roofed hump of black against the night sky. A huge tree, its leafy limbs silhouetted against the starry heavens, stood guard.

There was another flash of movement. Mad Dog felt rather than saw it. The hair on the back of his neck prickled.

His gaze narrowed.

Nothing moved. Not even a whisper of a breeze swept across the too quiet land.

Mad Dog relaxed. His fists unfurled.

He'd spent too many nights alone on the road, straining to hear the first sign of danger. Now he was imagining a threat where there was nothing but peace and stillness.

Bending, he picked up the empty plate and went to the door. Quietly he turned the knob and pushed the door open. A wedge of light snaked through the opening and warmed him.

Mariah was standing at the sink, staring out the window. Her eyes were dry, but he had a strange feeling that she was near tears. She didn't seem to notice that the door had opened.

Mad Dog's gaze followed hers out the window. He frowned. There was nothing out there except shadowed fields and the picket fence.

What was she looking at?

He studied her. Her normally erect carriage was curved somewhat, softened. Flyaway wisps of curly brown hair had fallen from the tight knot at the base of her neck, creating a wavery curtain along the pale flesh of her cheek. Her fingers were curled in a white-knuckled death grip on the sink's rim.

She reminded him of a woman he'd known in his youth. Etta Barnes. Etta had lost her husband in the war, and she'd never been the same afterward. Her skin had lost its color, her eyes their sparkle. And sometimes, if Mad Dog caught her just right, she'd have tears in her eyes for no reason at all.

But that was crazy. Mariah Throckmorton was a reserved, judgmental spinster. What loss could she have suffered, living her whole life on this safe farm? He had to be imagining the sorrow in her face. What trouble could she have had in her staid, well-ordered little life?

Probably planted petunias in the rose garden.

He cleared his throat.

She jumped and spun around. "Mr. Stone!"

"Sorry," he said softly. "I didn't mean to startle you."

"I-It's fine." She smoothed the hair from her face in a nervous motion. "I was just daydreaming, anyway." She smiled thinly. "Not a very worthwhile pastime, to be sure."

"I don't know. I dream all the time."

A change came over her at his words. She stiffened. Mad Dog felt as if the room's temperature had just dropped twenty degrees. "My point exactly."

They stared at each other in silence. Mad Dog didn't know what to say to her now. The softness was gone from her eyes, but the memory of it lingered in his mind, calling to him, beckoning. And all of a sudden she intrigued him. He wondered what kind of woman lay hidden beneath all that drab brown muslin.

"Breakfast is at five-twenty," she said finally. "Don't be late."

He grinned. "Five-twenty, huh? Not five-fifteen or five-thirty, but five-twenty. Rather regimented, isn't it?"

"That's the way I like it. If you don't—" she paused, looked at him hopefully "—you know where the door is."

"Just trying to be friendly."

She bristled and threw her nose in the air. "I hardly need a friend like you."

"I don't know," he said, watching her steadily. "Could be I'm exactly what you need."

"Go to bed, Mr. Stone. Tomorrow will be a long day." Her voice was cold and hard, but there was an underlying tremble in it that piqued his interest even more. As if she were working very hard to remain aloof. As if she were hiding something.

"Good night, Miss Throckmorton. I'll see you at five-nineteen."

"Good night, Mr. Stone. Hopefully I won't see you at all."

Jake stood at the fence, gazing out over the darkened fields. The farmhouse rose from the shadows like a pale white crown atop a sheet of brown wool. Smoke spilled from the chimney, its acrid scent riding on the night air. Red-gold light illuminated the windows, turning them into hazy, welcoming squares against the whitewashed walls.

A painful ache seeped through Jake's chest. The house reminded him of another place, another time. A time when he was never hungry or lonely or cold, a time when no door had ever been closed to him.

He shut his eyes. The lingering echo of musical laughter haunted him, brought the sharp sting of tears behind his eyelids.

She would hate what he'd become, hate what he was doing.

It's a waste of time, Jacob. You can't make someone care. . . .

He wished he could say that wasn't what he wanted, wasn't why he was here, but he couldn't lie to himself. Not in the long, cold, lonely nights on the road. He knew exactly why he followed Mad Dog, and knew, too, that it was a fantasy that would never come true.

He'd only be hurt again; he knew that, knew it with a certainty that made him feel sick and shaky inside. He'd tried for years not to care, tried not to believe in miracles and happy endings, but he couldn't manage it.

Somewhere inside him was a voice that never stopped, a heart that never gave up. His mother and grandfather had tried to make him see the truth a thousand times. A thousand times they'd failed. That secret part of him kept dreaming.

But the dream was beginning to tarnish, dulled by too many freezing nights and sweltering days and too much loneliness.

He glanced at the farmhouse again. At the sight of it, so warm and welcoming and homey, something inside him twisted hard. He wanted to belong in a place like this again, wanted to have someone tell him he was welcome.

Welcome. The word brought a quiver of response.

He squeezed his eyes shut, trying to be grown-up. But he was so hungry and alone and afraid. Life on the road was killing him slowly. He wanted to stop worrying that he would get sick and die alone, or that a train would run over him, or that he'd starve in the winter's coldness. He wanted someone to sit beside him and brush the too long hair from his eyes, or touch his forehead when he felt ill.

He wanted his mother back. . . .

Hot tears slipped from his eyes and slid down his cheeks. He barely noticed. They were familiar, these tears, as familiar as the cowardice that made him follow but never act. He was so tired of trying to be strong. . . .

Bowing his head, he turned away from the farmhouse that stirred too many memories. In the distance, an animal howled. The sound throbbed on the gentle breeze, then dwindled into nothingness.

He crept through the darkness toward the barn. Twigs

snapped beneath his heels, leaves crinkled, but other than the nervous nickering of the horse in the pasture, the world was still and quiet.

He passed an apple tree and grabbed several, stuffing the ripe, red fruit into his sack. Then he raced across the farm and disappeared in the barn.

Behind him, the huge, cross-beamed door slammed shut. Somewhere a cow mooed. Dusty darkness curled around him, thick and smothering. Gripping his bag, he cautiously crossed the hard-packed dirt floor and felt for the loft ladder. When he found it, he clambered up the creaking wooden rungs and flung himself onto the soft piles of hay.

He closed his eyes and smiled, inhaling the familiar scent. This was heaven. He hadn't slept on something this soft in the four months he'd been following Mad Dog.

He lay there a long time, almost falling asleep. Then hunger roused him. Sitting up, he burrowed through his pack and pulled out the apples. Greedily he ate three of them, then flopped back down and tried to sleep.

The spasms came on suddenly, clutching and twisting his stomach. He stumbled to the loft window and shoved it open, sticking his head into the cool night air. He retched until there was nothing more to throw up. The bile splashed on the dark ground below.

Trembling, he closed the window and crawled into the corner, curling into a tight, miserable ball. Tears stung his eyes and mixed with the clammy sweat on his face. Stalks of hay stuck to his damp cheeks. The sour odor of vomit hovered in the dusty air.

God, he was tired of this. . . .

He closed his eyes and prayed for a night without nightmares. He needed sleep, needed it something awful, because tomorrow it would start all over again. Mad Dog would leave this wonderful little farm and hit the road for some smoke-filled hellhole in the bad part of town. And Jake would follow.

He had nowhere else to go.

Chapter Four

Rass glanced at his precious specimens, now lined with military precision along the shelf above his desk. Mariah had been at it again.

He shook his head slowly and crossed to the window. Pushing aside the lacy curtain, he gazed outside. The land, his land, looked as it always looked in the first short evenings of autumn. Night was beginning to creep in. The sky was an endless lake of midnight blue studded with diamondlike stars. Greta's grave was a dim glimmer of pale gray against the velvet shadow of the grass. The bunkhouse was an indistinct white square against the advancing night.

He stared at the little building, wondering about the man within. Though he wouldn't have admitted it to Mariah, Rass had a niggling sense of worry. Of doubt.

He didn't know exactly what he'd thought when he tacked the slip of paper to the wall at Ma's Diner, but he knew what he'd expected.

A husband for Mariah. Someone to take care of her when Rass was gone.

What he'd gotten was an irresponsible drifter with a ready smile and itchy feet, a man who moved on but never moved in. At first, Rass had meant to tell Mad Dog the job was filled. He'd even opened his mouth to say the words, then he'd looked into Mad Dog's eyes. Really looked, in the way Greta had taught him. And there, beyond the cocky grin and the easy going manner, he'd seen the same quiet loneliness he saw when he looked in his daughter's eyes, or, lately, in his own.

Somehow, they were the same, the three of them. The surprising thought had come to him out of the blue. Then a breeze touched his forehead in almost a caress, and he'd sworn it carried with it the lavender-sweet scent of his late wife. And so, without even thinking, he'd invited Mad Dog into his home.

But now, without the breeze, he wasn't so sure.

Sighing, he rested his forehead on the cold window. "What do I do, Greta? I've got to take care of her. . . ."

For a split second he found himself actually waiting for an answer. But, of course, there was nothing; no sound in the lonely room except for the whispered cant of his own breathing. He was alone, he reminded himself for the millionth time in the eight months since Greta's death. There was no one to bounce his ideas off of, no one to give him the advice he needed so desperately.

He drew away from the window, let the curtain flutter back into place. The house was depressingly quiet, without even an echoing remnant of the laughter that had once filled its walls. Without Greta, it had lapsed somehow from a home to a house, and he had no idea how the transformation had occurred. He knew only that he missed what this place had once been, missed it desperately. Without Greta's guiding hand, he and

Mariah had become strangers, hearing without listening, talking without communicating.

Somehow, everything he said to his daughter was wrong, or her reaction made it feel wrong. He knew it, could see it in the stiffening of her back or narrowing of her eyes; he could hear it in the reedy, defensive tone of her voice. He knew instantly when he'd said something wrong, but he didn't know how to correct it. She was so . . . remote sometimes. And she was hurt so very easily.

Ah, Mariah, he thought, feeling a familiar surge of regret. They were together now, but someday she'd be alone, rattling around in this big house with no one to talk to.

He was an old man, and old men died.

And what would she do then? That was the question that had prompted him to tack the ad to the diner wall.

He couldn't leave her alone and lonely and closed off from the world around her. He'd let her hide here with him too long. Years ago, when she'd first come back, humiliated and emotionally battered, he should have forbidden her to return. He should have forced her to recuperate in the real world, instead of allowing her to lick her wounds here, in safety. Because he and Greta had been so soft and forgiving and safe, Mariah had never healed.

For a while, they'd thought she was improving. Her smile came back; the bounce in her step returned. She was, if not the impetuous, passionate child of her youth, at least content. Then they noticed her reluctance to leave the farm. At first it was a family joke. Mariah couldn't open the gate. Mariah couldn't go to town.

Greta and Rass had laughed loudly, then quietly, and then not at all.

He and Greta had handled it badly. He saw that now. They shouldn't have allowed her to remain within the safety of the white picket fence. They should have pushed her out.

It was a lesson well learned. They'd let her have her way because she was in pain. Because she'd lost so much.

No more, he vowed silently. Now the stakes were too high. No matter how hard he had to be or how cold, he had to force Mariah to break down her defenses. She'd grieved long enough—or not at all. He wasn't quite sure which. But either way, it was time for a change. Now, finally, she had to face the fear that kept her trapped behind the ordinary picket fence.

Maybe Mad Dog was a pisspoor choice. But he was here, and he was an interruption in the carefully ordered routine of her life. She couldn't ignore him. Maybe he'd make her laugh, maybe he'd make her cry, maybe he'd make her scream in frustration, maybe he'd scare the bejesus out of her. Rass didn't care. As long as he made her feel something.

For once, she wouldn't have her father looking out for her. No matter what happened, what Mad Dog said to her, how upset she got, Rass wasn't going to step in and protect her.

This time she was on her own.

At precisely five o'clock, the Bee alarm clock rang. Mariah was already awake, sitting stiff as a nail, her gritty eyes staring at nothing. Absently she swatted the clock.

Dark silence tumbled around her, broken only by the erratic, anxious cant of her breathing.

Day two with Mad Dog Stone.

She let out an irritated sigh and stood up. Shoving her feet in her slippers, she padded to the commode and poured a generous amount of water into the crockery basin, washing her face and brushing her teeth quickly. She finger-combed her unruly, ringlet-curled hair and coiled it into a thick, no-nonsense chignon at the base of her neck. Only the wispiest corkscrews escaped her practiced hand.

She'd made a mistake yesterday, a mistake she had no intention of repeating. She'd let Mad Dog get to her. She shuddered at the memory. It was inexcusable, and stupid to boot.

How could she have let him frighten her? She'd grown up a lot in the years since her girlish infatuation with Stephen. No one could hurt her like that again— and certainly not the same kind of shiftless, lying loser as before. Passion no longer beckoned her with a sly, seductive voice. She was content here, and she was safe. No drifter with an easy smile could threaten her.

She wasn't afraid of him, she told herself firmly. She was simply irritated by his presence. He didn't belong here, and she wanted him gone. She wanted everything to go back to the way it was before. Silent. Safe. Contained.

The walnuts hadn't worked. So she'd try something else. Anything else. She'd keep trying, over and over again with increasingly disgusting chores, until he went, screaming, in the other direction.

And she knew just what to try next.

Smiling at the thought, she went to the armoire and flung the mirrored doors open, reaching blindly into the darkness. It didn't matter what gown she chose; it never did. Ever since the day she'd returned home, she'd worn nothing but brown. The drab color made her feel unobtrusive. Safe. No one noticed a woman in brown.

She slipped into a coffee brown linsey-woolsey dress and tied a washed-out apron over it. Securing a brown and white striped bonnet loosely around her throat, she sailed out of her bedroom. A quick knock at her father's door wakened him, and then she was down the stairs.

Within moments, she had a fire going in the stove and coffee brewing. She hauled the heavy cast-iron frying pan out of the dresser and slammed it on the stove top. While it was heating up, she pulled some leftover cornbread and hard-boiled eggs from the Metallic Ice Rack. Packing them in cheesecloth, along with some pickles and cider, she stuffed everything into a wicker basket and headed outside.

She almost ran into Mad Dog on the porch.

His bare, hairy chest filled her vision. She tried to look away; her gaze dropped, and snagged on the sagging drawstring waistband of his drawers. Heat scorched her throat and fanned up her cheeks.

"Miz Throckmorton," he drawled, scratching his naked chest. "What a pleasant surprise."

She jerked her chin up—anything to keep from staring at his chest—and found herself gazing into warm, inviting gray eyes. He smiled down at her. The flesh around his eyes crinkled invitingly, his thick mustache bunched up. She drew in a sharp breath and stiffened, shoving the basket toward him. "Here's your breakfast."

"Thanks."

That was all he said, just "thanks," but in the dark, chilly beginnings of an autumn morning, his voice sounded warm and rich and . . . beguiling. Mariah shivered at the intensity of her reaction to it.

"You cold?"

She winced at his perceptiveness and felt suddenly exposed. "No," she snapped. "I am not cold, and it wouldn't be any of your business if I were." She crossed her arms and glared at him. "Get dressed and meet me here in one hour. Farm work starts early."

"That's only one of the things I hate about it," he said with a throaty, vibrating laugh. "I suppose you've concocted an especially enticing chore for me this morning?"

She felt just a tinge of satisfaction. "I have."

His cocky grin faded. "What?"

She smiled. "The pigpen."

By four o'clock that afternoon, Mad Dog realized he'd been lied to. All his life he'd heard that pigs were smart animals. But now, after mucking through their shit for six hours, he knew it was a hoax. Pigs were the dumbest, dirtiest animals on the face of the earth.

He jammed the shovel in the thick, oozing mud and rested against the wooden handle.

She was doing it to him again, trying to kill him.

He closed his eyes briefly, feeling the once comforting and now brutal warmth of the sun on his face.

Yanking his hat down over his eyes, he wondered fleetingly if a man could sleep standing up.

A hog bumped against his legs and sniffed at his crotch.

He stumbled sideways. His boots caught in the pungent muck and he fell, face-first, into the goo. When he looked up, he saw a pair of prim, lace-up canvas boots.

"Need a hand, Mr. Stone?"

Gritting his teeth, Mad Dog planted his bare hands in the mud and pushed upward. Through a painful blur, he saw Miss Button-up looming in front of him like some evil brown bird of prey.

She was standing behind the low-slung slatted fence, her feet ankle to ankle, her small, pale hands at her sides. A dull brown-striped sunbonnet shielded her face, but nothing could hide her superior smile. It was as bright as the sun. And her eyes were glitteringly hard.

She was gloating again.

He moved fast. Launching himself forward, he took hold of her hand in a greasy, oozing grip and hauled himself to his feet. "Why, thanks, Miz Throckmorton," he said, standing directly in front of her, "a hand is exactly what I needed."

A look of pure horror twisted her face. She stared down at her muddy hand and skirt. Then she snapped her gaze to his, and this time there was no superior smile, no condescension. Only white-hot anger. "I should have known . . ."

He grinned and tipped his filthy hat back. "Of course you should have."

"Are you finished?"

He nodded and swept a hand toward the pen. "The

containers are clean, the water trough is fixed, the beds are raked, the manure's piled, the mud is chunkless, and those goddamn hogs are as pink as a baby's butt."

She gave him a curdled, disapproving frown. "Good."

"And best of all, I'm still here." He clapped his hands together. Mud flew on impact. "Now—"

She lurched backward a second too late. Dark, slimy specks splattered her dress.

"Sorry about that." He smiled broadly. "Guess you shoulda stayed away from the work area."

"I didn't think there'd be one."

"Seems I'm making a habit of proving you wrong."

She said nothing, just glared at him.

He tried to brush the muck off his pants, but it just smeared down his legs. "Christ, I smell like—" he grinned and looked up at her "—shit."

"Don't worry, it's not a noticeable change. Supper's in thirty minutes. Don't be late to pick it up."

Before he could answer, she was off.

Mad Dog watched her leave. Her back was ramrod-straight, her hands fisted at her sides. He didn't need to see her face to know that it was screwed into an irritated pinch. Those full lips of hers were probably pressed into a pale white line.

He smiled. She might look like a tall, unforgiving bird, but that butt of hers sure twitched nicely beneath all that washed-out brown skirting. . . .

Brushing off his hat, he strolled to the pump and washed in the painfully cold water, getting as much shit and mud out of his hair and clothes as possible. He wished like hell he hadn't lost his razor in Abilene. He could use a shave.

He twisted his wet shirt and stared at the meticulously tended farmhouse. Absently he tugged at his drooping mustache. He still couldn't quite figure out why he was still here. It went against everything in his nature—working like a common laborer and taking shit from Miss Button-up. Pig shit.

He should be on his way to Sonora by now.

But there wasn't anything in Sonora that was half as fun as ruffling the schoolmarm.

Challenging her, testing her mettle, was beginning to be downright fun. She was a surprisingly worthy opponent. She had the tenacity of a goddamn bulldog.

He bounded up the porch steps and skidded to a stop at the front door. Before he could even knock, the door banged open.

Rass stood in the opening grinning wide. "There you are, son. I was just coming to get you."

Mad Dog gave his shirt another good twist and then put it on. The damp fabric stuck to his flesh. "No need for that, professor. I'm just here to pick up my supper."

Rass stepped back across the threshold. "Pick it up? No need for that, son. You're welcome to eat inside. Surely Mariah invited you. . . ."

Mad Dog grinned. He could practically *hear* Mariah grinding her teeth. "Naw, she musta forgot to mention it."

"Well, come on in."

Mad Dog followed the professor into the warm house. A darkly paneled foyer curled around him, offering a beautiful embroidered bench to the weary. A gaslit hallway led to two closed doors. To his right was the parlor, a cozy room painted the color of summer roses and cluttered with ornate mahogany furniture. Family pictures covered the wallpapered walls and littered the tables.

Rass turned to the left and went into the kitchen. It was a large, square room with a glistening hardwood floor and an oval dining table. A huge, six-hole stove and free-standing sink lined the left wall; above the sink, a small window flanked by faded yellow curtains overlooked the porch and farm. Dozens of pale yellow crockery plates, pitchers, bowls, lay in perfect array in a polished oak dresser. A small icebox was tucked in the corner alongside the sink. The walls were papered in demure yellow and rose stripes.

Mariah eyed him, a small frown pulling at her mouth.

He grinned at her, tipped his hat. "Evenin'."

She stared at him, unmoving.

Rass smiled at his daughter. "You forgot to invite him in for supper last night. But I remembered."

She tried to smile. "I'm so glad."

"Well . . ." Rass's gaze bobbed from Mariah to Mad Dog and back to Mariah. The silence stretched between them, became uncomfortable.

"Sit down," she said finally, turning back to the stove.

Mad Dog followed Rass to the table and took a seat. Mariah dished up supper and sat down across from him.

Mad Dog stared at the food on his plate, feeling strangely uncomfortable for a moment. He felt Mariah's eyes on him. She was no doubt waiting to see if he'd eat like an animal. And he probably would. He didn't know shit about table manners.

In his childhood, there'd never been a table; no

mother teaching table etiquette. He just grabbed some bread off a passing cart and shoved it down his throat. And lately, on the train line, it had been no different. He couldn't remember the last time he'd sat down at a table to eat a meal.

He didn't look up, didn't make eye contact with anyone. Slowly, hoping like hell he wasn't doing something wrong, he picked up his fork.

He cast a quick, surreptitious glance around. Mariah was quietly spearing a chunk of potato with her fork, and Rass was using his spoon to shove all his food into a single, unappetizing pile.

Mad Dog let out his breath in a relieved sigh. He wasn't being watched at all, no one cared in the least about his manners. The irritating sense of discomfort disappeared. Smiling, he picked up his knife and started sawing through the sugar-glazed ham.

"So, son," Rass said, his mouth full. "Where are you from?"

Mad Dog took a satisfying taste of potato before he answered. "Chicago."

"Do you have family there?"

"Nope."

"No folks?"

Mad Dog smiled. Something inside him softened for a second, remembered. "My ma died when I was a boy."

Rass closed his eyes in sympathy, then said softly, "I'm sorry. How 'bout your dad?"

"He left one day for a tin of tobacco and never came back. I heard tell he died."

His gaze caught Mariah's across the table. She immediately lowered her lashes. "I . . . I'm sorry."

"Don't be. He was a lousy drunk who couldn't hold down a decent job."

She tilted her chin up. Their eyes met again, but neither said a word. He felt a sudden jolt of communion with her, as if she knew what it felt like to be abandoned, which was absurd.

The rest of the meal passed in a comfortable silence. When it was over, Mariah stood up and began clearing the dishes from the table. At the sink, she stacked the dishes on the slopstone and turned on the spigot. Water gushed from the indoor pipe and splashed into the metal bucket in the sink. "Mr. Stone," she said over her shoulder, "tomorrow is washday. You may leave your things on the porch."

"What if I don't have anything to wash?"

Wiping her hands on her apron, she turned to face him. Her narrowed gaze swept him from head to foot, noting the smearing of dirt on his sleeves and shirt. "You do."

"Then I'll do it."

She gave him a grim smile. "I'm sure you will . . . someday. I'd just prefer it was done—" she sniffed delicately "—quickly."

He shrugged. "Okay. If you want to wash my underwear that bad—"

She gasped. Embarrassment or anger—he wasn't sure which—stained her cheeks. She opened her mouth—no doubt for a stinging retort.

He grinned. "Yes, Miss Throckmorton?"

Her teeth came together with an audible click. He

could almost *see* her fighting for composure. "Mr. Stone, I believe I'll let you harvest the apples tomorrow morning."

He frowned. *Let you harvest the apples?* She made it sound as if she were granting him a rare, undeserved, treat.

"It's a difficult task, of course, but I suspect that if you concentrate, you'll do an acceptable job. The whole orchard takes about a week to harvest. We may as well begin while you're here."

He understood now. She thought he was dim-witted. "A difficult job . . . picking fruit?"

She gave him a sour look. "It is not as easy as it sounds, Mr. Stone. First thing tomorrow morning, you will go to the root cellar. There you'll find five barrels. They're clearly marked: Red, mostly red, yellow, green, and rejects. You will then go to the apple orchard—it's in the west pasture, along the stream—and begin to pick and sort the ripe fruit. I'll check your progress every hour on the hour. Do you understand?"

"You want me to pick the apple, check its color, and put it in the barrel of the corresponding type?"

She positively beamed. As if she hadn't expected him to get it. "Exactly."

"Do you preserve by color?" he asked.

The question seemed to startle her. Her smile faded. "No."

"Sell by color?"

"No."

"Then why separate? No other fruit farmer I've worked for does that. And I've picked apples from coast to coast."

Mariah stiffened at the question. Irritation thinned her lips. "I don't care what other farms do, Mr. Stone. I have always harvested the fruit here, and that's how *I* do it. If you think that will present a problem—"

He laughed and stood up. "Naw, I can do it. I just wondered why I should, but I got my answer."

She eyed him warily. "You did?"

"Sure. Because you like things neat and tidy." He looped his thumbs in the baggy waistband of his jean pants and sauntered toward her. Just in front of her, he stopped, smiling broadly. "No wonder you have such a problem with me."

She tried to back away from him, but the sink held her in place. "Believe me, I have no *problem* with you, Mr. Stone."

He smiled and leaned closer. So close, he could see the smattering of freckles that dusted her nose like specks of cinnamon. So close, he could see the reddish gold flecks that lightened her brown eyes. "Good, then we should get along just fine."

She didn't move, just stood there, toe to toe with him. "That's where you're wrong, Mr. Stone. We won't get along at all."

Chapter Five

The tree blocked out the warm, early morning sun. Light streamed through the fluttering leaves and dappled the apple-littered grass.

Mad Dog watched Mariah work. She was standing on the bottom rung of a wooden ladder, checking apples for ripeness with the focused intensity of a general on the front line.

There was something about her right now that piqued his interest. Even on that silly, wobbly ladder, she stood as stiff as a marble statue, her chin cocked at a ninety-degree angle.

Restraint, he decided; that's what caught his attention. He'd never known anyone—especially himself—to show any restraint at all. Everyone he knew, male and female, drank too much, moved too often, and died too young.

Not Mariah Throckmorton. She'd probably never danced or drunk or screwed in her whole life. And she was no spring chicken. She was so damned . . . fenced in. So controlled. And yet, even with all her rigid discipline, there was sometimes a softness to her that surprised and intrigued him. Like the other night, when he'd seen her staring out the kitchen window at the darkened farm. She'd looked . . . different. For a second there, he'd wondered about her, wondered what kind of woman lay beneath the schoolmarm's drab brown dresses. She'd looked—absurdly—like a woman who'd had trouble in her life.

He studied her, wondering what she was really like. *Could* she be the kind of woman with a secret past? Or was she exactly what she appeared to be: a judgmental, iron-hard spinster who didn't like her routine upset.

The question alone grabbed him. For some strange, illogical reason, she beckoned him. Not with the usual come-hither glances and welcoming breasts of most of the women he knew, but with something more subtle . . . and infinitely more intriguing. She was a mystery and a challenge.

He couldn't help wanting to break through that shield, just once, and see how human she was beneath it. If for no other reason than to see if he could.

Quietly, knowing how much it would irritate Miss Pay-Attention Throckmorton, he laughed.

She turned on him and crossed her arms. "And what, *precisely*, do you find so amusing, Mr. Stone?"

"I just love watching a woman work, Miss Throckmorton."

She gave him an uppity sniff. "No doubt it's the novelty of watching anyone work at all, Mr. Stone."

He gave her a slow, lazy smile. She was rising to the bait. She didn't want to; he could see it in the stiffening of her back, in the way she leaned slightly away from him. But she was responding anyway. "I expect you're right."

"Now, as I was saying, there's a chance this tree is ready to be picked." She frowned a bit. "For storage, of course."

"Of course."

She turned, gave him a knowing nod. "Some apples are best when stored for a while."

He gave her a pointed once-over. "That's true of women, too."

She didn't flinch, but her gaze hardened. "A fascinating observation, Mr. Stone. Now I must turn your attention to the work at hand." She peered down at him from her elevated position on the ladder. "You did catch that word, didn't you? W-O-R-K. You'll be doing some today if you want supper tonight. Unless you think it's time to just move on . . ."

"Now, Miss Throckmorton, I wouldn't want to disappoint you."

"Believe me, Mr. Stone, that's impossible."

He crossed the small field of grass that separated them and came up beside her. Close. With her on the ladder, they were of equal height. She stiffened, but didn't draw away, although he was certain she wanted to. "Are you ready to begin working?" she asked, careful to avoid eye contact.

"Yeah, I'm ready." With a sigh, he yanked the shirt over his head and tossed it on the ground.

Her eyes bulged. She looked at his bare chest for a second—maybe two—then quickly looked away. "P-Put your shirt back on, Mr. Stone."

He was so close, he could see the tiny pulse beating frantically in her throat. She was afraid. He could see it in her eyes, in the sudden flaring of her nostrils. But she didn't try to move, didn't back against the ladder. She looked him square in the eyes.

Afraid . . . of him. Mad Dog felt an unfamiliar stirring of shame. Silence stretched between them. From somewhere came the chattering cadence of a small bird. A breeze came up, rippling her heavy skirts.

He wanted to say he was sorry, but the words stuck in his throat. Instead, he picked up his shirt and put it on.

He heard her sigh of relief.

"So," he said, "what do you want me to do out here?"

She stared at him for a heartbeat longer, a small, frightened frown lingering in the corner of her mouth. Then she tilted her chin and turned toward the ladder. "You reach for the apple like this, and take hold of it with your thumb and middle finger. It comes off with a gentle twisting motion. Ripe fruit parts easily from the stem. If you have to try too hard, let it go. It's not ripe."

"Sorta like sex," he said without thinking.

She jerked back as if she'd been struck.

He winced. "I didn't mean to say that—"

Slowly she turned to him. Her face was as cold as carved marble, and there was no hint of emotion in her eyes at all. "I'm sure you find yourself very amusing, Mr. Stone. No doubt whores from here to Abilene think of you as God. But here in Lonesome Creek, things are a little different."

"Really? How's that?"

She ignored him and plucked the apple. Tasting it, she nodded. "It's ripe, Mr. Stone. You may pick the tree."

An hour later, Mariah was finally ready to begin the laundry. She dumped the last bucketful of boiling water into the metal washer. Steam spiraled upward, pelted her face as she added the soap. A film formed on the surface. Gradually the water turned a dull, opaque gray.

She pulled a heap of petticoats, undergarments, and shirts from the wicker laundry basket at her feet. One by one, she dropped the garments into the soapy water.

As she waited for the blob of white to submerge, she glanced toward the orchard. Mad Dog was about sixty feet away from her, half-buried in the big apple tree. He'd been working steadily for the last two hours.

It was the first time she'd actually watched him work, and she had to admit, she was surprised.

But then, everything he did surprised her. It surprised her that he was here at all, and it downright floored her that he stayed. A man like him *never* stayed on a nowhere little farm like this for three days. Hadn't she learned that truth the hard way?

He moved away from the tree, saw her staring at him, and he waved.

Without thinking, Mariah waved back.

Her hand froze in midair when she realized what she'd done. She yanked her hand back down and plunged it in her apron pocket.

Damnation.

What was it about Mad Dog Stone that pushed so easily past her defenses and made her respond?

She shuddered at the memory of what had happened in the orchard. Things had been going along well, she thought. She had instructed him clearly in what was expected from him, had kept her distance, had even ignored some of his taunting remarks. All in all, she'd been sticking to her decision fairly well.

Then he'd taken off his shirt.

She swallowed hard, even now feeling a little queasy at the remembrance.

She shouldn't have looked at his naked skin, should have torn her gaze away.

But she hadn't been able to move. She'd felt frozen, trapped like a rabbit beneath the searing, unerring eye of the hawk. Her breathing quickened, became a painful thumping in her ears.

God help her, in that minute, that second, she'd wanted to touch him, to feel the wiry softness of his hair and the tanned smoothness of his skin.

She forced the image away and grabbed the paddle. Gripping it hard enough to stop the shaking in her fingers, she rammed the fabric bubble of her petticoat beneath the water.

Somehow, Mad Dog Stone brought out her old self, the one she'd spent years trying to demolish.

She felt a suffocating wave of despair at the realization. It wasn't fair. She'd worked hard to suppress that passionate side of herself, binding up her fiery emotions so tightly, she'd almost forgotten their existence.

Until Mad Dog Stone reminded her with a simple wave or a casual remark. Or a bare chest.

Why? she wondered, but it was a feeble, empty question. She knew why.

The truth was painfully obvious—even to her. She hadn't really suppressed her passionate nature, after all. It had simply lain dormant at this peaceful farm, waiting for a challenge to draw it forth. And Mad Dog

Stone, drifter, vagabond, good-for-nothing vagrant, challenged her.

Sighing tiredly, she reached down for the last item in the laundry basket. A dirty gray shirt lay in a lonely heap at the bottom.

His shirt.

Reluctantly she picked it up. The coarse fabric felt rough against her fingers. Its sweaty, masculine scent mingled with the humid fragrance of the steam and curled, thick and heavy, around her. She couldn't seem to help herself. She closed her eyes and held the shirt close, inhaling the sharp, unfamiliar scent of it. It had been so long since anything foreign, anything unexpected, had come into her life, and she couldn't totally deny how it made her feel.

For a hazy, unreal moment, she felt as if she were part of a dream. As if the man working on her property were *her* man. For a second—just a second—she forgot the pain and humiliation in her past and imagined a future she'd never even let herself consider. A future in which she was something other than a crazy old spinster hiding out from scandal.

"You gonna smell all my laundry?"

Mariah froze. Fire crawled up her throat and fanned across her cheeks. Humiliation burned in the pit of her stomach.

She exhaled slowly and forced herself to look at him. "Are you here for a purpose?"

"Is that a philosophical question?"

Her eyebrow arched upward. "That's a large word for you, Mr. Stone."

He grinned. "I'm full of surprises."

Ignore him. "I'm sure you are. Now, what do you want?"

He held out an apple. "Red or mostly red?"

She studied it with a practiced eye. "Red."

"This one?"

Suddenly she understood. Her eyes narrowed. "Mr. Stone, are you toying with me?"

A slow, deliberate smile curved his lips. "Miss Throckmorton, when I'm toying with you, you'll know it."

The illicit, completely improper remark caused a red-hot spark of response. A shiver worked itself down Mariah's stiff back. She swallowed dryly. "I hope you aren't suggesting you may toy with me in the future."

"I don't know you well enough to say."

She pushed the damp hair away from her face and tried to smile. "Honesty. What an unusual approach."

"I'm always honest."

She snorted. She'd heard *that* one before—and from a man remarkably like the one standing in front of her. "Sure."

He shrugged, as if he didn't care a whit if she believed him—and somehow that made her believe him.

She studied him, intrigued in spite of herself. "You *always* tell the truth? Even if it hurts people, or makes someone think badly of you?"

"Sometimes the truth hurts. That's life."

"That makes you a very dangerous man, Mr. Stone."

He shook his head. "Only if you expect something from me. Fortunately, no one does. So what about you, Miss Throckmorton. Are you honest?"

She almost answered, but didn't. She thought suddenly about the dowdy spinster in brown, hiding behind a white picket fence. "No," she said, and the quiet confession surprised her, "I suppose I'm not."

He smiled and walked away. At the pump, he paused and turned back around. "Mariah?"

"Yes?"

"A real liar would have said yes."

She couldn't help herself. She laughed.

Grinning, he yanked his hat down and walked away without another word. Mariah watched him leave.

It wasn't until later, much later, that she realized he'd called her Mariah.

Rass kneeled awkwardly and laid a hand on the carved granite of Greta's headstone. The stone felt smooth and cold and comforting.

Sighing, he leaned back against the giant oak tree that shaded his wife's grave from the hot sun. Above his head, colorful leaves rustled in the late afternoon breeze. Every now and then one dropped, twisting and floating as it fell to the ground. Strands of sunlight shot through the branches and hit the grassy earth, moving and dancing in a ceaseless golden pattern.

Hi, Greta.

The breeze picked up, ruffled his hair in a caress. He felt her presence in the wind. And in the sun and the rain and the silence. She was here with him, sitting invisibly beside him.

He squeezed his eyes shut and took her hand. In the emptiness of his own fist, he felt her warmth and it gave him comfort.

From his perch on the grassy knoll, he stared down at

the farm. Mariah was standing in front of the wash-house, doing the laundry. At her feet was a wicker bas-ket; to her left, the clothesline, now empty. Soon it would be filled by billowy garments snapping in the breeze.

A quiet sense of sadness pervaded him at the thought. So much the same as every Saturday for sixteen years . . .

Ah, Greta, what are we going to do with her?

He coughed hard. When it was over, he sagged back-ward. God, he was tired, and there was a persistent, nagging pain in his left shoulder.

It was hell to get old.

Lately he was tired and sore and coughing all the time. He even woke up tired.

Down the hill, a movement caught his eye.

His gaze followed it. Mad Dog was walking toward Mariah. He stopped at the washbasin and held out an apple. Then a second one. A few moments later, he heard the unmistakable—incredible—sound of Mariah's laughter.

Rass sat up straighter. "Did you hear that, *liebchen*? She laughed." He shook his head. "Our little girl laughed."

The sound recalled a dozen hazy, treasured memories of Mariah's childhood. She used to laugh all the time. She'd been so passionate about life, so spirited. It had taken all of Greta's strength to keep up with her head-strong daughter.

And now, here she was laughing again. For the first time in years.

Rass whistled softly. Maybe he'd done the right thing

after all. Maybe Mad Dog Stone was exactly what Mariah needed.

She *laughed.*

He shook his head. It might not be earth-shattering, might not be a wedding, but, by God, it was a start.

Chapter Six

Mariah wrung out Mad Dog's now white shirt and slapped it over the top rung of the wooden clothes bar. Fat, clear droplets slid down the sleeves and plopped on the golden grass. Beside and below the shirt, petticoats, shirts, pantalets, and sheets shimmied in the cool breeze.

She stepped back, blinking at the eye-splitting field of white. A tired sigh escaped her lips as she stretched her aching, chapped fingers.

Lord, she was exhausted. Saturdays were the worst day of the week for her. Carrying bucket after bucket of boiling water from the stove to the washtub, turning the tub's wooden-handled crank for endless, back-breaking hours, wringing out dozens of heavy sheets and feeding them through the Economic Starcher. And she wasn't even finished. On Monday she'd spend countless hours hunched over a hot iron.

Just the thought of ironing made her feel weak. And hot.

And ready for a swim.

Sighing, she dipped her hands into the now cool rinse water and splashed her face.

When she opened her eyes, Mad Dog Stone was standing directly in front of her. He looked as tired as she felt.

"Christ," he said, sopping his brow with his sleeve, "what a day. It was hotter than shit for fall."

Mariah managed a weak smile. She was too tired to argue with him over his language—or anything else. "Picking's hot work."

"So's laundry."

She smoothed the damp hair from her face with fingers that shook with fatigue. She knew he expected a response, but she was too tired to make the effort. Even an insipid nod was beyond her.

Lord, that swim would have felt good today. . . .

"Well, if you're finished with me, I'm gonna lay down for a while."

Mariah perked up slightly. "Really?"

He swiped his brow with his sleeve again. "Yeah. Unless . . ."

"Unless what?"

He tried to look casual, but didn't quite manage it. "Unless you'd let me take a real bath?"

Mariah felt a stunning sense of relief. She couldn't have concocted a better plan. "Certainly, Mr. Stone. A shower and a rest would be perfect for you." In a resurgence of energy, she spun around and bounded up to the house, racing down the shadowy hallway for the bathing room.

For a moment, she was alone. She grabbed two thick Turkish towels from the washstand's cupboard. As she reached for the soap, she heard him come up behind her. He didn't say anything, but she felt his gaze, hot and pointed, on her back. She froze, knowing she'd need an excuse for the second towel.

She couldn't think of a single one.

Mad Dog stared down at Miss Prim and Proper. She was burrowing through the towel closet as if it held the crown jewels. And muttering.

Now, one thing he knew: Mariah Throckmorton was not a muttering kind of gal.

"Something wrong, Miss Throckmorton?"

She popped to her feet and slowly turned around. "W-What do you think of the bathing room?"

For the first time, Mad Dog noticed his surroundings. "Holy shit . . ."

She flinched at his foul language. "How . . . eloquent, Mr. Stone."

Mad Dog didn't respond. He couldn't. He was stunned by the unexpected grandeur of the room. He'd heard, of course, of houses that had bathing rooms like this, but that was back East. And he'd never actually seen one.

It was big, as big as an ordinary bedroom. Forest green wallpaper covered the top half of the wall, melting into a boldly carved mahogany wainscoting. The burgundy tile floor gleamed like the flat facet of a huge, single ruby. Atop it lay a green and burgundy and black Oriental carpet with golden tassels. The faint scent of gas wafted from the brass-sconced fixtures along the wall. Ovals of shimmering light slid down the dark walls and puddled on the elegant floor.

And the bath. Mad Dog let out a soft, appreciative

whistle. It was a long way from the town water pump he usually used.

The shower/bathtub combination was completely encased in carved mahogany. Within the dark wood, porcelain glistened like an open oyster shell, clean and smooth and inviting. A row of six shining brass knobs was the only adornment on the otherwise flawless wood.

"I know it's extravagant . . . but my mother loved her baths." Mariah's voice was soft and wistful. It pulled Mad Dog in, made him want to hear more.

He tried to find the right words. "She's . . ."

"Passed away last winter," she said quietly.

"I'm sorry . . ." Immediately he regretted the pat, too easy words.

She shook her head and looked up at him. Though she tried to hide it, sorrow clung to her, a wispy veil that softened her gaze. "My father's razor is in the commode's top drawer. I . . . wish you'd use it, but you don't have to."

He studied her. She was asking a favor of him, not demanding or judging or condemning. Simply asking. The moment seemed suddenly fragile, worth saving. "Thanks, I will."

She handed him a towel and a bar of Dirt Killer soap. "Well, I guess I'll leave you to your privacy."

She started to leave.

For some crazy reason, he didn't want her to go. "Wait—"

Slowly she turned back to him. "What?"

He had nothing to say to her; he'd acted without thinking. He glanced at the towel clutched to her chest and said the first thing that came to mind. "You want the shower first?"

"No!" The word burst from her, then she laughed shakily. "No, thanks. You go ahead. I'll wait."

Mariah felt his sharp, penetrating gaze on her face. She shifted uncomfortably. "Well, I'd best go." Before he could respond, she turned and hurried from the room, closing the door behind her.

In the empty hallway, she sagged against the closed door for a heartbeat. Then she smiled. She'd done it.

She hugged the warm towel and barreled from the house. Outside, the still hot sun hit her hard in the face, but this time the heat was welcome. Although she was dying to run, she forced herself to walk across the yard. At the barn, she paused and glanced back. Mad Dog was nowhere to be seen.

Grinning, she dashed around the barn and raced through the fragrant orchard. Deep in the back pasture, she came to a bend in the river that created a still, green pool.

For as long as Mariah could remember, this place had been her refuge. As a child, full of mischief and energy, she'd come here to play, to splash around in the water, to laugh and yell, to be free. Now, as an adult, this place was her escape from a dull and ordinary life. From the detached, emotionless woman she tried so hard to be.

Here, in the cool quiet of the pool, she could let her stiff facade slip away, let it be lost in the swirling current. For a few precious moments a week, she could be herself.

She stood there a long time, relaxing, enjoying the

feel of the breeze and the sun on her face. It felt almost like a touch, and she shivered in response. It had been so long since anyone had touched her, really *touched* her. Years . . .

She closed her eyes, trying not to think about it, battling the wave of sadness that accompanied the thought. It was the price of safety, she knew. Isolation meant safety, but safety meant loneliness. It was a truth she'd known, and tried to accept years ago. But sometimes, like now, she felt her loneliness, her disconnection from the world, so sharply, so keenly, that she wanted to cry.

It was such a simple thing, being touched, and yet it would mean so much. . . .

She pushed the depressing thoughts aside with practiced ease. She crossed the river where it was shallow and went to her usual spot on the other side. Slowly she unpinned her heavy hair and shook her head, reveling in the feel of her loose, unbound tresses. Finally she peeled off the ugly brown dress and kicked it aside. A breeze molded the thin linen undergarments to her body.

She shuddered at the caressing touch of the wind. The lacy eyelet of her undergarments fluttered against her flesh. She unlaced her canvas boots and threw them aside. They landed in a heap with her stockings and dress.

Leisurely, her arms at her sides, she walked into the river, giving herself over to the one purely sensual pleasure in her regimented life. Cold water seeped through the flimsy linen of her underclothes. The fabric clung to her goose-bumped flesh.

She went in, deeper. Deeper.

Water lapped at her knees, her waist, her breasts,

swirled around her like a lover's gentle touch. A cool breeze pushed the water in ever-widening circles around her. She dropped her head back into the water. Droplets slid along her forehead and gathered on her lips. She tasted the clean, pure freshness of it, and imagined for a moment—just a moment—that she was being kissed. She dragged her tongue along her full lower lip, savoring the water's sweetness.

Behind her, the rope lay in readiness, as it had every Saturday for years. She took hold of it, feeling the coarse texture of the knotted hemp beneath her slick palms. She let her feet go out from under her; they drifted upward, floated weightlessly toward the surface of the pool.

She closed her eyes and lay there, motionless, floating, feeling the caressing lick of the water against her flesh and the stirring touch of the breeze on her damp face. Her every sense felt heightened. The air seemed clearer, cooler; the earthy, fecund scent of the bank filled her nostrils.

She let out her breath in a deep, contented sigh. Lord, this felt good.

Mad Dog crept through the orchard behind Mariah. He knew he shouldn't be following her—he had no right. But he couldn't help himself. She'd been so damned *odd* in the bathing room, so unlike herself. He sensed that she was hiding something, and he had to know what a woman like Mariah Throckmorton had to hide.

The rushing babble of the river became louder and

louder. At the last lonely apple tree, he stopped and peered around.

She was standing beside the river, where a curve in the land created a smooth, jade green pool. Beside her, a huge, wind-sculpted oak tree stood guard, its golden-red leaves flickering gently in the breeze.

She closed her eyes and reached up. One by one, she pulled the pins from her hair. Unbound, the thick, curly brown mass tumbled downward, framing her face. Sunlight caught dozens of reddish strands, turning her dull, ordinary brown hair into swirls of mahogany fire.

She shook her head for a moment, smiling, then reached behind her again.

Mad Dog swallowed hard. His throat dried up. His heard pounded hard and loud against his rib cage. He started to back away. He shouldn't be here, shouldn't invade her privacy—

The baggy brown dress slid down her body and landed in a heap at her feet. She kicked it aside.

He froze, unable to move. *Holy shit.* Mad Dog let out his pent-up breath in a sigh. His hands started to shake. He shoved them in his pockets.

She opened her eyes.

He lurched behind the tree, waiting in silence for her to march up to him and slap his face.

Finally he couldn't stand it anymore.

Heart pounding in his ears, he peered around the tree. At first he didn't see her.

He edged a little more away from the tree. Just enough to watch.

She was standing in the water now, shivering, wearing nothing except a creamy, scoop-necked chemise and matching drawers. The thin fabric clung to her curves, sculpted her tall, lithe body.

Mad Dog's reaction to the sight of her was swift and hard. He let out his breath slowly. Jesus, he couldn't believe the transformation. Relaxed, without that god-awful pinched expression on her face, she was almost beautiful. The harsh austerity of her features seemed suddenly sculpted, classically chiseled.

She walked into the water, submerged, until all he could see was her pale throat and face, and her hair, fanned out and floating atop the jade water. She dropped her head back, wet her hair, and came back up.

Droplets of water slid down the sides of her face. She licked at one, tasting it. Her wet hair was the color of rich coffee; it made her skin look impossibly pale, her lips incredibly pink. And her eyes . . . Christ, her eyes were like brilliant topazes against the creamy softness of her skin.

Reaching behind her, she grabbed hold of something. Her body angled upward, floated on the surface. She lay as still as a fairy-tale princess, her body moving in the undulant rhythm of the current. Her small breasts rose and fell in gentle, even breaths, the hard peaks straining through the wet fabric.

Mad Dog stared at her. It was impossible to look away. There was no trace of the prim, proper spinster in the woman floating so calmly on the surface of the water. In her place was a woman as sensual and powerful as nature itself.

A woman who could have a big secret in her past, a pile of trouble behind her.

Mad Dog felt the hardening ache of desire. It throbbed, made his jeans feel tight.

For a crazy moment, he pictured himself going to her right now. He closed his eyes, imagining the creamy soft feel of her skin, the hard pinkness of her nipples.

A soft groan escaped him. God, he yearned to take her in his arms right now, to drag her against his hardness and kiss her. She would taste of innocence, freshness, and surrender.

Suddenly he wanted to know her. The real her, not the facade she presented to Rass and the rest of the world. He didn't want to know the spinster; he wanted to know the wood sprite who floated half-naked in a lonely pool of water. The woman who might have had "trouble" in her life, the woman with secrets.

He smiled. Who would have thought a nice, quiet little farm like this would hold an honest-to-God mystery?

Goddamn, it was intriguing. And the longer he stared at her, the more he wanted to know the truth.

Under all that drab brown fabric and starched blouses was a woman of fire and passion. A woman he wanted to know. Maybe even needed to know.

He pushed away from the tree. Turning, he headed back to the farm. With every step, he thought about her, wanted her. By the time he got back to the house, he had an honest-to-God goal. He was going to strip the facade from Mariah Throckmorton and see the real woman.

He grinned, feeling a surge of anticipation. This was gonna be fun.

Jake saw Mad Dog follow the stiff-looking lady across the orchard. He waited a long time—maybe too long—until Mad Dog disappeared down by the river.

It was Jake's chance. With a quick glance both ways,

he made a beeline across the yard and raced up the steps.

At the door, he paused and looked around, then cautiously eased it open. It creaked loudly.

Jake drew in a hard breath.

No one yelled at him, or came running.

He let out his breath and slipped inside the house. The mouth-watering aroma of simmering stew drew him toward the kitchen. His stomach rumbled loudly. Saliva rushed into his mouth.

He surged to the icebox and skidded on his knees, wrenching the wooden door open. Inside, he found some leftover ham and cold potatoes. He jammed the food under his arm and closed the icebox.

He was halfway to a stand when he heard the front door open.

He froze for a heartbeat, then dove beneath the table.

"Rass, are you home?" Mad Dog's voice called out from the other room.

Jake huddled against the table leg, the precious food crushed to his heaving chest.

The front door squeaked shut, then clicked. Heavy-heeled footsteps thudded down the hallway. Another door opened, closed.

Jake sat there, waiting, his every sense strained to the breaking point.

He closed his eyes and banged his head back against the sturdy table leg. He was getting so tired of this, tired of running and sneaking and stealing and hiding. Tired of *wanting*.

He wanted to belong in a house like this one, wanted to sleep in a real bed and feel safe at night.

He shook his head. He should do it right now, before Mad Dog had a chance to get away again. Jake closed his eyes, picturing for the millionth time how it would go. He'd walk up to Mad Dog and demand—

Demand what? The familiar question sparked a red-hot flood of frustration. He didn't even know what he wanted from Mad Dog—so how in the world did he think he'd get it?

Maybe tomorrow, he thought dully, but as usual, the words had no sting, no bite. He didn't believe them for a second. Tomorrow would be no different from today, or yesterday, or the day before that.

The sound of running water leaked into his thoughts.

He crawled out from underneath the table and paused, looking around. Then he lurched to his feet and ran for the front door.

He opened it gently and peered out.

The place looked deserted. He clutched the stolen food against his empty stomach and ran from the house.

He was so wrapped up in his own pain, his own fail-ure to do what he'd set out to do, he never saw the pair of eyes that watched him run back to the barn.

Chapter Seven

Mariah stood at the range, cooking supper. The sweet and sour scent of baking sauerbraten filled the warm kitchen. Boiling water popped at her from the big black pot. Pale globs of *spaetzle* dough bobbed in the roiling surf. Beside it, butter slid back and forth in a small cast-iron pan, leaving streaks of thick, boiling gold in its wake. On the shelf above the range sat a crockery bowl full of bread crumbs. Everything was on schedule.

She smiled. The reassuring organization made her feel good, added to the sense of well-being she'd felt since this afternoon.

She was so proud that she hadn't let Mr. Stone's presence deter her from her swim. It was important to her, *necessary*. Without it, she ended each week feeling like a raw nerve.

The tension started first thing Sunday morning—with her first reluctant glance at the graves—and built day by day, until by Saturday afternoon, she was close to screaming.

The swim removed it all. Now she felt strong enough to take on the world. Or one weary, ill-mannered drifter.

She was sure she could keep her passionate responses to herself now; she wouldn't react to Mad Dog's taunting.

"Go ahead," she murmured with a smile, "take your best shot. I'm ready for you."

"I'm ready for you, too." Mad Dog's quiet voice came at her from the doorway.

Mariah winced. *Damn him for sneaking up on her.* She stiffened and reluctantly glanced at him.

He was standing in the doorway at a casual slant, one shoulder rested against the doorjamb, arms crossed, hat pulled low over his eyes. She was unaccountably reminded of a lion, waiting in the shadows for its prey.

He stepped out of the shadows, and her breath caught. She stared at him, unable for a moment to tear her gaze away. He'd shaved and changed his clothes. The drooping, too thick mustache was gone, as was the brown stubble that furred his cheeks. His face was strong, with a blunt, squared jawline, and a damnably sensual mouth that was curved in a dazzlingly white smile. He was wearing a clean white shirt that hung loosely on his broad shoulders and gaped at the throat. Faded, worn Levi's, bleached to the color of foam, hugged his long legs. Blond hair lay curled, thick and soft-looking, against his limp collar.

Sweet God, he was a good-looking man.

Nothing could have irritated her more. "It isn't polite to sneak up on people," she said stiffly.

"Did you really expect politeness from me?"

A traitorous smile tugged at her mouth. She immediately bit it back. *Damn him for making her smile.* "No."

He pushed his hat back and sauntered toward her, slowly. His bootheels clicked on the planked floor, his even, gentle breathing filled the air between them. His eyes were fixed on her, as if he were searching for something.

She smoothed a nonexistent wrinkle from her apron and turned away from him. "You may sit down, Mr. Stone. Supper will be ready in a few moments."

He peered into the pan. "Looks like maggots."

"Lovely comparison. Of course, if anyone should recognize a maggot, Mr. Stone, it'd be you."

He laughed.

The rich, rumbling sound grated on her nerves. She'd meant to insult him. Almost involuntarily, she glanced up.

He was beside her. Close. So close, she could smell the clean, masculine scent of his skin and the just-washed freshness of his clothes. His face filled her vision. Intense, pewter gray eyes stared into her own. She felt somehow invaded by his look, penetrated.

She dragged her gaze away from his eyes. And accidently glanced at the vee where his collar lay open. Curly, coffee brown hair darkened his suntanned flesh. The sight of it taunted her, tempted her.

She yanked her chin up and forced herself to meet his eyes again. "Was there a reason you came over here?"

"Yeah."

She knew instinctively that she shouldn't ask, but she couldn't help herself. "W-What is it?"

He leaned closer. Mariah's heartbeat sped up, whether from fear or some darker, more dangerous, unknown emotion.

"I want to get to know you."

"What?"

He laughed softly. "I'm curious about you, that's all."

Oh, *that's* what she needed. She straightened, careful not to look at his eyes. "I don't want you to be curious about me, Mr. Stone."

"I know you don't. That's why I am."

She gave an impatient sigh. "Are you *trying* to irritate me, Mr. Stone?"

"No. It just comes naturally. One of my few gifts."

"Your mama must be proud." One second too late, she remembered that his mother had died. "Oh, Lord, Mr. Stone, I'm sorry. . . ." She turned to him, not knowing what else to say.

He stared back at her, and for once he wasn't smiling. Their eyes met, held. There was something in his gray gaze that surprised her. A depth of emotion, of loneliness, that seemed vaguely familiar. Then it was gone.

If it had ever really been there at all.

"You're forgiven."

Mariah refused to think about what she'd seen in his eyes. "Well, that was easy," she said with a brittle laugh.

His smile was back, stunning in its warmth. "I'm an easygoing guy. Just remember it when I offend you."

"Oh? Are you planning to offend me?"

He shrugged. "No, but it'll happen. That's my other gift."

"That's it—only the two?"

"Well, I throw a mean right punch."

She stirred the *spaetzle*. "My, my, what a repertoire of skills. It must be a simple matter to find employment."

"I rarely look for work."

"Unfortunately for me, you occasionally find it."

He leaned toward her. For one terrifying moment, she thought he was going to touch her. She tried to back up, but couldn't move.

He didn't reach for her. His only touch was with his eyes. And somehow that look, that glance, was more intense and physical than any touch she'd ever known.

"You're not what you seem, are you, Miss Throckmorton?"

The quiet words pierced Mariah like tiny, poison-tipped arrows. She tried to think of a flip, sarcastic remark, but nothing came to mind. She stared at him, her lips parted for words that never came.

Behind them, the kitchen door creaked open. "Hi, you two," came Rass's gravelly voice from the foyer.

The spell shattered. Mad Dog backed up.

Shaking, Mariah turned away from him. "Hi, Rass." Her voice was sandpaper-rough and soft. Even breathing was difficult.

Rass inhaled deeply and patted his stomach. "Smells like sauerbraten and *spaetzle*. My favorite. Give me an extra helping, will you?"

"Sure, Rass." She bent down and opened the oven door. Waves of heat hit her in the face as she eased the big roasting pan from the oven and set it on the range top.

She stared down at the steaming roast, barely seeing it. Anxiety curled around her insides, cold and hard. She didn't want to be studied by Mad Dog, didn't want him testing her limits, asking her questions that hadn't been asked in years. Questions she had been unable to answer in the first place. She didn't want to be "known" by Mad Dog Stone.

Her past was hers, damn it. He had no business probing into things that didn't concern him.

She told herself that's why she was shaking, why she was afraid of Mr. Stone. She wanted her secrets kept secret. Just that and nothing more.

But she couldn't make herself believe it. There was something besides fear that made her tremble in his presence, something she hadn't felt in . . . sixteen years.

Mad Dog was chipping away at her resolve, getting past her rigid defenses. He made her angry, made her smile, made her *laugh*, for God's sakes.

He made her feel alive again.

It had been so long since she'd felt anything for a man. And then she'd done it all so badly, given her heart completely and asked for so little in return. Her own emotions had devastated her.

She didn't want to feel alive again, didn't want to respond to Mad Dog as a woman reacts to a man. She wanted to be employer-employee, nothing more. Anything else would hurt too much.

Of that, she had no doubt. There was no percentage in caring for a man like Mad Dog Stone. The worn, holey soles of his boots told her everything she needed to know about him.

He was exactly like Stephen. And he was making her feel things, just like Stephen had. . . .

But then she'd been a young girl, practically a child. The words calmed her, soothed her somewhat. She wasn't sixteen anymore and she didn't want the same fairy-tale life she'd wanted then.

Now, she was older, wiser, the exact opposite of that starry-eyed adolescent. She saw the world as it was, a cold, inhospitable place where danger lurked behind every corner.

She was stronger. Mad Dog might make her feel things—she couldn't deny that—but he couldn't hurt her unless she gave him her heart.

And God knew she wouldn't do that.

Mad Dog scooted his chair up to the table.

Across from him, Mariah sat as stiff as a plank, her hands demurely in her lap, her gaze on her plate.

She was trying to ignore him right now, to pretend she didn't care at all if he delved into her past. But she couldn't quite manage it—either that, or he was getting to know her well enough to see the tiny pleats of worry at her brow and the barest of trembling in her fingers.

There was something in her past. As hard as it was to imagine, Mariah had a secret. He was becoming more and more certain of it, and the more he thought about it, the more intrigued he became. The more he wanted to know the truth.

But he couldn't learn anything about her if she wouldn't look at him. Right now she was staring at her plate as if it held the crown jewels of England. She was trying to ignore him—and he couldn't stand that.

He cleared his throat and poked at his food with a fork. "These maggots sure look tasty."

Her head jerked up. "It's *spaetzle*, Mr. Stone."

Rass glanced. His blue eyes had a dreamy, faraway look. "Did someone mention maggots?"

"Of course not, Rass. Mr. Stone was just telling us

about his friends." She gave Mad Dog a too sweet smile. "It's an understandable mistake." Before he could respond, she turned to her father. "You've hardly touched your supper. Are you feeling well?"

Rass stabbed a slippery *spaetzle* and brought it to his mouth. "Um ... good," he said, chewing noisily.

She smiled. "Very funny."

Mad Dog stared at her, amazed again at the transformation a smile made on her face.

She seemed to feel his gaze and turned. "What are you looking at?"

"I was just thinking how pretty you are when you smile." He said the words softly, surprised by the truth in them.

She stiffened. Her lips pressed in a hard line and she looked away.

Mad Dog frowned. "I meant it as a compliment."

She ignored him completely and stared at her food.

He plopped his elbows on the table and steepled his fingers, studying her. She was trying to retreat into herself, trying to pretend he wasn't even at the table. He had no intention of being ignored. "So, Miss Throckmorton, how long have you lived here?"

She tensed, but didn't look up. "Most of my life."

"Mariah doesn't leave the farm," Rass said matter-of-factly.

Mariah gasped quietly. "I ... I'm sure Mr. Stone isn't interested in our private affairs, Rass."

Mad Dog leaned forward, smiled encouragingly. "On the contrary, Miss Throckmorton, your *affairs* are of the utmost interest to me."

He'd gone too far. He knew it instantly.

Everything about her changed. She straightened. Her cold brown eyes fixed on him as if he were a spider on clean sheets. One eyebrow lifted derisively. "I can't imagine why, Mr. Stone."

Rass set his fork down with a clank and sighed impatiently. "All this mister and miss is getting tiresome. Your names are Mariah and Mad Dog. Use them."

Mariah looked at Mad Dog.

He gave her a challenging smile.

She didn't return it. "I cannot call a . . . human being Mad Dog. What is your given name?"

The question caught Mad Dog by surprise. It had been years since someone had asked his name; years more since he'd answered. He'd become accustomed to traveling in anonymity, unknown and untraceable. He *liked* being one of the nameless.

He leaned back in his chair and gave Mariah his best sexy smile—the one that always worked. "Come on, Mariah, you can say Mad Dog if you really try."

"Certainly I *can* call you Mad Dog, but I choose not to." She leaned forward, setting her elbows on the table. "So, Mr. Stone, what is your given name?"

He swallowed hard. For the first time in years, he felt a flash of uncertainty around a woman. "It doesn't matter."

She sat back in her chair, her gaze still fastened on his. "It seems, Mr. Stone, that you have a few secrets of your own."

Mad Dog turned his attention back to his food. She'd gotten close there for a minute, too close.

And suddenly he didn't feel quite as cocky as he had before.

* * *

Lord, she was exhausted. Today had been the longest day of her life. Even the bath hadn't helped in the end. She felt worn-out and hollow. Empty.

Mariah stood at her bedroom window, staring down at the dark, quiet farm. Twilight pushed thick shadows through the orchard and drizzled orange remnants of light atop the bunkhouse's pointed roof.

I was just thinking how pretty you are when you smile.

She flinched at the memory of his words.

She hadn't meant to react, hadn't meant to show him such an obvious reflection of her soul, but his words had sucked the strength from her. The sentence, so close to one of Stephen's lies, had cut through her self-control like a blade, leaving her exposed and bleeding.

He was getting to her, getting past her guard. The truth was painfully obvious and undeniable. She could feel it, feel him, creeping through her like a virus, leaving a trail of weakness in its wake.

No matter how many times she thought about it, how often she tried to rationalize away her awareness of Mad Dog, the seductive pull of his presence remained.

"You're attracted to losers," she said aloud.

But that wasn't quite it, and she knew it. She wasn't really attracted to Mad Dog Stone. She was . . . *aware* of him, drawn to him in some sick, twisted way. There was a difference—at least she prayed there was.

How could she not be aware of him, here on this dusty little farm in the middle of nowhere where nothing of importance had happened in years? He was like a hot, pulsing tornado on a calm fall day.

How did one ignore a tornado in her own backyard?

Tightening her arms, she went to her bed and perched stiffly on the edge.

She had to stop reacting to him. It didn't really matter if he found out the whole sordid secret of her past. He wouldn't care, he'd probably laugh anyway.

A tightness squeezed her chest at the thought. It surprised her that still, after all these years, the truth had the power to shame her.

She squeezed her eyes shut, wishing—for once—that she could cry.

She needed a good cry right now, needed to release the pent-up frustration and anger that gripped her. But she hadn't cried in years, not since that afternoon so long ago when she hadn't been able to stop crying. Even when her mother had died, she'd stood at the gravesite, cold and devastated and achingly alone, and unable to cry. Her grief had been an icy block of pain pressing against her chest.

She heaved a tired sigh and slumped forward. He was beating her down, she could feel it, but she couldn't stop it. She was so tired of it all, of lying and hiding and pretending. It had been a drain before, with Rass, but now, with Mad Dog, it was becoming unbearable.

If only she had courage—just a little bit. She had everything else: a strong will, a strong mind, a wagonload of grit and determination. Everything but courage. That, she'd lost a long time ago, and she'd never been able to regain it. If she had, she might not even be here. No stupid white picket fence would stop a person with courage.

"Oh, God . . ."

She didn't know what to do about Mad Dog. How to keep her distance. How to make him keep his. All she wanted was to be left alone, for things to go back to the way they used to be.

She wanted to feel safe in her own home again.

Was that asking so much?

Chapter Eight

Rass stood in the kitchen, listening to the quiet creaking of the floorboards upstairs.

His breath expelled slowly. Mariah was in her room.

He went to the icebox and pulled out the leftover slab of sauerbraten. He sliced up the meat and fanned it on a speckled tin plate, placing a couple of potatoes and some cooked carrots around it. Then he tucked a bottle of cider under his arm. Straightening, he cast a last anxious glance at the stairway. It was still empty.

Moving as quietly as possible, he went to the front door and eased it open. Cold evening air, redolent with the sweet scent of ripe apples, greeted him. The farm lay wreathed in darkening shadows; the fruit trees were jet black skeletons against the gray night sky.

He quietly pulled the door shut behind him. The latch clicked into place. Head down, hands curled tightly around the food, Rass hurried to the barn.

He stopped in front of the closed door. Anticipation quickened his tired old heartbeat, made him feel young again. There was a mystery inside his very own barn. He'd known it the minute he'd seen that young boy skulking across the farm this afternoon. Someone hiding on the Throckmorton farm was a riddle too exciting to ignore.

He balanced the plate of food on his palm and gave the door a hard push. It shuddered away from him, scraping the hard-packed dirt floor in its arc to the back wall, where it hit with a *thud* that shook the wooden structure.

Up in the loft, something moved.

Rass ventured to the center of the barn and looked up. Pale, blue-gray moonlight seeped through the small second-story window, casting the barn in shades of onyx and steel blue. The loft was a looming black ceiling.

He went to the ladder and rested a boot on the bottom rung, peering up into the darkness. "Hello there."

Nothing.

"I've got some food for you."

A board creaked overhead. Dust and bits of hay rained through the cracks, pattering Rass's upturned face. "I saw you today." He paused, choosing his words carefully. "I mean you no harm. I just thought you might be hungry."

Silence answered him, yawning and endless. Rass was just about to try again when something—someone—inched across the loft toward the ladder. Slowly, slowly. The old boards creaked.

Rass held his breath. Excitement pounded through his old man's heart. *He's coming, Greta. He's coming. . . .*

A small face peered over the edge of the loft. Rass couldn't make out the boy's features amidst the shadows. But a tousled thatch of reddish gold hair caught and held the moonlight. "Whatcha got?"

"Sauerbraten, potatoes, cooked carrots."

"What's sauerbraten?"

"Does it matter?"

The boy shook his head. "Naw. I reckon I'd eat dead spiders about now."

Rass nodded and started to climb the ladder.

"Hold on—"

Rass looked up.

The kid flung a leg over the edge and stared down at Rass. "You're . . . old."

Rass blinked up at him in surprise. "Uh-huh?"

The kid shrugged. "I . . . think maybe I should come down to eat."

Rass grinned and stepped back from the ladder. That told him all he needed to know about the stranger hiding out in his barn. The boy had heart. "I'd appreciate that, son."

The boy turned around and climbed down the ladder.

Rass went to the workbench and lit a lantern. Flames flickered to life in the glass globe and filled a small section of the barn with tenuous, throbbing light.

The boy peeked around the ladder, eyeing Rass speculatively.

Rass walked toward him. "I'm Rass Throckmorton," he said, coming to a stop.

The boy edged cautiously away from the ladder and took the plate of food from Rass. "I'm Jake."

"Well, Jake, shall we sit down while you eat?"

Jake glanced down at the plate in his hand. Naked hunger passed through his eyes, but he didn't take a bite. "What do you want from me?"

Rass was saddened by the question. He set down the

lantern, then slowly sat down. "Nothing," he said softly. "I just thought you might be hungry."

Jake seemed to think about that for a moment, then awkwardly he sat down beside Rass. Pulling the plate onto his lap, he stared down at the food for a long, wordless moment, and Rass thought he saw the sheen of tears in the boy's eyes. Then he dove into the sauerbraten and chewed noisily.

Rass watched him eat, and once again he was filled with sadness for this boy who knew what it meant to be alone and frightened and hungry.

"How old are you?" he asked quietly, when Jake had finished.

Jake took a messy, dribbling swallow of the cider and backhanded the moisture from his mouth, giving Rass a sheepish look. "Sorry. I've got better manners than that. I'm fifteen—sixteen in March."

Rass was surprised that the boy had even heard the word *manners*, much less be chagrined by his own lack. "Where are you from?"

A guarded look crept into Jake's green eyes. It looked absurdly out of place on his open, honest features. "Last place was Abilene."

It wasn't an answer, but Rass let it go. Reaching into his pocket, he pulled out a small leather bag and opened it. Treasures glittered in the pale lamplight: an arrowhead stone, the wispy remnants of a rattlesnake skin, a small gray wasp's nest.

Jake picked up the wasp's nest, studying it.

Rass saw the beginning of wonder in the boy's eyes, and his chest tightened with emotion. It was like his old teaching days at Public School No. 27 in New York. It

had been so long since he'd had an eager young mind
in his charge, since someone had wanted the useless
stockpile of information in Rass's brain. Not since he'd
taught geology and history to the Digby boy. Now,
there was a mind, he thought with a smile, and wondered whatever had happened to Larence.

"I found that in the eaves of an abandoned farm out
toward town. Maybe tomorrow you'd like to go collecting with me—"

Jake shook his head. "Naw. I'd best be moving
on. . . ."

"I need an assistant," Rass interjected eagerly.
"Someone to catalog my finds and carry them for me."

Jake stared at the arrowhead. A small frown pulled at
the edges of his mouth. "When I was a kid, I used to
love rock collecting."

When I was a kid. Rass's old heart gave a painful
twitch. What a sad sentence coming from a fifteen-year-
old. "I'm seventy-four and I still love it."

"My mom gave me a book about rocks. Told all
about the different kinds."

"She must love you very much."

"Yeah." He paused, looked down. "She did."

Did. Rass understood the sadness now. He wanted to
say he was sorry, but he knew how useless the words
were, how pointless. So he said something else instead,
the only thing he could. "You could stay for a while.
Move on anytime you wanted."

Jake looked at him. In the flickering golden light, his
young face appeared pale, almost fragile. There was a
hint of uncertainty in his eyes. "I . . . I'd like that,
but . . ." He glanced down at his hands.

"But what?"

"I saw that stiff-looking lady and . . . the man who lives here. . . ."

Rass winced at the description of Mariah. "That'd be Mariah, my daughter," he said quietly, "and our new handyman, Mad Dog Stone. They won't bother you."

Jake shook his head. Something like fear darkened his eyes. "I wouldn't want . . . anyone to know I was here. I'm not ready for that yet."

Rass understood. No doubt it had been a long time since the boy had felt at home somewhere. The barn felt safer for him. "Well, that wouldn't be such a problem. It could be our secret for a while."

His green eyes widened hopefully, as if he hadn't dared to hope for that answer. "Really?"

"Really."

Slowly Rass pushed to a stand. "Well, I guess I'd best be getting back to bed. Growing boys and crotchety old men need their sleep. I'll bring breakfast to you about seven o'clock."

"Thanks, Rass."

"You're welcome." Turning, Rass walked out of the barn and shut the door behind him.

The darkness of the night curled around him, comforting in its familiarity as Rass walked back to the farmhouse. Later, alone in the huge feather bed made for two, he stared up at the darkened ceiling.

You sent him to me, didn't you?

For a tantalizing moment, he thought Greta was going to answer. He waited, acutely sensitive, for the scent of lavender and the touch of the wind.

But tonight there was no answer, save the one in his

heart. Still, he smiled. For the first time in months, he looked forward to the morning.

Mad Dog made a bed for the first time in years. He spread the crisp, clean linen across the bumpy mattress and smoothed it out carefully. His hand strayed along the fabric, feeling its unfamiliar texture.

Eagerly he stripped out of his clean clothes and slipped into the bed, drawing the blankets high on his chest. The cool sheets and heavy blankets wrapped around him, cocooned him in a kind of comfort he hadn't known in years.

God, it felt good.

He let out his breath in a sigh and stared up at the ceiling, trying to see into the darkness that huddled above the rafters. But it was impossible. The blackness was impenetrable; he might as well have been staring into space, trying to pierce the distance between the earth and moon.

For no apparent reason, he found himself thinking about Mariah Throckmorton again. She'd be in her bed now, the blankets pulled up to her chin, her hair fanned out across the sheets like strands of mahogany fire.

No, he decided. Braided. She'd have that soft, beautiful hair coiled and twisted and controlled. Always controlled.

He smiled just thinking about her. There was something special about her. She intrigued him. No, more than that. She . . . drew him. He wondered what she thought about, what she dreamed about. Wondered if she was anything like him at all. If she ached for something more in her life than she had on this dusty little farm, that elusive, formless *something*.

He'd chased that need for years, trying to track it down, turn it into something tangible and real, but it was still nothing more than a hazy dream, a longing. He was no closer to it now than he had been fifteen years ago.

And yet still he searched for it, and for some strange, inexplicable reason, he thought maybe Mariah would understand his restless longings.

Strange . . .

He closed his eyes and stretched out. The cool linen chafed his bare skin, caressed it. The sensation was foreign and vaguely erotic. Heat curled in the pit of his stomach and radiated into his groin. He turned restlessly, trying to sleep.

But it was too late. He was thinking about Mariah again.

The next morning, Mariah scraped leftover sausage, sauerbraten, and potatoes from the cutting board into the hot frying pan. Adding spices and onions, she smashed the mixture into a hash. The thick, pungent aroma of frying onions blasted up at her, bringing tears to her eyes.

Absently she wiped away the stinging tears and stirred the hot mummix. The roiling, formless mixture bubbled and popped. Behind it, a tin of freshly baked cornmeal hoecakes sat warming on the stove top.

Not once did she turn away from the stove or glance back at the table.

Then she heard the soft rumble of laughter.

Ignore it. Ignore him.

But she couldn't. She turned slightly and cast a surreptitious glance at the table.

Mad Dog was sitting in *her* chair, with his elbows on the table. He was chatting with her father as if they were the best of friends.

Her gaze slid along his profile, noticing the strength in his squared jaw, the softness in his lips. Sunlight shone through the window behind him and wove through his long, sun-streaked hair.

Mariah's heart felt heavy in her chest. Loneliness slid into longing and moved through her body.

She looked away. It wasn't Mad Dog Stone that caused the ache in her soul, she reminded herself sharply. It was simply his presence, here in her home, talking so intimately with her father, smiling, joking.

Mariah had never had a gentleman caller. It was a fact that had never bothered her until now, this moment. Now, when she looked at Mad Dog, so at home at her kitchen table, she felt a wrenching sadness. A regret for the life she didn't have, would never have.

She couldn't deny that deep in her heart, she wanted a man in her life, wanted the endless, undying love Rass and Greta had shared. Mariah had grown up believing in that fairy-tale kind of love, had seen it every day in her parents' eyes, had expected it.

Now, of course, she knew better. Though, even now, in the long, cold winter nights, she lay in her lonely bed, staring up at the darkened ceiling, and she ached for its loss.

But Mad Dog Stone wasn't the answer to her loneliness. She had to force herself to remember that. Though he stirred something in her—that was undeniable—it was only loneliness that made her respond to him. That, and nothing more.

She forcibly tore her thoughts away from Mad Dog and focused instead on the breakfast. Pushing the hash to one side of the pan, she cracked six eggs into the hot grease.

When the eggs were done, Mariah dished up breakfast and sat down opposite Mad Dog, careful not to meet his gaze. She focused hard on her food, studying each bite intently.

But she felt his gaze on her, hot as fire, stinging as a slap.

She kept her head bowed and bit her lower lip to keep it from trembling. Her heartbeat was erratic, and she couldn't seem to draw an even breath.

She felt . . . vulnerable. It should have angered her, should have made her mad enough to bury the debilitating emotion beneath an avalanche of cool animosity. That's how it had worked for years, whenever anyone— even Rass—had gotten too close.

For years she'd made herself unapproachable and distant. It had been her armor against an unkind world and a passionate, thoughtless nature.

But this time she couldn't make it work, couldn't shut off her emotions with a mental demand and a steel will.

The strange feelings kept creeping back, insinuating themselves into every fiber of her heart and soul. Inside her, she felt a darkness growing, consuming her, eating through the self-control she'd always fought so desperately to maintain.

She was finding it harder and harder to ignore him. Some part of her, some little silent part she'd thought she'd buried long ago, came sputtering to life in his presence. Something about him pushed past her reserves and made her see the aching, desperate lack in her life, the loneliness, the isolation. Just looking at him, at his easy smile and ready laughter, made her remember what it felt like to be free and unafraid. To be touched and held and loved.

God help her, sometimes when she looked at him, she remembered what she wanted to forget. She remembered how good it felt to be held in a man's arms, how comforting it was to be touched.

And it scared her to death.

Chapter Nine

"It's time for church," Rass said, pushing his empty breakfast plate toward the center of the table. "Your mother is waiting." He gave Mariah a bright smile. "She was never a patient woman."

Mad Dog frowned. "I thought—"

"My mother's dead," Mariah said matter-of-factly. "But Rass still visits her every Sunday."

"Sometimes more often," Rass added.

Mariah softened at the quietly spoken words and smiled at her father. "*Usually* more often."

Mad Dog pushed his plate away. "No church for me, thanks."

"It isn't what you expect," Rass said quickly.

He looked at the old man. "How do you know what I expect?"

Mariah laughed and stood up. "It isn't what anyone expects."

He was stunned by the sound of her laughter. It was so unlike her, soft, musical, and yet throaty. Somehow it conjured images of dark nights and steamy passion.

She frowned at him. "Is something the matter, Mr. Stone? You look rather pale."

He couldn't believe he'd reacted so strongly to something as innocuous as a laugh. "Nothin's wrong."

She started to turn away, *wanted*, he thought, to turn away, but she didn't. She stood there. Their gazes locked. Something passed between them, something . . . compelling.

Then, abruptly, she turned away from him.

He blinked. The strange connection with Mariah faded so quickly, he wondered if he'd imagined it. He tried to remember what they'd been talking about.

Oh, yeah. Church.

He glanced at Rass. "Sorry, Rass. I try not to be a hypocrite."

Rass frowned at him. "What do you mean?"

"I don't believe in God."

"I suppose you believe in the devil?"

Mad Dog laughed. "*Him*, I've seen proof of."

"What if I could show you God?"

Mad Dog felt a grin start. "He lives here, does he? In Lonesome Creek?"

Rass nodded seriously. "Of course he does. You could just come and see. . . . That wouldn't be hypocritical."

He shrugged. What the hell. At least he'd get to be with Mariah—maybe even see her smile. "Okay, Professor. Let's go find God."

"Is that what you're wearing to church?" Mad Dog asked Mariah as she came down the stairs an hour later.

She gave him a cold look. "What's wrong with it?"

His gaze swept her from head to foot. She was standing perfectly erect, her small, gloved hands properly pinned to her midsection. An austere stand-up collar, unrelieved by lace or adornment, hugged her pale throat. Dozens of round black buttons—the only color other than dirt brown on the entire dress—marched from her absurdly high collar to her narrow, belted waist. Pointed brown boots peeked out from beneath the plain hem. Her hair was drawn back from her head so tightly, he wondered if it was nailed in back.

He brought his gaze slowly back up her body and looked into her eyes. "Nice dress," he said blandly.

She gave him a delicate sniff and walked out the door.

He was certain that she wanted to slam it behind her, but she didn't.

Plunging his hands in his pockets, he idly strolled out of the kitchen and followed her onto the porch.

Rass was standing in front of the house, holding a bunch of vibrant purple flowers. He looked . . . younger, as if the prospect of going to church erased a dozen years from his face. Gaiety lit his watery eyes with brilliant blue light. "Are you ready, Mad Dog? Mariah?"

"I'm ready," she answered crisply.

Mad Dog glanced around for the wagon, but there wasn't one to be seen. "You want me to hitch up the buggy?"

Rass laughed, a big, good-natured sound that echoed across the lonely farm. "We don't need horses to see the Lord, Mr. Stone. Follow me." Without another word, he took off across the golden fields.

Mad Dog cast an uncertain look at Mariah. "Where's he going?"

She didn't look at him, but he thought he saw the

barest hint of a smile touch her lips. "God lives in the west pasture, Mr. Stone."

He, too, started to smile. "Not in the back twenty?"

"There, too, of course, but we visit Him in the west pasture."

He moved toward her, drawn irresistibly by the sarcasm that limned her words. "You believe that, Mariah?"

She closed her eyes for a moment, then tilted her chin. When she spoke, her words were as soft as the early morning breeze. "What I believe is none of your business, Mr. Stone."

And she stepped past him.

He watched her walk on ahead of him, her body held unnaturally erect. The round, thick oval of hair anchored to the base of her neck glinted like a coil of dark fire in the pale sunlight, reminding Mad Dog of the heat that lay beneath all that stiff propriety.

He smiled. Slowly and with great relish, his gaze slid down her slim back, past the tight indentation of her waist, to the gently rounded curve of her butt. The often-washed linsey-woolsey of her dress clung enticingly to her backside, swishing with each step.

Tilting his hat back, he followed her.

They made their way to a small knoll some distance from the house. The windswept rise should have been no more than a hump in the unending golden fabric of the field, but even to Mad Dog it seemed to be more; a place, not just a bump.

An ancient oak tree stood guard over the spot, its gnarled limbs reaching protectively toward a small iron-work settee. Beside the chair, a rounded headstone pushed up from the well-tended grass, its white marble gilded by the sun's uncertain rays. In front of it sat a pottery bowl of dying purple dahlias.

Mad Dog glanced at the inscription on the stone. *Here lies the body of Greta Wilhemina Throckmorton. Wife, mother, friend. April 17, 1820 to December 23, 1893.*

A sharp pain shot through his insides. He squeezed his eyes shut. Aw, Christ . . .

A whisper of wind worked through the oak's leaves, chattering, welcoming. Slowly he opened his eyes, and found Mariah staring at him.

For once, there was no animosity in her eyes, and no guarded distance. "Are you all right?"

He felt a sudden urge to reach out to her, to tell her he understood. But he couldn't move, didn't move. He just stood there like an idiot, staring at her, feeling her pain mingle with his own to become a cold, heavy block against his lungs.

In the end, all he said was, "Fine."

She eyed him a moment longer, then turned away. Moving slowly, as if each step were dangerous, she crossed to the ironwork settee and took a seat. She perched stiffly on the scrolled edge, her ankles pressed tightly together, her hands in her lap, her face downcast.

Rass moved eagerly toward the tombstone. Kneeling, he replaced the dying flowers with fresh ones. "Sit down, son." Then he started talking to the gravestone in quiet, murmured tones.

Mad Dog walked around the gravesite and came up beside the settee.

Mariah didn't look up.

He inched past her knees—brushing them slightly—

and sat down beside her. The metal creaked beneath his weight.

She stiffened and scooted to the very edge of the seat.

Beside them, still kneeling on the ground, Rass cleared his throat. "Hi, Greta." His voice was lower and softer than Mad Dog had ever heard it before. A quiet kind of emotion suffused it—love, maybe, or reverence. The gentle greeting had a surprisingly strong impact on Mad Dog. It reminded him of the way his mother had spoken to him so long ago.

"We have a visitor with us today, Greta," he whispered. "Mr. Stone. I have great hope for him. What do you think?"

Mad Dog glanced sideways at Mariah.

She sat as stiff as a hat pin, her gaze stoically focused on the gloved hands folded primly in her lap. She didn't so much as look at her father or the tombstone. Even in profile, he could see the tension that held her rigid. Her mouth was drawn into a thin, unforgiving line. A network of worry wrinkles creased the corners of her eyes.

She seemed . . . agitated—even more so than usual. As if she were holding on to her precious self-control by a fraying thread.

A sweet, lavender-scented breeze ruffled through the grass. Rass closed his eyes and inhaled deeply. A slow, potent smile worked across his face. "I think so, too," he whispered, though the words were lost almost immediately on the breeze.

He turned, looked up at Mad Dog. "Do you feel it?"

Mad Dog forced his thoughts away from the woman

sitting so silently beside him, trying not to care why she looked so sad and alone and lost. "Feel what, Rass?"

"Close your eyes."

"Okay." He did as he was asked.

"Listen. Hear the wind . . ."

Overhead, the leaves chattered together, the breeze was a melodic, whistling echo.

"Smell the fruit. The apples, the pears . . ."

The sweet fragrance of the orchard engulfed Mad Dog, filled his senses. A reluctant smile pulled at his mouth.

He heard Rass's slow, shuffling footsteps crunching through the grass toward him. Then came the quiet creaking of old bones, and a gusting exhalation of breath.

Mad Dog opened his eyes and found Rass kneeling directly in front of him.

"That's God," the old man whispered. "He's not in some church, some *building* erected by hammer and nails. He's in us, in the goodness we show to one another. In the love we let ourselves feel."

Mariah snorted. "Ha."

Pain glazed Rass's eyes. He sat back on his heels and drew his blue-veined hands into his lap. "My daughter doesn't believe." There was a wealth of tired sadness in his words.

She stared down at him, her face curiously devoid of emotion. "I did once."

Rass met her cold gaze with his own warm, caring one. "God isn't like a game, Mariah. You don't roll the dice once and then give up if you lose."

She didn't even flinch. "Let it go, Rass."

"*You* let it go."

She rose slowly to her feet. "I'm done with church for today." Her gaze flicked to the tombstone and stuck. "Tell Mama hello for me."

"Tell her yourself."

Mariah didn't answer, didn't seem even to hear. She was staring at the small patch of clipped grass beside her mother's grave. Something glinted in her eyes, something dark and agonized, then she looked away. Without another word, she picked up her heavy skirts and left for the house.

Both men watched her leave, Mad Dog sitting on the half-empty settee, Rass kneeling in the grass at his feet. Neither said a word.

Then, when she disappeared into the house, Rass sighed tiredly and pushed to his feet. Walking to the edge of the mowed grass, he stared down across the farm.

Mad Dog went to the old man and laid a hand on his rail-thin shoulder. He wanted to say something to comfort Rass, but such a thing was so alien, so totally foreign, he had no idea how to go about it. So he stood there like a fool, his hand planted on Rass's shoulder.

"Ah, Greta," Rass whispered to himself. "Our little girl is hurting so bad. . . ."

Mad Dog said nothing. There was nothing to say.

Then, suddenly, Rass turned to him. "You could help her."

He frowned. "I don't even know her."

"That's an excuse."

Mad Dog wanted to laugh or turn away, but the blue fire in the old man's eyes held him in a steel-edged grip. "Maybe," he said evenly.

The keen intensity faded from the old man's eyes. A

caring warmth replaced it. "Excuses have a way of catching up with a man. Even on a backwater farm in the middle of nowhere."

Mad Dog stared over Rass's white-haired head. A question hung on his tongue, heavy and demanding. He knew he shouldn't ask it—shouldn't care—but he couldn't help himself. Something in Mariah's face had touched him, and he wanted to know why. "What's wrong with her?"

"You'll have to ask her that yourself."

"She won't tell me."

"Maybe not the first time. Try again." He looked up at Mad Dog, captured his gaze. "You're a fighter, aren't you?"

"Not in that ring."

Rass gave him a perceptive, probing look. For the first time in years, Mad Dog felt . . . vulnerable. Like the frightened, lonely kid he'd once been.

"Not yet," Rass remarked.

Mad Dog knew he should let the conversation die its uncomfortable death right there, but there was something else he needed to know. He tried to ask the personal question casually. "That patch of grass by your wife's grave—what does it have to do with her . . . problem?"

He knew he hadn't fooled the old man. Rass looked up at him, a smile curving the edges of his pale lips.

Mad Dog felt—crazily—that Rass was pleased by the question.

"Everything," Rass answered softly, and then he walked away.

Mad Dog stood there a long time, listening to the

cant of the breeze through the autumn grass. Colorful
leaves tumbled across his boots, swirled and danced
above the golden carpet in a wash of green and burgundy and brown. The wind was a low, mournful dirge.

The old man was wrong. Mad Dog couldn't ease the
sorrow from Mariah's face, couldn't lift the burden
from her shoulders. That was something he'd learned
about problems. You had to solve your own.

He put his hands in his pockets and focused on the
strand of smoke spiraling up from the chimney. If he
closed his eyes—and he was careful not to—he could
have imagined Mariah inside the house. Her skin would
be pale, almost translucent, her hands would be shaking. She'd be moving slowly from room to room, her
back stiff, her hands clenched, looking for something to
take her mind off her troubles.

Surprisingly, he wished that Rass were right, that he
could help her.

Mariah stood at her bedroom window, staring down
at the bunkhouse. A headache pulsed behind her eyes;
every now and then her vision blurred from the force of
it. She rubbed her throbbing temples with her fingertips.

Leaning forward, she pressed her forehead against the
comforting coolness of the pane. God, she felt so vulnerable and alone. The shield she'd cultivated for many
years was gone, shredded. It had left her the moment
she looked at that tiny patch of clipped grass beside her
mother's grave.

Oh, she'd lost her armor before—every Sunday, in
fact—and she knew she'd get it back. But right now,
without its steel protection, she felt empty and afraid.

Especially with Mad Dog Stone lurking behind every corner, pushing her—always pushing her—making her feel things she didn't want to feel. Making her want things that scared her to death.

And Rass. God bless him, but he didn't understand. To Rass, death was a doorway; a momentous, anticipated experience in a person's life. He had no doubt that he and Greta would be reunited, and less doubt that his wife was in a better place than he. He couldn't wait to join her.

But Mariah hadn't believed in God, or in heaven, in a long, long time. Ever since the first time she'd stood by that small patch of grass.

At the memory, pain surged through her; pain so blinding and intense, it almost brought her to her knees. She sagged against the window and squeezed her eyes shut.

"No," she murmured desperately. "No . . ."

But the images came anyway; she was too weak to fight them off. Red-gold hair and murky blue-gray eyes. A pale blue blanket . . .

Thomas.

A strangled sound of grief escaped her. The memories battered her senses, left her shaken and defenseless. His tiny, quavering wail. The doctor's horrifying words, *I'm sorry, Miss Throckmorton, there's nothing we can do. . . .*

And the blood. Sweet Jesus, the blood . . .

"Oh, God . . ."

She covered her face and stood there, swaying in the center of her empty, lonely bedroom. She wanted to cry, *ached* to, but the tears were trapped in a cold, hard block in her chest.

"No more," she whispered shakily. Her hands slid slowly away from her face and dropped lifelessly to her sides.

She wouldn't think about Thomas anymore. She couldn't.

If she did, she'd go mad.

Mad Dog stood by the table, his gaze fixed on the stairway that led upstairs.

To Mariah.

He backed away from the table, shaking his head. It wasn't his business. Whatever memories haunted Mariah Throckmorton were her own.

From upstairs came a whimpering, choked sound of despair.

"Christ," he muttered.

He knew what was wrong with her now, at least part of it. He'd known when he saw the headstone. And sweet God, he understood her pain. He'd felt it himself, still occasionally felt it. Even now, after all these years.

He found himself wanting to say something to her—he didn't even know what. Just ... something. And it wasn't because he wanted to rattle her or taunt her or make her react. He just wanted to let her know he understood.

He didn't know why—didn't want to know why—but suddenly it was important.

Slowly, knowing he shouldn't and yet unable to help himself, he climbed the stairs. Each step was a creaking reminder that he was invading another person's grief, going where he wasn't welcome. It was something he'd never done in his life; he was welcome in too many places to go where he had no invitation.

Still, he kept moving. With each step, his stomach tightened.

On the landing, he paused. There were three open doors and one closed one. Instinctively he knew that Mariah's bedroom door would be closed. Always.

He stared at the closed door. *Now's the time to back out, Stone.*

He couldn't believe he was doing this. He shouldn't do it, shouldn't reach out to someone he had no intention of actually *touching*, but he couldn't seem to stop himself.

Fisting his hands, he moved slowly toward the door and knocked.

Nothing.

Then came the shuffling sound of hurried feet. "Just a minute, Rass," she called out.

The door swung open. Mariah stood in the doorway. She took one look at him and gasped. Her nostrils flared, her eyes widened. She lurched for the door and tried to slam it in his face.

His hand snaked out, grabbed the door. She stumbled back, then stopped herself and stared at him through despair-darkened eyes.

She was a mess. Her hair was an uncontrolled mass of thick, wavy curls that lay half-pinned, half-dangling down her back. Her skin was deathly pale, almost gray, and her lips were a thin, colorless line.

She looked desperate and vulnerable . . . and achingly beautiful.

She swallowed hard. "Wh—What do you want?"

He moved awkwardly toward her, close enough to touch her but careful not to. He looked down, met her frightened, desperate eyes. He opened his mouth to speak, and found that he had nothing to say.

"Please," she said in a soft, quivering voice. "I don't want to play your games right now."

It was now or never. He took a deep breath and forced himself to say the words he'd never said before. "I . . . my mother . . . she died on Christmas Eve."

Mariah's mouth slipped open. Surprise chased some of the sadness from her eyes. "I'm sorry."

"I didn't come up here for your sympathy."

"Why did you come up here?"

"I . . . aw, hell, it's crazy—" Awkwardness suffused him. He turned to leave.

She reached for his arm. Her fingers curled around his forearm, tightly. He felt the warmth of her skin through the worn cotton of his shirt. A shudder of longing spilled through him at her touch.

Slowly he turned around, his eyes drawn irresistibly to her hand, so pale and soft against the tired fabric of his black shirt. Somehow her touch gave him strength, made it easier to face her and say what he'd come to say.

He looked at her. Their gazes caught, held. "I just wanted you to know I . . . understood."

At his quiet confession, her eyes widened. A gentleness filled her eyes, the emotion so warm and soft, it made Mad Dog's heart sting with longing. She tried to smile.

He saw the slight trembling of her lips and almost groaned aloud. An aching tenderness unfolded within him. Christ, he felt something he'd never felt before. He wanted to kiss her, to take her face in his hands and kiss the sadness from her mouth.

"Does it go away?" she asked softly.

He knew he'd never forget this moment, never forget the sad luminescence of her eyes. Her honesty, like her pain, touched something deep inside him, something he'd forgotten even existed. "It fades," he said softly.

"It fades." She repeated his words quietly, staring up at him.

Mad Dog watched the movement of her lips, mesmerized. He wanted to say something else to her, something profound and relevant that would relieve some portion of her pain. But there was nothing; he knew that. Grief wasn't soothed by pretty words or flowers or notes of sympathy. It simply faded in its own time, in its own way. If it ever did.

But he had to do something to save this moment. It was so special, so suddenly fragile. He felt a connection he'd never felt with a woman before. As if some part of her understood some secret part of him.

"Maybe you'd like to go for a walk?" he said.

Chapter Ten

Maybe you'd like to go for a walk?

Mariah stared at Mad Dog, feeling absurdly relieved. The suffocating weight of grief eased away from her heart; without it, she felt . . . light. It was such an ordinary request, *go for a walk*, but it had been so long since someone had expressed a desire to simply be with her.

She remembered long ago, when she was a young girl, waiting desperately for her father to ask her to join him on his adventure walks. But he never had. He'd walked with Mama for hours, tramping through the grassy pastures, strolling through the sun-dappled orchards. Mariah remembered watching, always watching, from the loneliness of her bedroom, until one day she'd stopped waiting to be invited.

Now, finally, someone had asked her. A smile pulled at her lips. Lord, she'd forgotten how powerful and potent it was to feel wanted. And how dangerous.

That's why she'd run off with Stephen, because *finally* someone had asked, someone had said, "I love you. . . ."

She knew she should say no, should decline graciously and withdraw into the private sanctity of her room. But she didn't want to do the safe thing right now. She wanted to feel connected to the world, appreciated and cared for and cosseted.

That's what his offer was: a chance to pretend to be something other than a frightened old spinster with a sordid past. A chance to be someone else—if only for a few moments.

She could no more deny him right now than she could cry.

"Let me get my bonnet. Wait here." She left Mad Dog standing in the doorway and hurried into her room. She grabbed a handful of hairpins from the cracked china saucer on her dresser and re-coiled her hair as she walked back to the door.

Mad Dog stood in the doorway, waiting.

She smiled and pulled a hairpin from her teeth, ramming it into the tight coil at the base of her neck.

"Mariah?"

She eased another pin from her mouth. "Uh-huh?"

"Don't."

She frowned and glanced up at him. "Don't what?"

He touched her wrist, curled his long, warm fingers around it, and gently pulled her hand away from her hair. "Let it be."

She almost swallowed her hairpins. "Let it *down*, you mean?"

He laughed. It was a rich, rumbling sound that heated her insides and made her stomach feel fluttery. "For me."

She tried to laugh. "That's highly improper."

"Of course it is."

A small smile tugged at her mouth. She was tempted. He smiled at her. "Come on, Mariah . . ."

Her name sounded soft and feminine and pretty on his lips—all the things she wanted to be, used to be, and never would be again. All the things she wanted to pretend to be right now.

"What could it hurt?" he added.

What could it hurt? The seductive words pulled the starch from her defenses. It was a new way of looking at things. Usually her first question was how much will it hurt.

"What indeed?" she said softly. Then she smiled. She'd probably pay for it tomorrow, but today she didn't care. For once, she wanted to be herself. She tugged the pins from her hair and tucked them in her pocket.

Mad Dog stepped toward her, his eyes fastened on hers. For a moment, she couldn't breathe. He reached out, pushed his fingers through her hair, and loosened it, fanning it out around her shoulders. "That must feel better," he breathed, stepping back.

"It does," she admitted.

"Then shall we go?"

She smiled brightly, feeling suddenly like a young girl at her first dance. She nodded and followed him from the house.

They emerged into the warm, sunlit afternoon and walked side by side down the creaking wooden steps. Together they strolled down the path. The air was fragrant with the smell of flowers and dirt and sunlight.

Mariah couldn't think of a thing to say. Neither, apparently, could Mad Dog. They walked in silence, listening to the sounds of the afternoon: the whisper of the breeze, the repetitious creak of the porch swing, the chatter of the birds. It didn't seem to matter that they didn't speak. The silence was companionable, comfortable.

Mariah glanced down to her right, seeing the burgundy, purple, and amber smear of her autumn flowers. Saucer-sized gold chrysanthemums waved in the slight breeze. The heady fragrance of the flowers filled her senses. She felt herself lapsing into a lazy, whimsical state that was completely out of character. For a second—perhaps no more than a heartbeat—she felt like a woman out strolling with her man. She felt . . . special.

A gate creaked open.

Mariah jerked to a stop and snapped her chin up. Her heart started beating faster, drummed in her ears. Fear caught her hard, stabbed through the pit of her stomach. She couldn't swallow, couldn't breathe.

Mad Dog was a foot or so ahead of her, his hand on the gate's glinting silver latch. He pushed the gate slightly. It squealed in protest and swung backward, smacking against the picket fence in its arc. "Milady?"

She stared at the gate, unable to look away.

He frowned at her. "Mariah?"

His voice seemed to be coming at her from a million miles away. Involuntarily she took a step backward. She told herself she wasn't afraid. She couldn't breathe because of the flowers; suddenly they smelled sickeningly sweet. The ceaseless, annoying chattering of the birds battered her ears and gave her a pounding headache.

For a terrifying moment, she thought she was going to be sick.

He came up beside her, touched her chin. "Mariah?"

She yanked her gaze away from the gate and focused on his eyes, only his eyes. Her heart was beating so loudly, she could hardly hear his words. "Yes?" She tried to sound casual, but her voice was strained and uncertain.

He looked down at her. "Is something the matter?"

The concern in his eyes almost broke Mariah's heart. Suddenly the magic of the afternoon was gone, melted into the pains and frustrations of her past. She shook her head, wet her impossibly dry lips.

It fades. . . .

His words came back to her. Reassuring, pretty words, filled with the hope she'd lost so long ago. She wanted to believe them, ached to believe them, but now, standing here beside the gate, she knew they were a lie. For her, the heartaches of the past would never fade.

He touched her chin, tilted her face to his. "What's going on here?"

She looked up into his handsome features and wished for an insane, desperate moment that she could be what he wanted. That he could be what she needed. But neither one of them could change that much. She let out her breath in a tired sigh and tried not to feel broken. "I . . . have to start supper."

He frowned. "I see."

Do you? she wanted to say. *How could you—when I don't even understand it myself?* But she said nothing. So she just stood there, staring up at him, wishing—oh, God, wishing—things were different.

Suddenly he looped an arm around her and drew her close.

She knew she should pull away. It was wholly improper to let him touch her this way. More than that, it was fraught with risk.

But right now, standing in the empty yard, it felt good to have someone—to have him—beside her. The silent, unquestioning support was something she'd never had in her life, and it made her feel warm and safe and ... however inappropriately, cherished. She leaned infinitesimally toward him, resting against the hard ball of his shoulder.

In his arms, she felt safe. The irrational fear of leaving the farm receded again, slunk back into the darkness in the back of her mind. It wasn't that she couldn't leave, she told herself. She just didn't want to. Not now. Not yet.

Maybe tomorrow she'd feel like leaving. And if she really wanted to go, the damn gate wouldn't stop her. Nothing would ... not if she really wanted to go.

Her eyes fluttered shut. A quiet sigh escaped her lips. "Thanks," she said quietly, "I needed that."

He tightened his hold. She felt each finger like a curl of fire through the worn fabric of her sleeve. "You need a hell of a lot more than that, Mariah, but I guess this'll do for now." Before she could respond, he leaned toward her and planted a moist, openmouthed kiss in the tender flesh beside her ear.

She shivered at the heat of the contact.

Then he turned and walked away.

She stared after him. She wanted to look away and knew she should, but she couldn't.

Something had changed with them today. It had started when he'd come to her bedroom. Not to fight with her or scare her or tease her, but simply to say that he understood what it meant to feel lost and alone.

It meant so much to her, that moment of intimacy, perhaps more than any moment she could remember in the last ten years. He'd reached out to her, however tentatively, and touched her soul. It was a kindness she wouldn't have expected from a man like him.

A man like Stephen, she thought immediately, but the thought carried no weight this time, no sting. And no truth.

Mad Dog wasn't like Stephen. True, they were both footloose wanderers who couldn't stay put, but where Stephen was dishonest and self-centered, Mad Dog was honest and caring.

He wasn't like Stephen.

She squeezed her eyes shut, feeling a breathless sense of panic. She wanted to believe he was like Stephen, *needed* to believe he was like Stephen. Then she could keep him at arm's length. Without the negative comparison, she didn't know what to do, how to handle him, how to protect herself.

But he wasn't like Stephen, she knew that now. Knew it with a certainty that terrified her.

"Oh, no . . ." She brought a cold hand to her mouth. *Please, God,* she thought, *don't let me start feeling that way again. Don't let me think he might be different.*

But it was too late. God help her, it was too late.

Rass leaned back against the oak tree and drew his legs up to his chest. Curling his arms around his ankles, he stared down at the farm he'd helped to build with his own two hands.

Sadness tightened his chest. A dull pain throbbed in his left shoulder.

There's so much left to do.

So many things he'd never gotten around to.

A small, wistful smile pulled at his lips. The loafing shed had been the first thing he'd built. What did he know about building—a geology professor from New York? But he'd found the supplies—books, nails, hammers—and he'd done his best.

The first effort had fallen down in a hard rain. The second lasted almost through the winter. And the third, well, it was still hanging on to existence by a thread.

He'd been able to laugh about it, then and now, because of Greta. He remembered standing alongside her during the rainstorm, both of them soaked through to the skin, rain streaming down their faces as the shed crashed to the ground.

The memory of her throaty laughter rang through his mind, reminding him how they had stood there, hand in hand in the drenching rain, and laughed at his failure.

But where had Mariah been that day? Questions like that plagued Rass more and more as he got older.

He had so many memories of Greta, and so few of Mariah. Somehow they'd excluded her. They hadn't meant to. Jesus, they hadn't meant to. . . .

It was just that they'd come together so late in life. Neither of them had ever thought they'd fall in love, and it had been such a precious, all-consuming gift. They'd never expected to have children, never wanted to, and with Greta's age, they'd never worried about it.

Then Mariah had come, all red-faced and crying and demanding.

They'd loved their daughter, deeply and completely. But had they ever told her, ever showed her in the thousand tiny, wordless ways they showed each other? God help him, he couldn't remember. . . .

She was lonely now, so damned independent. Exactly the woman two middle-aged parents had raised her to be. Strong, defiant, aware of her own intelligence.

But they hadn't taught her how to love or how to be loved.

He felt another sharp, twisting pain in his heart at the thought. God, how could they have been so blind?

He shook his head, staring through stinging eyes at the dull brown grass.

She'd never called him daddy, not even as a child. She went straight from "father" to "Rass" at the age of six. And for a year after that fiasco with Stephen, she didn't call him anything at all. Didn't even speak to him.

Why the hell had he let her retreat so far into herself? Last night he'd looked into Jake's eyes—a stranger— and Rass had seen pain. How had he missed so much in his own child?

"Why didn't we see it, Greta?" The words slipped past his chapped lips.

It had never mattered before that Mariah called him Rass; hell, he'd been proud of her pride and defiance.

But now, damn it, it mattered. There were many things he wanted to tell her, lessons yet to teach her.

He didn't even know where to begin.

He sighed, disgusted that he knew perfectly well how

to reach out to a stranger, but had no idea how to connect with his own daughter.

It should be simple and straightforward.

I'm sorry, Mariah. I love you.

Tears stung his eyes again. Not so simple, he thought with an unfamiliar bitterness. Not with Mariah.

Somehow, he and Greta had created a child who didn't hear those words well, didn't want to hear them.

Had they forgotten to tell her as a child? Had she stood alone in their happy home, waiting for a declaration her parents had taken for granted?

He'd never once told Greta that he loved her. His own parents had never said the words, and yet he'd known, just as Greta had known. He'd always thought of love that way, as a look, a touch, a smile. Not a word to be passed from one to another like a Christmas gift.

But now he wondered. What was love to Mariah? Had she waited, lonely and aching and afraid, for the simple words that had never come? Had she run away with the first man who said them to her because she was so starved to hear it?

A dark, sadness filled him. He didn't know, might never know what he and Greta had done wrong. And, perhaps it didn't matter. Perhaps all that mattered was making it right now.

He had to get past the silent wall of her defenses. Maybe then he could figure out a way to say the hundreds of things that needed saying.

Or maybe just the one.

It was almost nightfall when Rass finally came to the barn. Jake heard the old man's voice, calling out to him, and relief rushed through him. He'd been lonely today, tired and sad. He couldn't wait to sit and talk with Rass. When he was with the old man, Jake felt safe and cared-for.

"Hey, Jake," he said from the doorway, "come on down."

Jake frowned. Rass sounded . . . tired.

He crawled to the corner of the loft and peered down. "Hi, Rass."

Rass smiled weakly. "Hi, Jake."

Jake got a really bad feeling in his stomach that something was wrong. His frown deepened. "You don't have any food with you."

Rass shook his head. "Come on down."

Jake clambered down the ladder and dropped onto the floor. "What's going on?"

Rass walked toward him, his feet making a shuffling, scuffing sound on the hard-packed dirt floor. There was a sheen of moisture in his rheumy blue eyes. "I've been thinking, Jake."

Jake licked his lips, trying to banish a rising sense of apprehension. "Oh."

Rass glanced sideways, staring hard through the small, dusty window in the barn's left side. "It's not right that you hide out here."

"But—"

He waved a veiny hand. "But nothing. I try not to make the same mistakes twice. And I know better than to let you hide from whatever it is you don't want to face."

Jake froze. Emotions—fear, anxiety, anticipation—hurtled through him, left him winded and reeling in their wake. "Wh—What makes you think I'm hiding from something?"

"Believe me, Jake, I've learned to read the signs."

"I'm not hiding from anyone." He flushed, realizing his mistake instantly. "I mean, anything."

Rass's eyes narrowed at Jake's words. The old man studied him for a long, uncomfortable moment before he spoke. "Good. Then there's no reason to stay in the barn."

Jake shook his head. He tried to swallow, but his throat was dry. He was afraid his obvious fear was revealing to much, but he couldn't help himself. "I don't think so. . . ."

Rass laid a firm, comforting hand on his shoulder and squeezed gently. "It's time for you to meet my daughter . . . and Mad Dog. Time to quit hiding."

It's time. Jake sighed heavily. How many times had he thought those exact words? Maybe Rass was right; maybe it was time to stop running and hiding and being afraid. He'd followed Mad Dog for months now, too scared to actually say hello.

"Come on," Rass said gently, and turned for the door.

Jake couldn't move. His feet felt as heavy as stones. *You don't have to follow him.*

He could turn around right now and run. Just forget the whole thing.

But he'd tried that already.

For ten years he'd tried to forget about the legendary Mad Dog Stone—tried and failed.

He had to go with Rass; he knew that. He *had* to go. He'd been following Mad Dog for months, dreaming incessantly of this moment. He couldn't let it slip through his fingers now because he was afraid.

"Rass?"

The old man stopped, turned around. "Uh-huh?"

Jake wet his lips nervously. "Stay with me." He tried to say the words in a flippant, casual tone and failed. They came out weak and pathetic-sounding.

Rass nodded and gave Jake a soft knowing smile. "I will."

Jake squeezed his eyes shut and said a quick, silent prayer. Then, silently and side by side, they walked out of the barn and headed toward the house.

Jake's stomach was twisted into a throbbing, nauseous knot. He tried not to be afraid, but it was impossible. He was scared to death.

Finally, after all these years, he was going to meet his father.

Chapter Eleven

Mariah stood at her mirror, pinning her hair into a tight coil at the base of her neck. She rammed one hairpin after another into the thick chignon, securing it until a hurricane couldn't bring it down.

Today she'd let Mad Dog get too close. Far too close. Just thinking about it made her feel queasy and vulnerable and afraid. She'd let him inside her today, just a little bit and for no longer than a heartbeat, but she'd let him in all the same.

A tremor passed through her, made her fingers tremble. His quiet confession had touched something in her, made her feel warm and liquid inside, as if maybe things would someday be all right again. It was a thought she hadn't had in years, hadn't let herself have.

For a few precious, magical moments, she had almost believed in her old dreams, almost believed her life could be different.

She sighed. Feeling infinitely tired and old, she left her bedroom and descended the stairs. In the kitchen, she went through the motions . . . started a fire in the stove and pulled the food from the ice rack. But even as she buried herself in the familiar, comforting routine, she couldn't make herself forget.

What a fool she'd been.

It had been crazy to let herself pretend. She knew the cost of looking at life through rose-colored spectacles. Mad Dog Stone offered her an easy smile and a moment's comfort. Nothing she needed, nothing she could count on. She had to remember that. Always. He wasn't the answer to the aching loneliness that gripped her in the long hours of the night.

He was a drifter, just passing through her life.

Maybe he wasn't exactly like Stephen, but in the end that wouldn't matter, wouldn't save her from heartache. Because he was enough like Stephen.

He'd leave.

Her heart gave a tiny lurch at the thought. Without him around, she'd go back to her old life, lonely and isolated and afraid of everything.

But that was what she wanted, she reminded herself. What made her feel safe. She had to protect herself from Mad Dog and from herself. She had to make sure that when he left—and he *would* leave—he didn't take her heart with him. She couldn't survive that again. She wasn't strong enough.

And the only way to be sure he didn't take her heart with him was not to give it to him.

She hauled a big cast-iron skillet from beneath the stove and dropped it on the range top. It landed with a loud clang. She added a dollop of lard and a bunch of sausage and leftover mashed potatoes and onions. The foods slid together in a splattering, popping mixture.

Suddenly the front door creaked open. "Go on into

the kitchen. I'll be right back," came her father's voice from the foyer.

Mariah's heartbeat sped up at the thought of seeing Mad Dog again. *Please help me be strong. . . .*

Stiffening, she picked up the pepper sprinkler and added a healthy dose to the food. "Hi, Rass. Mad Dog," she called out, careful not to look their way. "Supper's almost ready."

The front door clicked shut. Quiet footsteps moved through the foyer and into the kitchen. "H-Hi."

Mariah glanced at the doorway. And found herself staring into the face of a young boy with large, frightened green eyes and tousled red-gold hair. He was thin, too thin, his face all hollows and sharp points, looked almost elfin. But he had strong cheekbones and a squared jaw that would someday make him a handsome man. He was wearing a dirty, patched blue work shirt and oversize wool trousers, hitched around his small waist with a thick black belt.

Her heart skidded to a stop. The aluminum pepper sprinkler slipped through her nerveless fingers and clanked on the hardwood floor. For one crazy, terrifying moment, she thought she was looking at a ghost—an image created by her own guilty, lonely mind. "Thomas," she whispered throatily.

The boy licked his lips nervously. "I'm Jake," he said in an unsteady voice. "Mr. Throckmorton invited me to supper. I'm his new assistant."

Mariah blinked in confusion. "I don't understand. . . ."

Rass shuffled into the room. "Ah, Mariah, I see you've met our young guest."

Slowly the tilting world righted itself. Mariah's hopeful, impossible image slid into reality.

She stared at the boy, really seeing him this time. Disappointment poured through her, leaving her shaken and desperately sad in its backwash. No ghost, she realized; just a young man. A dirty, ragged-clothed boy with strawberry blond hair and green eyes.

Not Thomas.

Of course it couldn't be Thomas. . . .

She swallowed hard, fighting to regain her equilibrium. "Jake." As hard as she tried, she couldn't make her voice anything but a tremulous whisper.

"He's going to help me catalog my fossils."

Mariah nodded, too stunned to even point out that she cataloged her father's fossils. Too dumbfounded to even feel criticized. "That's . . . wonderful." She moved hesitantly toward the boy. Her fingers stung with the need to touch his cheek, to push the dirty hair from his eyes. To be the mother she never had been, never could be.

She came up short, stopping before she made a complete fool of herself. She glanced at her father. "Where did you find him?"

Jake threw a frightened look a Rass.

Rass shrugged. "He . . . uh . . . answered my other ad at Ma's Diner. He's just passing through and needed some extra money."

Just passing through. Mariah tried not to be hurt by the familiar words. She shrugged, wondering what she could say to this boy. He was probably at least fifteen years old; far too old to need a mother or mothering. And yet her instincts were so strong, almost overwhelming. It took all her strength and self-control not to move toward him or offer to wash his clothes. "Oh . . ."

"I-Is that okay with you?" Jake asked.

Mariah looked at the boy, seeing the nervous tensing of his mouth and the way he kept rubbing his palms along his wool pant legs. An aching tenderness unfolded within her. He was alone in the world; somehow she was sure of it. As alone as she and Rass. She wished she could take the pain of that away from him. No one so young should ever be alone or lonely or afraid.

She gave him a soft smile. "Of course it's all right. You're welcome here, Jake." The words echoed back at her, filled her with desperate longings she thought she'd forgotten years ago. She crossed her arms. Her empty, empty arms.

So welcome . . .

He glanced down at the floor. A thick lock of hair fell across his eyes. "Thanks."

"Here," Rass said, showing him to the table. "I'll set you a place."

Mariah stared at the boy a moment longer, then forced herself to turn away. Moving stiffly, she went to the stove and added more sausages and potatoes and onions to the pan.

But her hands were shaking and her heart was racing. Between Mad Dog's touch and Jake's presence, she felt frighteningly out of control, as if the world she'd spent fifteen years creating had just tilted on its end. And everything she wanted, everything she believed in and had fought for, was slowly, irrevocably sliding into the darkness of the unknown, the unmanageable.

Things were changing too fast. She was feeling things she hadn't felt in a lifetime, and it scared her to death.

God, help me . . .

But this time the words didn't help. She didn't even know what to ask for.

Jake sat at the table, his back stiff, his knees held tightly together. He stared down at his hands, pressed palm-down on his thighs. His heart was hammering so hard, he couldn't hear anything else.

"You been . . . outta . . . long, Jake? Jake?"

He blinked hard and snapped his chin up. Across the table, Rass was peering at him intently, the old man's bushy white eyebrows drawn in a concerned vee above his blue eyes.

"Uh . . . sorry, sir. What did you say?"

Rass smiled. "I didn't say anything. Mariah asked if you'd been out this way for long."

Jake glanced over at the woman. She was standing by the stove, staring at him in the soft, gentle way his mother had. He swallowed hard, feeling a rush of embarrassing emotion. She looked . . . caring. Almost as if he mattered. But that was crazy. "Sorta long."

"Oh." She gave him a smile that made his insides feel like they were melting.

He tried to think of something else to say, but before he could, someone knocked on the front door.

Jake froze. His fingers coiled into a sweaty ball of nerves. Suddenly he wasn't ready to do this. He wanted to sneak back into the shadows and put off the inevitable. Mad Dog wouldn't accept a long-lost son, wouldn't care. Jake had no business here. . . .

"Will you get the door, Mariah?" Rass said.

Jake's anxious gaze cut to Mariah; he hoped she'd do something to stop Mad Dog from coming in.

For a second he thought she might stop the inevitable. She looked as nervous as he felt. But in the end, she didn't. She smoothed her hands on her wrinkled apron and left the room.

Jake heard the door creak open, then came the rumbling sound of Mad Dog's voice. Then the woman said something he couldn't hear. Her voice sounded fluttery and nervous—just like Jake felt.

Oh, God, Mama . . . Oh, God . . .

Mad Dog sauntered into the warm, cozy kitchen. He stood in the doorway, hat tilted back on his head to reveal a smiling, suntanned face. His threadbare black shirt drooped on his broad shoulders, the open collar exposing a gaping slash of dark chest. Old, faded blue jeans hugged his long legs.

"Well, well," he said with a deepening smile. "Who we got here, Mariah?"

Jake lurched to his feet so fast, the chair skidded out behind him and crashed to the floor. Heat crawled up his neck and fanned across his cheeks. He yanked his fingers apart and forced his hands to his sides.

Mad Dog swept the hat from his head and tossed it on the Peerless creamery. It landed with a muffled *thwack*. Running a hand through his shoulder-length, sun-streaked hair, he strolled toward the table.

Each *thud-thud-thud* of bootheels on the planked

floor seemed thunderously loud. Jake flinched at every step.

Mad Dog held out his hand in greeting. "Hiya, kid. I'm Mad Dog."

Jake's throat went bone-dry. He stared at the hand extended toward him and thought of his own sweaty palms. He cleared his throat and tried unobtrusively to wipe his hand on his pant leg, then reached out.

Mad Dog's long, strong fingers curled around Jake's and squeezed hard. "You got a name, kid?"

Jake's chin snapped up. He looked into Mad Dog's gray eyes and felt a surge of emotion so strong it was almost overwhelming. He'd never been this close to his father. It was a moment he'd dreamed of all his life, but never actually believed would happen. Longing spilled through him in a sickening wave.

"I'm Jake," he said quietly, afraid his voice would crack if he tried more.

Mad Dog started to extract his hand, but Jake couldn't let go. He clung to his father's hand for a heartbeat too long, desperate to maintain the connection he'd waited all his life to find.

Mad Dog frowned, pulled a little harder.

Jake forced his fingers open and withdrew his hand.

"So." Mad Dog turned to Mariah. Looping his thumbs inside the waistband of his frayed jeans, he turned his back on Jake and headed for the range. "What's for supper tonight?"

Jake stared at the man's broad-shouldered back and felt a rush of anger. He'd been dismissed, forgotten.

One thing you gotta remember about your daddy, Jake. Mad Dog forgets things easy. It's just the way he is.

His mother's words came back to Jake, calmed him. He let out his breath softly, and felt the anger dissolve. It wouldn't be easy getting Mad Dog's attention, and even harder to keep it. He'd known that all along. His mother had told him so. Mad Dog was a loner who never stayed in one place too long and never cared about anyone but himself.

Jake tried to ignore the pinch of pain in his chest at the thought. He'd known about Mad Dog. Always.

Mama had told him long ago that his father was incapable of making a commitment.

But love, she told him. *That's not the same thing. Your father knows how to love—in his own easygoing way. He just doesn't know how to stay. . . .*

Jake swallowed hard. That's all he wanted, all he needed. It was so simple, it sounded stupid, but he couldn't force the need away. It had lodged in his heart the first time he heard about his daddy, and through all the years since, it had held fast. And since Mama's death, it had grown stronger. All he wanted now was a little bit of love.

That couldn't be asking too much.

Mad Dog sat at the table, his legs stretched out in front of him, his ankles crossed. The boy, Jake, sat across from him, still sitting as stiff as a knife, and Rass was sprawled in his chair, half-asleep. Mariah was at the sink, washing dishes.

He couldn't take his eyes off her. There was a new softness about her, a lessening of the rigid propriety. He was mesmerized.

She turned away from the sink suddenly, her damp

hands twisted in the wrinkled linen of her apron. Across the room, their gazes met.

Her eyes widened. He waited for her to turn away, but she didn't. Slowly she eased her hands from the apron and let them fall to her sides.

She looked incredibly beautiful right now, and somehow vulnerable. A dangerous, potent yearning swelled in his groin at the sight of her. All of a sudden he wanted to kiss her. *Needed* to kiss her. *Jesus* . . .

Rass's chair creaked loudly. He leaned back and lit up a pipe. The acrid-sweet odor of tobacco floated through the room. Threads of gray smoke drifted across Mariah's face, obscuring her for a heartbeat.

"Sit down, Mariah. I have an idea," Rass said, puffing on the pipe.

She moved stiffly to the table and sat down beside Mad Dog, careful not to make eye contact. Her chair was close to his, so close he could smell the soft fragrance of vanilla that clung to her clothing.

"We could play a game," Rass suggested. "We've got that new Electoral College Game." He grinned at Mad Dog. "It teaches the method of electing our president."

Mad Dog tried to smile—he really did. "Uh-huh. Sounds great."

"I don't know, Rass," Mariah said quietly, "Mr. Stone probably doesn't like board games."

"I think *bored* is the key word," Mad Dog remarked blandly.

Mariah didn't look at him, but he felt, oddly, as if she were disappointed. She started to rise.

Instinctively he reached out and grabbed her wrist. Her skin felt cool and soft beneath his chapped fingers.

She gasped quietly and turned to him, slowly lowering back to her seat until their faces were a handspan apart. Her lips parted in surprise. A tiny breath escaped.

His gaze held hers in a strong, velvet grip. She didn't look away. Slowly her tongue peeked out, dragged nervously along her lips. Moisture glistened on the puffy pinkness of her mouth.

He almost groaned aloud.

"I didn't say I didn't want to play," he said quietly. "I just don't want to play that."

"What did you have in mind?"

"How about something more ... interesting. Like poker?"

Rass thumped his fist on the table. "Great idea."

She pulled back her hand. He resisted for a heartbeat and no more, then grudgingly let go.

"All right," she said, smoothing a nonexistent wrinkle from her skirt. "We shall try poker."

Rass set his pipe down and leaned forward. Resting his elbows on the table, he steepled his fingers and peered at Mad Dog. "How about making it more ... interesting?"

Mad Dog grinned. *Strip poker.* He bit back the entirely inappropriate response just in time. "What did you have in mind?"

"Team poker," he said. "You and Mariah against Jake and me."

He glanced at Mariah and grinned. He couldn't have planned it better himself. "What'll we play for?"

"How about a fish breakfast? Winners catch and cook," Rass said.

Mariah frowned at her father. "Winners?"

"Do you have a problem with that?"

"I just thought—"

"No problem." Mad Dog cut her off seamlessly.

Rass grinned triumphantly. "Perfect." Then he patted Jake on the back. "Come on, partner, let's talk strategy."

Mad Dog smiled. Rass and Jake could talk strategy from now until morning, and it wouldn't help. Mad Dog was gonna win this game.

Nothing—but nothing—was gonna keep him from spending the morning with Mariah. Even if he had to fish.

"I fold." Rass slapped his cards down on the table.

Jake grinned. "Me, too." His cards landed alongside his partner's.

Mariah glanced down at the ten facedown cards. She had a strong urge to sweep them into her hands, but Rass had been firm on the "no peek" rule.

Mad Dog fanned his cards out in front of him. "What a surprise. I win . . . again. And with a pair of threes." He turned to Mariah. "What about you?"

Mariah laid her cards down and frowned. She was starting to get extremely nervous. She and Mad Dog were winning with unbelievable regularity. She was beginning to suspect that Rass was letting them win. And she did *not* want to win. "Not even a pair. Ten high," she said in a tight voice.

"Well, you're too good for the likes of us," Rass said, scooting his chair back and standing. He stretched and yawned, clamping a veiny hand over his mouth.

"We're not done playing!" Mariah almost yelled.

Rass grinned. "Yes, we are. You two won." He turned

to Jake, still smiling triumphantly. "Lord, I'm tired. How about you, Jake?"

The boy grinned up at the old man. "Dead tired."

Mariah glanced at Jake, and felt a squeeze around her heart. "You want to sleep in the guest room?"

The boy cast a nervous look at Mad Dog. "N-No. I got my stuff in the barn already."

She frowned, wondering what Mad Dog had to do with Jake's decision to sleep in the barn. "Well, if that's what you'd prefer . . ."

Rass smacked the boy on the back. "I love a good fish fry. Don't you?" Then he glanced down at Mariah and Mad Dog. "We'll be down for breakfast around 6:00. Will you be ready?"

Mad Dog shrugged. "It's fishing, not flame throwing. How hard can it be?"

"I believe the last time you said that, you were talking about picking apples . . . or was it the pigpen?" Mariah reminded him dryly.

He laughed. "That's work. Fishing's fun."

She gave him a wry look. "Is it?"

He turned to her. "Isn't it?"

"Certainly. What could be better than getting up before dawn to squish a bunch of slimy living animals onto metal hooks?"

He leaned toward her. "Will it be dark?"

She frowned. "Of course."

He gave her a slow, dangerous smile.

God help her, she reacted. Anticipation crept down her spine in an icy shiver.

"Then, believe me, Mariah. It's gonna be fun."

Chapter Twelve

Mariah sat on the porch's top step, her knees drawn in close to her chest. Beside her lay two fishing poles, a willow trout basket, and a top-of-the-line Borcherdt's tackle box.

She closed her eyes and leaned against the wisteria-twined porch post. The dry scent of dormant leaves teased her, reminded her of spring, when the thick, twisted brown vine had been leafy green and ripe with pale purple clusters.

It was still in the hour before dawn, preternaturally quiet. No crickets chirruped their mating calls, no frogs called out from their hiding places in wet thickets along the river, no birds chattered to one another. The darkness was unbroken, a black blanket thrown across the rolling fields.

A whistle cut through the silence, riding gently, lightly, on the air. Then came the quiet crunching of bootheels on the loose rock path.

Her stomach tightened, anxiety spilled through her. Reluctantly she lifted her head and looked up, trying to see Mad Dog in the darkness, but she couldn't. She could hear his footsteps, imagine that easy, loose-hipped walk of his. Then the footsteps stopped.

"Helluva goddamn time to get up," his said in a scratchy morning voice. "That coffee I smell?"

She nodded stiffly. "I packed a flask."

"And you filled it with coffee?" There was a pause, and Mariah was somehow certain that he grinned. "Tequila warms you a lot quicker."

Mariah laughed in spite of herself. "I don't believe I want you that warm, Mr. Stone."

He moved toward her. *Crunch, crunch, crunch.*

Her gaze narrowed, tried to pierce the darkness, but he was no more than a shadow against the night, a presence felt but unseen. "Too late, Mariah," he said in a voice so intimate, it sent shivers down her spine. "I'm already hotter than you want me to be."

His silken words caused a red-hot shudder of response. Deep inside her, where no man had touched in years, and no man genuinely, she felt something. A spark of emotion that was powerful, but completely foreign—need, desire, she wasn't sure what.

Yearning, she realized suddenly. That's what it was. Deep down she yearned for something, for someone. She always had.

And you always will, she reminded herself sharply. Mad Dog Stone, drifter-vagabond-boxer, was not the man to fill the void in her empty soul. He didn't want anything from her that he couldn't get from a dozen women. And he wouldn't stay long enough to find out what she wanted.

Somehow, that made her sad. Then angry.

"Mr. Stone," she said tightly, "I cannot stand this

constant banter. Will you please save it for a woman more interested in hearing it?"

There was a breath-laden pause before he answered. "I think you like to hear it, Mariah."

Her heart skipped a beat. And that second of reaction made her angrier still.

"Obviously you've made a mistake, Mr. Stone. You've confused me with one of the big ... built, easy women with whom you no doubt spend your time."

"What makes you think I like big tits?"

Mariah knew immediately that she'd erred. "I really do not want to have this discussion with you, Mr. Stone."

He climbed another step.

Mariah steeled herself for his sensual assault. Her arms curled around her knees and locked hard.

He stopped. She heard his breath, just above her head, slow and easy, each breath a silent invitation.

In the distance, the horizon caught fire. A low, hazy line of red-gold sunlight blurred through the black night, sending feelers of warmth through the dark sky.

Slowly he dropped to one knee in front of her. The step sagged beneath his weight.

"It so happens I like smaller breasts, Mariah." Her name fell from his lips in a whispered, disembodied caress. "With pale pink nipples that get hard when I—"

"Stop!" She lurched to her feet so fast, he was caught off guard.

With a muttered *shit*, he half fell, half stumbled down the steps and landed with a thud in the flowers.

Mariah spun around and picked up the fishing gear. Ramming it under her arm, she yanked up her skirts and headed down the stairs. She was almost to the wash-house when she heard him call her name.

"Mariah?"

Reluctantly she came to a stop. "Yes?"

"It's darker than hell out here and I have no idea where the river is."

Mariah ground her teeth in frustration. He was right, of course. There was no way he could find the river without her assistance. She hugged herself tightly and tapped her foot impatiently.

Don't let him get to you, Mariah. Keep your distance.

"Fine, Mr. Stone. I'm waiting."

He loped up behind her. She felt each crunching step like a slap.

"You there?"

"Right here."

He moved toward her. She felt his hand close around hers; strong, long fingers slid gently between her own.

She stiffened, tried to yank her hand away.

He held fast. "I wouldn't want to get lost," he said with a soft laugh.

Mariah tried not to notice how good it felt to be touched by him, how warm his skin felt against hers. "F-Fine," she said. "Let's go."

He pulled her close and whispered in her ear. "Yeah, let's."

A flurry of emotions hurtled through Mariah as she led Mad Dog through the darkened orchard. Her senses seemed heightened in the shadowy half world of time that was neither night nor day. His fingers, curled warm and protectively around her own, felt like a lifeline in the darkness. A connection to another human being that she hadn't had in years.

It had been so long since a man had touched her. Even in passing. And now someone was holding her hand. She felt a hundred intense, unexpected emotions all at once—giddy, desperate, frightened.

The feelings were foreign and yet frighteningly familiar. She tried to convince herself that she didn't desire Mad Dog Stone, not even a little bit. That any woman would feel a spark of response in this situation. And she even knew that on some level it was true. Any woman would respond to a man like him.

But there was more to it. God help her, even after everything that had happened to her, with everything that she knew about Mad Dog, he still touched something inside her. Something that hadn't been touched in a lifetime and was desperately in need of warmth.

By the time they reached their destination, dawn had dressed the farm in pinks and golds. Strands of rosy dawn light slid through the shadowy orchard and licked the foamy swirls of the river. The quiet *lap-gurgle-splash* of the water against the muddy bank was the only sound in the world.

For a split second Mariah hesitated to tell Mad Dog they'd reached the fishing hole. She knew he'd pull his hand away then, and she'd be as she was before. A woman unconnected and alone.

She sighed, and in the silence the sound was achingly pathetic. Was she really so lonely that holding a man's hand—even Mad Dog's—could reduce her to silent lies?

"We're here," she said, wishing she could put a

stronger spine in her words. Instead, they sounded wistful and vaguely disappointed. Exactly the way she felt.

He waited a heartbeat, then let go of her hand. The cool breeze immediately rushed in, chilling flesh that moments ago had been warm and damp and joined.

She dropped the tackle box and rods. They hit the grassy earth with a jangling thud.

Mad Dog sat down and stretched his long legs out. Leaning back on his elbows, he grinned up at her.

Reaction set her fingertips trembling. God, how long had it been since a man had looked at her like that? As if she were young and beautiful . . . as if she mattered. The warm humor in his eyes snagged a corner of her heart, made her yearn again for that amorphous *something* that she'd never known.

"You gonna stand there all day?"

Mariah felt as if she were melting. She swallowed hard, trying to remind herself that he was a no-account drifter who offered nothing but pretty words and a quick good-bye.

Their gazes met. The cocky grin faded slowly from his lips. He gave her a look so smoldering and intense, Mariah's knees almost buckled.

"Mariah," he whispered. Straightening, he reached a hand up to her.

She couldn't have drawn back her hand to save her soul. She placed her fingertips on his warm palm. A shiver went through her at the contact. Slowly she sank to her knees beside him.

Please, she thought, drowning in his steel gray eyes. *Touch me before I remember you're someone I can never have. . . .*

But it was too late. She'd already remembered.

Trembling, she drew her hand back and tried to smile. "You want a cup of coffee?"

"That's not what I want, and you know it."

She pulled her gaze away from his compelling eyes and stared hard at her lap. "Don't look at me like that."

"Like what?"

Reluctantly she eased her chin up and met his gaze. "Like you want something from me."

"But I do. I want—"

She brought a hand up. "Don't say it. Please."

She was kneeling in the cold, damp grass beside him. Moisture seeped though her woolen skirt and thick winter underwear, but she barely noticed. Her every sense was focused on the man sprawled casually beside her.

He half turned, half rolled toward her. "You intrigue me, Mariah. Is there something wrong with that?"

A quavering heat moved through her body at his simple words. They were exactly what she'd come to expect from him. Not a false proclamation of love, not even a declaration of desire. Simply a devastating statement of fact. *You intrigue me.*

Suddenly she was afraid of him, afraid with every particle and fiber of her being. She might be able to defend herself against pretty words, might even be able to thwart her own desires, but his honesty was somehow stronger, more potent, than she could bear.

She squeezed her eyes shut, fighting for control. Trying to find the casual armor that would keep him away from her . . . keep her own yearnings at bay. She forced a brittle, frightening laugh. "Mr. Stone, must you say everything that comes into your head?"

"Yeah."

Mariah had no answer for that, no quick self-defensive comeback. After a few interminable, heart-thumping seconds, she opened her eyes.

And found him staring at her.

Her breath caught. She became achingly aware of the sounds of the dawn: the water's current, the wind's caress, his even breathing. The unfamiliar soap and woodsmoke smell of him filled her senses.

"Come here," he whispered.

She stared into his eyes and felt as if she were falling. She wanted to back away, *needed* to back away, but she couldn't.

Slowly—so slowly—she leaned toward him.

His hand came up. She felt his fingers, damp with dew and roughened by dirt, curl around her neck. His thumb brushed along her jaw in a feather-stroke. He drew her toward him, closer, closer, until she could feel his every breath like a caress against her tingling mouth.

Their lips touched. His tongue darted out, breezed along her lower lip.

Mariah started to tremble.

"Mariah," he whispered, his lips moving gently against her own. "Don't . . ."

She pulled backward, ashamed and humiliated and desperate. Her hands curled into tight, trembling fists in her lap. "I c-can't."

"Can't what?"

She refused to look at him. "You know."

He touched her chin with his forefinger, forced her to look at him. "Say the words."

She looked into his passion-darkened eyes and almost cracked. He wanted her. It was a dizzying, exhilarating sensation that soared through her blood like a burst of hot sparks.

Her self-control started to spiral away from her. She was inches—centimeters—away from throwing caution to the wind. She had to do something to keep him from kissing her again. She searched frantically for something to keep them apart, and came up with words. "I can't . . . kiss a man whose name I don't even know."

Surprise widened his eyes. The lazy, promise-laden smile dulled. Frowning, he drew back.

Mariah's pent-up breath released. She'd done it, made him pull away. *Thank God.*

"You're good at it," he said softly.

Mariah shivered beneath his perceptive look. "Good at what?"

"Protecting yourself. The name bit was particularly clever, I'll give you that. But it won't work—at least, not for long."

"W-Why not?"

He leaned close enough to kiss her again, but he didn't. She felt his slow, even breathing like a whisper of promise against her mouth. "Because you want me."

Fear cascaded through her in an icy cold wash. She jerked to her feet. Stumbling through the fishing gear, she put some distance between them. "No I don't."

He grinned up at her. "Pretty fast moving for a lady who has no interest."

Get away from him, now. Before you do something stupid—

Mariah snatched up her skirts and headed back towards the house. "Catch your own fish, Mr. Stone. I have better things to do."

The rich, rumbling strains of his laughter followed her, nipped at her heels. She couldn't outrun it, couldn't ignore it.

Damn him—and damn her lonely soul. She knew why she couldn't outrun his words, couldn't forget the feel of his lips on hers. It was painfully, humiliatingly obvious.

He was right.

And they both knew it.

Mariah ran up the porch steps and flung the front door open. Skidding into the comforting darkness of the foyer, she sank onto the cushioned bench and let out her breath in a quivering sigh. She slumped forward and covered her face with her hands.

Her whole body was trembling, and she couldn't stop it.

"Oh, God . . ." she whispered into her hands, feeling the moist, humid heat of her own breath. For a second there she'd forgotten everything, her past, her pain, her future. She'd wanted him to kiss her, wanted it with a desperation that left her shaken and weak and defenseless.

She'd come so close to destruction. . . .

But not close enough. She forced the harsh words into her mind. She hadn't succumbed; that's what she had to focus on, that's what she had to remember. She had to focus on the success; not how close she'd been to failure. She'd *felt* vulnerable, but she hadn't let herself be vulnerable. Thankfully, there was a difference.

She'd been tempted, but she hadn't given in.

Gradually her breathing normalized. Her fear slid back into the dim recesses of her mind. Slowly she pushed to her feet and headed into the kitchen.

In the doorway, she came to a stumbling halt. Jake was at the kitchen table, alone. He sat slumped in his chair, his elbows rested on the oilclothed table, his face cradled in his hands. He looked sad and lost and alone. Exactly the way she felt.

Her heart went out to him, twisted hard. Where were his parents? Who cared for him when he was sick and kissed his cheek when he was depressed? Who darned his socks and answered his boyish questions about the world?

The concern helped her, made her focus on his pain instead of her own. Before she knew it, she was moving toward him. Beneath her feet, the floorboards creaked.

He looked up, startled. "Miss Throckmorton—"

She smiled. "Call me Mariah."

His hands plunged beneath the table. "R-Rass told me to meet him here before breakfast."

She poured two cups of steaming, fragrant coffee and went to the table. Setting one down in front of him, she sat beside him. "You don't have to explain, Jake. You're welcome here."

His eyes rounded. Then slowly his shoulders sagged. A tired, lonely breath escaped him. "Thanks."

Mariah's own breath caught. She could tell how much her simple words had meant to him. She wondered again about his life, wondered if he'd ever belonged anywhere. And again she thought of Thomas, and the promise of his life.

He blinked at her, and a thick lock of dirty hair fell across one eye. He blushed and pushed it aside. "Sorry," he mumbled, "my hair's sorta long. . . ."

Mariah reacted immediately to his shame. Hope niggled through her, a fraying thread. She wet her dry lips and tried to sound casual. "I . . . I could cut it for you."

He looked up, surprised. "You'd do that . . . for me?"

"Certainly, but—" She glanced down at the table, uncertain suddenly. A host of sad memories took hold of her for a heartbeat before she could push them away.

"But what?"

She swallowed and met his gaze. "I've never cut a young man's hair." *I should have, but I haven't. . . .*

"I just do it with a razor."

The quiet, matter-of-fact words lifted her from her moment's sadness. "I have shears."

He smiled; it was a slow, tentative smile that matched her own emotion. "I'd sure appreciate it."

Mariah looked at him, and knew somehow that this moment was as important to him as it was to her. It felt potent and right . . . almost like a beginning, though she was afraid to really believe it.

She got to her feet and filled a bucket with warm water, then lugged it back to the table. As she set it down, water spilled over the bent metal rim and puddled on the oilcloth cover. "Go ahead and sit on this chair," she said, indicating the butter stool. "I'll go get a comb and shears."

He glanced at her nervously. "Okay."

Mariah turned and bolted up the stairs, grabbing the shears and comb from her dresser. When she returned to the kitchen, he was sitting on the stool in the middle of the room.

She wrapped a towel around his neck and dampened his hair. Standing behind him, she studied his dirty, unkempt head. "How long do you like it?"

"My mama used to cut it along my collar." His voice was quiet, almost wistful. "She liked it a little long."

With shaking fingers, she touched his hair, running her index finger along the ragged, uneven ends. Again she wondered how he came to be here. Once, he'd obviously had a mother who cared, who cut his hair and took care of him. Who wouldn't have wanted her little boy's hair to look like this.

She picked up the comb and tugged the tangles from his hair. For a dreamy, unreal moment, she was flung back to a time that never had existed but should have. *Thomas* . . .

Jake made a soft, gurgling sound in his throat.

She paused, pulled from the dream by the quiet noise. "Did I hurt you?"

"No." His voice sounded thick, embarrassed. "It felt . . . good."

Mariah started to smile. "Oh." Slowly she combed his knotted hair and massaged his scalp with her fingers. Then, biting her lower lip, she began to cut along his collar.

Snip. Snip. Snip.

She tried to think of something to say to him, but it had been years since she'd made small talk, and never with a young man. It was suddenly important that he like her; she didn't want to say the wrong thing and ruin everything.

He was like her, she could tell. Alone and lonely and afraid. She wanted desperately to connect with him, to forge some kind of a friendship, but she didn't know how. For many years she'd been unconnected to people, a loner. She had no idea how to change that.

"Jake ..." She said his name softly, unaware even that she'd spoken until he answered.

"Uh-huh?"

She froze, trying to think of something to say now that she'd started. "I ... uh ... notice there's a rip in your shirt. I could sew it for you."

"I'd really appreciate that, Miss ... Mariah. Thanks."

She felt a surprising rush of relief. It was a beginning, anyway. More of one than she'd made in years. "Good."

His body relaxed, lost some of it rigid stiffness. "I'm not too good with a needle and thread." His voice was soft and quiet, almost casual. And she thought perhaps he'd smiled.

Yes, she thought in amazement, *it's a beginning*. For both of us.

Chapter Thirteen

Mariah stirred the thick, bubbling oatmeal and stared out the window, watching dawn creep through the orchard in a rising curtain of rose-gold light. She tried to tell herself that she wasn't looking for anything—or anyone—in particular. But her gaze kept veering toward the creek.

"Is this enough ham?" Jake asked, turning expectantly toward her.

She glanced at him and smiled. He stood beside her, carefully slicing ham on the slopstone. He looked like a different boy than he had just half an hour ago. He'd taken a bath, and his shorter newly washed hair shone like a copper penny in the early morning light.

Her heart squeezed at the sight of him. For a second, just that, she felt as if he belonged here. As if maybe he'd even stay. She swallowed a lump of emotion and nodded at him. "That's just right, Jake. Thanks."

"You want me to put it in the frying pan?"

"Sure." She sidled away from him, making room.

He scraped a scoop of bit-studded leftover lard from the battered blue speckled tin and slapped it in the hot pan. The gray-white smear slid across the pan in a hissing trail.

"You helped your mother cook, didn't you?"

Jake looked up at her. Their eyes met, and in the green depths she saw a heartbreaking sorrow. "Yeah."

Mariah wet her lips and smiled down at him, feeling a sharp sting in the region of her heart. This time she did reach out and brush the hair from his eyes. "She's a lucky woman to have a son like you."

He started to say something, but before he could get a word out, the front door opened.

Jake gasped and jerked back. His eyes rounded. "Mad Dog's here."

Mariah's heart lurched, her breathing sped up. Anxiously she glanced at the doorway. "Go on and sit down, Jake. I can finish it from here."

"Okay." He grabbed his lukewarm cup of coffee and hurried back to his chair. There was a squeaking groan of wood and wire as he sat down.

Mariah stiffened, breathing deeply. *Calm down, Mariah. Don't let Mad Dog rattle you. What happened at the river was nothing. Nothing at all.*

But it was a lie, and she knew it. No amount of rationalization could change the truth. Her time with Jake had given her a brief respite from thinking about this morning, but now that respite was over, and the truth of what had happened hammered her until she could hardly breathe.

God help her, she'd wanted that kiss today, wanted it with a desperation that left her dizzy and out of control. And fool that she was, she wanted it still. She couldn't see him right now, or speak to him. She was too damn vulnerable and needy to be strong. She didn't have the strength to keep her distance. If he looked at her right, or touched her, she was afraid she'd melt into his arms.

She jerked back from the stove and spun to leave. She had to get away from him, now before he made her forget again.

He strolled into the room and stopped in the doorway. He angled against it, resting one shoulder against the jamb. "Hiya, Jake." He tipped his hat slightly and grinned at her. "Mariah."

Her step faltered for a half second and no more. She tilted her chin up and started to push past him. "Excuse me."

He grabbed her wrist and pulled. She stumbled against him, making a small, quiet sound of protest.

"It won't work," he said softly.

Almost against her will, she looked up at him. He was smiling, but it was an easy, gentle smile without mockery or sarcasm. Just a smile. She wet her lips. "What won't work?"

"You can't run from it."

She wished to God she misunderstood him, but his meaning was crystal-clear. "It?" She tried to sound haughty. To her horror, her voice was breathy and weak-sounding.

He leaned infinitesimally toward her. "There's something between us, Mariah."

She stiffened and tried to pull away. He held her fast. "There's nothing between us. I don't know what you're talking about."

"You're lying."

She licked her dry lips and stared up at him, breathing too quickly. "I don't want there to be anything between us."

He gave her a look that was so sad, so filled with compassion and understanding, that for a moment, she felt light-headed. "That's not the same thing, is it, Mariah?"

She made a strangled, gasping sound of fear and wrenched herself away from him, running blindly from the house.

Mad Dog watched her leave, shaking his head as the door slammed shut.

Turning back around, he strolled into the kitchen and poured himself a cup of coffee. "Hiya, kid," he said, taking a seat across from the boy.

Jake spit up his coffee. "H-Hi."

"Women," he said, shaking his head again.

The boy didn't say anything, he just sat there, staring at Mad Dog through wide, questioning eyes.

Silence pressed into the room, thick and awkward. Mad Dog felt increasingly uncomfortable. "You fight much?" he said, for lack of anything better.

"Nope." Jake set down his cup and stared at Mad Dog as if he were waiting for something.

"Like fighting?"

"Not anymore."

"How 'bout baseball? That's a helluva game, huh? The Cincinnati Red Stockings are my team."

"Naw."

He set down his cup. "Christ, kid, help me out here. I'm just trying to make small talk. What *do* you like?"

Jake shrugged. "I dunno. Reading, talking, being home. You know, regular things."

Mad Dog grinned. "Not too excitin', kid. Didn't your dad teach you anything?"

For a second, Jake seemed to stop breathing. Slowly he set his cup down and stood up. "No. My *dad* didn't teach me anything."

Mad Dog frowned. "Look, kid—"

But Jake wasn't listening. He shoved away from the table and ran from the room, leaving Mad Dog sitting alone.

"Jesus Christ," he said into the silence. "The kid's as touchy as she is."

Mariah bolted breathlessly down the loose rock path, trying to regain control. Then suddenly she stopped.

Ahead lay the white picket fence. She stared at it, trying suddenly to remember how it felt to be on the other side.

That gate used to be nothing to me. . . .

She tried to imagine reaching for the latch, turning it, pushing through.

Fear set in immediately, suffocating her. Her heartbeat sped up, her breathing stalled.

She swallowed hard and turned away from the fence. Clasping her hands together, she ran toward the orchard.

Maybe tomorrow, she thought desperately. *Maybe tomorrow you won't think twice about leaving. . . .*

But the words were hollow, empty, and she knew it. She hadn't wanted to leave the farm in years; not since she'd come back years ago, humiliated and ashamed and pregnant. Then, she'd closed the gate behind her and tried to forget about the world that lay beyond the safety of this farm. She'd never meant to stay here, never meant to hide, but somehow she hadn't left.

She squeezed her eyes shut and felt a drenching wave of despair. Involuntarily she remembered the last time she'd closed that gate behind her. She'd been sixteen and full of fire and dreams.

Stephen.

She sank slowly to her knees in the dewy grass and bowed her head. Memories of that time, that life, surged through her mind, and she was too tired to fight them off, too weak to make herself forget.

The night she'd met Stephen she'd been in town with her parents for a performance of *Romeo and Juliet* by a troupe of traveling European actors.

Stephen had, of course, been Romeo.

She hadn't been able to keep her eyes off him. He was larger than life onstage, and blindingly handsome. When he smiled at her, Mariah's bones seemed to melt into the rickety bench upon which she'd been sitting. No one had ever noticed her the way he had, no one had ever smiled at her quite that way before.

She remembered the night so clearly. Thousands of stars twinkled in the late summer sky. After the performance, she'd walked idly toward the bridge, kicking a stone, waiting for her parents. It had taken her a long time to realize that they'd gone home without her.

Even now, she felt a stab of pain in her heart at the realization. She knew then, as she knew now, that they loved her. They simply loved each other more.

She sat on the timbered bridge, letting her feet dangle into the cool darkness of the night, feeling lonely. Palms pressed to the scratchy wood, she stared up at the blanket of stars and tried not to cry.

"What's a wee pretty girl like yourself doin' sittin' out here all alone?"

Mariah still remembered the lilting softness of his Irish brogue.

He'd been so handsome, her Stephen. So charming and beguiling. A twenty-two-year-old actor with a ready laugh and a gentle touch. To a lonely sixteen-year-old girl, he was a dream come true. She'd been lonely then, starved for the words "I love you." And when he said them, whispered them in her ear with a sweet, laughing kiss, she'd been lost.

She shook her head, feeling the start of a small, bittersweet smile. If only his laughter had lasted, or she had depended upon it less ...

She blinked hard and forced her eyes open. She tried to push the long-suppressed memories back into the shadows from which they'd come, but she couldn't find the strength.

She'd fallen in love so damn easily, and asked so little in return.

Please, God, don't let me make that mistake again. Help me to be strong. . . .

She lay back in the cool, damp grass and closed her eyes, reveling in the feel of the sun on her face.

She was almost asleep when the sound of footsteps awakened her. She opened her eyes and looked up.

At first all she saw was a shadowy silhouette, backlit by the rising sun. Then she saw the hat, the smile. A shiver moved through her.

Mad Dog.

She tensed, pushed up to her elbows.

"Naw, don't get up." He dropped to a sit beside her.

Part of her wanted to get up and run—a really big part. But for some reason, Mariah didn't move.

He stretched out beside her.

She inched away from him.

"Ask me something, Mariah," he said softly. "Anything you want."

She stiffened. "What makes you think I have any questions about you?"

"You do."

"What if I ask something that's too personal?"

"You can't."

She allowed herself to glance his way. He was sprawled out beside her, arms wishboned behind his head, legs crossed at the ankles, staring up at the pale rose sky. It took her breath away, just being this close to him. She ached suddenly to push through the barriers of her past and let herself care about this man.

She realized instantly that she was being a fool, and with the realization came a sinking sense of sadness. "There are always things too personal to talk about," she said quietly.

"Not for me, Mariah. I'll tell you anything you want to know."

"Why?"

He shrugged. "I don't have any secrets."

She pushed up a little, still staring at his profile. "All right. You said you never lied. So what's your sin?"

"What do you mean?"

"Well, for most everyone, lying is their big sin. What's yours?"

He paused a minute, thinking. "I leave."

She frowned. "That's not a sin."

He turned to her. There was a surprising vulnerability in his eyes. "It is the way I do it."

Slowly Mariah leaned back again and gazed up at the sky. Silence stretched between them, but it was oddly companionable, as if they were both thinking about what he'd just said.

It is the way I do it.

She shivered, though the morning was getting warm. It sounded like a warning. As though he wanted to ensure that she never expected anything different.

But that was crazy. Why would he want to warn her? Why would he care what she expected?

"Your honesty always surprises me, Mr. Stone," she said without looking at him.

"I'll never lie to you, Mariah."

She squeezed her eyes shut, trying not to be romanced by that simple sentence.

"Now it's my turn to ask a question about you."

Every muscle in Mariah's body tightened. "I don't recall saying I'd play this little game."

"It's not a game, Mariah," he said with a soft laugh. "It's called conversation."

She tried to relax. "Oh. All right, then. Ask a . . . nonpersonal question."

"Why don't you leave the farm?"

The question caught her off guard. She tensed, expecting to shatter at the words. But, amazingly, nothing like that happened. She felt almost relieved.

No one had ever asked her that question, and deep down, some part of her wanted to answer.

She was tired of pretending it was nothing. Tired of being afraid all the time. Maybe if she tried, just this once, to answer the simple question, things would finally begin to change. Maybe if she could *talk* about the gate, she could someday open it. And who better to confide in than someone who wouldn't be around to remind her of her shortcomings if she failed?

She took a deep breath and tried what she had never tried before. "W-When I was younger—" she laughed bitterly "—much younger, I wasn't afraid of anything."

She squeezed her eyes shut. "Anyway, I—" *Fell in love with a loser and ran away with him.*

She tried desperately to form the words, but the confession wouldn't come. Humiliation clogged in her lungs and washed across her cheeks. God, she couldn't say the words. Not even to a drifter who didn't care and had no one to tell and no right to judge. Her hands curled into tight, impotent fists.

Defeated, she pushed up to a sit and stared dully at her tired brown skirts. "I went as far as Walla Walla." She forced a brittle laugh—that much was true at least. "Then I came home."

"Something happened in Walla Walla."

"Something." Her voice was as dead as the leaves strewn on the drying grass.

He rolled over onto his stomach and looked up at her. His face was surprisingly earnest. "I know you don't think much of me, but if you ever want to talk about it . . ."

Heat crept through her body at his simple offer—one no one else had ever made. She wanted to lean toward him. Their faces were close now, and if she moved—

even a little—they'd be close enough to kiss. The realization sparked a girlish sense of giddiness—and then an older, wiser woman's fear.

Yearning pulsed through her body, made her fingers shake and her throat go dry. God, she wanted to touch him right now, to run her fingers through his too long hair and pretend her past was only that.

But, as always, she didn't have the courage. She couldn't give him anything of herself. But she could give the truth, and surprisingly, she wanted to.

"It's not you," she said.

He frowned. "What's not me?"

"I've been unfair to you, treated you badly because . . . of someone else."

"Someone who hurt you?"

"Yes. He was a lot like you. . . . But perhaps not as much as I first thought."

"In what way? Handsome, charming?"

At his easy smile, weakness washed through her, calling to her in a sly, seductive voice. *Touch him. . . . Just try it.*

"Come on, Mariah," he said softly, "how am I like the other guy?"

She swallowed hard. "You'll . . . leave."

His smile fell. He looked at her with uncharacteristic seriousness.

Their gazes locked. His eyes were warm gray pools of promise, drawing her in. Her heartbeat sped up. Suddenly she wanted to be touched by Mad Dog, ached to be touched by him. She wanted to reach out, unafraid, and feel the rough texture of his flesh.

Make me a promise, she thought desperately. *Even if you won't keep it . . .*

"You're right," he said. "I will leave."

Pain crushed through her, though she should have expected it. She squeezed her eyes shut. What a fool she was, wanting him to lie to her. A bigger fool for thinking—even for a second—that Mad Dog might offer something more than his smile and a touch or two. "Thank you for that, at least."

"Open your eyes, Mariah, and look at me."

Reluctantly she did.

They were so close she could see the tiny green flecks that darkened his gray eyes. His breath was a whispered caress against her mouth. "You're looking at this all wrong."

"What do you mean?"

He reached up and pulled a pin from her hair.

She gasped quietly but didn't draw away.

His hand came up again, and again. One by one he removed the pins, until the tight little knot collapsed. A waterfall of thick, wavy hair cascaded down her arm and puddled on the grass.

He caressed the soft pool of hair for a long moment. The quiet between them grew, intensified, until Mariah thought she could hear a slight buzzing in her ears. She stared, mesmerized, as his fingers moved over her hair, stroking in a gentle circle.

Then he looked up. Their gazes caught, held. "Mariah." Her name hung in the air between them, creating a sense of intimacy.

Mariah longed to say something in response, but she

knew that if she did, if she reached out to him even that much, she'd be lost.

He gave her a slow, promise-laden smile that sent feelers of warmth to the cold reaches of her soul. Leaning closer, he plucked up a stalk of grass and put it in his mouth. It was a long, crooked green line against the beguiling fullness of his lips. Then slowly, so slowly, he drew the stalk from his mouth and dragged it across her lips.

The touch was soft and rough at the same time. Mariah was achingly, desperately, aware of it, of *him*. Her every sense was stretched taut, heightened to the breaking point. The simple touch to her lips sparked a dozen forbidden memories and needs. She swallowed hard.

"I could be the best time you ever had," he drawled. "And no one would ever have to know."

Mariah stood at her bedroom window, staring down at the bunkhouse, her arms wrapped tightly around her body to ward off an inner chill.

I could be the best time you ever had.

Over and over again she heard Mad Dog's indecent proposal. The words chased after themselves in her mind, grinding a groove of frailty through her stiff self-control.

Every time she thought about it, she felt hot and cold and frightened and alive. She felt as if she were drowning in a warm, seductive pool of her own desires. She could barely keep her head enough above water to breathe.

"He'll leave." She whispered the familiar words to her own rippling reflection in the glass.

She'd said the words to herself a thousand times since yesterday. At first they'd sounded strong and sure—the way she felt—and they'd given her comfort. Now they were getting weaker and weaker with each passing minute.

I could be the best time you ever had. And no one would ever know.

It was amazing how compelling those words were. They cut through her anxiety like a hot knife and filled her with giddy, tingling anticipation. They seduced her, intrigued her.

She would never have thought that such a simple sentence could romance her so completely, could make her feel so . . . free.

But they did. Nothing she did with Mad Dog would be held against her, or even remembered by anyone except herself.

Not like before, when she'd been so public about her passion . . . and her heartbreak.

No one would ever know.

She shivered. Seductive words indeed.

Chapter Fourteen

Mad Dog threw a dark apple into the "red" barrel. It hit with a thunk that sent tiny bits of fruit flying. Absently he stared at the boy picking apples in the other tree. For some strange reason, he felt bad about what had happened in the kitchen that morning.

"Hey, kid," he said, tossing another apple in the barrel.

Jake paused in his work and peered through the colorful leaves. "Yeah?"

"About this morning . . ." Mad Dog shrugged, not quite sure what to say. "I'm sorry if I said something that upset you."

Jake stared at him for a long minute, then slowly smiled. "Yeah, me, too. I guess I acted sorta dumb."

Mad Dog grinned. "Hell, I do that all the time." He waved the boy over. "Come on, let's take a break."

Jake scrambled down from the ladder. Gently placing his sack full of apples in the "mostly red" barrel, he followed Mad Dog to the sagging wooden fence.

Mad Dog yanked his canteen from around the fence post and took a long, gulping drink of water. The cool water felt good dribbling down his exposed throat. "Ah, that's good." He handed the canteen to Jake. "Course, it'd be better if it was tequila, but sometimes a guy just has to make do."

Jake stared at him. A tight frown worked its way across his serious face. "What do you mean?"

He grinned. "Don't take me too seriously, kid. It's just a saying."

Jake took a quick sip of water. Wiping the moisture from his lips, he looked up at Mad Dog through earnest green eyes. "You're a fighter, aren't you?"

"Yep." He smiled, ran a hand through his hair, and unbuttoned his shirt. The cool afternoon air breezed across his sweaty chest, fluttering the edges of his shirt. "You follow me?"

Jake paled. The canteen slipped through his fingers and hit the grass. "Huh?" The word was a high-pitched squeak.

"You follow fighting?"

"Oh." Jake's scrawny chest caved in. Something that looked like relief flashed through his eyes. "Yeah, I guess."

"Seems people think it's sort of romantic."

"Don't you?"

Mad Dog snatched a towel from the fence rail and wiped the sheen of moisture from his brow. "Nothin' glamorous about hittin' a man, kid."

"Why do you do it, then?"

He sat down in the warm grass and idly ran his hand through a pile of multicolored autumn leaves. "Money, I guess. Same reason a man does anything."

"My grandfather used to say a man should let honor guide his actions."

Mad Dog snorted. "Yeah, I've known men who'd say a fool thing like that. Most of 'em never missed a meal in their life."

Jake moved toward Mad Dog hesitantly and sat down a respectful distance away. "Have you? Missed meals, I mean?"

"More than a few."

"When you were a boy? I mean, that would explain—"

Mad Dog looked at Jake sharply. "You ask a lot of questions."

Embarrassment stained the boy's cheeks. He looked away, stared hard at the grass. A glaze of something that looked suspiciously like tears sheened his eyes. "Sorry."

"Oh, for Christ's sake, don't take it so personal. I just meant, there's some things a man doesn't like talking about. Some things *I* don't like talking about." He smiled at the boy. "So tell me something about yourself. Where you from?"

"Wisconsin."

Mad Dog couldn't think of a damn thing to say about that. "Oh."

"M-My grandfather's name was Jacob, too." He glanced up, stared at Mad Dog through eyes that looked impossibly big against his small face. "You ever know anyone by that name?"

He felt a surprising jolt of emotion. It had been years since he'd thought of old Jacob Vanderstay. A bitter smile thinned his lips. "Yeah, I knew one once. He was a mean son of a bitch, too. Wanted everyone to live by his rules. And I never knew a person who had so many rules."

"How did you meet him?"

Mad Dog leaned back against the wobbly fence rail. A dozen images, long forgotten, surged through his mind, bringing a bittersweet smile to his lips. *Laralee*.

He shook his head. Christ, how long had it been since he'd thought of her? "I knew his daughter."

"How come you're smiling?"

"She was something else. I wonder what ever happened to her."

"Your wife?"

"Almost." He grinned at the boy. "But I made a clean getaway."

The boy frowned. "Did you ever go back to see her?"

"Naw." He stretched his arms across the top rail and stared up at the endless blue sky. "She was rich and spoiled as hell. Her dad thought I was a lousy bum who might be redeemed by hard work in the family business." He leaned toward Jake, grinning. "You know what the family business was?"

Jake looked like he was going to smile. "What?"

"Funeral parlor." He laughed. "The old man wanted me to take it over if I married his precious daughter." Mad Dog shuddered dramatically. "It wasn't for me. And Laralee and her dad made it clear: If I married Laralee, I was an embalmer in training. So one night I just packed my stuff and moved on. But for a long time I wondered what happened to her."

"You could've gone back to see." There was a strange bitterness in the boy's voice.

Mad Dog shrugged. "What for? She wouldn't have

wanted to see me again—not after the way I ran out. Believe me, kid, women are funny about shit like that."

Jake looked at him through green eyes that were strangely sad. "She would have wanted to see you . . . I bet."

"Could be." Mad Dog pulled his gaze away from Jake's face. There was something unexpected in the boy's eyes, a pathetic edge of pain that was too deep, too agonized. . . .

Mad Dog tried to tell himself it didn't matter; the boy's pain didn't concern him. But even so, an odd, prickling sensation worked down his spine. It took a supreme act of will not to look at Jake again.

He felt . . . ashamed. As if he'd somehow let the boy down.

But that was crazy. Jake and Mad Dog had nothing in common except a kindred wanderlust that brought them both to the same small farm in the middle of nowhere.

Besides, he told himself, what did he know about sixteen-year-old boys? Maybe they were all a little sad and pathetic. Especially before they got laid.

He leaned sideways and grabbed the canteen, taking a long, satisfying drink. Then he thumped Jake on the back. "Well, kid, let's get back to work." Uncurling slowly, he dragged his tired body to his feet and headed toward the tree.

But all the way there, he felt Jake's gaze on his back, a warm, tangible presence that seemed to demand something in a sly, silent voice. It was goddamn disconcerting.

* * *

Rass sat beside Greta's grave, with his hand laid casually, lovingly, on the cool headstone.

He closed his eyes and held his breath, waiting for the scent of lavender and the gentle touch of the breeze. But it didn't happen this time, and without its magic, he felt depressingly alone.

Sweet Jesus he missed her. . . .

He let out his breath in a tired, lonely sigh.

"Snap out of it, old man," he told himself. He couldn't let go now, couldn't crawl into the shell of sorrow that had encased him since Greta's death. Now, more than ever, he had to be strong for his daughter. For once, she needed him. And by God, he wouldn't let her down again.

Mariah. Her name filled him with regret.

"But she's getting better." He said the words aloud, allowing himself to take some small measure of comfort from them. This time they weren't just words to assuage his guilt. They were true.

She *was* getting better. She no longer stood as stiff and rigid. She'd even loosened that ridiculously tight chignon of hers. She smiled at Jake and laughed with Mad Dog.

She'd taken a first step down the road to healing, a single, trembling step.

Now he needed to kick her in the butt. Metaphorically. Anything to make her take another step. And he had to do it quickly. Instinct told him he didn't have a lot of time.

But how? That was the question that had brought him to Greta in the first place. How could he force Mariah and Mad Dog to see what Rass saw so clearly?

The sound of Mad Dog's rumbling, baritone laughter seeped up from the orchard, where he and Jake were picking apples. The two of them were starting to get along, Rass thought. Probably because of the time they spent working together.

And suddenly Rass had an idea. A slow, thoughtful smile tugged at his lips.

"What do you think, Greta? Am I on the right track? Could a little time alone together be the answer?"

This time the breeze came, ruffling through the fallen leaves in a chattering, dancing swirl. It smelled of sunshine and warm earth and lavender.

Rass smiled. He had his answer.

Whistling softly, smiling, he said good-bye to Greta and headed down to the orchard. As he came over the rise and dropped down into the thicket of trees, he heard the *crack-thunk* of an apple hitting a barrel.

He peered around a large, leafy tree and saw Jake first. The boy was burrowed high in the tree, carefully plucking ripe apples from the branches. Mad Dog was at the next tree, throwing apples, one at a time from the pile in his arms, into the various barrels.

Rass shook his head. Fortunately Mad Dog was an honest, good-hearted man, because he was pure disaster as an apple picker.

Rass stepped away from the shielding foliage of the tree. "You trying to go straight from picking to applesauce in a single step?"

Mad Dog spun toward Rass's voice. He had the good grace to wince at being caught. "Shit. Sorry, Rass."

"Well, I guess there's too many rules around here, anyway."

Mad Dog grabbed his hat from the fence post and cocked it on his head, grinning at Rass. "It's a specialty of mine—breaking rules. One of the few things I do well."

Jake climbed down from the tree and headed toward Rass. "Hi, Rass." He set a few apples into the "mostly red" barrel and reached for the canteen.

"Hey, Jake," Rass said, "I thought I'd go to town for a few things. Do you know how to drive a buggy?"

Jake nodded. "Sure, Rass. I used to drive my mama to the doctor's."

"Good. Run on down to the pasture and catch Cleo for me. She's the swaybacked black. You can't miss her."

Jake reached down for his slouch hat and crammed it on his head, then started walking. Rass and Mad Dog watched silently as the boy turned down the gravel road and headed for the barn.

They stood in companionable silence for a long time. The sun was just beginning its lazy descent. The blood-red shadows of twilight clung to the darkening horizon.

Memories came flooding back to Rass, filling the cold, dark places in his heart with remembered warmth.

"Greta used to love this time of day," he said softly. "She called it the magic hour. More than day and less than night."

"She must have been quite a woman, Rass. I'm . . . sorry."

"Nothing to be sorry about."

They lapsed into silence again. Somewhere a bird chirped. Wind whispered through the leaves of the trees, stirring the crispy, fallen reminders of autumn. From the hidden recesses of the river came the first bulging ribbits of lonely bullfrogs.

Tears burned Rass's eyes, turned the shadowy fields into a golden-red smear. "I never thought she'd die. . . ."

Mad Dog gave Rass's shoulder a comforting squeeze, but didn't say anything.

Rass gazed out across the orchard, feeling Greta's presence beside him. He fisted his hand, knowing that her essence, some ephemeral part of her soul, lay within his grasp, had always lain within his grasp. It gave him strength and purpose and a sense of quiet well-being. "Sometimes, when I stand under the tree on the hill, I see her. She's waiting for me."

Mad Dog shifted his weight from side to side and looked away.

"Am I making you uncomfortable?" Rass asked with a crooked smile.

Mad Dog let out his breath in a relieved gust. "Very."

"I know you don't believe me. Mariah doesn't either. That's because you've never been in love, either one of you."

Mad Dog laughed. "No surprise there, Professor."

"One day you'll feel what I felt for Greta, and then you'll know. That feeling just doesn't go away. Not even if one of you dies."

"I wouldn't bet on me feeling that, Rass."

That's exactly what I'm betting on. Rass cleared his throat and stared up at Mad Dog. It was time to say what he'd come to say. "Will you take care of Mariah for me while I'm gone?"

Mad Dog laughed. "How long you gonna be gone?"

Rass frowned at the answer. "Does it matter?"

"Sure it does. You're gonna be gone for supper, maybe overnight, I'll say yes. You're leaving till spring, I'd say find someone else."

"I thought you liked Mariah."

"I do . . . a hell of a lot actually. What's that got to do with it?"

"Well . . . I thought you'd sort of like to stay. After all, you're still here."

"You haven't paid me yet."

Rass eyed Mad Dog speculatively. The young man was trying like hell to appear disinterested, but he couldn't mask his emotions completely. Deep in his eyes, Rass saw what he wanted—needed—to see.

Mad Dog wasn't as detached as he tried to appear.

Rass fished through the baggy, lint-softened interior of his pants pocket for his wallet. Flipping it open, he pulled out a crisp ten-dollar bill and handed it to Mad Dog. "Here you go. I'm paying you—more than I owe you for the week. You going to leave now?"

Mad Dog stared down at the paper money for a long, silent moment, then slowly he looked up and met Rass's gaze. "No."

"Why not?"

Mad Dog flinched. "I'm not ready to move on, I guess."

"And that has nothing to do with my daughter?"

He sighed quietly and ran a hand through his shaggy hair. "I wish it didn't, Professor."

Rass did his best not to smile. "But it does."

Mad Dog squeezed his eyes shut. "Yeah, it does." He looked up suddenly, his gaze sharp on Rass's face.

"Don't make too much of it, Rass. I'm not the kind of man who stays anywhere too long."

"Maybe this time'll be different."

A grim smile pulled at Mad Dog's mouth. "I've had plenty of women say that, but somehow it never is."

Rass thought about saying more, but knew it wasn't the time. There were certain discoveries a man had to make for himself. "Well, I'm just going into town for a few hours. I thought I'd take Jake out to that Chinese restaurant for supper. But I don't like to leave Mariah alone on the farm. You know, in case there's trouble."

Mad Dog smiled. "Sure thing, Rass. I'll keep an eye on her for you."

Rass thumped him on the back. "I knew I could count on you."

Mad Dog laughed. "Now, *there's* a first."

"What?"

"No one counts on me, Professor."

He looked up at the younger man's face. "Like I told you, maybe this time is different."

Rass let the sentence sink in, with all its possibilities, then he turned and walked away.

Chapter Fifteen

Mad Dog yelled for Mariah, but there was no answer. She was probably hiding someplace, trying to keep out of his way now that they were alone on the farm.

He couldn't say he blamed her.

Grabbing his towel and soap from the bunkhouse, he headed to the house for his nightly shower.

He bounded up the sagging porch steps and rapped hard on the door. He didn't expect an answer, but he knocked just the same. Mariah always made a point of not being around when he took his regularly scheduled shower.

No one answered.

He reached for the brass knob and turned it, easing the door open. It creaked on its hinges and swung inward.

He poked his head into the shadowy house. It was a deathly quiet void. He slipped through the door and lit a lamp. Golden light cut a path through the shadows.

He closed the door behind him and went to the base of the stairs. "Mariah? Are you up there?"

Still no answer.

"If you are, I'm gonna take my shower." He started to turn away from the stairway, then stopped.

Mariah's room was at the top of stairs.

Up there, just a few short feet away, lay her secret sanctuary. Somewhere, amongst her personal items, was the trinket or doodad that would explain the sadness in her eyes and the bitterness in her smile.

Before he knew it, he was walking up the stairs. At the landing he paused and looked around again. The corridor was dark and empty.

"Mariah?" He called her name tentatively, hoping now that she wouldn't answer.

She didn't.

He crept toward her bedroom and gently turned the knob. With a single push, the door swung inward on its arc.

The room was austere and cold, lit only by the bloody red haze of a dying sun. No fresh flowers brightened the dresser, no scrap of lace softened the scratched wood of the washstand. A white coverlet lay stretched across the four-poster oak bed like a layer of new-fallen snow. Not a single wrinkle marred the stark linen. There was no hint, no evidence at all, of the woman who slept beneath it.

He felt . . . disappointed but had no idea why.

The dresser caught his eye. Slowly, feeling keenly out of place, he crossed the shadowy room. The top of the dresser was empty but for a meticulous pile of hairpins in a cracked china saucer, and a wooden hairbrush. There were no knickknacks, or photos, or mementos. No dried rose from a long-ago love affair.

Gently he eased the top drawer open and found it filled with precisely folded undergarments. He closed the drawer quickly and opened the others, one by one.

It wasn't until the bottom drawer that he found anything even vaguely enlightening.

There, folded in a small, neat square, was a thin blue blanket, its edges lovingly embroidered in yellow and green flowers and puffy white lambs. Beside it lay an old-fashioned baby bottle and a tarnished silver rattle.

He thought of the hours that embroidery had taken, the time that someone had spared to make the hem just right, the blossoms perfect. Greta, no doubt. The woman had made certain that the blanket was just right for her baby. And Mariah had saved it all these years along with her bottle and rattle. Wasn't that how women did things? Pass special items down from generation to generation.

For the Throckmorton women, it all ended here in a half-empty, forgotten drawer. Mariah had no children to wrap lovingly in the blanket. But she kept the baby things all these years, obviously hoping for the future.

Frowning, he eased the drawer shut. Did she still hope for a child, had she ever? Or was this the resting place for forgotten dreams? The questions made him feel edgy, opened the way for feelings he didn't want to have.

Straightening, he moved cautiously toward the armoire. He knew what he'd find before he opened it, and he wasn't disappointed. It was filled with dozens of drab, brown dresses and tired aprons.

She didn't even own a dress of another color. Why? he wondered. Why was she so obsessed with looking drab and unobtrusive?

Feeling unaccountably sad, he left the room and went into the hallway, closing the door behind him. He was halfway down the stairs when he realized why he felt uncomfortable.

He stopped and glanced back up the stairs. It dawned on him, what he'd found in her room.

It was a room exactly like his. Empty, impersonal. The room of a person who chooses not to exist. It was a place with a bed, but no memories. A place to sleep; not a place to dream.

His frown deepened. He'd made a mistake in coming here tonight. He'd wanted to see a room filled with ruffly knickknacks and lacy gewgaws. A room like any other, to indicate that she was a woman like any other.

What he'd found was the lonely, empty refuge of a woman strikingly disconnected to the world.

A woman he understood all too well.

Mariah strode briskly from the washhouse, a set of clean sheets wedged under one arm. In her other hand, she held a half-full wash bucket and a broom. Soapy water sloshed over the metal rim and splashed her feet as she walked.

She needed something to keep her busy while Jake and Rass were gone. Anything to keep her from thinking about the fact that she and Mad Dog were alone here.

Hard work, she decided, was the best defense to runaway nerves. So, bucket in hand, she headed for the bunkhouse. Today was cleaning day; it always had been, and she refused to allow her careful routine to be upset by Mad Dog's presence.

She'd carefully scheduled his showers—every night at seven-thirty—and he was always in the bathing room for at least thirty minutes. Thus, she figured she had at least half an hour before Mad Dog finished his shower and came looking for her. And she knew from experience that she could clean the bunkhouse in less than twenty minutes.

When she came to the small, darkened outbuilding, she paused and set down her bucket and broom. Without bothering to knock, she pushed the door open.

Dark silence tumbled back at her.

She straightened her spine and went to the bedside table. Lighting a lamp, she looked around and made a quiet, *tsk*ing sound of displeasure, then went to work.

The bunkhouse was small, and took no time to clean. She swept the floor, washed the window, swiped the dusty dresser, and shook out the curtains.

Then she paused, breathing hard, swabbing the sheen of sweat from her brow. What now?

Glancing around the room, she saw a gray-white bag slumped in the corner. It was *his* bag, she realized instantly. The only thing he'd brought with him.

She wondered what was in it, what he valued enough to carry from place to place.

"Maybe I'll just unpack for him," she said aloud.

Yes, that was reasonable. A friendly thing to do.

Cautiously she moved to the corner and kneeled down. She pulled on the fraying rope drawstring. The bag fell open. A threadbare black shirt, twisted into a tight, wrinkled ball, rolled toward her, hovering at the canvas lip.

She pulled it out, staring at it a long moment before she folded it and put it in the dresser's middle drawer. One by one, she drew out his belongings—two pairs of faded, holey blue jeans, a patched flannel shirt, a ragged

oilcloth coat, socks, and underthings. She folded and
put them away, then opened the bag wider and peered
in. A collection of tattered notebooks and loose sheets
of paper lay in the bottom. She pulled one of the notebooks out and it fell open.

She tried not to read it, but the words leapt out at her,
drew her in.

*The ravages of poverty are all around me, haunt-
ing the train lines with the pathetic, pitiful wails of
hungry children, the quiet whimpering of desperate
parents. The country is falling apart, one homeless,
wandering person at a time. How can this, the great-
est nation on earth, allow its people to go uncared-
for, unfed?*

There the entry stopped. Frowning, she flipped
through to another page.

*The winter of '92–'93 was relentlessly cold for the
thousands of men who camped along the boggy
beaches of Lake Michigan. They worked for endless,
backbreaking hours on structures that, once finished,
would rise into the cloudy Illinois skies like the spires
of a magical fairyland. Together, they dreamed, and
the country, it seemed, dreamed right along with
them.*

*But like all dreams, the much-anticipated World's
Columbian Exposition of 1894 had a dark, nightmar-
ish side to it. And like all nightmares, it has been
pushed aside by the strident light of day, to be forgotten.*

The fair opened on May first, and what a glorious opening it was. White-pillared palaces rose from a six-hundred-acre oasis of lagoons, courts, and plazas. The whole world gazed at the midwestern United States in awe. It ran for six months, then closed. The elegant, breathtaking white fairyland came down one piece at a time.

And what was left after the magic had run its course? A hundred thousand jobless, dreamless men, women, and children wander the cold, empty streets of Chicago, huddling around street corners and begging for scraps of food. They stand in endless, desperate breadlines, battered tin cups outstretched. Babies and young mothers sleep in open doorways and beneath damp blankets of newspaper.

Never has the chasm between progress and poverty been so hauntingly large in this country as it is today. We are in the clutches of an economic depression so carnivorous and insatiable, it's eating the very fabric of our lives. We are sacrificing our children to it, our future. And no one, it seems, is listening. . . .

Mariah closed the book, shaken. His images were potent and unforgettable. She'd known, of course, of the depression that gripped the country, but she never dreamed it was so urgent, so bleak.

She swallowed thickly, feeling sick for the children—babies—living without food or shelter.

His words moved her more than she would have imagined possible, told her something about the man who'd written them. These weren't the musings of a carefree drifter with an easy smile. This article was written by a man who knew the taste of tragedy, the feel of it. Knew it as intimately as she knew sorrow and despair. They were the words of a dreamer, someone who wanted to change the world. A man who understood pain and sorrow and death . . . and hope and redemption and second chances.

A man who believed in love.

Mariah was mesmerized by the thought, drawn to it like a moth to a burning flame. Somewhere behind the cocky grin and drifter bravado lay the true Mad Dog—or whatever his real name was.

Absently she pulled the notebooks from the bag and gently piled them in the bottom drawer, then shut it.

Folding the bag, she slid it under the dresser and reached for the sheets, then crossed the room and started to make his bed.

In quick, practiced motions, she stripped off the wrinkled old sheets and tossed them outside. Then she whipped the bottom sheet in place and started smoothing it out.

The sound of footsteps interrupted her concentration. She froze.

A shadow crossed the open door.

She glanced sideways. He stood in the doorway, arms crossed, wearing his dirty black cowboy boots and a Turkish towel. And nothing else.

She gasped. "Oh, my Lord . . ." The top sheet slipped through her fingers and slumped on the bed.

He grinned, his teeth startlingly white amidst the shadows. "Now, ain't this a surprise. . . ."

She couldn't speak. Not for the life of her.

His left eyebrow cocked upward. "A pleasant surprise."

"Good evening," she managed, though there was no air in her lungs.

She stared at him, unable to glance away. At the look in his eyes, seductive and predatory, her control started to unravel. All the questions about him, about her, about *them*, spiraled through her mind so fast, she felt lightheaded. And his words *I could be the best time you ever had* hung in the air between them, tense and heavy. He might as well have said them again.

"Here, let me help you." He strolled to the bed and stood at the other side. The crisp white sheets spread between them, cool and inviting. Mariah tried not to look up, tried to concentrate on the bed and only the bed. But no matter which way she turned, she saw the flat, well-muscled flesh of his stomach, and the soft, coffee brown hair that furred his chest. The acrid scent of lye, softened by masculinity and woodsmoke, hovered between them.

He bent toward her. A long lock of damp, wheat blond hair fell across one gray eye. She tried not to look at him, but couldn't help herself. He was so devastatingly handsome. His eyes were crinkled in the corners, dancing with seductive gray light. Deep, grooved laugh lines bracketed his full lips. Without the scraggly stubble of beard, his jaw was strong and squared.

He grinned at her and leaned closer. Their gazes fused above the blinding whiteness of the sheet. She swallowed hard and dropped her gaze. His hand moved in a seductive, circular motion on the sheet, smoothing out the wrinkles.

Mariah watched his hand, mesmerized for a moment by the contrast of his deeply tanned skin against the stark linen. Then she realized what she was doing. Jerking away from the bed, she nervously brushed the curly wisps of hair from her face. "There. It's done."

"Thanks." His voice sounded soft, intimately beguiling. It reminded her of the words she'd read, dreamer's words, and she felt herself soften inside.

She looked up, met his intense, burning gray eyes. A shiver coursed through her, brought goose bumps to her arms. "I . . . I cleaned the bunkhouse." She glanced down. Heat spread across her cheeks. She knew she shouldn't say the next words that came to her mind, knew, too, that she would. "For you."

He glanced around, smiling. "It looks—" Suddenly his smile faded. A frown creased the tanned flesh of his brow. "Where's my bag?"

She cast a guilty glance at the corner of the room. "I put your belongings away. The bag's under the dresser."

He pinned her with eyes as cold as a winter sky. "You pawed through my things?" His voice was quiet.

She licked her lips nervously, wishing she could melt into the floorboards. Anything—anywhere—so she didn't have to look into his eyes. "Not p-pawed. I just—"

Then, as quickly as it had come, his anger dissolved. The dark intensity in his gaze vanished, leaving sparkling gray pools that whispered of passion. Screamed of passion. He gave her a crooked grin. "Oh, well. I'm hardly in a position to be angry."

The heat of that smile hit Mariah hard, worming through her insides like a trail of fire.

He sauntered around the bed toward her, his fingers looped casually inside the towel. A silvered droplet of water clung tenaciously to the end of his hair.

Mariah stared at the tiny bubble, focused on it, trying to drown out the rest of him. But she couldn't quite succeed. With every step he took, she was acutely aware of him. The soft thud of his bootheels on the floorboards; the quiet, even tenor of his breathing; the easy rise and fall of his bare chest.

"Mariah . . ." On his lips, her name was a whispered caress, a promise of something yet to be.

He stopped in front of her.

She stared at the drop of water, watched it quiver for a moment at the wet tip of his hair, then plummet downward. It splashed in the thicket of chest hair and zigzagged down the hard, washboard length of his stomach, disappearing in the thick white fabric of the towel.

Her gaze followed it, lingering a half second too long at the sagging waistband of the fabric.

His hands moved to the towel. "I could take it off. . . ."

Fear chilled her. She snapped her chin up and met his smoldering gaze. "No!"

A slow, mocking smile curved his lips. "Ah, Mariah . . ."

She stumbled backwards and hit the wall.

He moved toward her. "Don't be afraid. I won't hurt you."

A hysterical bubble of laughter escaped her. She clamped a hand over her mouth, mortified that the insipid, childish sound had come from her.

He leaned toward her, slowly—so slowly—bringing his hands toward her face.

She pressed against the wall. The erratic, pounding beat of her heart thundered in her ears.

Casually he placed his fists against the wall, one on either side of her head. Then he leaned toward her. The tip of his nose brushed hers.

The simple touch jolted Mariah to the core. Her eyes widened. She swallowed hard, unable to tear her gaze away from his face. "Wh-What do you want?"

He kissed the end of her nose. "You know what I want."

She cleared her throat and tried desperately to sound calm. "N-No, I'm sure I do not."

His head lowered, just a fraction.

Mariah's heart stopped beating. Time seemed for a moment to pause.

He kissed her, a soft, gentle brushing of lip against lip that lasted no longer than a heartbeat. "I want you, Mariah." He drawled the words against her mouth. He closed his eyes, leaned infinitesimally toward her. "God help me, I shouldn't want you, but I do."

She felt the tender movement of his lips against hers, and a violent shiver cascaded through her body, leaving a trail of goose bumps in their wake.

He pulled back slowly. "Come to bed, Mariah." The invitation was whispered against her ear. His parted lips felt soft and moist against her flesh.

She froze. Fear spilled through her, left her cold and shaken and trembling.

His words came back to her, mocked her. *No one would ever know.*

What a fool she'd been to even consider them. *She* would know. What was left of her after he'd finished would know, would always know. . . .

She shook her head, trying to say something. But her throat was as dry as old ash, and no sound came out except a pathetic whimper. The progress she'd made recently dissolved in a puddle of familiar fear. It felt good, that fear, comforting. It was an emotion she understood.

With a quiet gasp, she ducked out from his arms and ran for the door, slamming it shut behind her.

Mariah didn't stop running until she reached the picket fence. There, she sank to her knees on the cold, hard ground, and bowed her head in shame. God, she wanted to cry, needed to cry.

I want you. The soft, shattering words came at her from a hundred different directions.

A tiny sound of despair lodged in her throat.

She wanted him, too. There was no longer any point in denying it; she was weary of trying. She wanted him to kiss her. God help her, she'd ached for his kiss, dreamed of it. From the moment she met him, he'd taunted her, upset her, angered her, touched her. Her world hadn't been the same since he strolled into it last week, and it wouldn't be the same when he strolled out.

When he strolled out.

The words spiraled back at her, burrowed into her heart. He would leave soon, and her life would go back to the way it was. This brief interruption of passion would be forgotten.

Forgotten.

Never, probably, to come again.

Pain welled through her at the thought of Mad Dog leaving her. Tears threatened, burned her eyes, but of course, didn't fall.

Her shoulders caved downward, her spine rounded. She squeezed her eyes shut, imagining all the moments with Mad Dog that mattered. The ones she'd remember long from now, during the endless winter nights when she was alone and lonely. She'd remember everything about him—his gestures, his smile, his touch. The way it had felt when he curled his arm around her and held her close. The feel of him, the smell of him, the taste of him . . .

Oh, God, the taste of him . . .

Could she really let all that go? Could she stand by, afraid and lonely, and let him simply walk out of her life?

He'd never stay. . . .

Once, the words had had the power to hurt her. Now they simply stated a bald, unemotional fact. He wouldn't stay. She couldn't go. In those simple words lay everything that stood between them.

It was so much . . . and it was nothing at all.

The truth, when it came to her, was blindingly obvious. She couldn't let him go, not now, not yet, without ever tasting the passion he offered. She'd been alone for so long, her passion pent up beneath starched layers of linen and too many hairpins. She didn't want to be alone anymore. She wanted, needed, just this once to be touched by something more human than the wind. . . .

She took a deep, steadying breath and stood. Her legs felt rubbery and unstable—whether from kneeling or from the decision she'd made, Mariah wasn't sure, and it didn't matter. Straightening her spine, she headed back to the bunkhouse.

With each crunching step, her fear increased. So did her resolve.

She stopped at the door. The thick, white-planked portal filled her vision. It was the only thing that stood between her and passion. Her and pain. If she knocked now, her life would never be the same.

Do it.

Don't do it.

She let her breath out slowly, forcing her hands apart. There was really no decision to be made. She didn't want her life to be the same anymore. She was tired of being alone and isolated, tired of being lonely. Her soul ached for the warmth of a touch. For years she'd thought of nothing but the past; she'd worried about it, agonized over it, tried to atone for it. Now, for once, she wanted to think about the present.

Before she could change her mind, she knocked.

"Come on in," came Mad Dog's deep, masculine voice.

Mariah's knees almost buckled. She jerked her chin up and opened the door.

On the bed, in a pool of golden light amidst a mass of wrinkled white sheets, lay Mad Dog. He was sprawled casually across the mattress, one leg stretched out, one leg bent, with the Turkish towel across his midsection.

Surprise flashed through his eyes. "Mariah." He said her name in disbelief. Then came the smile, a slow, steady curving of lips that made Mariah's heartbeat quicken.

She swallowed hard and tried to smile back. She almost succeeded. "Am I going to regret this?" she asked in a voice so quiet and shaking, she wondered if he could hear it.

He sat up straighter. Across the wide expanse of wrinkled sheets and naked skin, their eyes met. There was no laughter in his gaze this time, only a searing honesty. "Probably."

"Will you?"

He grinned. "Probably not."

In that instant, with that answer, Mariah felt her last crumbling remnant of resistance disappear. She laughed, and it was a musical, velvety sound that surprised her. "Mr. Stone, I do so admire your honesty."

It was true, she realized. That's what had drawn her to Mad Dog, what drew her now. It wasn't his handsome face or ready smile or teasing words. It was his honesty.

He was recklessly, fearlessly honest. His integrity touched something in her, made her yearn for the days when she, too, used to be forthright. Unafraid.

She wanted that again, wanted it with a desperation that left her winded. And maybe, with Mad Dog beside her—even for a fleeting night of passion—she could find that kind of honesty within herself again.

And she was going to start right now.

She looked at Mad Dog, an honest, wide-eyed stare that held nothing back. "I want you, too."

Chapter Sixteen

Holy shit, she was serious.

Mad Dog sat up, yanking the towel tighter against his hips.

She was standing in the open doorway, as stiff as a blade, her hands balled at her waist. Fear had pulled the color from her skin and tightened her full lips into a thin, quivering line. With the moonlight drizzling through the doorway and bathing her in elysian light, she looked young and frightened and impossibly vulnerable.

Vulnerable.

He bit off a curse. Christ, she was such an innocent, standing there, quietly asking for something she couldn't possibly understand. He could give it to her—longed to give it to her—but she wouldn't be able to live with the consequences. And, surprisingly, he wasn't sure that he could, either. He liked Mariah, genuinely, honestly liked her. He didn't want to hurt her. She wasn't the kind of woman for him. She didn't deserve to be dallied with and then deserted. She deserved better than he could give her.

That shocked the shit out of him. He ran a hand

through his hair and shook his head. For the first time
in his life, he was going to be a goddamn hero. He
couldn't believe it.

He tightened the towel around his waist and eased
carefully from the bed, walking slowly toward her.

She didn't back away, just stood there, as still as
stone, haloed by ivory moonlight, her huge eyes focused on his face. A tiny pulse beat frantically at the
base of her throat.

"Go home, Mariah."

She squeezed her eyes shut for a moment, then
opened them slowly. "Don't make this any harder on
me. Please."

The soft plea coiled around his heart and squeezed
until it hurt to breathe. "You don't know what you're
asking. . . ."

She looked up at him suddenly, met his gaze. "I'm
no . . . virgin."

He was so surprised, both by her words and her atti-
tude, that it took him a second to answer. "You're not?"

"No," she said with a hint of something in her
voice—perhaps pride, maybe pain. "So you won't be
'ruining' me. That job's been adequately handled by
someone else. And—" she hesitated a heartbeat, then
went on steadily "—I can't have children, so you've no
problem on that account."

He heard the pain in her voice, and knew what that
confession had cost her. It moved him immeasurably,
her gutsy attempt at courage. He knew how easy, how
safe, it was to be casual about the important things. It
was a defense he'd used a hundred times in his life. Hit
'em before they hit you.

Obviously Mariah was a woman who'd wanted children, desperately. He remembered the baby blanket, and suddenly it all made sense. She'd embroidered it long ago, waiting, hoping.

Sadness tightened his chest. Once again he felt that strange, inexplicable need to comfort her. He brushed a strand of hair from her lip. "I'm sorry ... about the children. But doctors can be wrong. . . . They're wrong all the time. . . ."

"I don't want your pity." She smiled, but it was a strained, hurting expression. "I want your body."

He laughed in spite of himself. "Jesus, Mariah—"

Her smile faded. She gazed up at him with heartbreaking seriousness. "I've been stuck on this farm for years, running away from everything and everyone. I don't want to run anymore. Please ... make love to me, Mad Dog. . . ."

The softly spoken words hit him like a punch to the gut. Christ, he'd never had a woman say that to him before. *Make love to me* in that quivering, desperate voice. It tore through his resolve and started a red-hot fire in his groin.

He looked away, balled his hands into painful fists.

She shouldn't be standing there, looking so damn beautiful and vulnerable, asking him to make love to her. Not a lady like her; not to a man like him.

He should get the hell out of here, right now, just grab his shit and hit the road and never look back. Walk. Run. Ride. Anything to keep her from looking at him again, from touching him, from uttering those shattering words: *Make love to me.*

"Have . . ." Her voice fell to a throaty whisper. "Have you changed your mind about wanting me?"

He laughed sharply and looked away. "Hardly."

His answer seemed to give her courage. Slowly she moved toward him, until she was standing close enough to be kissed. The heat from her body was a tangible, erotic presence that filled his senses. She smelled of soap and water and wildflowers.

She looked up; he looked down.

"Is something . . . wrong with me?"

He flinched. "You're not easy, goddamn it. Don't you see?"

She tried to smile. "I believe I'm being extremely easy right now."

"I'm no good for you," he whispered in a harsh, throaty voice.

"I don't care. . . ."

"I'll leave you."

"Don't you think I know that?" Her voice was reed-thin, almost frightened. "All I want is a night—one night—to keep me warm on all the long winter nights when I'll have no one. Is that so much to ask?"

He stared down into the warm bourbon of her eyes and felt like he was falling. Jesus, suddenly it hurt not to touch her. He wanted her so badly.

"You're worth more than that, Mariah."

She made a tiny, gulping sound. "Don't . . . don't make me beg. . . ."

"Christ, Mariah, I'm not trying to humiliate you. I just don't want you to hate me in the morning. I like you too much for that."

"I'll hate you more if you say no."

He wanted to back away from her, but he couldn't move.

Slowly, as if she were scared to death, she tilted her face up to his. "Kiss me . . ." Her voice broke slightly, her lips trembled.

"Aw, Christ." The curse burst from his lips in a gust of breath. He couldn't stop himself. Without thinking, he grabbed her shoulders and pulled her toward him. His lips came down on hers in a hot, hard kiss that drove the breath from his lungs.

And at that first intoxicating taste of her, Mad Dog was lost. His one and only attempt at being a hero shattered into a million desire-tipped shards.

A tiny, contented sigh escaped her, slipped from her mouth to his. He pulled back slowly, staring down into her eyes. A slow smile moved across his face.

"God, you're beautiful, Mariah."

A prickly heat crawled up her throat. Without warning, she was reminded of Stephen and his lies. Pained by the memories, she looked away. "You don't have to say that."

"I know."

She felt his gaze on her face, pointed and searching, and reluctantly she looked at him. There was something in his eyes she hadn't seen before, a sadness. "What?"

"You think I'm lying, don't you?"

"You . . . lie?" She gave a laugh that sounded fragile even to her own ears.

"Come here." He pulled her to the old oval mirror that hung above the lopsided dresser. Maneuvering her to stand in front of it, he slipped behind her. "What do you see?" he whispered against her ear.

She rolled her eyes. "Oh, for God's sake. What does this have to do with—"

"What do you see?"

Reluctantly she let her gaze move back to the mirror. "I see my face. And half of yours."

He placed his hands on her shoulders and began to knead her taut muscles. The rough-skinned pads of his fingertips moved gently up and down, massaging. "What color are your eyes?"

It was hard to concentrate when his hands were working such seductive magic on her shoulders. A strange sensation spilled away from his fingers, sliding down her body until she felt light enough to fly. "Brown," she said without even looking.

"Wrong."

She frowned and looked at him in the mirror. "You're saying my eyes aren't brown?"

He shook his head, smiling at her reflection. "Your eyes are far from ordinary brown. Now, what color are they?"

"Well, they have a little . . . gold in them."

He kissed her cheekbone, letting his lips loiter against her skin as he spoke. His breath was hot and moist against hers. "They're the color of fine bourbon or warmed maple syrup," he murmured. "What about your hair?"

"Brown. Well . . . reddish brown."

He eased back from her face. His hands slid across her shoulders and up the long, straight column of her throat. One by one he pulled the pins away. As if from a great distance, she heard them hit the floor with a tinny ping.

When they were all gone, he fanned his fingers through her long, curly hair, shaking it loose.

She blinked in surprise at her reflection. A riotous mass of wavy, mahogany-hued hair swirled around her pale face, softening the hard lines of her cheekbones. Lamplight caught her hair and gilded it. Her eyes looked golden-brown and liquid against the creamy smoothness of her skin.

"You're beautiful, Mariah."

A thrill zipped through her. For the first time, the words didn't echo of the past or hint of mockery. She *felt* beautiful. A slow, trembling smile shaped her lips.

Smiling, he turned her around.

The passion in his gaze sent waves of heat undulating through her body. Her quivering smile faded.

Slowly, without saying a word, he began to unbutton her dress.

Mariah felt his fingers brush the soft flesh of her throat and she flinched. Anticipation and anxiety fluttered in her stomach. Her breathing sped up. She fought the urge to bat his hands away.

The buttons fell away, the fabric gaped. Cool night air slid in, caressing her skin in a tingling touch.

She squeezed her eyes shut.

As if by magic, the dress peeled away from her body and swished to the floor in a heap. She stepped out of it, kicked it aside.

"Open your eyes, Mariah."

She shivered. He made her name sound like something out of a love song. Slowly she opened her eyes and stared up at him.

He smiled. "I want you to see me kiss you." He bent toward her.

At first it was just a feather-stroke, a touch that lasted no longer than a heartbeat. A quiet sigh escaped her parted lips. It was different from the first kiss; that one made her feel desired. This one made her feel loved.

She closed her eyes, letting herself pretend—just for now—that they loved each other.

His mouth moved against hers. She felt the firm softness of his lips forming to hers, melding, joining. At the slow, steady contact, she felt the first pulsing strands of desire.

He drew back slightly, so that their lips were a hairsbreadth apart. She frowned and strained toward him, wanting more.

His tongue dragged lazily along her lower lip, tasting, exploring the full curve, then dipped into her mouth. The warm, liquid tip of it flicked against hers, causing a lightning bolt of heat to lodge in her chest.

He pulled her against him, hard. The kiss turned hot and demanding and passionate.

Mariah's heart slammed against her rib cage and pounded a breathless, stacatto beat. A deep, formless longing engulfed her, made her ache and pulse and need, for . . . something.

The feelings scared and exhilarated her. She felt blissfully alive. She wanted to touch him, to explore his body, but she couldn't force her arms to move.

His hands slid down her neck again, and she shivered uncontrollably as first one, then another finger slipped beneath the lacy eyelet of her chemise. He moved gently, with excruciating slowness, peeling the fabric back from her tingling flesh.

Half-naked, she shivered.

He grabbed her wrists and pulled them up, forcing her hands around his neck. She clung to him, feeling the soft steel of his neck, burying her fingers in his hair. The kiss deepened, became painful and intense. She pressed herself against him wantonly, achingly aware of his coarse, wiry chest hair on her nipples.

With a groan, he swept her into his arms and carried her to the bed, letting her settle gently into the mounds of twisted sheets and blankets. The harsh, thick wool felt scratchy beneath her naked back, the sheets smooth and cool.

In the grip of her awakening sensuality, she noticed everything. The softness of the sheets, the coolness of the air on her skin, the moonlight spilling through the silvered windowpane.

Mad Dog kicked the door shut and came back to bed. But he made no move to join her; he just stood there, staring. His eyes were narrowed, and as dark as tarnished steel. Everywhere he looked, she felt singed.

She lay there, breathing hard, half-naked. She should have felt shame or fear, or any one of a dozen debilitating emotions. But she didn't. Desire drugged her, made her feel sleepy and wide-awake at the same time.

He reached for his towel and unwound it, letting it fall to the floor in a heap of white.

Mariah stared at his aroused, naked body in awe. A tingling heat crept through her blood and splashed in fiery strokes across her cheeks. The dull throbbing inside her sharpened, took on a painful, needy edge. "Oh, my . . ."

A slow, lazy smile spread across his face. "See what you do to me, Mariah?"

He leaned toward her and pulled at the sagging drawstring waistband of her pantaloons. The flimsy linen slid away from her ticklish flesh, leaving her bare-skinned and exposed to his burning, intense gray gaze.

A shiver tore through her body.

"Don't be afraid," he breathed, tossing the undergarment over his shoulder and crawling into bed alongside her. The old mattress sagged beneath his weight, the metal frame creaked.

"I'm not. . . ." She breathed the incredible words aloud.

He pulled her to him. Their naked bodies came together in a wall of searing heat.

She tilted her chin up and looked at him. A slow, seductive smile curved his lips as he bent down for a kiss.

Mariah closed her eyes, waiting for the moist, welcoming feel of his mouth.

His lips molded to hers, a soft caress that she answered with boldness, touching her tongue to his. She heard the hiss of his indrawn breath, and the sound filled her with a giddy sense of her own sensuality. She coiled her arms around him, held him tight and pressed her breasts against the hard wall of his chest.

She kissed him with all the passion she'd hoarded for years. She licked him, laved him, nipped at him with her teeth. Her tongue met his, coaxing, teasing, probing, until they were kissing with blind, desperate passion.

The roughened pad of his fingertip grazed the tender

flesh beneath her breast, tracing the pale globe with tormenting slowness. Then, in agonizing inches, he moved his knuckle upward, gliding toward the straining pink peak.

Mariah's breath caught, held in a quivering gasp. Anticipation tumbled through her in an excruciating wave. She shivered, squeezed her eyes shut. Her body turned liquid, melted, as his thumb and forefinger closed around her pebbly nipple, drawing it out in a few gentle—then not so gentle—plucks. He squeezed the hardened tip and twirled it lightly back and forth before cupping the fullness of her flesh in his hand. The damp heat of his palm enveloped her breast, sending shooting sparks of fire throughout her body.

Mariah's breath broke into short, breathy gasps that burned all the way up her throat. The dull throbbing in her stomach radiated outward, lodging hot and hard between her legs. Restlessly, needing something she couldn't name, she writhed in silent agony.

Fire filled her body, scorched her senses. The rapid, deafening beat of her heart hammered in her ears, matched the dull throbbing of her desire.

He drew back and let out a shaking breath. "Touch me, Mariah. . . ."

She wanted to. God, she wanted to. "I . . . I don't know how."

"Try." He said the single word quietly, on an exhalation of breath that wafted across her damp forehead.

She moved her hand slowly upward. Wincing, biting down on her lower lip, she touched his neck.

"Lower," he said in a smiling voice.

Her fingers slid into the hair that furred his chest. She

closed her eyes, reveling in the feel of him. Each strand of his chest hair seemed separated from the rest, wiry and soft. Her breath released in a quiet sigh of wonder. It filled her with a heady boldness, this right to touch his body at will.

"Lower."

She moved her hand downward again, through the thicket of his chest hair, over the hard rim of his last rib, to the soft, muscular concave of his stomach.

He shuddered. Goose bumps patterned the skin beneath her fingertips.

"Lower." His voice was ragged, his breathing labored.

She wet her lips again and pushed her hand down, down.

Suddenly the soft, firmly muscled expanse of his stomach was gone. Instead, she felt the mound of hair that grew between his legs.

"Oh, God . . ."

"Lower."

She took a deep, trembling breath and curled her fingers around him, surprised by the velvety texture of his skin and the steel-hardness of his desire.

She *felt* how much he wanted her, and it filled her with an unexpected sense of her own power. All of a sudden she felt beautiful and sexy and desirable—all the things she'd never been before. She tightened her hold on him and stroked him.

A quiet, animal-like growl erupted from his throat, and the sound, so primal and passionate, lodged like a spark of fire in Mariah's heart.

He sank deeper into the covers. His pelvis pushed up into her hand. "Holy Christ . . ."

She looked up at him uncertainly. "Am I doing something wrong?"

He touched her face with trembling fingers. "Not hardly." Before she could say anything else, he pulled her into his arms.

His lips crashed down on hers in a powerful, passionate kiss that drove the breath out of her lungs and left her trembling with need. Restlessly she pushed against him, pressing against the hard length of his thigh.

His mouth moved away from hers, slid down to her chin, then moved on again, trailing moist, openmouthed kisses along her throat, over her collarbone to the soft swell of her breast.

The wet tip of his tongue flicked against her nipple. She gasped and arched toward him, her arms coiling around his back.

Wave after wave of hot, aching sensation spilled through Mariah, becoming a pulsing ball of fire between her legs. She trembled with longing, arched against him, grinding her mound against the hardness of his thigh. She couldn't keep still, couldn't keep quiet. She moaned his name as his hand moved down the quivering, sensitive hollow of her stomach.

"Oh, God . . ." She swallowed thickly and threw her head back into the pile of pillows behind her.

His fingers pushed through the curly fleece between her legs and kept moving, searching, probing for a point of pleasure. He found it, slid his long, hard finger against her.

Mariah gasped. Her body shuddered and turned liquid, melting in readiness.

He rubbed his finger against her. She groaned and closed her eyes as his hand moved in a frenzied, focused circle against her hot, wet flesh. She clung to him, her arms shaking with need, her palms slick with sweat. Her fingernails dug into his flesh, scoring it.

The thudding beat of her heart roared in her ears. Sensations hammered her body, spilling through her in hot, liquid waves of fire. She thrashed restlessly, her every sense focused on his hand and the delicious, forbidden things he was making her feel. She arched up, driving her hips against his palm, pleading in a voice that sounded weak and desperate and frayed. "Please . . . please . . ." She didn't know what to say, what she wanted him to do. She only knew that she was desperate for something, some relief.

With a low, groaning sound, he pulled her beneath him and covered her body with his own. She felt his hardness between her legs, pressing into her.

He pushed up on his elbows and stared down at her. Their eyes locked.

In one sharp thrust, he entered her.

Pain stabbed through Mariah. It felt as if her insides were being stretched apart. With a small, surprised gasp, she tried to sink into the mattress to get away from him, but his heavy body had her pinned in place. At his back, her fingers curled into tense fists and pressed against him.

He stilled. "Are you okay?"

She blinked up at him, feeling the embarrassing sting of tears in her eyes. "It . . . hurts a little."

"I thought—" He shook his head. "Jesus, you said you weren't a virgin."

"I'm not . . . precisely." She bit her lower lip and stared up at him. "I hope you're not disappointed. . . ."

His gaze softened. "I would have done it a little differently, that's all." He bent his head down and kissed her again, a soft, gentle kiss that filled Mariah with a raw, painful sense of loss.

She hugged him, desperate suddenly for the feel of him, the smell of him. He made her feel so alive, so beautiful and wanted and sexy. All the things she'd never been in her life and never thought she could be.

Slowly his hips moved against hers. The physical pain of their coupling eased in the wake of the hot need that coiled around her insides, throbbed between her legs. She clung to him, her legs wrapped around his, her shoulders coming off the bed.

Gasping, moaning, she writhed beneath him, matching him thrust for thrust.

"Oh, God," she whispered. The need took on a sharp, painful edge. She reached, strained, arched for something she didn't quite grasp, a relief she couldn't imagine. "Oh, God."

"That's it, Mariah," he whispered against her forehead. "Come on, baby, come on. I can't . . . wait. . . ."

He plunged into her, filling her with a scalding, pumping heat that pushed her over the edge.

She clutched his sweaty shoulders with talon hands, her head fell back. Control spiraled away from her, left her whole body shaking with need. She clung to him, her torso arched, quivering, trembling. . . .

For a breathtaking second, she felt poised on a sharp, quivering tip. Her body spasmed, went rigid.

Relief came in a red-hot, dizzying wave that sent her flying into a warm, dark nothingness of pure pleasure. Her body rocked, throbbed in a timeless, undulating rhythm.

Slowly it pulsed away. With a quiet sigh of wonder, she collapsed back onto the pile of twisted sheets and blankets, her body shaking in the aftermath of passion, her arms and legs numb and limp.

His arms curled around her, held her close. She felt warm and spent and infinitely safe. "Is it always like that?" she asked softly.

He laughed, and the sound filled her with happiness. "No. It's almost never like that."

She looked up at him, her eyes steady on his. There were so many things she wanted to say to him, but she knew she couldn't say them yet. Knew that perhaps she could never say them. "You were right."

Tenderly he pushed a damp lock of hair from her eyes and curled it around one ear. "About what?"

"You *are* the best time I ever had."

He grinned. "I told you I never lie."

Chapter Seventeen

It was the best sex he'd ever had.

Mad Dog glanced down at the woman sleeping peacefully in his bed and still couldn't believe it.

She lay sprawled beside him, one arm curled possessively across his chest, the other bent awkwardly beneath her body. Her face was a pale, perfect cameo against the grayed fabric of the sheets. Silky mahogany curls lay spread out across the pillow and mattress like a waterfall of fire.

He watched her sleep, amazed by the joy he took in such a simple thing. She was so unlike the other women he'd slept with. Course, they were whores, mostly, but still he wouldn't have thought there was such a difference. The women he knew slept like lumberjacks, their painted mouths hanging open, their breath thick with the odor of old tequila and tobacco smoke. During the night, their face paint smeared so badly, they looked like they'd been punched in the eyes.

Naturally, with that sort of thing waiting for him, Mad Dog got out of their beds early.

But now he felt differently. He *wanted* to sleep with Mariah. Really sleep. He wanted to curl alongside her and hold her tightly and be there with her in the morning when the sun came tapping on the glass.

He gazed down at her. Her skin looked as soft and exquisite as ivory silk, her ears small and delicate. She breathed evenly, ruffling the linen pillowcase with each exhalation. Her pink lips were parted slightly, her dark eyelashes fluttered every now and again.

He focused on her lips, remembering with electric intensity how she'd kissed him, touched him, licked him.

Is it always like this?

Her innocent words came back to him, and this time he realized their full impact.

What had he said to her? He couldn't remember if he'd answered at all. But now, naked and beside her, the truth exploded at him.

It wasn't always like that.

It was *never* like that.

He frowned at the thought. The difference between Mariah and the other women seemed suddenly important.

He couldn't put his finger on the difference, didn't know exactly what it was, but it scared him. He *liked* whores; he always had. They were easy, forgettable conquests that had no hold on him when daylight came. And *sleeping* with them had never held any appeal at all.

He pushed away from Mariah and scooted back in bed, staring dully at the whitewashed bunkhouse walls. For the first time, the room didn't seem even a little bit confining.

A strange queasiness settled in his gut. He'd been here almost a week now. The walls should be pressing in on him. This place should be feeling cramped instead of . . . cozy.

Cozy? The word came at him from nowhere. He almost smiled at its absurdity.

But it wasn't funny. It was scary as hell.

He looked at the closed door.

He should use it. Now.

He thought about it, thought about easing his way out of bed and dressing silently. He could just flip his bag over his shoulder and be gone. He'd done it a million times, and never once had he looked back or regretted his decision. It was simple to leave women, easy.

Reluctantly he glanced down at Mariah. The truth came to him, stunning in its intensity.

Not so easy.

"Aw, shit." Thumping his head back against the wobbly headboard, he ran a hand through his hair.

What the hell was happening?

A niggling, expanding sense of anxiety crept through him. Something was wrong. The damned bunkhouse felt *cozy* and he didn't want to leave—even after he'd slept with her.

Yet, he told himself firmly, and the simple word offered considerable comfort. He didn't want to leave yet. That didn't mean he wanted to stay.

It wasn't the same thing at all.

Mariah came awake gradually. The tail end of a pleasant dream tickled her, made her smile. Stretching contentedly, she yawned and opened her eyes.

A round, flat nipple studded with coffee brown hair filled her vision.

She was curled against Mad Dog's naked side, her cheek resting on his chest, her arm tucked lovingly around his waist.

The night came rushing back on her. Wanton images tumbled through her mind. Heat flooded her cheeks as she thought about her behavior in bed. She'd been wild, aggressive—both times.

A smile tugged at her mouth. *Third time's a charm* . . .

She couldn't believe how good she felt, how incredibly relaxed. Tonight she'd broken through one of the biggest barriers of her past—her sexuality—and it felt marvelous. She felt like a new woman. A free one.

Smiling broadly, she tilted her chin and stared up at the man who'd given her back her ability to laugh.

He was gazing at the door, his eyes narrowed and hard-looking. Something seemed to be bothering him, but Mariah felt too good to care what it was.

She stretched her arms, feeling the sting of exertion in every muscle. "Lord, I hurt."

"It gets better," he answered almost distractedly.

Wiggling up to a half sit beside him, she rested her chin on the smooth curve of his shoulder and looked up at him. "I think it would help if we did it again." She kissed his shoulder, tasting the warm, salty tang of his skin.

He turned and looked down at her. Surprise widened his eyes. "You want to do it again? Now?"

Mariah knew she should feel shy and hesitant and afraid—a "nice" girl would—but she didn't feel any of those familiar emotions.

She felt . . . free. And giddy with anticipation.

She smiled at that, almost laughing out loud. Imagine

her—*her!*—feeling giddy. It was an incredible, heady sensation that made her bold. She'd just opened the door on a whole new side of herself, a side she liked, and she didn't want to close it yet. It had been shut for far too long.

She peeled back the sheets to expose his naked, aroused body. "I don't think I'm alone in wanting it. . . ."

Mad Dog laughed. "It would appear not." Sliding down beside her, he took her in his arms. "So, Mariah, tell me this: How does someone who is 'not precisely' a virgin manage to get so horny?"

She blushed at the crude word, but didn't look away. "You do it to me."

"Only me?" he teased.

She sobered. It was suddenly important to her that he know the truth, that he understand the gift he'd given her tonight. "Only you."

He frowned, and she knew instantly she'd said something wrong. "Mariah . . ."

Fear brushed through her. She didn't want to hear what he had to say. Tightening her arms around him, she rolled on top of him. Her legs slid around his hips, her ankles locked around his. The hard evidence of his desire pressed against her thigh. "Let's do something different this time."

He slipped his arms around her, letting his fingers splay across her naked fanny. "What would you recommend?"

She pulled back in surprise. "Me?"

He gave her a crooked grin. "You must have learned *something* interesting when you lost your virginity."

Incredibly, she laughed. She knew then, without a doubt, that she'd made the right decision tonight. In all the years since Stephen, she'd never been able to remember their physical relationship without a searing sense of shame and humiliation. Now all that was gone.

"What's so funny?"

She shook her head, feeling totally, deliciously liberated. For once, the past was in perspective. "Let's just say this. A two-minute egg takes longer than my . . . experience did."

He grinned. "That's your big 'I'm not a virgin.' Two minutes?"

"Maybe less. It was too dark to look at my watch."

"Did you want to?"

"Have sex?"

He laughed. "Look at your watch."

"Oh, that." She smiled broadly. "I believe I counted seconds instead."

"How many?"

"Not enough."

He pulled her on top of him, curling his arms around her naked back. "Well, that's a pisspoor memory to carry around with you. How 'bout we change the record?"

"What do you mean?"

He came toward her. "One, two, three—"

Their lips melted together in a long, searing kiss that reignited the flames of their desire.

Mariah gave in to the passion completely, utterly. She didn't think about Stephen, or the past, or even the nagging fear that Mad Dog would leave her.

Right now, she didn't care. All she cared about was

the wonderful, exhilarating things he was making her feel. She closed her eyes and tumbled into the searing, satisfying world of pure physical pleasure.

Rass quietly closed the door behind him. The minute the lock clicked into place, he sagged, feeling tired and infinitely old. The porch planks creaked beneath his feet in a whining protest that seemed absurdly loud in the silence of the night.

"Rass? You out there?"

Rass lifted his head and stared at the buggy parked in front of Doc Sherman's house. Now, in the silvered moonlight, it was a shadow cast in streaks of ash gray and jet black. Cleo, the horse, was invisible against the dark night sky, and Jake was a slim reed of blackness that shot up from the charcoal seat.

Rass tried to smile for the boy. "I'm here, Jake." Tiredly he pushed away from the door and shuffled down the creaking steps, across the gravelly path to the buggy.

Jake bounced down from the driver's seat with the exuberance of youth and held out his pale hand. "Can I help you?"

"Thanks." Rass grabbed Jake's hand and hauled himself up the springy metal steps, settling slowly on the padded leather seat.

Jake bounded in beside Rass and snapped the reins. Cleo put her big head down and began a slow, even plodding toward home.

Moonlight illuminated the wide swath of dirt road that cut through the endless acres of grass and wheat. On either side, black fences stood in sharp contrast to the blue-tinged fields. Sounds filled the night: the steady clomping of Cleo's hooves on the hard-packed dirt, the wheezing snort of her breathing, the squeaking whine of well-sprung buggy wheels turning toward home.

"Thanks a lot for supper, Rass. The food was great," Jake said.

Rass attempted a smile. "It would have been better at the Chinaman's place."

Jake shuddered dramatically. "I couldn't eat that stuff. It looked like gooey grass."

Rass laughed unexpectedly and found his mood lightening a bit. "Well, Ma's Diner is good, too."

"Yeah. Service sure is slow, though. It must be eleven o'clock.'

"We're in no hurry." Rass leaned against the tufted leather seat and let out a tired breath. For the hundredth time tonight, he found himself thinking about Mariah and Mad Dog, hoping he'd done the right thing in leaving them alone.

The two of them were perfect for each other; Rass was more sure of the fact with every passing day.

But Mad Dog was a bad bet, and Rass had known that from the minute they met. Usually Rass pushed the realization aside, buried it beneath a thick layer of optimism. But at times like this, when he felt weak and sick and alone, Rass fell prey to the fear that Mad Dog would leave her . . . and Mariah would fall back into the bleak pit of her own despair.

And this time she'd never come out of it.

Ah, Greta, he thought, squeezing his eyes shut. *Am I doing the right thing?* The vision of his wife came to him as clear as day, her face implanted in his soul like a treasured photograph.

Bittersweet memories hurled themselves at him, and he sighed. He was too tired tonight to fight them, too tired to be strong. Loneliness pressed in on him from all sides, crushing his lungs until he could barely breathe. Tears stung his eyes.

Ah, Greta . . .

"Are you okay, Rass?"

Rass wiped his eyes with his sleeve. "Fine. Why?"

Jake cocked his head back toward the house. "That was a doctor's place." He shrugged. "I saw the sign and, well, I just wondered . . . you know, if you were all right."

"Doc Sherman's a friend of mine."

It wasn't an answer at all, but Jake seemed not to notice.

"Oh."

"But let's not tell Mariah I saw him, okay?"

"Okay."

Rass stared at the boy, studying him in the weak, eerie light of the moon. Jake sat as tall and straight as a nail, his elbows resting lightly on his knees, his fists hung over the rim of the buggy on the reins. His hair was a smooth, precisely cut red-gold fringe that hung out from beneath his hat.

Surprisingly, Rass found himself remembering someone else with the promise of red-gold hair.

He ran a shaking hand through his white hair. Thomas would be sixteen about now, just Jake's age. Pain rippled through Rass at the thought, escaped his chapped lips as a quiet whimper. Even now, all these years later, he couldn't think about the baby without aching for the loss of his tiny life.

"Rass ..." Jake's quiet, tentative voice cut through Rass's old man's memories.

He swallowed, tried to find the courage to speak. "Yes?"

"I need your help with something."

The simple question was a gift. With it, Rass was able to push aside the painful thoughts and focus instead on something real, on something that mattered. The bitter memories fell into the background of his mind. "Sure, Jake. If I can."

Jake stared hard at Cleo's butt and swallowed. "I . . . haven't gotten to spend much time with Mad Dog."

"Uh-huh."

"And I, well, I came here to get to know him. . . ."

Rass straightened. Now *that* was an unexpected bit of information. What was Mad Dog to Jake? "You did?"

Jake winced. "Didn't I tell you that?"

Rass chewed his lower lip, studying him intently. The boy was sitting even straighter than before, but his hands were shaking on the reins, his mouth was trembling. "No," he said slowly, "you didn't tell me that."

"I . . . uh, musta forgot." He tried to laugh. It was a strained, hollow sound that didn't fool Rass for a second.

"Uh-huh."

Jake licked his lips nervously. "Anyhow, I came here to meet Mad Dog." He turned to Rass. "He's a famous fighter, you know."

Rass nodded slowly, but again, he wasn't fooled. Jake didn't want to meet Mad Dog because of his fame.

"Uh-huh. So what's the problem? He's on the farm, you're on the farm. Get to know the man."

Jake's gaze skidded away. A redness that looked like embarrassment—or shame—crept up his cheeks. "He doesn't seem to want to get to know me."

"I see. So, you want to know *how* to get close to a man who doesn't seem too inclined to get to know you."

Jake let out his breath in a relieved sigh. "Yeah."

"That's not too hard. If the mountain won't come to Mohammed, then Mohammed best head for the mountain."

"What does that mean?"

"Simple. You're here to get to know Mad Dog. If he's not sniffing around your door, you'd best knock on his."

Jake shook his head. "He wouldn't like that."

"So? What do you care?"

Jake turned to Rass suddenly. The boy's eyes were big as quarters. "You mean just follow him around till he *does* talk to me?"

Rass shrugged. "Why not?"

"What if he punches me?"

"Punch back."

Jake rolled his eyes. "He's a professional, remember? He'd kill me. I don't know the first thing about defending myself, either. My mama made sure I didn't know how to fight. She thought it was a useless waste of time."

"All women think that—it's a genetic deficiency."

"Oh . . ." Jake frowned. "She never mentioned any-

thing about a deficiency. She just said fighting was stupid and didn't solve anything."

Rass stifled a smile. "Maybe Mad Dog would teach
you to fight. That'd get you two together for a while."

Jake grinned. "That's a great idea, Rass."

Rass felt the last niggling bit of grief slide away. His
natural optimism bounced back, bringing a smile. "I'm
a professor," he said proudly. "Ideas are my life."

Mariah came slowly awake. Yawning, she arched in
a long, lazy stretch. Pain twisted through her muscles at
the movement.

She groaned. Her body felt pulverized and pounded . . .
and wonderful. Memories of last night seeped through her
sleepy brain, warming her once again.

She blinked lazily and opened her eyes. Sunlight
streamed through her bedroom in a thick, dusty slash of
gold. Through the half-opened window, she heard the
chattering call of a barn swallow and the distant echo of
voices.

She stretched again, rolling out of bed. Her feet hit
the cold floor with a muffled thump. Smiling—she
couldn't seem to stop herself—she reached for her flannel wrapper and put it on.

Then a question hit her with the force of a blow.

Wrenching the fabric belt around her waist, she hurried to her bedroom window and yanked it open. Cool
morning air hit her in the face.

Please be here, please . . .

She shoved the lacy curtains aside and stared down at
the bunkhouse. The door was open.

Her heart picked up speed, thudded anxiously in her chest. Her throat went dry. He never left the door open.

She poked her head out the window, her eyes desperately scanning the small farm.

She found him. He was standing alongside the water pump, washing his face, wearing a faded pair of blue jeans and nothing else.

Relief poured through her. She clutched the window ledge with shaking fingers and bowed her head. "Thank God."

Slowly she brought her head up and looked down at him. Emotion tightened her heart, and she swallowed hard, wondering what exactly she felt for Mad Dog this morning.

She knew what she felt about herself—for the first time in years, she was excited about the day, eager to see what would happen. She felt young and free and unafraid to reach for what she wanted.

And what she wanted was Mad Dog.

It was simple, really. She wouldn't have him for long, wouldn't feel this way when he left. So she had to seize the time they had together and cling to it, enjoying every moment. It didn't matter how she felt about him; it never had. What mattered was how she felt about herself.

She smiled. Lord, it felt good to simply *enjoy* something, to ask nothing from it, expect nothing. To simply accept.

He looked up suddenly and smiled at her, waving.

Mariah felt the effect of that smile all the way on the second floor. Memories of last night washed through her, leaving her tingling and warm in their wake. She shoved her hand out the window and waved back at him. "Morning, Mr. Stone."

"Morning, Miz Throckmorton," he called back, his smile broadening.

Down by the picket fence, Rass pushed to his feet and started walking toward Mad Dog. He was saying something Mariah couldn't hear. All she caught was the word "clouds."

Mad Dog turned to him.

And Mariah saw the red scratch marks that crisscrossed Mad Dog's back. Horror rounded her eyes. With a gasp, she stared down at her stubby fingernails, unable to believe she'd actually done that to his skin.

Then she looked at her father.

"Oh, my God!" Her hand flew to her mouth. Rass was going to see the damage she'd done to Mad Dog's back. And he was going to know what had gone on last night.

"Oh, my *God*."

She ducked back in the window and ran for her armoire. Yanking out a plain brown skirt and shirtwaist, she dressed quickly and raced down the stairs, her bare feet thumping on the sagging steps.

She lurched into the kitchen and saw the remains of breakfast sitting on the table. God, she'd missed breakfast.

She ran through the room and half stumbled down the porch steps. When she finally reached Mad Dog and her father, she was red-faced and winded, clutching the stitch in her side.

"Hi." The word came out as a high-pitched squeak.

Rass looked at her briefly, frowning. "Mornin',

Mariah. We missed you at breakfast." He started to say something to Mad Dog, then slowly turned back to Mariah. "Your hair's down."

She gasped, plastering a hand to her unbound hair. "I . . . I misplaced my hairpins."

Rass gave her an odd look. "Now, *that's* a first."

Mad Dog laughed. "Not precisely."

Mariah rammed her elbow into Mad Dog's side. He made a satisfying grunt of pain and covered it with a cough.

She tried to smile at her father.

Rass stared back at her. A small frown pleated his forehead. "Everything go okay around here last night?"

Mariah felt the color drain from her cheeks. "Fine."

They all stood there for a moment longer, staring at one another, nodding. No one said a word.

Finally Mad Dog turned to leave. "Well, I'd best—"

Mariah grabbed his arm. "Don't go."

He frowned at her.

She realized suddenly how foolish she must look. A middle-aged spinster, hair a tangled mess, clinging to the naked arm of a man she barely knew. As if she had a right to touch him.

Forcibly, gritting out a smile, she released her hold on Mad Dog and reached for the black shirt heaped on the ground. "I simply wanted to remind Mr. Stone to wear a shirt." She turned to him, shoved the shirt at him with a pointed look. "It isn't fitting to go about half-clothed."

"Really?" The single word was steeped in irony. She had no doubt whatsoever that he was picturing her as she was last night—naked, laughing, astride him.

Heat splashed across her face. "Really."

Rass whistled cheerily and shook his head. "Why is it I feel like I'm missing something?"

"Can't imagine, Rass," Mad Dog said, slipping into his shirt.

Mariah let out a relieved sigh as his back was covered. "So," she said, searching for something to say, "did I hear the word 'clouds'?"

Rass nodded. "I was just about to tell Mad Dog about cloud-watching. It's a grand day for it."

Cloud-watching. Mariah felt a warm rush of bittersweet memories. "We haven't done that in years. Not since . . ." Her voice snagged, caught.

Rass gave her a smile. "Not since you were a child." He turned to Mad Dog. "It used to be one of our favorite pastimes."

Mad Dog turned to Mariah. "Do you want to do it?"

His words were spoken quietly, with a concern that wrenched Mariah's heart. She looked at him, wanting desperately to touch him, to say thank you for so many things. But all she said was "Yes."

In companionable silence, the three of them walked toward the knoll alongside the river. As they passed the barn, they saw Jake, painting fences. Rass called out to him, waving the boy over. "Come on, Jake. We're going on an adventure."

Jake set down his paintbrush and hurried over to the group, falling into step between Rass and Mad Dog.

Rass led them all to the grassy rise and then stopped. "Okay, everyone lay down. We want to make a cross formation, with the tips of our heads touching."

The four of them lay down, forming a cross in which

Rass lay north; Jake west; Mad Dog south; and Mariah east. In the center, their heads touched in a connecting circle.

"You start us off, Mariah," Rass said quietly.

Mariah closed her eyes. The chilly wind rippled across her skirts and fluttered against her cheeks. As she lay there in the cold, drying grass, she felt herself falling back into the past. Once again she was a child. . . .

They had done this for endless hours, she and her parents; it had been one of their great family adventures, a time to explore hidden dreams and find forgotten laughter. A time to share and talk and giggle.

Their heads had to be touching, she remembered, because Rass believed they could meld their thoughts that way, that within the family, a magical, timeless connection could somehow be made.

She smiled at the memory. As a child, she'd believed absolutely that they could read one another's minds; it *seemed* as if they could. But then, as she got older, she stopped believing. Her adolescent mind questioned everything, and her heart began to see the truth. Somehow, in some quiet, intangible way, she was excluded from the circle of love. Even though her head was touching, she couldn't read her parent's thoughts anymore. But they could read each other's, always.

That's when she'd stopped playing this game. She told her parents it was because she was too old, that she didn't—couldn't—believe anymore, that it was a silly waste of time. It was the first of many self-protective lies she told herself, and them.

She thought that they'd stop playing, but, of course, they hadn't. They'd played on without her.

Somehow, that had been the most painful part of all. She remembered standing on the porch, watching them walk, hand in hand across the fields, lying down together. They didn't seem to miss her at all.

"Mariah?" Rass's soft voice brought her back to the present.

She blinked hard, feeling the sting of tears. She squeezed her eyes shut, fighting for control. Gradually the hot moisture dissipated, leaving her dry-eyed once again. She cleared her throat and studied the heavens.

Today the sky was an unbroken curve of cerulean blue, interspersed with puffy, floating white clouds.

A snowman-shaped cloud broke free of its moorings and drifted to the left. "I see a little boy in a bowler hat. . . ." Her voice cracked. Memories of Thomas seeped into her heart, squeezing until it hurt to breathe.

Beside her, there was a whisper of movement in the grass. Before she'd identified the sound, Mad Dog's hand curled around hers, warm and reassuring.

Her whole body seemed to dissolve at the comfort of that touch.

She turned her head toward him and found him staring at her. Their faces were close, separated only by a studded thicket of browning grass. He didn't say anything, just stared at her, his gray eyes filled with an impossible understanding.

Mariah felt a surge of gratitude and caring. For the first time in her life, someone had reached out to her, said—however silently—that she wasn't alone.

She wanted to weep at how much that simple touch

meant to her. But, of course, she didn't. She smiled and squeezed his hand, saying nothing.

She didn't even know what to say.

"What's the boy doing, Jake?" Rass said, moving the game forward.

Slowly Mariah turned her attention back to the sky. So did Mad Dog, but he didn't draw his hand away.

"He's leaving home," Jake said. "That big cloud—that's home. The other one, the skinny one, that's his father. He's moving toward his dad, but he can't catch up. The wind is taking them in different directions."

"I don't see a dad," Mad Dog said. "I see a barmaid with big breasts and too much hair. She's chasing the dad, too." He grinned, pointed up. "The dad's slowing down for *her.*"

Jake laughed, and with that buoyant, juvenile sound, the pallor of old sadnesses evaporated, floating away in the apple-scented air.

For hours, the four of them lay in the fragrant, drying grass, amid a blanket of fallen autumn leaves, staring up at the blue, cloud-strewn sky.

Never once did Mad Dog let go of Mariah's hand.

Chapter Eighteen

Jake felt acutely conspicuous as he stood by the bunkhouse, waiting for Mad Dog. He flexed his fingers, then curled them tight, then flexed them again. Nervously he bounced on the balls of his feet.

He tried to make himself smile, tried to feel confident.

He could do this, he could. He'd just tilt his chin up, meet his father's eyes, and ask him. It was just a question, after all. Just a stupid question.

Mad Dog, would you mind teaching me to fight?

He frowned. No, that wasn't right. Too formal. His father would probably laugh and keep walking.

Hey, Mad Dog, you wanna box?

It sounded like he was offering him a present.

He flexed and unflexed his hands again. He needed something just right; the perfect words to make Mad Dog notice him.

That was the key.

Jake tried not to think about how much that hurt.

Mad Dog hadn't noticed him yet. Oh, he'd spoken to Jake, he'd even laughed with him a couple of times. But they hadn't ... connected. The magical father/son tie

Jake had always believed in didn't seem to exist. At least not between him and Mad Dog.

Even yesterday while they'd watched clouds together, there'd been nothing special between them. They'd laughed and talked some, but it wasn't what Jake had dreamt of all his life. What he ached to find. Even his obvious hint about the cloud/boy searching for his father had fallen on deaf ears.

"Hey, kid, you're lookin' pretty down in the mouth. What's up?"

Jake's head snapped up. Mad Dog was standing in front of him, smiling.

Mad Dog walked toward him. "You okay?"

Jake couldn't move, couldn't even nod. Humiliated, he started to turn away.

Mad Dog touched his sleeve. "Hey, kid, did you want something from me?"

Jake froze. Reluctantly he glanced at his dad. "Wh— What do you mean?"

Mad Dog laughed. "Well, you're hangin' around my place, I just thought, you know, you wanted something."

Surprise shot through Jake when he realized the importance of what had just happened. Mad Dog hadn't just walked on past, uncaring. He'd stopped, asked Jake what he wanted. Almost as if Jake *mattered* to him.

Hope spilled through Jake in a dizzying wave.

This was it. He had to do *something* to get to know his dad. He looked up, trying to keep the hope from his eyes, and knowing he failed. "I was just thinking . . . er, wondering . . . I mean . . . hoping—"

"Yeah, Jake?"

He licked his lips nervously, clenched his hands. "W-Would you teach me to fight?"

Mad Dog frowned. "You want to learn to box? Why?"

He hadn't laughed! Jake felt a pounding sense of relief. Taking a deep, steadying breath, he surged ahead with the plan. "I-I'd want to be able to protect myself if something happens." His gaze fell. "You know . . . be like you."

There was a long silence before Mad Dog said quietly, "You don't want to be like me, kid."

"Yes I do."

Mad Dog gave him a surprisingly sad smile. "I've made . . . mistakes in my life, kid. Big ones. I'm no one to look up to."

Jake's heart seemed to stop beating. He leaned forward. "What mistakes?"

"Nothing worth talking about. Just mistakes."

Jake knew his next question shouldn't be asked, but he couldn't help himself. "Do you . . . have any kids?"

Mad Dog snorted. "No, I'm not that stupid. That's the sort of mistake you can't walk away from."

Disappointment crushed through Jake. He looked away. Tears burned his eyes and he fought to blink them back. He shouldn't have asked the question.

Fool. Idiot.

Jake swallowed a thick lump of tears. It shouldn't have surprised him; it was what his mother had said all along. To Mad Dog, kids were just mistakes. *He* was just a mistake. But Jake had never let himself believe it. Always, always, he'd believed that Mad Dog would welcome him.

"Kid? You all right?"

No, Jake wanted to say, to scream. *I'm not okay. I'm your son. Your mistake.*

Mad Dog laid a hand on Jake's shoulder, squeezing lightly. "You got something in your eye?"

Jake sniffed hard; his shoulders felt weighted down by years worth of useless dreams and endless nighttime prayers. It had all been a waste of time. All the traveling, the lying, the hiding, were for nothing. When Mad Dog learned the truth, he wouldn't care. There wouldn't be any big, tearful reunion, no bear hug and welcome.

Jake was just a goddamn mistake.

Mad Dog *would* walk away. And Jake would end up as alone as he was right now, with nothing to show for all of his stupid little-kid dreams.

"You really want to learn to fight?" Mad Dog's voice was soft, tentative, as if he didn't know quite what to say.

Jake looked up dully. "Huh?"

Mad Dog smiled encouragingly. "Okay, let's go. Supper won't be for another hour."

"Really?" Jake felt something inside him come to life. Hope—that insidious little nugget of hope he'd nurtured always—crept back into his heart. He smiled, and even though he knew he was being a fool, knew Mad Dog would never really, truly care about his son, Jake felt himself start to believe in the dream again.

He shook his head, smiling a sad, trembling smile. He was as crazy as his mother. She'd never stopped believing in Mad Dog either.

Silently Jake followed Mad Dog to a secluded spot over by the springhouse. There, Mad Dog stopped.

"Okay, kid, we'll start with the basics. How much did your old man teach you about fighting?"

The question caught Jake off guard. "Huh?"

"Your father, how much did he teach you about fighting?"

"N-Nothing," he stammered. Then he realized he could use the question as a beginning. There was so much about his father Jake didn't know. "Did . . . your dad teach you how to fight?"

Mad Dog stiffened. An uncharacteristic bitterness hardened his eyes. "I suppose you could say that."

Jake saw something on Mad Dog's face he didn't expect, didn't understand, and it reeled him in. He took a cautious step toward him. "What did he teach you?"

Mad Dog laughed, but it was a hard, humorless sound. "My old man taught me how to take a punch." He cleared his throat, and blinked, and the moment was over. Grinning again, he cocked his head to the left. "Okay, stand over there. Feet apart, back straight, arms at your sides."

Jake tried to do everything Mad Dog asked of him.

"You look a little tense, kid. Trying jumpin' around a little, loosen up."

Jake hopped once, feeling foolish.

Mad Dog grinned. "I'll close my eyes, okay? Jump till you feel relaxed."

Jake felt a surge of relief when his father closed his eyes. He hopped around, wiggling his arms until the tension he'd felt earlier melted away. "Okay," he said at last, "I'm relaxed."

Mad Dog opened his eyes. "Great. Now bring your fists up like this."

Jake copied his dad, bringing his fists up to his chest.

"Okay, we'll start with your reflexes. When I punch, you duck."

Jake's eyes bulged. "We're going to start right out with punching?"

"It's fighting, Jake. Not brain surgery. Hitting's all there is."

"Oh." He started to feel a little sick to his stomach. "Will . . . it hurt?"

Mad Dog arched one eyebrow. "It will if you don't duck."

Mariah sneaked up the stairs, wincing every time the floorboards creaked. "Rass," she whispered harshly, "are you up here?"

Nothing. No answer.

She came to the top of the stairs and peered into the hallway. It was dark and silent. Her father's bedroom door was closed.

She crept around the corner and moved silently down the corridor, past her bedroom, past her father's office and his bedroom, to her mother's sewing room. Every step felt weighted and painful. There, at the closed door, she paused.

Her heart thumped like a jackrabbit's. In the eight months since her mother's death, Mariah had never once gone into this room, not even to clean. Right after the burial last year, steeped in silent, agonizingly sharp grief, she'd come into her mother's sanctuary, alone.

Through a pounding headache caused by unshed tears, she'd boxed up her mother's life. Then she'd closed the door and walked away. Never once had she ventured back. Until now.

You can do it, she told herself firmly. *You can go in here. It's just a room. . . .*

Straightening, she reached for the doorknob; it felt cool and slick and unfamiliar in her hand. Turning it, she pushed the door open.

Late afternoon sunlight pulsed through the big window on the east wall, filtering through the expensive lace curtains her mother had ordered through the Bloomingdale's catalog. White sheets covered the furniture in a series of macabre, ghostly shapes.

For a moment, she couldn't move. Then, taking a deep breath, she stepped into the room and closed the door behind her. The gunpowdery scent of old dust and cobwebs filled Mariah's nostrils. Coughing, she walked woodenly to the white heap below the window and flung the dusty sheet aside.

Her mother's desk.

She reached out, touched the scrolled woodwork along the top of the oak parlor desk. Images came to her hard, hammered her self-control.

This is a dress for you, baby. For my special little girl . . .

Mariah forcibly shoved the memories away and closed her mind off to more. She couldn't think about her mother. Even now, almost a year later, she couldn't think about her. If she did, she'd start crying and she'd never stop.

Carefully she eased the desk's top open. The inside was almost empty, as Mariah knew it would be. Once, it had been cluttered with stacks of nothings—pencils, papers, photographs in elaborately scrolled frames. Once it had smelled of lavender, for her mother always kept a sprig or two inside it. Now it smelled like wood and dust and disuse.

All Mariah had left in it was a stack of old, yellowing copies of *Godey's Lady's Books*.

She leaned forward, propping the lid open with the top of her head, and took a handful of magazines. Then she eased back, quietly closing the desk. Pushing slowly to her feet, she whipped the sheet back in place and walked stiffly from the room.

The door shut with a crisp little click that almost broke her heart. Her control wavered.

She squeezed the magazines to her chest and raced for her bedroom, slamming the door shut behind her. Inside her own safe sanctuary, she leaned back against her door, breathing heavily. Memories came at her from a dozen angles, trying to pierce her defenses. She didn't let them through.

Gradually her breathing normalized and she walked to her bed. Perching rail-straight on the edge, she started flipping through the magazines for a hairstyle to replace the tight chignon she'd worn for years. She thought about her hair, only her hair, and after a while the suffocating sense of loss began to diminish.

She sighed, relieved. She'd beaten it once again, held it back by sheer force of will.

She was halfway through the third magazine when she heard a strange sound come through her partially open window.

Frowning, she set the book down and crossed the room. Opening the window, she leaned out.

And saw Mad Dog punch Jake in the jaw. The boy yelped and stumbled backwards, slamming into the springhouse.

Mariah gasped. Anger exploded through her, displacing the last nagging sense of grief. Ducking back inside, she raced from her bedroom and ran from the house, erupting through the front door with a bloodcurdling scream.

Hair flying, she hurtled across the gravelly path. "What in the *hell* are you doing?" she screeched at Mad Dog.

He turned to her, slack-jawed in surprise. "Huh?"

"A *brilliant* response." She glared at him, flinging her pointed finger toward Jake. "You hit this child."

"I'm no child! I'm sixteen years old."

Mad Dog smiled at Mariah. "Well, well, Jake. Appears we got us a riled-up mama hen." He reached out to touch her.

She smacked his hand aside. "Don't you try to sweet-talk me. You *hit* him."

"Course I did."

Mariah blinked at him in surprise. "What kind of excuse is that?"

"It's no excuse. Do I need one?"

"He was teaching me to fight, Mariah," Jake said, holding his reddening jaw.

Mariah turned to Jake. "Teaching you to fight? Why?"

Mad Dog grinned. "A boy needs to know how to defend himself. It's a manly thing."

Mariah refused to be swayed by his smile, though she

felt the heat of it all the way to her toes. "You don't need fists for protection," she said stubbornly.

"Not when you've got the butt end of a shotgun, eh, Mariah?" Mad Dog said softly. The whisper of his breath brushed her throat, and for a split second, she forgot what she was arguing about.

Jake surged toward her, too. "I want to learn how to fight, Mariah. Really, I do."

She gazed into Jake's wide eyes and saw something that looked like desperation. A small, uncertain frown pulled at her lips. She sighed and crossed her arms. It was obvious that Jake wanted this, wanted it a lot.

You're not his mother. The words came at her, hard. She flinched and slowly lowered her arms. She might want to be a mother, but she wasn't. What did she know about the needs of a young man?

Jake looked at her beseechingly, as if begging her to understand. "I just didn't duck fast enough, that's all."

She turned to Mad Dog, trying not to sound as motherly as she felt. "I don't . . . want you hurting him."

Mad Dog sobered. "If he's not fast enough, he's gonna get popped. That's a plain and simple fact." He turned to Jake. "You want to keep learnin'?"

"Yes." He nodded fervently. *"Please."*

Mad Dog turned back to Mariah. "Gettin' hurt is part of life, Mariah. Pretending otherwise is stupid. The boy needs to learn how to take care of himself, but the lessons're gonna hurt. Can you understand that?"

A wave of sadness spilled through her at his quiet words. They were so like him, so damned honest and heart-wrenching. He saw everything clearly, without the blinders she'd worn for years. "I understand," she said quietly, and she did. Better than he could ever know. If there was one thing she understood, it was life's painful lessons.

Their eyes met, her wide with old sorrows, his filled with infinite tenderness. "Ah, Mariah . . ." He reached out.

She shivered, anticipating his touch.

But he didn't touch her. He leaned toward her, close. She felt the caressing strands of his breath along the side of her face. Then, slowly, he put a hand at her waist and drew her toward him, whispering words to be heard by her alone. "You did the right thing, stepping in when you thought I was beating him. Most . . ." His voice cracked, thickened. "Most women would've been too scared. You would have made a hell of a mother."

Mariah's ability to breathe died for a single, exquisite second. Joy filled her heart and almost made her weep at its poignant sharpness. Nothing he could have said would have meant more to her. Her throat burned with unshed tears, her eyes glittered with them.

She looked at him, met his searingly honest gaze and knew that he meant it. Suddenly she wanted to tell him about Thomas, to share with him the excruciating burden of her sadness and let her soul be comforted by the simple act of talking.

"Come on, Mad Dog, let's fight." Jake's youthful voice shattered the moment, sent it spiraling into the oblivion of lost chances.

Mariah forced a bittersweet smile. "*Try* not to hurt him," she whispered throatily.

Mad Dog didn't smile. He just looked at her through

those heart-wrenchingly honest gray eyes. "I always try not to hurt people."

"But it happens," Mariah said quietly.

Mad Dog sighed. They both knew exactly what they were talking about, and it had nothing to do with boxing. "It happens."

It was the first time Mariah had ever despised honesty.

Mariah checked her appearance in the mirror. Again. Nervously she tucked a stray lock of hair into the loosely woven braid that streamed down her back.

It wasn't much of a hairstyle; she'd tried for hours to match the hoity-toity chignons and rolls in the magazines, but without success. Finally she'd given up on looking sophisticated and elegant, and chosen instead to look relaxed.

It might have worked if she could unclench her jaw.

She forced herself to take a deep, calming breath. It was just a braid, she told herself. Women had been braiding their hair for years. She had no reason to feel self-conscious.

But she was. She'd done this for Mad Dog; tried to look pretty. And now she didn't know which scared her more—that he would notice or that he wouldn't. She hadn't cared about her appearance in years, and she realized now what a blessing that was. Just thinking about Mad Dog's response made her stomach knot up.

She almost hoped he didn't notice.

Stiffening, she smoothed her damp palms on her brown apron and turned away from the mirror. Head up, braid swinging, she marched down the stairs and sailed from the house.

Outside, the fires she'd started earlier were burning brightly, belching smoke up around the sooty cast-iron caldrons that squatted above them. Jake stood at one caldron, stirring the bubbling applesauce with a long, wooden-handled paddle. Rass was sitting beside him, his folded body propped against the side of the spring-house. His soft, rumbling snores wafted through the air.

Jake looked up at her and smiled. "Gosh."

She paused, fighting the urge to tuck the stray hairs from her face. "What is it?"

"You look pretty with your hair that way."

An unfamiliar heat crawled up Mariah's throat. An uncertain smile pulled at her mouth. "Thanks."

He eased the long paddle from the applesauce and carefully laid it on the makeshift canning table Mariah had set up earlier. "Wait here, okay? I'll be right back." Without waiting for her response, Jake tore off across the farm and disappeared in the barn.

Mariah smiled. All of a sudden, she *felt* pretty. Whistling softly, she headed for the canning table and started peeling the last few apples of the harvest.

Jake came out of the barn at a dead run. Breathing hard, he raced across the orchard and skidded to a stop beside the table. "M-Mariah?"

She glanced at him. "Uh-huh?"

He chewed on his lower lip and swallowed hard. His knobby Adam's apple slid up and down his throat. "I wanted you to have this." He held out his fist. Slowly his fingers unfurled. On his palm lay a frayed, wrinkled pink ribbon.

Mariah stared down at it, feeling an absurd urge to cry.

Jake glanced down at his feet. "It belonged to some-one I loved a lot. I want you to have it."

Mariah stared at him, standing there so alone and frightened-looking, his hand outstretched, his face downcast, and felt a powerful rush of emotion. God, she wanted to surge toward him and take him in her arms and tell him how very much that scrap of a ribbon meant to her. But she was afraid of frightening him away, afraid she was blowing a molehill of a gift into a mountain of emotion.

"It's just a dumb old ribbon. . . ." he said in a thick voice.

Mariah realized how long she'd stood there, staring at him, saying nothing. She reached out and took the ribbon from him. It felt warm and satiny in her palm. "Would you tie it on for me?"

He looked up then, and she saw the sheen of tears in his eyes. "You'll wear it?"

She swallowed hard. "I'd be proud to wear it, Jake."

He came up beside her and took the ribbon back. She turned around.

Hesitantly, he pulled the coil of twine from the tail of her braid and replaced it with the ribbon.

"There," he said, stepping back.

She turned around. He looked up at her, his green eyes filled with the same aching, tender emotion that filled her heart.

There were so many things she wanted to say to him right now, but somehow nothing made it up her thick-ened throat. It had been so long since she'd expressed her emotions, she didn't know how to anymore. So she just stood there, staring at him, hoping he could read her mind.

He gave her a slow, hopeful smile.

And, crazily, she thought that he had.

Chapter Nineteen

Mariah stood at the kitchen window, staring out across the quiet farm. Dawn was breaking along the horizon, sending plumes of purple and pink into the midnight blue sky.

She watched, mesmerized, as light broke across the land. A glittering layer of hoarfrost clung to the acres of dead grass and shimmered on the fencing. Cleo stood at the paddock gate, waiting to be grained, her breath visible in the cold air.

Any day the snow would come, blanketing the dormant grass with a layer of sparkling, pristine white.

They were ready for it. The hard, backbreaking chores of the harvest were done. The fruit had been picked and preserved and stacked and stored, the fields had been readied for the coming winter, the last colorful autumn leaves had fallen. Now the farm was an endless thicket of skeleton-bare trees huddled against the frosty air.

And Mad Dog was still here.

Mariah smiled to herself. Even now, she couldn't believe it. Every morning she raced to the window first thing and wrenched her curtains aside.

And every morning she'd seen smoke coming up from the bunkhouse chimney.

Today was no exception.

She leaned forward and glanced through the rippled glass, seeing the small, white building. Just the sight of it filled her with almost unbearable hope. They would have another day together, at least one more.

Whistling softly, she went to the icebox and pulled out the eggs and bacon.

Behind her, the stairs creaked, and then came the shuffling, slow-moving sound of Rass's slippers on the hardwood floor. "Mornin', Mariah," he said in a raspy, slightly slurred voice.

"Morning, Rass." She went to the stove, poured him a cup of steaming coffee, and met him at the table. "Here you go. Breakfast will be ready in about fifteen minutes."

He collapsed on the chair and took the cup from her. Curling his shaking, big-knuckled fingers around the warm china cup, he rested his elbows on the table and took a grateful drink. "I hope I make it to mealtime."

Mariah laughed at the familiar morning complaint. "Let me know before I serve up," she quipped, heading back to the stove. She slapped a slab of bacon down on the slopboard and began slicing it into even strips.

The front door creaked open, then clicked shut. Jake hurried into the kitchen. "Morning Rass. Mariah."

She turned to him, smiling. "I'm making your favorite this morning."

Rass groaned. "Oh, God, Mariah, not more apple pancakes."

"They're Jake's favorite," she defended.

Rass feigned disgust. "I know, but every morning is a bit much." He turned to Jake. "Don't you like *anything* else?"

Jake grinned. "Apple fritters."

Rass shook his head. "You were destined to live on an apple farm."

Mariah felt a rush of emotion at her father's poignant words. She smiled at Jake. "On *this* farm, I think."

Jake stared back at her, his smile slowly fading. A hint of moisture glittered in his eyes. "I don't have any other place to live."

Mariah set down her knife and wiped her hands on her apron. "You always have a home here, Jake. I hope you know that. I—" She glanced at Rass and corrected herself. "*We* need you. In fact, it's getting colder now, and I was thinking that you might like to move into the guest room downstairs."

He swallowed hard. "Thanks. I'd like that."

They all stared at one another in silence.

Behind them, the front door creaked open and slammed shut. Hard bootheels sounded on the wooden floor.

"Christ," came Mad Dog's voice from the foyer. "Not more apple pancakes." He walked into the kitchen, grinning.

Mariah's heart swelled with quiet happiness at the sight of him, standing so casually in her kitchen, as if he belonged here. The wonder of it all rushed through her, warmed her as it did every morning. Fleetingly she wondered if he felt it, too, this growing sense of belonging, but she pushed the question aside with practiced ease. She'd made a point of not asking such things; not of him, and not of herself. For now, she was content to simply accept the gift of their time together.

"You're spoiling the kid," he said, leaning against the doorjamb.

"If you had an acceptable favorite breakfast, I'd spoil you, too," she responded.

He gave her an affronted look. "What's wrong with a shot of tequila?"

Rass snorted. "One more apple pancake and I'm going to start siding with Mad Dog."

"I love 'em," Jake piped up, beaming.

Mad Dog crossed the kitchen toward Mariah. She heard each footfall, felt each step. Anticipation shivered through her. Her heart beat erratically in her chest, her breathing sped up. Their gazes met, locked. She saw the carefully banked fire in his gaze, and knew it mirrored the look in her own eyes.

She spun back to the slopboard, focusing on the bacon so her father wouldn't see her eyes. It was getting harder to hide her feelings for Mad Dog. They had slept together several times since that first night. They sneaked around the farm like errant adolescents, laughing, looking for privacy. But no matter how often she loved him, she wanted more.

The need for him was like a living, breathing presence inside her. Every time she looked at him, she ached; when he touched her, she felt as if she were melting.

He came up behind her. She felt the heat of his body like a prickling fire against her back. "Morning, Mariah," he whispered.

She squeezed her eyes shut, fighting the urge to lean back and let him hold her. "Morning, Mr. Stone."

The soft tendrils of his laughter curled around her heart and squeezed. "I was thinking, *Miss Throck-morton . . .*"

She caught her breath. "Yes, Mr. Stone?"

He leaned toward her. She felt his breathing ruffle the back of her unbound hair, slide along the back of her neck, heavy and moist. "My schedule is free tonight," he murmured in a voice so quiet, only she could hear it. "Again."

Response washed through her in waves, radiating to the very tips of her fingers. She turned around and stared up into his smoldering, passionate gray eyes.

She swayed unsteadily. Lord, she wanted to kiss him. Right here, in the middle of her kitchen with her father and an impressionable boy looking on.

She tried to look calm and unaffected. But her knees were knocking so loudly, her father could probably hear them. "Tonight," she mouthed.

He leaned toward her. "It's getting damn cold by the river," he whispered.

His breath was warm against her forehead. She shivered and fought the urge to close her eyes. "I'll get rid of Rass and come to you tonight."

He smiled. "I'd rather you come *with* me tonight."

She couldn't help herself. She laughed.

Rass peered toward them, trying to see past Mad Dog's broad back. "What're you two giggling about over there?"

Mariah spun around and started hurriedly chopping

bacon. "Nothing, Rass. Mr. Stone just asked for my . . . coffee recipe."

Mad Dog turned toward the table and started walking toward Rass. At Mariah's feeble lie, he paused and glanced back at her. "Yeah, Rass, I gather recipes wherever I go. It's hobby of mine."

There was a moment of stunned silence, then all four of them burst out laughing.

Mariah bent down for the wicker basket heaped with clothing. Looping an arm through the handle, she picked up her sewing box, and headed outside.

Opening the front door, she stared out at the farm, washed now in the amethyst shades of early twilight. Over by the springhouse, Mad Dog and Jake were boxing. The crunching *smack* of their punches echoed across the silent, still acreage.

A tingling warmth spread through her at the sight of them. Her fingers tightened around the scratchy wicker of the basket, her throat closed up. It felt so right, coming out of the house on a cold autumn evening to see her boys boxing in the yard.

The moment swelled inside her, pushing at the edges of her heart until it felt overflowing. *Her boys.* For a moment she let herself imagine that they really were her boys out there, that Jake was her son and Mad Dog her husband, that they all belonged together.

She squeezed her eyes shut and tried to banish the foolish dream, but it wouldn't go away. The last few days of autumn had been magical, a season of impossible dreams. She could almost believe it would last.

"Come on out, Mariah."

She glanced sideways and saw her father sitting slumped in the porch swing. "Evening, Rass."

He scooted sideways, patting the slatted space beside him. "Join me."

Mariah glanced down at him and smiled. Lord, it had been so long since she'd sat with her father on the porch swing. Her heart ached with longing at the thought of joining him, sitting beside him. Belonging . . .

"You used to love the swing. I built it for you. Remember?" The single, tantalizing word lodged in her heart. *Remember* . . .

Clutching the basket and flat sewing box, she moved to the swing and sat down. It creaked loudly beneath her weight, welcoming her in the way it had since childhood.

They sat in silence for a while, then slowly, gently, Rass began to rock. The swing glided back and forth, back and forth, taking Mariah back in time with its easy, familiar motion. She found herself relaxing, slipping back into a place and time that had no heartache, no loss. For a few heartbreakingly perfect moments, everything was the way it used to be. The way it should have been.

There was only one thing missing. *Mama* . . .

Her mother sat in this swing for hours, darning her husband's pants, her daughter's socks. And laughing, always laughing.

"What is it, Mariah?" her father asked quietly.

She reached down and pulled a pair of Jake's pants into her lap, staring down at the patched, brown woolen pant leg so hard, it smeared. She thought at first that she wouldn't answer her father, couldn't answer him.

She squeezed her eyes shut, feeling an overwhelming sadness. She licked her lips and stared out across the farm.

"Mariah?" He said her name softly, almost whispered it.

And suddenly, sitting here on the porch, beside her father, she felt a flash of courage, a momentary strength. She turned to him, knowing her eyes were wide with pain, and for once, not caring. "Do you . . . miss her all the time?"

Rass let out a soft breath. "Every moment of every day."

Mariah felt tears swell in her throat. They clung, burning, to her eyes and refused to fall. "Me, too."

Rass reached out, laid his trembling hand on her shoulder. "She loved you, Mariah. Jesus, she loved you so much."

Mariah felt the warmth of that touch all the way to her soul. "I know that. I just . . . wish I'd told her more often."

He squeezed her shoulder reassuringly. "She didn't need to hear the words. She knew."

"I needed to say them." Mariah's fingers clenched the coarse fabric. Grief curled around her throat, made breathing almost impossible. The porch swing kept up its gentle rocking motion, creaking back and forth.

Mariah stared dully at the pants. Tears burned in her throat and behind her eyes. She knew that if she could turn now, in this instant, to her father and say *I love you*, it would all change. Or if he could move toward her and take her in his arms the way he used to . . .

But she couldn't and he didn't. There were too many

years of quiet distance between them, too deep a layer of awkwardness. She didn't know how to reach out to anyone, least of all her own father. And so their silence grew heavy and uncomfortable, rang with ghostly reminders of the laughter that used to fill this porch at night.

She told herself it was all right, that someday she'd make it right with her father. She was getting stronger every day. Soon she'd be able to say the words that burned in her heart. Maybe even tomorrow . . .

"Ow, shit!" Mad Dog's yelp of pain rang through the silence.

Mariah's head snapped up. Mad Dog lay sprawled in the dirt, arms flung wide, legs spread. Jake was crouched beside him, shaking him.

She dropped the pants and lurched to her feet, screaming Mad Dog's name.

He sat up and gave her an infuriatingly cocky grin. "The kid's gettin' good," he said, rubbing his jaw. Then he smiled up at the boy. "I'm proud of you, Jake."

Jake beamed. The two of them bent their heads together and started talking. The unintelligible garble of their lowered voices drifted through the still, chilly air.

Shaking, Mariah slumped back onto the swing's slatted seat. Tiredly she reached down and retrieved the pants.

"He's a good man," Rass said softly.

Mariah didn't even pretend to misunderstand. "Yes, he is."

"Do you love him?"

The question surprised Mariah. It was one that had knocked gently at the door of her mind a hundred times in the past few days, but she'd never let it in. Every day it took more strength to ignore, though, and she was getting weaker by the hour. Every time she looked at him, she wondered if she loved him.

He didn't love her, of course; she knew and accepted that. But somehow, that seemed almost unimportant. She wanted—needed—to know if she loved him. Sometimes, when she looked up into his smiling face, or felt the warmth of his touch, she felt . . . something more than sheer physical response.

She turned to her father. "How would I know, Rass?"

He smiled. A dreamy, faraway look crept into his eyes. "You'd know."

Mariah sighed. "Well, it certainly wasn't love at first sight for Mad Dog and me."

"I don't know," Rass said with a smile. "Cracking a man's jaw with a shotgun is a form of courting in some cultures."

Mariah couldn't help smiling. "I guess I don't love him, but . . ." Her voice trailed off.

"But what?"

She licked her lips nervously and looked at her father. In his rheumy blue eyes she saw something she never remembered seeing there before. Unconditional love and acceptance. It stunned her. Fleetingly she wondered if it had always been there or if it was something new. She didn't know, didn't care. What mattered was the fact that now, for the first time ever, she didn't feel like a failure in her father's eyes.

Her heart swelled with aching emotion. She felt suddenly younger and filled with hope for the future. "But I think I could love him . . . if I let myself."

An infinite sadness crossed his eyes, and Mariah thought—crazily—that he took responsibility for her inability to love. "Don't be afraid of going out on that limb, Mariah. It's where the fruit is."

"I don't know if he can love me back. I . . . I don't think he can."

Rass smiled sadly. "We never know that, Boo."

Mariah glanced at him sharply. Emotion tightened her throat. "You haven't called me that in years."

Sadness filled his eyes. "I should have."

Mariah swallowed hard and stared at him.

"You know what I think?" He leaned toward her. "I think he could love you, too."

"If he stays." She said the three terrifying words aloud.

Rass's smile faded. Slowly, tiredly, he leaned back against the porch swing. Even Rass, the eternal optimist, couldn't pretend to have an answer for that one. "If he stays."

With that, they lapsed back into silence.

Mad Dog dried himself off and stepped out of the shower. Whistling softly, he wrapped the towel around his waist and headed for the steamy mirror.

Anticipation shivered through him. Mariah had made good on her promise; she'd found a way to give them some time alone. Jake was harnessing Cleo right now. Any minute, Rass and the boy would be leaving for town.

Still smiling, he reached for Rass's razor and started to shave.

Outside, someone screamed.

Mad Dog dropped the fancy pearl-handled razor. It clattered in the porcelain sink. He yanked the towel away from his body and grabbed his blue jeans, stabbing his feet into the pants as he hopped to the door and ran down the hall. Breathing hard, half-dressed, he burst outside.

He saw the farm in a series of horrible images: Mariah, on her knees in the dirt; Rass sprawled on the ground; Jake, staring at Mad Dog with tears streaming down his face.

"Oh, Jesus." The quiet words slipped past his lips as he bounded down the steps and raced across the yard.

"Rass, Rass!" Mariah's shrill, desperate voice filled the silent air. She clutched her father's shoulders, shaking him hard. "Wake up." Her voice broke off into nothingness.

Mad Dog kneeled beside her, touched her shoulder. "What happened?"

She jerked toward him, staring up through huge, terrified eyes. "He just . . . collapsed." She brought a hand to her mouth, as if speaking the words made it more real. "Oh, God . . ."

Mad Dog reached for the old man's wrist. "There's a pulse," he said. Relief washed through him. "He's still alive."

Beside him, Mariah made a sobbing sound.

He squeezed her shoulder lightly, then scooped Rass into his arms. The old may lay limp and lifeless, his head lolled back. "Get a blanket," he said to Mariah.

She sat there, stiff as a statue, her head bowed, her hands curled into shaking fists in her lap. Her eyes were dull and vacant.

"Mariah!" he yelled at her.

Through a fog of fear and terror, Mariah heard Mad Dog yelling at her. With great effort, she lifted her chin. "Uh-huh?"

"Go get some blankets. Now!"

She snapped out of her incomprehensive state and spun away from him, racing into the house. She thundered up the stairs and barreled into her bedroom, snatching the blankets from her bed. Wadding them against her chest, she plunged back down the stairs and ran outside.

Rass was lying in the buggy's backseat, his lifeless, blue-veined hands folded against his chest.

"Oh, God . . ." Mariah made a choked, garbled sound of horror and skidded to a stop. The blankets fell from her numb hands and whooshed to the ground in a heap of white.

"Christ, Mariah." Mad Dog swiped up the blankets and threw them at Jake, who tucked the thick wool around Rass.

Then Mad Dog climbed up onto the buggy seat and yanked back on the reins. "Open the gate, Mariah."

The gate.

Mariah felt the words like a punch to the throat. She started shaking; her breathing shattered into short, choppy bursts that burned up her throat.

"Open the goddamn gate!"

You can open the gate, Mariah. You can.

Haltingly she moved toward the gate. The long silver latch glinted in the moonlight. She stared at it, unable to move. Her heart thundered in her ears, a headache pulsed behind her eyes. For a terrifying, debilitating moment, she thought she was going to throw up.

Come on, Mariah . . .

She reached out; her fingers trembled so hard, it took her a moment to grab hold. At the feel of it, so icy cold and unfamiliar, pure, primal terror washed through her. She wrenched her hand back.

She couldn't touch it, couldn't open it. Not even for Rass. *Oh God, oh Jesus . . .*

Behind her, something cracked hard. Hooves pounded toward her. The ground rattled beneath her feet.

"Whoa!"

Cleo skidded to a dusty stop, the buggy creaked. Mad Dog jumped down from the seat and shoved the gate aside, then he climbed back up into the carriage. "Get in!" he yelled.

Dully Mariah looked up at him. For a heartbeat, she didn't know what he was talking about.

"Get in, for Christ's sake."

She shook her head, trying to speak, but nothing made it past her lips except a tiny, mewling sound of terror. Despair pushed in at her from all sides, strangled her. It had been a lie, all these years. She thought she didn't want to leave; she'd never known she couldn't, never known she was so sick and twisted and useless. . . .

Mad Dog frowned. "Mariah? What is it?"

She felt as if she were being ripped slowly, painfully in half. She tried desperately to breathe, but she couldn't. "I . . . can't . . . leave."

"What do you mean?"

A scream welled up inside her. She shook her head, trying to hold it back. "I c-can't leave the farm."

Mad Dog ran a hand through his hair and sighed heavily. "I don't know what the hell you're talking about, Mariah. Get in the goddamn buggy."

This time she couldn't stop the scream. It ripped past her mouth and blasted through the night, a sound of elemental, animal grief. "I *can't*," she screamed, her hands clenched into fists at her sides.

"Mariah—"

"Just go, goddamn it." She lifted her face to Mad Dog's, saw him through a blur of hot tears. "T-Take care of him, please. . . ." Her voice shattered into a pathetic whimper. "Please, he's all I have. . . ."

"I know where the doctor lives," Jake said from the backseat.

Mad Dog looked at her one last time, then snapped hard on the reins. Cleo bolted forward. The metal buggy wheels skidded through the loose gravel in a bone-crunching whine and turned onto the dirt road, hurtling toward town.

Chapter Twenty

Darkness closed in on Mariah, pressed against her lungs until every breath was a wheezing, hurting gasp. Pain pulsed through her body, wringing her heart, twisting her soul into reed-thin rope that snapped beneath the pressure.

Rass was dying. Rass, who'd held her hand when she was a little girl and dried so many of her tears. Rass, who loved to explore roads and found joy in a bit of white quartz. Her daddy.

"Oh, God . . ." With a strangled sob, she sank to her knees. Out on the road, the buggy sped into the thickening bank of shadows. Wheels crunched through the loose stones, Cleo's pounding hooves hammered in a thundering beat.

Then it was gone. The buggy disappeared into the night, and even the sounds faded away. She was left in an aching, sightless void, utterly alone.

She should be with him. Jesus, she should be with him—

She screamed until her throat was dry and parched, until the wailing keen melted into a scratchy, pathetic whimper. The spiked slats of the picket fence seemed to pulse ominously, mocking her with silent laughter.

Self-loathing surged through her in a crippling wave. She clamped a hand to her mouth and staggered upright. Her feet caught in her skirts and she tripped, falling hard against the fence. It creaked and sagged beneath her weight. The spiked tip of a slat bit into her hand, slashed into her palm.

Shame and guilt moved through her. She sank to her knees on the hard ground and bowed her head, dragged down by the overwhelming burden of her own uselessness.

I let you down, Rass. Oh, Jesus, I let you down. . . .

A strangled, burning sob wedged in her throat.

Please, God, let him live. Please . . .

She thought of this afternoon, when she'd blithely assumed she and Rass had years worth of time to talk. She hadn't said what she wanted to say to him, the words he needed to hear. She'd been afraid, and now he was near death—maybe dead—and she'd never said the words to him, never told him how much she loved him.

God, how much she loved him . . .

Grief exploded through her then, left her shaking and sick and desperately, desperately afraid.

She didn't know what to do, how to vent her emotions. They overwhelmed her, clawed at her coherency with talon tips. Hysteria built inside her heart, expanding with every heartbeat, surging with every breath.

She screamed again, but the sound came out strangled and gasping.

Oh God, oh God, oh God . . .

She squeezed her eyes shut and pitched face-first onto the cold, unforgiving ground. Slowly she curled into a fetal position and lay there, panting, trying desperately to cry.

Waiting for her father to come home.

The buggy skidded to a stop in front of Doc Sherman's house. Jake lurched out of the backseat and raced up the path, hammering on the door with his fist.

No one answered.

Fear spilled through him, chilled him to the bone. He pounded harder. "Doc . . . Doc, are you home?"

Finally the door swung open. A stoop-shouldered, bespectacled old man with gray-white hair stood in the opening. He squinted down at Jake. "Yes? Who are you?"

Jake flung his finger back toward the buggy, where Mad Dog stood with a limp, lifeless Rass in his arms. "We got Rass Throckmorton. He . . ." His voice cracked. Hot, embarrassing tears welled in his eyes.

Doctor Sherman straightened. "Get him the hell in here!"

Mad Dog hurried up the path and followed Doctor Sherman to a bedroom in the back of the house.

"Put him down," Doc said, reaching for his black leather bag.

Mad Dog laid Rass tenderly on the bed, then leaned over him, peering into the old man's waxen face. "Rass," he whispered. "Don't give up. Don't . . ."

"Scoot," Doc said, looping a stethoscope around his neck. "There's coffee on the stove. Have some." He looked at Jake through kind, concerned eyes. "It's gonna be a long night."

Jake shambled into the sitting room. He tried not to

think of the other times he'd been through this exact night, but the memories were insistent, worming their way through his thoughts with insidious strength. He'd lost other loved ones in his life; his grandfather, his mother. Once they got like this, they never lived through the night. Never ...

Tears scalded his eyes, dripped down his cheeks. He sank unsteadily onto the hard leather of a settee and buried his face in his hands. Memories and images winged through his mind, each one bringing a fresh lump of tears.

I thought you might be hungry. . . .

If the mountain won't come to Mohammed, then Mohammed best head for the mountain. . . .

You were meant to live on an apple farm. And Mariah's quiet invitation. *This apple farm.*

They'd made him so welcome, given him so much. With them, he almost felt like he had a family again, something he thought he'd buried with his mother. Rass was the grandfather Jake had never really had; the loving, gentle relative that Jacob Vanderstay had never been. A man who never got angry or demanded anything. A grandfather who laughed and loved and gave.

"Please, God," he said, tasting the salty moisture of his own tears. "Please don't take him yet. . . ." But his words were hollow and lifeless, without the spine of hope. He'd said them too many times in his life, and he knew the truth. God almost never answered at a time like this.

He squeezed his eyes shut. Tears burned down his cheeks and burrowed into the corners of his mouth, tasting warm and wet and hopeless. He'd never felt more alone in his whole life. And his father was right beside him.

"Can I get you a cup of coffee, kid?"

Jake snapped his head up, feeling a surge of anger at this man who was his father but wasn't. "Don't call me kid. My name is Jake."

Mad Dog dropped slowly to a squat in front of Jake. "My old man called me kid. I guess it's just a bad habit. I'm sorry."

Jake's irrational anger died as quickly as it had come. Without it, he felt cold and alone again. He slumped forward. His elbows hit his knees and he cradled his face in sweaty palms.

Mad Dog's touch was so gentle, so tentative, that at first Jake thought he'd imagined it, willed it somehow. But he hadn't. Mad Dog had reached out and touched Jake's shoulder, squeezing it gently.

"He's gonna be all right, Jake. He's a strong man."

Jake's head came up slowly. Tears burned in his eyes, turning his father into a blur of blond hair and tanned skin. And for an instant, just an instant, Jake didn't know if he was crying for Rass or for himself.

His father had touched him, comforted him. He bit his lower lip to keep it from trembling. It was nothing, really, just a meaningless little squeeze on the shoulder, but to Jake it meant the world. It meant his father cared—at least a little.

He swallowed hard.

Mad Dog withdrew his hand slowly. The moment started to slip away.

Jake surged forward, unwilling to let the connection fade. Suddenly now, on this tired old settee, with death so close, he could taste its familiar sourness, he felt a stirring of courage. He wanted to get to know his father.

He spoke before he lost his nerve. "What was your dad like?"

Surprise widened Mad Dog's eyes. "I dunno."

Jake refused to let it go. "Are you like him?"

Something dark moved through Mad Dog's eyes. He pushed to his feet and walked away from Jake, staring down at his own bare feet on the plush Oriental carpet. "Yeah," he said after a while, "I guess I am."

"You're lucky," Jake said quietly.

Mad Dog turned to him. "Why's that?"

Jake tried to keep his voice steady, but it was hard. "At least you knew your dad. My father ran out on my mama before I was born."

A sad, understanding shadow of a smile shaped Mad Dog's mouth. "My dad ran out on us, too." Slowly he walked over to the settee and sat down beside Jake, stretching out his long legs.

"Would you run out on your own kid?" Jake's breath caught at the simple question. He couldn't believe he'd asked it, but once he had, he felt anticipation course through him. *Maybe Mad Dog would say just the right thing . . . maybe he'd say he'd always wanted a child . . . a son . . . and he'd never leave one behind.*

Mad Dog leaned back. The settee creaked in protest. "I've thought about that, believe it or not. When I was younger, I wanted kids. I thought I could be a good father." He laughed easily, shook his head. "Then I grew up."

"What do you mean?"

"A good dad stays put, Jake, it's as simple as that. I leave."

"How do you know?"

The question seemed to surprise Mad Dog. A slight frown pulled at his forehead. "What do you mean?"

"Have you ever tried to stay anywhere?"

Mad Dog turned away from Jake and stared at the flocked, red-papered wall in front of them. He opened his mouth, then closed it.

"Are you gonna answer me?"

Mad Dog smiled, but it was forced. "It's a stupid question. I said I can't stay, so I can't. But at least I'm honest—my old man lied to us. He acted like he was gonna stay, then he left. I never lie."

Jake's heart twisted hard. "No, I guess you didn't."

"When I realized what kind of drifter I was, how irresponsible and all, I made myself quit wantin' a kid."

"So now you don't want one?" Jake's voice was so quiet, he barely heard it himself.

"Naw, I like my life the way it is. I go where I want, do what I want. I'm free. You'll know what I mean someday."

Jake shook his head. "I've been on the road awhile. I want a place to stay." He looked at his dad, stared into his gray eyes and tried to make him understand. "It's . . . lonely out there for me."

Before Mad Dog could respond, a door creaked open. Doc Sherman came shuffling out of the bedroom and walked into the sitting room, sinking into the big, over-stuffed chair across from them.

Jake froze, his eyes riveted on the doctor. *Please, God, let him be okay . . . please. . . .*

Easing the spectacles from his face, the doctor set them on his thigh and rubbed the bridge of his nose.

Mad Dog leaned forward. "How is he, Doc?"

Sherman sighed again, a deep, depressed sound. "Not good. It's apoplexy. His left side is partially paralyzed, and he's in a deep sleep. A coma, it's called."

Jake felt as if he were falling. A tiny whimper escaped his pursed lips. Mad Dog squeezed his shoulder again. The reassuring touch comforted Jake, gave him an anchor in the shifting world of his grief.

"Is there anything you can do for him?"

The doctor shook his head. "Rass and I talked about this a few days ago. He's been having the symptoms for a while now. He knew this was coming. He . . . he wanted to die at home."

The word *die* hit Jake hard in the stomach. He squeezed his eyes shut, shaking his head in denial.

"How long does he have?" Mad Dog asked.

"Who knows? Maybe a week; maybe a day."

"Sometimes miracles happen," Jake said quietly, staring at the doctor for confirmation. There was none.

Mad Dog gave Jake a slow, sad smile, and Jake knew that his father didn't believe in miracles any more than he did. "You just keep hoping that, Jake. Rass needs someone to believe in a miracle." Then he turned back to the doctor. "What should we do for him?"

Doc pulled a folded piece of paper from his shirt pocket. "I've made you a list." He handed it to Mad Dog, who skimmed its contents before he looked back up at the doctor.

"Anything else?"

"I don't think Mariah knew he was sick. Rass was so

protective of her." The doctor rubbed the bridge of his nose again and closed his eyes for a moment. "It's going to hit her hard. She has no one else in the world."

Jake looked up suddenly, feeling a tiny seed of hope in the darkness. *She has me.* He wanted to say the words out loud, tried to, but his throat was so thick, he could only make a useless, scratching sound.

"No one ever expects something like this," Doc went on, "and Mariah's . . . fragile. I wish there was someone to take care of her. Rass would've wanted that."

Jake opened his mouth to say *I will*, but the words were never heard. Someone else had spoken first.

"I'll take care of her," Mad Dog said.

Jake looked at his father, stunned.

Mad Dog was sitting hunched over, with his elbows on his bent knees, staring at the doctor. His eyes were filled with a quiet determination that surprised Jake. Mad Dog was serious. He *would* take care of Mariah.

Jake shook his head. If he hadn't been so devastated about Rass, he might have managed a smile. It must mean something, this unexpected commitment to Mariah. Something big.

But Jake didn't know what it was.

Mariah heard the buggy driving up the yard. She flew out of her bed and ran, hair flying, down the stairs and through the kitchen, bursting onto the dark porch.

Mad Dog reined Cleo in, bringing the buggy to a creaking halt.

She didn't look at him. Instead she stood there, stiff as a rail, her hands twisted together at her midsection. "He's dead, isn't he?"

"No . . . he's not dead."

Mariah lifted moist, hopeful eyes to Mad Dog's face. Her fingers uncoiled, fell back to her sides. "He's okay?"

Mad Dog's face crumpled, and Mariah's budding hope crashed all around her. And somehow the pain of losing that second of hope was more devastating than the hours she'd spent believing he was dead. "What is it?" she asked dully.

Mad Dog gave her a look of intimate sadness. Quietly he said, "Is his bed ready?"

She nodded. Fear and desperation closed in on her, in her chest, her heart, her throat. Her insides twisted and writhed, her pulse pounded in her ears. She was close to shattering, close to losing what precious little control she had. She drew in a sharp, shaking breath and tried to hold on.

Mad Dog jumped down from the buggy and scooped Rass into his arms. Her father's head lolled back, his arm slipped lifelessly downward.

Mariah gasped at the sight of him, so pale and wan. Her father, who'd always been there for her, always been healthy and robust, looked small and old . . . and dying.

Jake jumped down from the buggy and walked toward her. His eyes were red-rimmed from crying, and his skin was the color of candle wax. His mouth was drawn into a tight, trembling line.

She felt his sadness, knew he was as miserable as she was, and doing his adolescent best to hold back tears. Deep inside her, something stirred, some remnant of the woman she'd been a few hours ago, and she wanted to reach out to him. But she didn't, she couldn't. There was nothing inside her, nothing to offer to a young boy who needed comfort.

Sickened and saddened by her own weakness, she looked away from Jake's teary eyes.

Mad Dog cradled Rass in gentle arms and walked up the porch stairs. He stopped beside her, looked down at her through eyes filled with tender understanding. "Let's take him to bed."

She tried to nod, but even that simple action was beyond her.

"Jake," Mad Dog went on, "you go get a pitcher of warm water, a washrag, and a spoon. Doc says we're supposed to keep him drinking if we can."

Mariah knew she should feel grateful to Mad Dog for taking over, but she was so sick and numb, she didn't feel anything.

"Show me the way," he said gently.

She turned away from him and stumbled up the stairs, clutching the wobbly handrail for support. He followed slowly, his every footstep heavy and thudding on the creaking steps.

She stared through wide, gritty eyes at the darkened hallway and forced herself to keep walking. But every step caused a twisting spasm in her stomach. Her fingers trembled, her throat went dry.

The closed door loomed in front of her. This was her father's bedroom, and once, long ago, her mother's. It was *their* place, their sanctuary. She didn't want to go in there, didn't want to place her dying father in his bed and try to pretend she could survive.

Shaking, she reached for the knob and opened the

door. Pale moonlight slithered through the lacy white curtains and puddled on the fringed, dark blue carpet. A shadowy, four-postered bed huddled against one wall, its center a mass of white sheets and black blankets.

She moved woodenly into the room, her hands twisted nervously together. The quiet, shadowy room smelled of lingering lamplight, freshly washed sheets, and . . . lavender.

The unexpected scent almost brought Mariah to her knees. It was impossible, she told herself. It was only her imagination that added a hint of lavender to the air.

She lit two lamps and went to the bed, yanking back the blankets. The harsh scent of burning oil filled the shadowy room, obliterating the impossible fragrance of lavender.

Mad Dog followed her into the room and laid Rass down on the bed. He bent over, carefully tucking the blanket around Rass, drawing it up to his chest.

Mariah got her first real look at her father. Golden lamplight wreathed him in an amber, almost ethereal light, but even that couldn't add color to the bluish hollows of his cheeks. Shadows clung beneath his closed eyes, giving them a deathly, sunken look. His lips were gray, almost invisible against the lifeless pallor of his slack skin.

Grief hit her so hard, she felt dizzy. She clutched the bedpost, clinging to it for support.

Mad Dog appeared beside her, curled an arm around her shoulders, and drew her close. The steadying warmth of his touch penetrated the soul-deep chill inside her bones.

With an exhausted sigh, she let herself lean against

him. He reached for the settee beneath the window and dragged it to the bedside. Together, they sat down.

"Mariah?"

She winced, knowing what was coming next and not wanting to hear it. She licked her paper-dry lips and stared at the wooden floorboards. "Yes?"

Mad Dog let out a quiet sigh. "He's in a coma."

She nodded, feeling strangely as if she'd left the room. There was someone else inside her now, a remote inner core that made her body move, made her lips speak, made her head nod. But there was no feeling in her, no emotion, nothing except an icy coldness. She knew what he was going to say next. She'd heard it before. "Uh-huh."

He swallowed so loudly, she heard it. "Doc Sherman says he's . . . not going to get better."

"Doc's wrong." She tried to make the words sound strong, but they eked past her lips as a frail whisper.

"Maybe," he said quietly.

Tears scalded her eyes. "There . . . there could be a miracle," she said throatily.

"Do you believe in miracles?"

The question almost killed her. She sagged, feeling suddenly agonizingly brittle and unprotected. "No."

"Doc says he doesn't have much time."

She bit down on her lip, trying to hold on. "How long?"

"Maybe a week . . . maybe tonight." He placed his hand on hers, squeezed. "You need to say good-bye."

She turned to him suddenly, looked at him for the first time since they'd come into the room. He didn't understand. No one did. Loneliness and sorrow smothered her, pressed cold hands against her chest. "You think that will help?" she said, unable to keep bitterness from her voice. "Saying good-bye?"

"It's all you have."

She gasped at his words. "Oh, God," she whispered, feeling beaten and afraid. "I . . . I can't say good-bye to Rass, too." Tears clogged in her throat, burned in her eyes. A pounding headache filled her head. "I can't."

He stroked her hair gently. "I wish I knew what to say to you, Mariah."

The words touched nothing in her, left her feeling as cold and dull and dead as before. "There's nothing any-one can say."

"No," was all he said, but in that simple, single word, she knew he understood, knew he'd faced a loved one's death before. He curled his arm around her, held her close. "I'm here."

For now.

Mariah heard the words as clearly, as loudly, as if they'd been spoken aloud.

He was here with her for now. But soon he would be gone, Rass would be gone, Jake would be gone, and she would be alone.

Utterly, desperately alone.

She hung her head and wished she could cry.

Chapter Twenty-one

Mad Dog stood in the bedroom's open doorway. The room was bathed in light—Mariah had ripped down every curtain and lit every lamp. But the golden glow couldn't chase away the chill of death or warm the cold, sunken cheeks of the man who lay still and silent in the huge, four-postered bed.

Sadness crept through Mad Dog's chest, tightening it until every breath hurt. Tears burned his eyes, turned the sunlit room into a golden blur. He blinked, unashamed of his grief. Gradually the chamber came back into focus. And what he saw—and heard—broke his heart all over again.

Mariah sat beside the bed, the settee scooted close. She leaned slightly forward, one slim hand curled around her father's blue-veined, big-knuckled one, the other holding a book of poetry. The halting, quiet strains of her voice filtered across the room.

"All my past life is mine no more; the flying hours are gone like transitory dreams given o'er, whose images are kept in store by memory alone...."

She set the book down and bowed her head.

The sight of her, so sad-looking and defeated, twisted

something old and forgotten in Mad Dog's heart. He was seeing a rare moment of weakness, he knew. He'd watched her often in the past two days, stood here in the doorway in silence, wishing—Christ, wishing—he could do something for her.

But she wouldn't let him help. She just sat there by the bed, holding her father's hand and reading poetry. Sometimes—not often—she stopped reading and simply talked to him. Not about anything important, not about her fear or loneliness or despair, but about the weather, the farm, or the coming of winter.

It was a rare moment when she put down her book; rarer still when she allowed herself to bend as she was doing now.

For the past few days, she hadn't left his side. She didn't eat, hardly slept, never moved. Her sorrow was like a heavy gray shroud over her shoulders, weighing her down, pulling the color from her cheeks and the spirit from her soul.

And never once had Mad Dog heard her pray.

Now, looking at her, he could see the effects of her vigil. She was wan and strained-looking. Her skin had lost its creamy sheen; the healthy glow had given way to a lackluster ashen hue. Her eyes, once so sparkling with life, were dull and vacant.

Her sadness touched him more than he would have thought possible. It was crazy; but he hurt because she hurt. He wanted suddenly to go to her, to put his arms around her and hold her close.

But she wouldn't let him comfort her. He let out his breath in a frustrated sigh and knocked on the wall. "Mariah, I've brought you something to eat."

She didn't look up. "I'm not hungry." Her voice was as flat and lifeless as the hair that hung in a snarled mass down her back.

"You have to eat something," he said tiredly, knowing it was a battle he'd lose.

She placed her book, facedown, on the settee's cushion and reached for the washbasin beside her. Plunging her hands into the lukewarm water, she pulled out the rag and twisted it hard. Water streamed down from her fists. Then, carefully, she dabbed her father's slack mouth with the damp cloth.

Mad Dog had been dismissed.

Frustrated, he studied her downcast face. She was trying pathetically hard to remain in control, to appear invincible. But she couldn't quite manage it. He saw the quiver in her lower lip when she looked at her father, the trembling in her hands when she gently washed his face.

Her pitiful attempt at strength tore at his heart. He knew how she felt, knew how hard it was to appear strong when your spirit was gone. He'd sat in that same chair, helpless and alone, watching his mother wither and die.

He wanted to tell Mariah he understood, that she wasn't alone. But she wouldn't listen to him, wouldn't even look at him.

He knew why; knew and understood. When the pain was that sharp and the defenses so weak, a kindness— any kindness—was almost unbearable. She was terrified to let anyone be kind to her right now, afraid that if she gave in—even for a second—she'd fall into a pit of grief from which she'd never emerge.

He rubbed the bridge of his nose. There had to be something he could do to help. Something—

"Oh, my God."

He opened his eyes. "What is it?"

"He moved."

Mad Dog lurched into the room and came up beside her.

She squeezed her father's hand with both of hers. "Rass? Rass?"

Rass groaned. It was a quiet, rustling sound. His eyelids fluttered.

"I'm right here, Rass. It's Mariah and Mad Dog. We're right here."

He groaned again, ran his tongue across his teeth. Slowly, incredibly, his eyes began to open. "Mariah?" His voice was a scratchy shadow of itself.

"I'm right here, Rass. Right here." She squeezed his hand.

He frowned, tried to focus. "Mad Dog—that you?"

For a moment, Mad Dog couldn't speak past the lump of emotion in his throat. "I'm here, Rass."

A tired smile pulled at one side of Rass's blue-tinged lips. "Well, I'll be damned . . ."

"Rass, I want you to eat something. . . ." Mariah began.

Rass stopped her with a slow wave of his good hand. "No point in eating."

She gasped softly. "Rass, don't—"

"I want to sit on the porch swing," he said in a thick, slurred voice. "See the night sky one last time."

Mariah drew in an unsteady breath. "Don't say that!"

Rass turned sad, rheumy blue eyes on Mad Dog. "Carry me out to the swing, will you?"

Mad Dog felt the sting of tears. Rass looked so old and tired ... so unlike himself. His once vibrant smile was lopsided and slack. "Sure."

He bent down and scooped Rass into his arms, then gently lifted him. He weighed less than nothing.

"I'll be right there," Mariah said.

Mad Dog nodded. Cradling the old man carefully, he carried him down the stairs.

Mariah appeared on the porch a minute later, carrying pillows and blankets. She quickly made up a bed of sorts, pulling up a padded stool for Rass's feet.

Mad Dog eased Rass onto the swing.

"Sit with me, Mariah," Rass said in a wheezing, tired voice.

Mariah sat beside her father. He leaned against her, and she curled her arms around his frail body. Together, they half sat, half lay in the porch swing. It creaked slowly back and forth, filling the quiet night with sound.

Rass glanced up at Mad Dog through sad, knowing eyes. That look hit Mad Dog hard, stealing his ability to breathe for a second. He'd seen that look before, in his mother's eyes, just moments before she died.

"Get Jake ..."

Mad Dog swallowed hard. Sadness clogged in a thick lump in his chest. "Sure," he rasped. He waited a minute, afraid to leave, then slowly he turned and walked away. He knew where he'd find Jake; the boy hadn't left the barn since Rass had been brought home two days ago. He just sat up there in the darkness, rocking silently back and forth.

Mariah watched Mad Dog walk away. When he disappeared, she tightened her hold on her father. "I knew you'd come back to me. I knew . . ."

"You're going to have to be strong." Her father's breathy voice cut through her sentence.

She stiffened. "You're not going anywhere—"

He coughed. "I'm dying, Boo. . . ."

Tears welled in her eyes, moist and hot. She shook her head. "No, Rass. No."

He sighed tiredly and looked at her. In his watery blue eyes was a sadness that made her physically ill. "You've got to accept this, Mariah. You can't hide from it or run away."

She shook her head. "I . . . I don't . . . w-want you to say these things. *Please*."

"I was wrong to shield you for so long, Mariah. Your mother and I . . . we just loved you so much. We couldn't stand to see you cry." He squeezed his eyes shut. Tears squeezed past his lashes and streaked down his gray wrinkled cheeks. "So we didn't let you cry. I'm so sorry."

"Please don't be sorry." Her voice dropped to a pleading whisper. "Please . . ."

He opened his eyes and looked at her. In that instant she saw it all: the pain, the sorrow, the regret. She remembered all the times he'd looked at her, gazed at her with a father's quiet caring, and her heart broke.

He'd always been there for her, always, even when she'd been too stupid to reach for him. She couldn't imagine a life without him. . . .

"I love you, Boo."

It was as close to crying as she'd ever been. "I love you, too . . . Daddy. Please don't leave me."

He gave her a slow, watery smile. "You haven't called me that in years."

"I should have."

"Ah, Boo," he said quietly. Slowly he brought his shaking right hand up and touched her face. His palm felt papery and dry against her flushed cheek. "How does the hurting start?"

She shook her head, unable to answer.

They stared at each other for a long, long time. The muted sounds of the night faded away, leaving only the mingled duet of their strained breathing and the regular creak of the porch swing. Moonlight spilled across the farm and twined through the dead wisteria vines in shades of pearl and blue.

Mariah had the sudden, sickening thought that her daddy wouldn't be here when the wisteria blossomed.

The crunching thud of footsteps serrated the silence and pulled Mariah from her thoughts. She looked up and saw Jake and Mad Dog standing on the bottom step.

"Rass." Jake's voice was an awed whisper.

Rass smiled sadly. "Jake." Then he glanced down at Mad Dog. "Will you carry me back upstairs? I'm feeling tired again. Jake, come with me."

Mad Dog climbed the porch steps slowly and drew Rass into his arms, then carried him back to bed.

Wordlessly, trying to be brave, Mariah and Jake followed them to the bedroom.

"Jake, come," Rass said, waving his right hand tiredly. He turned to Mariah and Mad Dog. "Give us a moment."

Mariah gave her father a pleading look. *I have more to say. What if we don't have any more time?*

"We do," he said, reading her mind. "Now, go."

Rass settled into the comforting mound of pillows with a relieved sigh. It took a monumental effort to appear strong. His whole body ached, his mouth was ash-dry, even breathing hurt. And the paralyzed left side of his body was like a steady, dragging weight downward.

He closed his eyes, resting for a moment.

He might have dozed; he wasn't sure. Tiredly he forced his eyes open, and found Jake standing at his bedside, staring down at him through moist, red-rimmed eyes.

"Hi, Rass."

"Jake." Rass said the boy's name quietly, with love. "I wanted to say good-bye."

Tears welled in Jake's eyes, shimmering. One by one, they fell past his lashes and streaked down his face. "I don't want you to go."

Rass's heart gave a hard squeeze. Tears filled his eyes and slid down his temples in warm, wet streaks. "We don't have long, Jake. I'm really tired." He waved him over. "Come closer."

Jake kneeled beside the bed and peered eye-level at Rass.

"He's your dad, isn't he?"

Jake gave him a sad, trembling smile. "I should have known I couldn't hide it from you."

There were so many things Rass wanted to say, but he had no strength, and his will to live was beginning to wane. "Tell him the truth, Jake. It's your only hope."

"I'm afraid to."

Pain twisted Rass's insides. He winced, tried to keep talking. "I let Mariah use that as an excuse. I won't let you. Tell your dad the truth or . . . or I'll haunt you for life."

Jake tried valiantly to smile. "Okay."

"Promise?"

"I promise."

Slowly, with great effort, Rass reached up and touched Jake's cheeks. "I love you, son."

Jake started crying in earnest. Silvery tears ran in rivulets down his pale cheeks. He bowed his head, pressing his forehead into the soft pile of blankets beside Rass. "I love you, too, Rass."

Rass started to say something else, but before he got the words out, he forgot what he wanted to say. The pain in his heart came pounding back, thundering in his ears. Streaks of hot agony shot down his left arm and lodged, burning, in his wrist and fingers.

"Get Mariah," he gasped.

Rass sank into the bed, deeper, deeper. A strange feeling stole through his body, tingling like a thousand hot needles beneath his skin. He felt light-headed and weighted down at the same time. The blood pounded through his veins in an audible, throbbing rhythm.

His gaze took in the bedroom in a heartbeat; he saw it all, saw it and cataloged it in his mind.

This had been his room for so long. . . .

His eyes fluttered shut; it took such an effort to keep them open. A memory flashed through his mind, bringing the moist heat of tears. He remembered the day, almost twenty-five years ago, when he'd brought his bride here from New York. This room, this bed, had been their sanctuary and their playground.

Tears pulsed past his closed eyes and slid down his face.

He felt his body weaken. It felt as if he were sinking slowly, inexorably, into the bed, disappearing.

He tried to reach for Mariah. She had to be beside him, had to be calling out his name, but he couldn't hear her. His head was filled with a low, buzzing hum that obliterated everything, even the thudding beat of his heart. He couldn't lift his good hand; it felt incredibly heavy.

He opened his mouth, tried to say her name, but his throat was so dry, he couldn't make a sound. His tongue felt thick and useless and dead.

Gradually he became aware of a dull, amber glow. He frowned. The golden light increased slowly, matching the erratic beating of his heart, spilled from the window and crept across the shadowy floorboards.

Rass realized with a start that his eyes were closed. He tried to open them, but couldn't.

A shape appeared at the end of his bed. At first it was dark, no more than a shadow ringed in impossible light. But slowly the shadow melted and features came forth.

"Greta." The name slipped past his lips in a sigh.

She smiled. *Hello, love.*

He smiled, and the moment he did it, he knew it was a real smile, not a one-sided, half-paralyzed shifting of lips. "You're here. . . ."

You knew I'd wait for you. She reached out her hands. *Come on, love. It's time. . . .*

Rass looked down, and though his eyes were still closed, he saw the glow emanating from his own body.

The light behind Greta intensified, turned from a molten gold to a shimmering white. Heat caressed his cheeks and made him feel strong again. The pain of old age slipped away. Effortlessly he sat up, his hands outstretched. "Greta . . ."

"No! Daddy, don't leave me." Mariah's throaty voice broke through the haze in Rass's mind.

Uncertainty stabbed through him. He stopped, sank unsteadily back into bed. "Boo?" he whispered tiredly.

Something warm and strong curled around his hand, squeezing gently. "I'm here, Daddy. Don't go."

Greta held out her arms, a sad smile on her face. *It's time, love.*

With great effort, Rass opened his eyes. Mariah was standing beside the bed, holding his hand. Her eyes were teary, red-rimmed pools of agony against the ashen pallor of her cheeks. "Mama's here," he said softly.

"Oh, Daddy . . ."

"We love you, Boo."

Tears filled her eyes but didn't fall, and somehow that hurt Rass more than anything he could imagine. "Let yourself cry. . . ."

She'll be okay.

Rass felt, rather than heard, Greta's words, and they filled him with a quiet, steady peace. The hot white light moved toward him, filled his body with shimmering, joyous heat. He felt his eyes flutter shut, felt his breath exhale one last time.

Then suddenly he was in a different place, enfolded in the arms of the only woman he'd ever loved.

Chapter Twenty-two

Winter came to the funeral.

In the gray, soulless sky, the sun was a dull golden globe without power or heat. Snow lay heaped on the fence line and bare tree limbs, encasing everything in an icy layer of translucent white. A freezing wind lashed down from snow-covered hills and barreled across the plain in a howling, mournful dirge.

Mariah moved stiffly forward, her chin tilted, her eyes painfully dry. Every crunching footstep was a brutal, heart-wrenching reminder of where she was going today, what she was doing.

She held up the back end of the pine casket. The hastily skinned wood abraded her skin, poked into the soft flesh of her palm. Dully she realized that she should have worn gloves.

Ahead, Jake and Mad Dog moved with the same stiff-backed reluctance, their heads bowed, their breath coming in great pluming streaks. Mad Dog held the right side of the casket; Jake, the left.

Together, step by halting, heavy step, they made their way across the silent, fallow farm, and up the hill to the knoll where Greta and Thomas lay. Wind whipped through the stark, bare branches of the oak tree, rattling the limbs. The iron settee creaked and moaned at the force of it.

"Okay," Mad Dog said quietly. "Let's put it down."

The three of them bent and set the casket on the frozen, snow-covered ground. It hit with a muffled thud that echoed forever in the crisp silence.

Mariah straightened. The first thing she saw was the hole Mad Dog and Jake had dug last night.

Pain shot through her, hit her so hard, she staggered. She tried to push the obvious thoughts from her mind, but she wasn't strong enough. She didn't want her daddy going in there. . . . It was so cold and dark and . . . final.

She jerked away from the box, from the hole, and stood apart from everything, stiff and alone. Cold air buffeted her face, whipped thin strands of hair across her unprotected cheeks. She didn't pull the furred collar of her gossamer coat around her throat; she didn't care.

It felt as if she were being slowly, cruelly twisted in half. Every breath hurt, her eyes burned with the need to cry, but still she couldn't. Just like before, like always, the tears were locked in her chest in a throbbing, scalding ache.

She wrapped her arms around herself, trying to find some impossible warmth.

"Mariah?"

With great effort, she lifted her head. And found Mad Dog standing in front of her.

"Mad Dog." His name slipped out in a whisper of longing. With some distant part of her mind, she thought how easy it would be to go to him right now, to wrap her arms around him and let him comfort her.

But the effort was too much for her. She felt icy cold inside, as dead as her father. As if there were nothing beneath her skin but broken glass, nothing in her heart at all.

She no longer wanted anything to do with Mad Dog, or Jake, or anyone. She just wanted to be left alone with the memories of her father, left alone with the hammering grief that kept her wide-eyed all night and half-asleep all day. She didn't want to talk to anyone, or say anything, or hear anything.

She wanted to die.

"Mariah?" he said again.

She stared at him, feeling nothing. "What?"

"Do you want to say a few words?" He gave her a look of such gentle concern, it almost broke through her apathy. He reached for her.

She let him touch her cheek, felt the warmth of his touch. But it meant nothing. "Yes," she said, hearing the lifeless tone of her own voice. "I'll say a few words."

She moved past Mad Dog, feeling his gaze on her. He was worried, she knew. Once that might have meant something, and she knew it should still. But it didn't.

Standing beneath the skeletal winter remains of the oak tree, she stared dully at the gaping hole. At the sight of it, stark and terrifying against the snow white ground, she shuddered and closed her eyes.

"Rass . . ." She paused, bowed her head. A headache throbbed behind her aching eyes. "Rass would have said, 'Don't cry for me. I'm not here.' "

Great, wrenching pain coiled around her heart. She

brought her head up, stared at the farm he'd loved so dearly. "He believed that death was a gateway to another, better world. I hope he's right. He . . ." Her voice cracked. "He deserves it."

She kneeled on the cold ground and placed her icy hand on the splintery wood of his casket. Misery pulled her shoulders, dragged her head downward. It felt as if she were being slowly crushed by a wall of cold, unforgiving stone. Breathing became almost impossible. She stared at the planks of hammered pine through gritty, too dry eyes. "Good-bye, Daddy. I love you."

She squeezed her eyes shut for a long, pain-drenched moment, then slowly she opened them and pushed to her feet.

Mad Dog and Jake were looking at her. In their eyes, she saw the offer of refuge, the promise of comfort. And she knew that in that moment, they could come together, the three of them, and get through this grief with one another's help.

She didn't care.

She was too tired to try, too spiritually broken to even long for the comfort of a family anymore. Mad Dog and Jake would be leaving soon; she knew that. Rass was the glue that held them together. Without him, they were three strangers. She had already begun to think of her nights with Mad Dog as fantasy, a fairy tale without substance or truth.

She looked at him and Jake, standing so closely together, banded in the similarity of their grief. They almost looked alike.

Mariah felt achingly alone, separate. She wished she had the strength, or the courage to go stand with them.

But she couldn't.

Tiredly she picked up her skirts and headed away from the grassy knoll.

They didn't even try to stop her.

In the long days and even longer nights that followed Rass's death, the house slid into a bleak gully of despair. Dust piled up on the furniture, coated the windowsills. The kitchen sat in waiting silence, a cold and empty reminder that the heart of the farm had gone away.

No laughter floated through the air, no conversation rang out at mealtimes. There were no mealtimes. There was no conversation. There were only memories, dark, aching memories that seemed to be everywhere.

Mad Dog couldn't stand it anymore. He'd tried to give Mariah time, tried to give her the space she needed to grieve. But she wasn't grieving; she was dying. Slowly, day by day, inch by pitiful inch. He couldn't watch it anymore.

He had to either do something for her or leave.

That was the problem. He didn't know what to do and he didn't want to leave.

He stared down at the stew bubbling in the pot in front of him. Absently he stirred it. The rich aroma floated upward, streamed past his nostrils and scented the room.

The front door creaked open, then banged shut. Footsteps shuffled through the foyer and came into the kitchen.

Mad Dog turned expectantly.

Jake sauntered into the room, his hands shoved deep

in his pockets, his head hung. At the threshold, he stumbled to a stop and jerked his head up. "*You're* cooking?"

Mad Dog shrugged. "Someone had to. I was losing weight."

Jake cocked his head back toward the front door, a worried look on his face. "So's she."

Mad Dog set the wooden spoon aside. Running a hand through his hair, he went to the table and yanked out a chair. The wooden legs screeched along the planked floor. He sat down and stretched his legs out. "Yeah, I know. She looks like a goddamn scarecrow."

Jake pulled out a chair opposite Mad Dog and sat down. "She talk to you at all?"

Mad Dog shook his head. A tired sigh slipped from his mouth. "I don't know what to do, Jake. She's . . . wasting away."

"I know. Yesterday I gave her a geranium—it was the only one that made it through the snow. She didn't even take it. Just said thanks in that sad voice and looked away."

"Flowers, huh? I never thought of that."

"Well, it used to work for my mama, but she was a different kind of sad."

Mad Dog frowned. "What do you mean?"

Jake swallowed hard. He seemed to find it difficult to speak. "My mama . . . loved a man who didn't love her back. It made her sad all the time. She cried a lot." He looked away, stared at the wall. "She gave up on him finally, but she never forgot him, and she made sure I didn't either."

"Did she walk around like a silent ghost, like Mariah?"

"No, she was more . . . emotional."

"Yeah. Most women are." Mad Dog nodded, staring through the doorway to the darkened foyer. He didn't have to move to know where Mariah was, what she was doing. She was sitting in the damn porch swing, her back ramrod-straight, her chin tilted high, staring into space. Her eyes were glazed, vacant-looking, her cheeks were sunken and limned in bruising shadows.

He let out his breath in a sharp sigh. Jesus, she looked like one of the dead herself. The sparkling life in her eyes had gone out, the healthy glow of her skin was gone.

Mad Dog found, to his surprise, that he missed her. Not just her body, either. He didn't even think of her in that way now. He missed the very essence of her, the way she cocked her head when she smiled, the way she shivered when he was near, the way she laughed. He missed her laughter most of all.

He propped his elbow on the table and cradled his stubbly chin in his hand, shaking his head. "Hell, I've never stayed in any one place longer than three days. If a person had a problem, I walked away. I don't know how to help her."

"She feels . . . lost," Jake said quietly, and looked up. "You ever felt like that?"

I feel like that right now. The thought surprised Mad Dog, but he couldn't deny the truth of it. Without her smile, her warmth, her touch, he felt like a boat adrift on a dead calm sea. Going nowhere.

"Yeah," he said quietly, wetting his lips. "I've felt

that way a few times. When my mom died, I ..." He shook his head, trying to find the words to express what he'd never told another living soul. "I guess I wanted to die, too."

Tears glazed Jake's eyes, squeezed past the corners. "Yeah."

Silence stretched between them, thick with memories.

Finally Jake managed to find his voice again. "I don't think she hates us or anything. She just ... doesn't care about anything."

"So, how do we make her care?"

He gave a tired little shrug. "I don't know."

Mad Dog looked at him across the table. "How did you get yourself out of it when your mom died?"

Something that looked like pain darkened Jake's watery eyes. He looked at Mad Dog steadily, his gaze surprisingly intense. "I focused on something else ... the one thing that still mattered. My father. I went to find him."

"Oh ... shit." Mad Dog sagged. "That won't do us any good."

"No." Jake's voice was subdued, almost disappointed. "I guess not."

Mad Dog chewed on his lower lip and squeezed his eyes shut. Jesus, this was so damned important, and he didn't know what to do. Slowly he opened his eyes, looked at the boy across the table. "Help me, Jake. . . ."

Jake's head snapped up. He looked up at Mad Dog through wide, surprised eyes. "You want *my* help?"

"We're in this together, kid." He sighed, shaking his head. "Aw, Jesus, I don't know how to get through to her, how to—" Then it came to him. He slammed a hand down on the table and grinned. "I've got it."

"What?"

"You'll see." He shot to his feet. "You try to get her to eat some of this stew. I've got to run to town. I'll be back by nightfall."

Jake stood at the hot stove, carefully ladling stew into a chipped crockery bowl. The bubbling brown mixture blurred before his eyes, turned into a swirling smear of brown chunks and white china.

We're in this together, kid. Together.

He'd waited all his life to hear those words. They gave him a giddy sense of hope he hadn't had in years.

Tomorrow, he thought. I'll tell him the truth tomorrow. And for once, the words didn't ring false. Jake actually believed them. Tomorrow he'd tell his father the truth.

Smiling, he set down the metal ladle and held the hot bowl in two hands. Turning, he left the kitchen and went outside.

The first thing he noticed was the steady *creak-creak-creak* of the porch swing. His good mood fled, pushed aside by the sadness of seeing Mariah. Beside her, on a small, rickety table, a candle burned, sputtered. Its acrid scent filled the tiny porch, and banished the shadows of the night.

He stepped onto the porch and quietly shut the door behind him. "Mariah? I've brought you something to eat."

She didn't move, just kept rocking, staring into the night. *Creak-creak-creak.*

He moved closer, peered around the arm of the swing. "Mariah?"

She waved a wan, pale hand. "I'm not hungry."

"You have to eat something . . . you know, keep your strength up." That sounded good, he thought. A grown-up thing to say.

She laughed bitterly but said nothing.

Jake set the bowl down on the top step and moved into her line of vision. Crouching down, he stared at her, seeing the network of lines that drew down her mouth, the sadness that glazed her eyes.

"My mama died last year," he said softly, resting his palms on his bent knees.

She squeezed her eyes shut and sighed tiredly. "I'm sorry, Jake."

Jake felt a surge of hope. It was the biggest reaction he'd gotten from her in days. "You saved my life," he said quietly, "you and Rass."

She looked at him then, and he almost wished she hadn't. Her eyes were dulled by immeasurable pain, her mouth was a sad, downward curve. He felt like he'd been punched in the stomach just looking at her. "Please." The plea sounded torn from her throat. "Don't do this to me. . . ."

Jake didn't know what to do. Uncertainty flooded him. He wished Mad Dog were here to tell him what to say. "I—"

She turned away from him, stared unblinkingly ahead. "Just go. *Please*."

Confused, Jake pushed to his feet. "You said once that I always had a home here. Did you mean it?"

She waited a long time, then slowly nodded.

He stared at her, tried to will her to look at him, but she didn't move, stared past him into the falling night. "I . . . I love you, Mariah," he said quietly.

She winced, then stiffened. A tear beaded in the corner of her eye, caught the candlelight like a diamond, but didn't fall.

It was the only indication that she'd heard him.

Mariah was still sitting on the swing when Mad Dog returned from town.

He ran across the shadowy yard and bounded up the sagging wooden steps. The whole porch rattled and shook at the suddenness of his arrival.

He walked the length of the porch and stopped directly in front of her. Grinning, he slammed a dark brown bottle on the railing. "I'm back."

Mariah didn't even spare him a glance. She just sat there, stiff as a nail, saying nothing.

His labored breathing scored the quiet. He sat on the wide porch rail and studied her, his long fingers curled around the bottle beside him. "Enough is enough, Mariah."

She pushed slowly to her feet. "I think I'll go to my room now." Stiff-backed, staring at the floor, she started to edge past him.

He brought his foot up, slammed a cowboy boot down on the left side of the porch swing. The chain-links clattered together; the slatted seat tilted sideways. She was trapped between his leg and the porch rail. There was no exit except past him—and he had no intention of letting her go.

She lurched to a stop, staring down at his dusty boot

as if it were a two-headed snake. In the flickering, uncertain light of the candle, her profile was waxen and hard. "Please move your foot."

Slowly he brought the other foot up, crossed it over the first. "No."

She turned, fixing dull brown eyes on his face. "I don't feel like talking now ... yet. So if you don't mind ..."

A wave of empathy moved through him at the sight of her pale, ashen face. She looked young and achingly vulnerable; a woman in need of a friend. For the first time in his life, he wanted to be a friend to someone. Not a drinking buddy or a casual acquaintance, but an honest-to-God friend. He'd never seen anyone who needed one more. But first he had to get through to her, break past her wall of pain.

"But I *do* mind," he said, infusing a dark steel into his voice. "I'm sick of your little-girl theatrics and your poor-me whining."

She gasped, and if possible, her skin paled another shade. She brought a trembling hand to her midsection and pressed hard. "I lost my father last week."

"That's life. It's no excuse for acting like a child." He paused for effect, then said the meanest thing he could think of. "Your father would be disappointed in you right now."

She made a horrible, gasping sound of grief. "Why are you doing this to me?"

He drew back, tried to will her to look at him, but she didn't. She just stared down at his crossed legs as if it took too much energy to lift her head. "It needs doing," he answered softly.

She stiffened. "You have no idea what I need. Now, move your feet and let me pass. I'm tired and I want to go to bed."

"But you don't sleep, do you? I've seen you, sitting out on this damn swing for hours at night."

"That's my business," she said, but there was no sting in her voice, only a quiet sadness.

"I'm making it my business."

"You can't do that."

"Watch me."

She sighed and shoved a hand through the tangled mass of her unbound hair. "What do you want from me, Mad Dog?"

"I want your smile back. I miss it." His voice lowered, thickened with emotion. "I miss you."

Her eyes squeezed shut. She bowed her head. A curtain of snarled brown hair fell across her face. "Oh, Mad Dog . . ."

He reached out, touched her cold chin with his forefinger. Gently he forced her to look at him. Their eyes met, held. "Matt," he said quietly.

She blinked. "What?"

"My name is Matthew Jedediah Stone. My mother used to call me Matt." He smiled, surprised by the admission. "I haven't told anyone that in years."

"Why tell me?"

He paused, feeling a surprising sadness. "It's all I have to give you."

She shuddered, hugged herself, and looked away. "I don't want anything from you."

"Yeah, I know."

She looked pointedly at the front door. "Well . . . Matt, I appreciate your honesty, but—"

"Last week you would have cared," he said quietly.

"Yes, well . . . then you should have told me last week. This week I don't care about much of anything. Now, if you'll excuse me . . ."

"I have the cure for apathy."

Her dull glance flicked at him. "I doubt it."

He picked up the tequila bottle. "Hair of the dog," he said, grinning.

She gave a disbelieving snort. "You expect me to get *drunk* as a way of dealing with my grief?"

"It always works for me."

She almost smiled, but it was a bitter, humorless curving of the lips and no more. "It won't work for me. It's stupid and pointless."

"So?"

"So?" She turned to him, her eyes as cold as a north wind on his face. "So let me understand your plan here. I . . . no, we . . . get drunk, and when I wake up— feeling horrible and sick—my father won't be dead?"

Mad Dog's smile faded. He stared deeply into her eyes, hoping—praying—she could see the comfort he offered. "He'll still be dead, Mariah; it'll still hurt like hell. But maybe it won't hurt as bad. Maybe a good cry—"

Her eyes widened. "Alcohol can make you cry?"

"Sure."

A small, tight frown pulled her features. He could tell she was thinking about it, really considering it.

Come on, Mariah. Take a chance. Take a—

"Well," she said slowly, "maybe just one drink." She looked at him. "If you promise it'll make me cry."

Mad Dog felt like whooping for joy. It was a start. And no one drank just one shot of tequila.

Chapter Twenty-three

Mariah couldn't believe she'd said yes to tequila. In the past week she'd said no to food, to sleep, to talking, to everything. And now she'd said yes to tequila.

It was the possibility of crying that had trapped her.

She bowed her head, stared through burning, gritty eyes at the shadowy earth. She wanted to cry so badly, it physically hurt. She'd tried time and again to let go of the grief locked inside her heart. But she couldn't do it. The tears were a solid block of ice pressing against her lungs, riveted in place by years of rigid, desperate self-control.

She cast a surreptitious glance at Mad Dog. *Matt*, she reminded herself. He was walking beside her wordlessly, leading her to some secret destination in the center of the farm.

He'd tried to hold her hand, but she didn't let him. She didn't want to get that close to him again, didn't want to let him comfort her. She just wanted to go to some dark, secret place, drink a little tequila, and cry.

She couldn't afford to let herself care about Mad Dog again. It didn't matter what he told her, how many pretty words he murmured, the truth was constant. Soon he'd leave, and she'd be alone. Not so long ago, that hadn't mattered. Or at least she'd told herself it didn't matter. But then she'd had Rass. She wasn't alone.

Now, when he left, she'd be desperately alone, and she didn't want to send him off with any more of her heart than he already had.

He stopped suddenly and opened the bottle. "This is a good spot."

Mariah looked around. They were in the middle of the west pasture. Most of the snow had melted since yesterday, but the ground was hard and frozen. Black-shadowed earth rolled away from them on all sides, melting into the star-spangled, purple sky. Down to the left, the river was a gurgling ribbon of sterling silver, its surface illuminated by shifting strands of moonlight. Up to the right, she saw the barest outline of the old oak tree and a glimmering hint of ironwork.

She looked quickly away.

Mad Dog touched her. "It's okay. You'll be fine."

She frowned. "That's it . . . we just sit here and get drunk?"

"You could stand."

Mariah reached out. "Give me the bottle."

He handed it to her. The brown glass caught a glimmer of moonlight; the liquid inside swirled like gold. The sharp odor of alcohol assaulted her senses.

She wrinkled her nose in distaste. "It smells bad."

"Tastes worse."

Mad Dog plopped to a cross-legged sit in the spike-sharp grass. Then he patted the ground beside him. "Come on, sit down."

Slowly, stiffly, she knelt beside him. Staring down at

the bottle, she tried to tell herself she was doing the right thing.

"Second thoughts?" he asked softly.

"No." She tilted the bottle and brought it to her mouth. The thick glass felt cold and foreign against her lips. She squeezed her eyes shut and took a huge, dribbling gulp.

Tears sprang to her eyes. Fire burned down her throat and puddled, pulsing, in her stomach. She yanked the bottle from her mouth and wiped her sleeve across her lips. "Oh . . . my . . . *God.*"

Mad Dog grinned at her. "I told you you'd cry." He reached out and took the bottle from her. Taking a big drink, he handed it back.

She frowned at him. "Another one?"

"At least."

"Maybe I should wait. . . ."

"It's not gonna digest, darlin'. Take another drink."

Grimacing, she took the bottle and wiped the mouth of it with her sleeve.

He laughed. "Whatcha doin' that for? You know where my mouth has been."

Mariah ignored him and took another burning drink.

Mad Dog leaned back on his elbows and crossed his legs at the ankles, staring up at the endless, star-bright sky. They sat that way for an eternity, with him sprawled casually in the grass, her kneeling primly alongside him.

The tequila passed back and forth, back and forth, until Mariah started actually *liking* the taste. It was like swallowing a starburst, and after each sip, she felt warmer. The tension that had coiled around her spine for days melted into more manageable proportions.

"Come here," Mad Dog said after a while, patting the ground.

Mariah took another drink. "Huh-uh." Then she handed him the bottle and wiped her mouth with the back of her hand.

He took a quick sip and handed it back.

She frowned heavily. For a second—just a second—the bottle went out of focus.

He wiggled it. The liquid sloshed against the glass.

She reached out with both hands, curling her fingers around the slim, cold neck. "Gotcha."

Was that her voice? It sounded . . . slurred.

"You got me," he said quietly.

Her head snapped up. She stared at him through watery, burning eyes. He swam in and out of focus for a moment. She narrowed her eyes, concentrating.

Gradually she could make him out. He lay in the shadowy grass, propped up on his elbows. Moonlight tangled in his too long hair, creating a halo of fire around his tanned, smiling face.

Her heart gave a tiny lurch. God, he was handsome. She'd almost forgotten. . . .

But she *wanted* to forget. Didn't she?

"I don't want you," she said primly, and took another sip.

He laughed, and in the quiet darkness it was a rich, rumbling sound that curled around her heart. "Yes, you do."

For some absurd reason, her fingers started trembling. She slammed down the bottle into the cold, hard ground. "No, I don't."

He sat up.

Mariah felt his gaze on her, sliding down her exposed throat like a finger of fire. She shivered and tried to ignore the feeling.

Slowly he got to his feet.

She was acutely aware of his movements, the crick of his knees, the crunch of his heels in the frozen grass, the accelerated tenor of his breathing.

He took a step closer to her and stopped. His hand appeared before her in the darkness. "Come on."

She blinked up at him. "Where are we goin'?"

"Does it matter?"

She reached for the tequila and started to take a drink.

He grabbed her hand. "I think you've had enough."

She bristled. "*You* think I've had enough? Who cares?" A defiant half smile pulled at her lips as she took one last drink.

"Come on."

She ignored his hand and set the tequila down. The bottle fell with a thump and released the sharp scent of liquor. She giggled and tried to right it.

"Come on, Mariah."

"Oh, all right." She placed her hands in the grass and pushed awkwardly to her feet. The moment she stood, a tidal wave of dizziness swept through her, turned her legs into warm pudding. She staggered sideways, arms flailing, then crumpled to the ground.

She giggled again. "I can't stand up."

Laughing softly, Mad Dog swept her into his arms.

The sudden movement surprised her. Instinctively she wrapped her tingling arms around his neck and hung on.

He turned and started walking.

Mariah let out a deep breath. She had to admit, she felt pretty darn good. She tucked her face into the crook of his neck and closed her eyes. The steady movement of his body lulled her, relaxed her. She found herself drifting, drifting, not thinking about anything.

"We're here." Mad Dog stopped.

Mariah lifted her head, blinked heavily, trying to see in the darkness around her.

A naked, shivering limb caught her eye.

She gasped, brought a hand to her mouth. No, she thought drunkenly, he wouldn't have brought her here. Not here . . .

His arms loosened. She slid down the long, hard length of him. Her feet hit the ground with a quiet thump, her knees immediately gave way, and she sank unsteadily onto the grass.

Everything about this place was painfully familiar. She didn't need to see it in the full light of day to recognize her surroundings.

The sharp tip of betrayal stung through her. "Why would you bring me here?"

He kneeled beside her, slipping his hand through hers. Their fingers curled together, formed a warm, tight-knit ball of flesh. "You need to say good-bye, Mariah."

She turned to him. "I said good-bye at the damn funeral."

"You need to mean it."

She shook her head. "No."

"I'm right here with you."

"You think that makes a difference?" She laughed; it was a sharp, almost hysterical sound.

"Yeah."

His answer was so quiet, so genuine, that Mariah almost believed him. For a moment, a giddy, suspended moment, she wondered *what if*.

"Talk to him, Mariah," Mad Dog urged, squeezing her hand. "Say the things you left unsaid."

She swallowed hard and reluctantly turned back to the mound of jet black dirt against the shadowy grass. A headstone glimmered in the moonlight, its words emblazoned in her mind. *Here lies the body of Erasmus Throckmorton. Husband, father, hero.*

She hadn't known what to say about him. What did you say about a man who'd walked this earth for seventy-four years and never harmed a soul? A man who believed in God, and miracles, and second chances.

What did you say about your father when he was gone? So many years, so many memories . . . so little space on a cold slab of granite.

"He loved you, Mariah."

Her head felt suddenly heavy. She nodded. "He was my life," she said quietly.

"He wouldn't want you to give up living for him."

A small, bittersweet smile pulled at her lips, then slid, quivering into a frown. "How did you get to know him so well?"

"He was an easy man to know."

This time her watery smile stayed a heartbeat longer before melting downward. "Yes, he was."

"Talk to him," he said again. "Say good-bye."

"That's dumb."

"So what, you're drunk."

She almost laughed. Then, slowly, she lifted her heavy head and stared at the blank rectangle where no grass yet grew. Just looking at it made her feel sick and queasy. Her hands started to shake, her mouth curved downward. But she wanted to say good-bye to him, ached to do it. She wanted to say all the things she'd meant to say to him when he was alive, but somehow never had.

"I feel stupid," she said.

"Don't."

She licked her lips, and tried to look away, tried to ignore Mad Dog's seductive words. But her gaze kept coming back to Rass's cold, dark grave.

Sweet God, she missed him. There were so many things she wanted to say to him, so many things she should have already said. *Daddy ... I'm so sorry about the way I shut you out of my life. I thought ... I don't know what I thought. I guess I believed we had forever.* The formless, desperate words swirled through her head, brought back a million painful memories.

Tears seared her eyes, turned the grave into a wavering smear. A lump of emotion swelled in her throat. *I wish I'd told you how much I loved you ... and not just when you were dying. I should have told you a long time ago ... after Stephen and Thomas. After Mama.*

Mama. The word cut through her like a knife, bringing a steel-sharp stab of pain. A single tear slid down her cheek and splashed on the hand curled in her lap.

Oh, God, I miss you both so much. ...

She made a choking, gasping sound and started to cry. "Oh, God . . ."

Mad Dog curled his arms around her, held her tightly. Her body spasmed. Hot tears ran in rivulets down her cheeks and dampened his shirt. The salty, poignant smell of them filled her senses and made her cry even harder.

He stroked her tangled hair and the moist sides of her face. "It's okay." He murmured the soothing words over and over again, calming her.

"I miss them so much, Matt."

She cried and cried and cried, until her throat was parched and dry and a headache pounded behind her eyes. She cried for her parents, for her lost youth, for her baby. For all the things she'd never cried for before.

She smelled lavender.

Gasping, she jerked her head up. Overhead, the stars seemed to be shifting, merging into a huge, white-hot ball in the center of the sky.

"The stars are moving," she said, sniffling hard and wiping her eyes.

"Hallucinations. It's the second stage of tequila." Mad Dog dabbed the moisture from her cheek. "It'll go away."

She closed her eyes and then slowly opened them.

And saw her mother and father standing behind the iron settee.

She gasped. "Mama . . . Daddy . . ."

We love you, Mariah.

Mariah heard the words, felt them, as clearly as if they'd been spoken aloud. Her parents said nothing else, but in that instant, that heartbeat, Mariah felt their warm, unconditional love. It seeped through her, filling the dark, lonely spots in her soul.

She knew then, without question, that they understood. That they'd *always* understood. And they loved her.

Jesus, they *loved* her. With all her faults and mistakes and stupid silences, they loved her.

She looked up at them. "Thomas?" She whispered his name quietly, hopefully.

Her mother smiled. *His soul was reborn.*

New tears burned across Mariah's eyes, but this time they were happy, loving tears. For the first time in her life, she felt filled with hope and light. She brought a hand to her face and swiped the tears away.

And when she pulled her arm away, her parents were gone.

She felt a moment's sadness at their passing, but it lasted no longer than that. She smiled at Mad Dog, blinking through the tears. "Did you see them?"

He frowned. "See who?"

She pushed the hair out of her eyes. "I guess not," she said, laughing easily.

Mad Dog eyed her steadily. "Feel better?"

"Oh, God, you have no idea. . . ."

"Who's Thomas?"

Almost involuntarily, she glanced back at the small, grown-over patch near her mama's grave. For the first time in years, she looked at it without feeling a crushing, smothering sense of guilt. "He was my son."

Mad Dog made a soft sound of surprise. "Your son?"

She turned to him, looked into his eyes. "Remember my two-minutes loss of virginity?"

"Yeah."

"I got pregnant."

"Oh, Mariah." He touched her cheek, a feather-stroke touch of compassion that made her shiver.

"I wrote to Stephen when I found out—his acting troupe was in Spokane by then. He said he'd meet me in Walla Walla and marry me." Surprisingly, she felt no bitterness about Stephen now; only a thread of sadness at her own naïveté. "I shouldn't have believed him, but I did—I was only sixteen. Of course, he stood me up at the altar."

"How . . . how did Thomas die?"

She started to cry again, soft, melting tears that slid down her cheeks and splashed on her skirt. "He never really lived. I had him almost six weeks too early. He was so tiny. . . . There was nothing Doc Sherman could do. Doc . . . said there shouldn't be any more."

Mad Dog touched her cheek. "Shouldn't. Or couldn't?"

Mariah tried to smile. "He said I didn't 'carry' well and shouldn't have any more."

"My mom had four miscarriages before she had me. The doctors told her the same thing. And you were sixteen years old. You're stronger now."

Her breath caught, her eyes rounded. A quivering sense of hope, new and more powerful than anything she'd ever imagined, spiraled through her. "Maybe." That's all she said, just *maybe*, but the word freed something inside her, made her, for once, believe.

"Why isn't there a marker?"

She glanced back at the small grave, remembering the tiny little box that lay beneath the frozen grass. She shook her head, realizing for the first time why she hadn't purchased one. "I couldn't say good-bye."

Still staring at the grave, she pushed to her feet and stumbled over to it. Awkwardly she sank to her knees and leaned forward, pressing her forehead into the prickly blanket of winter grass. The smell of it combined with the fecund fragrance of the dirt and filled her senses. Overhead, the last remaining leaves whickered together; one fell silently downward and landed on Mariah's hair.

"Good-bye, Thomas," she said throatily, letting the cleansing tears fall. "I love you, baby."

She had no idea how long she sat there. It could have been minutes or hours. Then, slowly, she straightened.

Across the row of graves, her eyes met Mad Dog's. At the sight of him, sitting there in the darkness, waiting for her, she felt a surge of blistering emotion.

"Matt." She whispered his name and held out her arms.

He was beside her in an instant, picking her up. She snuggled close to him, burying her face in the crook of his neck. "Thank you," she murmured, tasting the salty, familiar tang of his skin against her lips.

Mariah breathed deeply and lolled her head back, staring up at the sky as Mad Dog walked away from the graves.

At the movement, nausea punched her in the stomach. She groaned in surprise and clutched her writhing midsection. The stars blurred, pulsed. "I don't feel so good all of a sudden."

Mad Dog's soft laughter enfolded her. "I'm not surprised."

She blinked sleepily, tried to focus. "Where are we?"

He stopped at a door and kicked it open. "At the bunkhouse. Home sweet home."

His hold on her loosened, and Mariah slithered bonelessly to the floor. "Oops." She giggled and tried to clamp a hand over her mouth, but she missed and smacked herself in the nose.

Mad Dog grabbed her by the forearm and hauled her to her feet. She leaned against him, clutching her stomach. Nausea lurched into her throat and lodged there, throbbing.

"Do you want to lay down?"

His voice seemed to come at her from a million miles away. Dully she nodded. The simple action seemed to take forever.

He started to maneuver her toward the bed, but at the movement, something in her stomach gave way. Without warning, she threw up all over his bed.

He stared at the bed. "Aw, shit."

She was horrified for a second, then she giggled. "S-Sorry."

He laughed and scooped her into his arms again, carrying her into the house. In the bathing room, he helped her brush her teeth, then hauled her up the stairs and put her in bed.

Then he started to leave.

She held her hands out, blinked sleepily up at him. "Don't go. I want you. . . ."

He smiled softly, brushed a lock of hair from her face. "You need sleep. And besides, you're drunk as a skunk." He gave her a wolfish, sexy grin. "Tomorrow, when you're sober, we'll talk. . . ."

"Then just sleep with me."

Mad Dog paused. "Just sleep?"

"Please . . ."

"Why not?" Smiling, he stripped out of his clothes and crawled naked in bed beside her, drawing her close.

She laid a cheek on his bare chest and smiled peacefully. "I'm sorry I threw up on your bed."

He stroked her hair. "Don't worry, you're not the first woman to do so."

"You're not supposed to compare me to other women."

He chuckled. "I didn't think it was important to be the first to throw up on someone."

She snuggled against him, curling her arm possessively around his body. The familiar soap-and-water scent of his skin filled her nostrils. A long, contented sigh escaped her mouth.

"I like tequila. . . ." Before the words had even left her mouth, she was asleep.

Chapter Twenty-four

Mariah woke slowly. She had a second of oblivion, then she remembered last night. Pain surged through her at the memory.

She blinked, feeling the warm, wet streak of a single tear as it fell down her cheek. She knew somehow that she would have many mornings in her life like this, mornings when she woke up and thought of her parents, her son; the loved ones she had lost. And though the pain was still there, still ached in her heart, for the first time in her life, she knew she could go on. Knew someday she could smile again.

She pushed to her elbows, staring down at the man beside her. Sunlight crept through the window and wreathed him in a halo of wavering gold. He lay on his back, one arm flung over the side of the bed, the other scrunched up protectively against his chest.

She loved him.

She didn't need her father to tell her how she felt anymore. His smile, his laughter, his gentleness, his honesty. They were all invisible threads that bound her to him like steels bands.

She thought about last night, about all that he'd given

her, and she ached to give something back to him. But she had nothing of value, nothing that he needed.

What about love?

The thought came to her out of nowhere, stunning her with its simple power.

Before she could stop it, hope crept into her soul and seized hold, refusing to be rationalized away.

Maybe beneath that swaggering, smiling exterior, he was as lonely as she, as tired of being alone. Maybe he needed her as much as she needed him. Maybe, someday, he could even learn to love her.

Please, God, let him stay. . . .

Tears stung her eyes. She didn't bother to wipe them away. Never again would she be afraid to cry. There would be no more hiding for her, no more emotional armor. From how on, she'd face life head-on and fight for her happiness.

She'd give him everything she had to give, her heart and soul and body, and hope that it was enough.

It was all she could do.

A pleasant, tingling sensation spread through Mad Dog's body. He shifted his weight, tangling in the warm sheets that curled around him. An unfamiliar scent filled his nostrils, teased him to a woozy state of semi-consciousness. He flung one arm sideways, stretching.

His arm landed across something warm and solid. Flesh, he realized groggily. He was sleeping next to someone.

Flesh. The realization ripped the last clinging clouds of sleep from his mind. He opened his eyes.

Mariah lay snuggled against him, her chin poised

lightly on his chest, her lips a hairsbreadth from his left nipple. He felt the whisper-soft caress of her breathing against his skin.

He almost groaned aloud at the sight of her. Heat slid through his body and landed in his groin.

She gave him a slow, lazy smile, and pushed a tangled skein of hair from her still sleepy eyes. "Morning," she said in a soft, throaty voice that made him think of sex.

He blinked, tried to sound casual. "Mornin'. I guess you're feeling better. . . ."

"I feel great." Her gaze melted into his. Slowly she pushed the tip of her tongue past her parted lips and licked his nipple. "And you," she drawled, "taste even better than I feel."

The warm, wet tip of her tongue scalded him. He shivered in response. Arousal hardened his body, saturated his senses. He'd never had a woman initiate sex before—not even when he paid for their attentions. Jesus, it was nice. . . .

She licked his nipple again, tugged at it with her teeth.

Another low, gravelly groan escaped him. "Where did you learn that?" he said, trying to force laughter into his breathless voice.

"From you." Her mouth closed around his nipple, teased it into hardness.

Mad Dog sank deeper into the pile of pillows and closed his eyes. Who in the hell would have known this felt so good? No one had ever done this to him before; he'd never thought to ask for it. One of the drawbacks of sleeping with whores, he thought lazily. You got what you paid for, and not a goddamn thing more.

But it was more than that, and he knew it. He was feeling something that went beyond physical sensation. She was touching his body with her tongue, and he felt it there, but somehow what she was doing went deeper. As if that gentle, moist tongue of hers were flicking his heart as well.

She looked up, smiling. Their eyes met, and in the bourbon depths, he saw a reflection of his own emotions. The power of the moment hit him hard. His chest tightened, his ability to breathe melted away.

"What are you doing?"

She stared at him through steady, honest eyes. "I'm loving you."

Before he could respond, she moved down. The blankets bunched up behind her, peeling away from him until more and more of his naked body lay exposed. Cool air breezed across his skin.

Her head slipped under the blankets.

"Oh, Jesus . . ."

The warm tip of her tongue traced the hard line of his pelvic bone, left a searing streak of fire. Goose bumps studded his trembling flesh. He squeezed his eyes shut. *Oh, God . . .*

She trailed moist, openmouthed kisses along his hipbone. Her movements were slow and leisurely, tasting, exploring, touching. Desire pulsed through him, made him tremble and ache and need. Never in his life had he felt this way . . . desperate and out of control.

He grabbed hold of her shoulders and yanked her up the long, hard length of his body. A tiny mewl of surprise slipped from her lips. It was the only sound she made before his mouth came down on hers.

He kissed her long and hard, with all the pent-up passion of a man who'd had sex a thousand times but never once in his life made love. He pushed his tongue into her mouth, tasting the exquisite sweetness that was hers alone.

She kissed him with abandon. Her tongue twined with his, explored the moist cavern of his mouth, traced his teeth. Her arms curled around his neck, her breasts pressed against his chest.

Everywhere they touched, there was fire. Their skin burned together, fused. Mad Dog had never wanted a woman more in his life. He wanted her inside him, wanted to feel the very essence of her body melting into his.

He fumbled desperately with the tiny buttons of her chemise, trying to force his shaking fingers to function. Frustration burst past his lips in a growl. He cursed, wanting to rip the flimsy fabric from her body.

She laughed shakily and drew back.

"Where are you going?" He winced at the breathlessness of his own voice.

"I'd rather take it off than have you rip it off," she answered in a voice that matched his own. With nimble, practiced fingers, she unbuttoned the lacy chemise and shrugged out of it. The ivory fabric slid down her silky arms, pulled gently away from her small, pink-tipped breasts.

He moaned at the sight of her. Need twisted his insides into a hard, throbbing knot.

He'd never really understood the full impact of that

word before; it had always been synonymous with simple desire, but now he saw the truth. There was nothing simple about it.

He needed Mariah, needed her in this moment more than he'd ever needed anyone in his life. And not just her body—though he wanted her with a desire that bordered on desperation. He needed her smile, her laughter, her ability to care. That part of her that couldn't say good-bye to the people she loved.

She let her gaze move away from his. Slowly, with a seductiveness she couldn't possibly understand, she began to untie her drawers. The creamy linen slid down the trim, concave curve of her hip. A shadow of curly brown hair peeked out from the sagging, beribboned waistband.

"Jesus, Mariah," he whispered, "you're beautiful."

She eased the undergarments from her body and threw them behind her. The chemise landed half-on, half-off the dresser; the pants draped across the bedpost like a flag of surrender.

"Come here," he breathed, his gaze locked on hers.

She shook her head. Her long hair brushed against her nipples, hardening the pink tips.

"But—"

She leaned down, pressed a finger to his lips. "Shhh . . ."

Slowly, she drew back the heavy coverlet and exposed his naked body. He lay there, legs partially spread, hands clenched at his sides, breathing heavily. Her hot, pointed gaze studied him, moved leisurely to the hardened shaft of his desire. He couldn't move, his body felt weighted down. His breath came in fast, choppy bursts that sounded like cannon-bursts in his ears. He licked his lips and tried to swallow, but he couldn't. He lay stiff and unmoving, feeling exposed, vulnerable, out of control.

And painfully aroused.

She leaned toward him, placed her hands on his chest. Sweaty dampness seeped from her flattened palms and scalded his skin.

She gave him a slow, enigmatic smile . . . and straddled him.

He shuddered hard and closed his eyes. Gently, feeling her way, she lowered herself onto him, encased him in the tight, velvet sheath of her body.

He grabbed her bare buttocks and pulled her toward him. She leaned closer, curling her fingers around the scrolled oak bedrail. Her breasts wavered before him, taunting him with their perfect, pebbly tips.

He pushed up, took one in his mouth.

A moan of pleasure slipped from her parted lips, ruffled through his hair. She started to move, slowly at first, as if unsure of what to do, then faster and faster.

Sweat broke out on his chest. His fingers curled into the warm, solid flesh of her buttocks, squeezing, holding, guiding. Her hips moved in an artless, instinctive motion that drove him crazy with need.

He sucked her nipples, first one, then the other, drawing the puckered peaks deep into his searching mouth. Above him, she made quiet, gurgling sounds of passion that plunged through him, aroused him even more.

Their bodies turned hot and slick and melted into each other, until he didn't know where she stopped and he began. They found a thrusting, grinding rhythm of flesh on flesh.

He couldn't breathe for wanting her. His every sense felt stretched and heightened to painful intensity. A dark emotion tugged at his heart, consumed him. For a heartbeat of time, he felt vulnerable and afraid.

She came down on him hard, twisting, thrusting, driving the air from his lungs. He clung to her, sucking one nipple, pulling the other with his fingers.

She writhed, moaned, arched. Her head flew back in a spray of brown hair.

He glanced up at her, saw her curved above him, her eyes sealed shut, her lips parted, her cheeks bright with passion.

He tried not to come. For the first time in his life, he cared about making this good for her. As good as it was for him.

Ah, Jesus, how good . . .

Agony twisted his insides at the effort, made him swell and ache and hurt. The urge to release himself inside her, lose himself in her hot, wet warmth, was a driving, burning need.

He gritted his teeth and held back. Her name may have slipped from his lips, he wasn't sure. His body shook with the effort of control, sweat burned across his forehead.

She thrashed atop him, whimpering, then suddenly she stiffened. "Oh God, oh God . . ."

She plunged down on him, grinding herself against his hips with moist, desperate abandon. Her hands left the bedpost and curled in his hair, clutching his head to her breasts.

He squeezed her buttocks and arched upward, driving himself deep into her body. She tensed, cried out. The rhymthic pulsing of her release squeezed him.

"Oh, God . . . Matt . . ." she moaned.

At the sound of his name, he was lost. He grabbed her hard and thrust upward again, arching off the bed. Relief exploded through his body, tingled all the way to his fingertips in waves of painful pleasure.

He clung to her sweaty body, feeling suspended, dizzy. Darkness hovered at the edges of his mind. Her name slipped from his lips in a sigh as he drifted slowly back to earth.

Exhausted, he sank into the mound of pillows and pulled her close. She snuggled up to him, slipped her arm around his waist, and buried her face in the crook of his neck. The harsh scent of sweat and the sweet smell of passion filled the air.

He had a moment's utter bliss, then reality crashed in. He frowned, remembering the things he'd thought about her, the way he'd needed her, and for the first time in his life, he was truly afraid. He'd never needed anyone in his life; it was something he made certain of. He lived without restrictions, without commitments. When he wanted to walk, he walked; when he wanted to stop, he stopped. No one and nothing told him what to do.

That kind of freedom was as necessary to him as breathing. He couldn't live without it, couldn't live in safety behind a white picket fence. Couldn't grow old on some nothing little apple farm in the middle of nowhere.

And yet, a few moments ago, he'd needed her. Not as a physical release, not as a way to pass the time. Really needed. For a few heartbreakingly perfect minutes, with him inside her, holding her, he'd felt . . . complete.

Ah, Mariah, he thought, groaning, *what are we doing? What in the hell are we doing?*

But he knew.

It wasn't just great sex. It was love.

Mariah curled against Matt, holding him tightly. He stroked her hair in gentle, sweeping motions but said nothing.

She was afraid again. Afraid that now, in the bright sunlight of this morning, he'd get up, get dressed, and leave her.

She squeezed her eyes shut, feeling the sting of tears. *Please don't go, Matt. . . .*

She wanted to say the words, ached to say them, but somehow they lodged in her throat. So she said something else instead. "I . . . I read your articles, Matt."

The hand on her hair stilled. His body stiffened. "You did?"

She twisted around until she could look up at him. Their eyes met, his narrowed suddenly and guarded. "Yes," she said quietly. "I thought they were brilliant."

A look of incredulity crossed his face. "You did?"

She nodded, unable to say anything past the lump in her throat. She couldn't believe that no one had ever told him that before. *He needs me,* she realized. *Almost as much as I need him.*

"No one's ever read my work. . . ."

"I hope you don't mind—"

"No." He touched her face gently and gazed down at her. "No." A small smile tugged at his mouth, but there was no humor in it, only a bittersweet sadness. "I always thought that one day I'd work at a newspaper, but somehow I never stuck in one place long enough to try it out."

He's leaving.

The two words ripped her heart out, left her weak and bleeding and afraid. She tried to rationalize them away, but she couldn't do that, couldn't look at life through blinders anymore. He was leaving her. She knew it was a certainty that left her feeling sick inside. "Matt . . ."

"What?"

She gazed up at him, pouring her heart and soul into a single, steady look. She'd never been more afraid in her life than she was at this moment. "I love you."

He paled. She thought for one terrifying moment, he was going to laugh it off. But he didn't. He just lay there, staring down at her through those sad, honest eyes.

His silence pinched her heart. She tried to smile, but couldn't.

"Mariah . . ."

She pressed a finger to his lips. "I didn't tell you because I expect an answer. But I can't go back to the way I was before, hiding everything I feel. It hurts too much. I love you, Matt Stone. I'm proud of that. Whether . . ." Her voice cracked. She blinked through a hot blur of tears. "Whether you love me back doesn't matter."

He looked away, stared hard at the glittering golden square of the window. "It matters."

She touched his chin, forced him to look at her. In his

eyes was a bleakness that closed around her. She stared up at him, feeling the heaviness of the moment like a stone against her heart. She knew she shouldn't say anything more, should simply snuggle up to him and accept whatever scraps of affection he had, for as long as they were offered. A week ago she might have been able to do that, might have been able to accept less than she was worth. But no more. Matt had changed the way she saw herself, the way she saw the world, and there was no going back.

She swallowed hard and blinked up at him through her stinging tears. "Stay." She said the word quietly, almost on a whisper, but it resonated through the bedroom like a scream.

He winced. "Ah, Mariah . . ."

She heard the sorrow in his voice, and something that hurt even worse. Regret. Tears slipped over her cheeks, burrowed into the corners of her mouth.

He wiped a tear from the corner of her eye and stared down at her. "Would you come with me if I asked?"

Her heart skipped a beat. A tiny thread of hope slid into her thoughts. "Are you asking?"

He broke eye contact and stared at the wall behind her. It was a long, breathless moment before he answered softly. "No, I guess not."

She squeezed her eyes shut and tried to smile. "I can't leave the farm anyway. Rass proved that."

"I never meant to hurt you, Mariah."

She slid away from him and sat up, dangling her bare feet over the edge of the bed. "I guess I'm not the best match for a drifter."

Behind her, the bed squeaked. His feet hit the floor. "I wish I knew what to say to you, Mariah."

She straightened her back but didn't turn to him. "You do know what to say, Matt. You just don't want to say it."

He stood there a long time. She felt his gaze on her back, moving across her bare skin like a touch of fire. Then, slowly, he turned and walked away. When the door closed with a quiet click, Mariah sagged forward and started to cry.

Jake sat at the kitchen table, waiting for Mad Dog to come into the house. Upstairs, the floorboards creaked, a door clicked open.

Mariah was getting up.

Uncertainty snipped at Jake's self-confidence. It would be hard enough to do this. He couldn't say what he needed to say in front of Mariah.

Maybe he'd just wait for Mad Dog outside, by the bunkhouse.

Yeah, that made more sense.

He pushed his chair out and stood up.

Mad Dog came thundering down the steps and barreled into the kitchen. He ran into Jake and almost knocked him over.

He grabbed Jake by the shoulders and steadied him. "Sorry, Jake."

Jake stared at his father. He looked . . . sad. There was no other word for it. Jake frowned up at him. "Is everything okay?"

Mad Dog laughed bitterly. "Great." Then he pushed past Jake and headed to the door. "I gotta go."

Jake reached for him, missed. "Wait!"

"Can't." Mad Dog pushed through the kitchen door and disappeared.

Indecision rooted Jake to the spot for a heartbeat, then he made up his mind. He'd made a promise to Rass, and to himself. Today Mad Dog was going to learn he had a son.

Jake shoved his chair back into its spot at the table and ran from the house, bounding down the stairs after his father. "Wait!"

Mad Dog didn't even slow down.

"Damn it." Jake fisted his hands and sprinted toward the bunkhouse. He grabbed Mad Dog's arm and spun him around. "I *said* wait."

Mad Dog stared down at him through a haze, as if he hadn't even heard Jake calling to him. "Huh? Look, kid—"

"Jake," he shouted. "My name is *Jake*."

Mad Dog rolled his eyes. "Sorry."

Jake steeled himself for rejection and stared up at his father. "Do you know why that's important?"

Mad Dog frowned. "No, why?"

He drew a deep breath, then said, "My legal name is Jacob William Vanderstay."

Jake knew the moment his words registered. Mad Dog's eyes narrowed, his mouth tensed into a thin white line. "What are you saying?"

Jake nodded. "Laralee was my mother."

Mad Dog winced. He took a stumbling step backward, as if to put distance between himself and the words that were coming. "Yeah. So?"

Jake followed him. "You're my father."

"That's impossible." The words shot from his mouth like deadly arrows.

Jake felt their sharp tips in his heart. He faltered for a moment, afraid. He'd never once thought that Mad Dog might not believe him. He fished through his pocket and pulled out a bent tin locket with a painted violet on its face. He held it out to Mad Dog. "She gave me this and said it came from my father."

Mad Dog stared at the locket for a long time. Then he closed his eyes and rubbed the bridge of his nose. His broad shoulders caved downward, his head bowed. "Oh, Jesus."

Jake stared at him. Everything inside him, every emotion and hope and fear, twisted into a ball in his stomach. He'd waited so long for this moment, all his life. He'd dreamed of it a thousand times, ached for it.

"Say something," he pleaded.

Mad Dog's hand fell from his face. He looked at Jake through moist eyes. "I don't know what to say. I didn't know she was pregnant."

"I know that."

He seemed to search for something to say. "How is Lara?"

Jake swallowed hard. "She died."

Mad Dog squeezed his eyes shut. When he spoke, his voice was raspy and tired. "Why did you track me down? What do you want from me?"

Jake heard the words, the question, but he didn't answer. There was no point. He saw the truth in his father's sad, tired eyes. It was the beginning of good-bye.

Jake had tried to prepare himself for this moment, had told himself a thousand times that it would end this way. But still it hurt, hurt more than he could possibly have imagined. "I wanted to get to know you."

Mad Dog shook his head. "I can't be a goddamn father."

"You're already a father," Jake answered without looking at him. Even to his own ears, his voice sounded old and dull. "What you mean is, you won't be a parent."

"I don't know how."

Jake wanted to say, ached to say, *we could learn together*. But he didn't. The words stuck in his throat, held in place by a hot lump of tears. Resignation pulled his shoulders downward. "Yeah, right."

Mad Dog sighed. "Look, Jake, this is all coming at me pretty fast."

"Yeah, I know."

"But I know how much it hurts to be abandoned. . . . I guess . . . maybe we should spend some time together, get to know each other. What do you say?"

Jake's head snapped up. "Are you kidding?"

Mad Dog almost smiled. "I was just leaving the place. Maybe . . . maybe you wanna come with me?"

Jake felt a moment's disbelief, then a crushing disappointment. "Leaving? Why?"

He shrugged, trying to look casual, but Jake saw the pain in his father's eyes. "I don't want to hurt Mariah any more than I already have. And it's time to move on."

Jake tried desperately to understand. It felt as if his world were slowly unraveling, as if Mad Dog had pulled a loose thread and ripped everything apart. "But you'll hurt her if you leave."

"She'll get over it." His voice dropped to a whisper. "So will I."

"But . . . but—"

"But nothin', Jake. There's no future for me here. I'm a man that has to move. If I don't keep moving, I'll die. It's as simple as that. So are you gonna come with me or not?"

Jake glanced back at the house. In the second-floor window, a shadow moved. *Mariah.*

His heart twisted at the thought of her, tears burned his eyes. In the past weeks she'd given him everything he'd ever wanted and never thought he'd find again. He felt safe with her, cared-for. He couldn't walk away from her, couldn't leave her here alone, sad and depressed. He loved her.

He turned to his father, blinking up at him through scalding tears. And realized in that moment what he'd been searching for all these months. It wasn't just his father. It was a home, a family, a sense of belonging. All the things he'd found with Mariah. "I . . . I can't do that. She'll be alone."

Mad Dog squeezed his eyes shut, as if in pain. Then, slowly, he opened his eyes and looked down at Jake. "I'm proud of you, Jake."

Jake felt the impact of those simple words like a blow to the stomach. The words should have lifted his spirits, made him feel, finally, that he'd gained some measure of respect from his father. But they had the opposite effect; they sounded like good-bye. Years worth of hopes and dreams and prayers tangled around him until he couldn't breathe. A sharp pain wrenched his heart, twisted his insides. He realized in that moment how desperately he wanted to love his dad. "Stay . . . please. We could be a family."

Mad Dog blinked and shook his head. "I can't."

The last kernel of hope shattered, lay broken at his feet. Jake nodded, feeling hopelessly alone and lonely. He sagged forward, too depressed to even cry. His father was leaving him. After all the years, all the dreams, it was going to end like this. On a little farm in the middle of nowhere, with a quiet pair of good-byes. And there was nothing he could say to change it.

They stood there for a long time, staring at each other, saying nothing. Then, miraculously, Mad Dog opened his arms.

Jake hurled himself into his father's embrace and hugged him tightly, wishing he didn't ever have to let go. He wanted his dad to stay, wanted it so badly, he felt sick to his stomach.

Mad Dog pulled back and stared down at Jake through eyes that were glassy and overbright. "I'll miss you, kid. But I'll be thinkin' of you. And maybe someday I'll be back."

Jake sniffled and wiped his tears on his sleeve. "Don't say that unless you mean it."

Mad Dog winced. "Good-bye, Jake."

It took everything inside Jake to say the next word. "Good-bye."

Chapter Twenty-five

Mariah felt numb. She walked around her room, seeing nothing, feeling less.

She glanced dully out the window, and saw Mad Dog talking to Jake. Her heart twisted painfully at the sight of him, standing on her land, looking for all the world like he belonged there.

Like he belonged there.

A small, helpless sob escaped her. God, she'd gotten so used to seeing him every morning, eating with him, laughing and smiling with him. In the past weeks he'd become twined around her soul, and it felt now as if vital strands were being yanked from her body, leaving her hollow and empty inside. How could she go back to her old life? Without him, the farm would be so damned, depressingly quiet. . . .

He gave Jake a smile that looked almost sad, and then, slowly, his shoulders sagging, he backed up and went into the bunkhouse, closing the door behind him.

Jake stared after Mad Dog for a long time. A deep breath pulled the starch from his spine and left him, too, looking broken. He plunged his hands in his pockets and gave the closed door a longing glance before he turned and walked to the barn.

She stared at the bunkhouse, wondering what Matt was doing in there, what he was thinking. If she closed her eyes, she could see him still. Leaning against the wall, smiling, so handsome he took her breath away.

Tears burned her eyes and slipped down her cheeks. With a sigh, she leaned forward, rested her forehead on the cool windowpane. Her breath clouded the glass. For a moment the world was hazy and dreamlike. And she was a little girl again, pretending her Prince Charming was down there, waiting for her. . . .

Maybe he's waiting for you.

She knew immediately that it was a mistake to think that. But once planted, the seed of hope found fertile soil. Maybe he was down there, waiting for her to stop him. . . .

Maybe . . .

She didn't give herself time to think about it. She raced to the armoire and yanked out a baggy brown dress. Throwing it on, she hurried down the steps and ran to the bunkhouse, skidding to a breathless stop at the closed door.

She wiped her sweaty palms on the rough linsey-woolsey of her dress and stared at it.

I don't know what I was thinkin', Mariah. I can't leave you. . . .

She squeezed her eyes shut, wanting desperately to believe her own fantasy. She took a deep, shaking breath. "Please, God, make him stay. Please . . ."

Then she knocked.

There was no answer.

Steeling herself, she opened the door.

What she saw hit her like a slap to the face. She gasped quietly and stumbled backward, clutching the doorframe for support. Her stupid, little-girl fantasy crashed down around her.

Mad Dog was kneeling in the corner, stuffing the last of his things in the white duck bag. He yanked the bag closed and stood up, slowly turning around.

She tried to smile. "Surprise." The word sounded small and pathetic and painful. Exactly like she felt.

He sighed. The half-filled bag slid from his hand and hit the floor with a thud. "Mariah . . ."

She clasped her shaking hands together, trying not to be hurt by the gentle, loving way he said her name. "Were you going to say good-bye?"

He looked up at her then, and in his eyes she saw her own pain, mirrored and magnified. It tore at her heart with tiny, shredding claws. She started to shake.

"I don't know."

She felt a blinding wave of regret. Her hands balled at her sides. "I shouldn't have asked you to stay."

He winced. "I'm glad you did. And I wish . . ." He looked away. "Jesus, I wish I could say yes."

"But you can't."

"No, I can't." He picked up the bag and slung it over his shoulder, walking slowly toward her.

She stared at him, trying to memorize everything about him. The crooked tilt of a smile that wasn't there, the shining laughter in eyes that now looked glazed with pain. She wanted to touch him, hold him, cling to his knees if she had to. Anything to make him stay. But she couldn't move, couldn't speak.

"I'm not the man for you, Mariah." The hushed whisper of his voice slid along her throat like a caress. "You deserve someone who'll promise to love you forever, and will keep that promise. A man who'll work these fields from sunup to sundown and never complain. A man . . . who doesn't mind the picket fence."

She gazed up at him, knowing her eyes glittered with all the aching, desperate love in her heart, and unable to change it. "Maybe . . . with you . . ."

He shook his head, and the gentleness of the action made her feel almost sick. "Only you can make yourself leave this farm, and you're not ready, are you?"

She looked away.

"It's nothing to be ashamed of, Mariah." He moved closer, brushed a lock of hair from her tear-dampened cheek. She couldn't help herself, she leaned into his touch, seeking the warmth of it. "It's part of what makes you so special. You never let go, never forget, never say good-bye. But . . . I don't want that from a woman. I *want* good-byes."

She let out her breath and pulled away from him. Her whole body sagged at the finality of his words. "I know that, Matt. I guess I've always known it."

"I never lied to you."

She squeezed her eyes shut. Even now, when he was breaking her heart, she couldn't help loving him, wanting him.

"That doesn't help much," she answered.

"I left you my articles. They're all I have."

She swallowed hard, fighting a surge of bitterness. "That should keep me warm at night."

He touched her chin and forced her to look up at him. Reluctantly she opened her eyes.

He gazed down at her, his eyes solemn. "Would it help if I told you I loved you?"

Mariah's whole world seemed to tilt. For the first time she felt a stab of pure, white-hot anger at his leaving. Without even thinking, she brought her hand up to slap his face. At the last second, she stopped herself and forced her hand back to her side. Her eyes locked with his. "No, Matt." She pushed the words up her throat. "That wouldn't help at all."

They were the last words she said to him before he turned and walked out of her life.

Mad Dog leaned back against the vibrating wall of the boxcar and drew his sore legs to his chest. Beside him lay a new notebook, its pages fluttering in the fast-moving air. The pages were white and empty; their blankness mocked him. No matter how many times he tried, he couldn't seem to write. Nothing interested him or fired his passion or made him care. He felt strangely dead inside.

A sigh escaped his cracked, bleeding lips. He banged his head back against the slatted wall.

He curled his arms around his bent knees and hugged himself against the bitter cold. But it was a wasted effort. The weather bit through his tattered coat and gnawed on his flesh.

Winter had come with a vengeance this year, blanketing the world in a cape of icy white, turning the empty boxcars into chilly coffins. He sighed long and slow. His breath hung in the air for a second, then dissipated.

He felt like hell. He was cold, hungry, and tired. He hadn't had a decent meal in the week since he left Lonesome Creek. There was no work to be found in frozen America in this year of panic. And damn little charity.

Years ago, when he'd first started riding the rails, it had seemed romantic; stowing away in empty boxcars, outsmarting the railroad workers, making camp wherever he wanted, fighting the local strongmen at every county fair between San Francisco and New York. Then, he'd felt free.

Now he felt . . . different. Where before the rails seemed to go everywhere, they now seemed to go nowhere at all. His life was without romance or excitement or purpose. Just a series of endless, hopeless hours spent in freezing boxcars, riding from one unwelcoming little town to the next.

He wiped his eyes with hands that were black with dirt and scooted back into the car. Curling into a warmth-conserving ball, he closed his eyes and tried to sleep. Tried and failed.

Cursing softly, he rubbed his aching eyes and let his head bang back against the wall again.

For the first time in his life, he knew what it meant to miss someone, miss her so badly, you ached. He'd grieved for his mother, but that was different. Death was a loss that, with time, slid into memory.

Not so with Mariah. Every day he missed her more.

She was out there, a warm, living, breathing presence. When he closed his eyes, he saw her smile; when the coldness of winter touched his flesh, he remembered her warmth; when the silence enfolded him, endless and unbroken, he heard her laughter.

She was probably at the stove right now, cooking supper, the mouth-watering aroma of stewing meat seeping from the oven, filling the kitchen. Jake would be behind her, setting the table.

Christ, he could almost hear the quiet clinking of silverware and the muted music of their voices.

The house . . . Mariah . . . Jake . . . they were all back there, warm and cozy and welcoming. . . .

But that wasn't what he wanted, he reminded himself for the thousandth time since leaving. He wasn't a man who cared for "cozy" or wanted safety. He loved this life, out here all alone, going wherever he wanted, doing whatever he felt like. He'd always loved it. He needed his freedom like other men needed air.

It was just taking longer to get over them than he'd thought. But he *would* get over them. Pretty soon—any day now—these little quirks of longing would start to fade, and he'd be back to his old self.

Any day now.

He picked up his pen and notebook again and stared down at the cold, white page. Without thinking, he started to write something. When he looked down at what he'd written, he felt a chill that went clear through to his spine. There was only one word on the paper.

Mariah.

He threw the pen across the car, heard it hit the wall with a tinny crack and tumble to the floor.

It was only a matter of time before this idiocy would end and he'd forget Mariah. Soon he'd be back to his old self, writing articles, drinking tequila, screwing whores, and laughing.

Any day now.

It was three full weeks before Jake found the courage to tell Mariah the truth.

They were sitting on the porch swing, as they did every night after supper. Twilight lay in a heavy purple blanket across the farm. Stars glittered in the darkness, cast a million shimmering reflections on the new layer of snow.

He cast a surreptitious sideways glance at her.

She was sitting hunched over, her hands curled in her lap. Pale-faced, sad-eyed, she stared out across the land. He knew that she was searching the fields, waiting for Mad Dog to return.

"I think he loved you," he said softly.

There was a long, quiet moment, and then slowly she nodded. "So do I, Jake."

They lapsed back into a familiar silence. He dug deep for the courage to say what needed to be said. "My mama loved him, too."

She turned to him, surprised. "What?"

Jake tried to smile. "I'm his son."

She seemed for a moment to stop breathing. Her eyes widened. "Does he know?"

He nodded. "He asked me to go with him when he left."

A sad smile shaped her lips. "That sounds like him. Why didn't you?"

He gazed steadily at her. "I . . . I guess I thought you were as much a mother as he is a father."

"Oh, Jake . . ." She breathed his name, too moved by his simple words to say more.

"He'll be back."

She shook her head, dashed away tears with the back of her hand. "No, honey, he won't be back."

"I'm not just saying that. I've gotten to know him. He'll be back."

She gave him a fragile smile, but didn't say anything.

Jake wouldn't give up so easily. "He'll be back." He said the words over and over again, trying really hard to make himself believe them.

Two short, sharp blasts of the train's horn roused Mad Dog from a restless, dreamless sleep. He blinked blearily and pushed away from the cold, shuddering boxcar wall.

Running dirty fingers through his equally dirty hair, he sat up and glanced outside. The countryside whipped past him in a freezing white blur. He had no idea where he was; the landscape looked like Texas, or Arizona, or New Mexico—any of a dozen places he'd been in the last few weeks. The days and nights were beginning to blur together in his mind, merging into a hazy, forgettable collage of snow-covered towns and empty train cars.

Jesus, it was cold. He rubbed his hands together and blew into them, trying to create the momentary illusion of warmth.

The horn blared again; its piercing wail hovered for a split second in the frosty air, then melted into the wheezing chugs of the locomotive and disappeared. Giant iron wheels locked and screeched, grinding and bumping along the tracks as the engine began to slow down.

The train's speed decreased, and the whipping air faded into a gentle, snow-scented breeze. Without the wind, the pungent smell of the boxcar became overpowering. Old horse dung, musty burlap . . . human sweat.

Mad Dog winced. Christ, he needed a bath. He tugged on the wiry hair at his chin, and stared outside. Before he knew it, he was thinking about Lonesome Creek again.

Mariah.

Her name came to him on the breeze, winging through his mind like a breath of fresh air. He'd done that a lot lately, thought of Mariah and Jake and the farm. It was strange; all his life he'd thought about where he was going. Every new town was like an unopened Christmas gift, a treasure just waiting to be found. But lately things were different. He was thinking more about where he'd been and what he'd left behind. And more and more, that place, that time, felt like the unopened present.

He sighed, shoving his hand through his hair again. He'd never done that before, looked back, and he didn't like it.

He'd done the right thing. Of course he had. Sooner or later, he'd forget Mariah. He always forgot women. It was one of his gifts.

That and offending people.

The memory of their conversation came at him out of the blue, surprising him with its bittersweet punch.

Irritated, he grabbed hold of his bag and clutched his hat to his head. With a holler, he jumped off the slow-moving train, landed hard. Pain ricocheted up his legs and lodged in his knees.

"Jesus Christ," he cursed, bending over until the pain passed. Then, slowly, he straightened.

And found himself on the outskirts of Albuquerque.

He smiled. "Well, I'll be damned." Albuquerque. It was one of his favorite towns. There was a hell of a tavern here, and the prettiest little whore on the whole line.

This'll clear your head, he thought with a smile. Now, finally, he'd start to forget the only woman he'd ever remembered in the first place.

He strolled through the thin layer of new, airy snow, kicking it as he walked down Main Street. It was a quiet day for Albuquerque; no people running through the square, no Indians selling their crafts along the boardwalk. He walked through the new section of town and into the old.

As he neared the Tip 'Em Back saloon, familiar noises and smells spilled into the street, drawing him in, welcoming him in the way this town had a dozen times before. He tilted back his hat and pushed through the swinging half doors.

And was thrust into the seedy, smoking tavern. He coughed, blinking hard to see through the thick layer of gray haze that coated the room. From somewhere came the musical thumping of hard hands on a tinny piano. The clattering din rose above the boiling cacophony of raised voices, laughter, and hacking coughs.

He let the door swing shut behind him. The smoke greeted him like an old friend. Familiar smells assaulted his senses, reminded him that he had been away for a while. The sharp tang of tobacco, the musty odor of a place that hadn't been aired out in years, and the pungent stench of human sweat and dirty clothes.

It was raucous and loud, jam-packed with people who didn't ask names and didn't care where you were from. Just the kind of place Mad Dog had always belonged.

He tossed his bag into the corner and watched it land. Then he crammed his hands in his pockets and ambled to the long oak bar.

He was halfway there when a male voice boomed above the melee. "Jee-sus Christ, it's Mad Dog Stone back from the dead!"

Mad Dog glanced up and saw old Freddy Tomlinson still tending bar.

Freddy grinned, showing off a full set of yellow, rabbit-large teeth. "Hell, Stone, I figured you died."

Mad Dog sidled up to the bar and sat down on the cracked, painted stool. "You shoulda known better than that, Freddy. Only the good die young."

Freddy laughed hard, his hand pressed against his wobbling girth. "Yeah, you're right there." He slapped a wet rag on the bar and started sloshing it back and forth.

Mad Dog grinned. "You gonna make me ask? What's the point of bein' a regular if the bartender can't read your mind?"

Freddy tossed the towel down. It landed with a moist *thwack* and slid toward Mad Dog. Turning, Freddy grabbed a bottle of tequila and a shot glass from the mirrored shelves behind him and clanked them down in front of Mad Dog. Then he went back to wiping the bar.

Mad Dog frowned at the shot glass. Had they always

been dirty? He couldn't remember. He'd never even thought about it before, never wondered. Never cared.

The realization that he cared now made him angry. What the hell difference did it make if the glass had a little dust or dirt on it? Who cared?

He curled his fingers around the tequila bottle and poured himself a healthy shot. The pungent, eye-watering scent of the alcohol floated to his nostrils. He tipped the drink back and downed it in a single swallow.

Then he poured himself another.

He leaned back in the chair and stretched out his legs, glancing around him. The place was filled with familiar faces. Men hunched over dirty tables, playing poker. Painted women standing alongside them, cheering for whoever paid them the most money. Cards snapped on wooden tables, chips clattered together, men cursed.

It was too goddamn loud in here.

He frowned at the thought. He'd never thought saloons were too noisy or too smoky or too anything. Everywhere else had seemed dull and boring in comparison. But now, sitting here alone at the bar, sipping bad tequila, he found that he missed the quiet. . . .

He shook his head, disgusted. "Jesus Christ, Mariah, are you going to ruin *this* for me, too?"

Somewhere, a woman shrieked. "Mad Dog Stone, as I live and breathe!"

Mad Dog winced and glanced toward the wide stairway. Martha—or was it Matilda?—was shoving her way through the prostitutes and patrons on the steps, making her jostling, shrieking way to the bar. She half ran the last ten feet and came up beside him, breathing hard.

She smiled down at him, a practiced, pretty smile that for some reason set his teeth on edge. She fluttered her heavily kohled eyes and pressed a hand to her heaving cleavage. "Well, my, my," she sighed, dragging her tongue along her painted lower lip. "I was beginnin' to wonder if you forgot me."

Mad Dog frowned up at her. He'd slept with this woman a dozen times over the years, and he'd always had a hell of a time. He'd always thought she was pretty in a loud, overblown sort of way. But now he saw her as she really was. A young woman aged before her time by booze and a bad life.

"Buy a girl a drink?" she purred, patting her bleached blond hair.

"Sure." He shoved the bottle at her.

She frowned prettily. "No, thanks. That stuff makes me puke."

Mad Dog smiled in spite of himself, remembering. "Yeah, it has that effect on some women."

You shouldn't compare me to other women.

I didn't know it was important to be the first to throw up on someone.

The woman—Margaret?—touched him. "It's been a while, Mad Dog. Where you been hidin' out?"

He took a drink, let it linger for a second on his tongue before he swallowed. "I wasn't hidin' anywhere. I was just—" *Home.* The thought stunned him, confused him so badly that for a moment he couldn't speak.

"Just where?"

He shrugged, pushing the thought away. He didn't

want a home, didn't want to think he had one. He *liked* his life on the road, goddamn it. He loved it. "Nowhere. So how've you been?"

"Fine." She pressed against him, rubbed her satin skirt against his thigh in a slow, erotic invitation.

It left him cold. She smelled of old sweat and cheap perfume, of tawdry back rooms and hasty couplings.

"You wanna go up to my room?" she whispered throatily against his ear. Her gloved hand dove beneath the table and settled between his legs, squeezing lightly.

He almost said yes without thinking. But when he looked up at her, into her sharp, painted face and emoticnless blue eyes, he knew he couldn't.

The realization shocked him. He didn't want her, and she didn't want him. Not really. They wanted . . . a connection. A time to pretend they felt something they didn't feel. Once, that hadn't mattered to Mad Dog. Hell, he'd *liked* that cold anonymity, enjoyed women who cared nothing for him and less for themselves. Women who asked nothing of him and didn't care if he forgot their names.

But he was different now. Mariah and what they shared had changed him. He knew the difference between sex and love—Jesus, the difference—and he couldn't go back to the old way anymore.

He looked away, unable to face her, and took another sip of tequila. "Sorry, M . . ."

"Millie," she said softly. There was a quiver of hurt in her voice he never would have noticed before.

"Sorry, Millie. Not this time."

She sagged beside him, dropped an elbow on the table and stared at him. "You find yourself a woman, Stone?"

He couldn't answer.

She tossed back a shot of tequila and shuddered, wiping her mouth on the back of her sleeve. "If you have, and you care enough about her to stay away from me, then what the hell are you doin' here on Christmas night?"

Her jerked his head up. For the first time, he noticed the dying, empty tree leaning in the corner behind the bar. And the music. That tinny piano was banging out a staccato version of "O Holy Night."

Millie's face softened into an honest smile. "You didn't know?"

He shook his head. "Huh-uh."

She patted him on the back and turned to leave. "Well, Mad Dog, Merry Christmas. I'd best get back to work."

Mad Dog barely heard her good-bye. He stared into the mirror behind the bar, seeing his shaggy, unkempt appearance, and wondered what Jake and Mariah were doing right now. He could imagine the house, decorated with ornaments and evergreen, smelling of turkey and dressing and pumpkin pie. He could hear their laughter and the quiet rustling of paper as they opened their gifts.

He stared accusingly at his reflection. *What the hell are you doing here, alone, drinking, and dirty? You have a place to go. You have a home. . . .*

He took a burning gulp of tequila, right from the bottle. "Holy shit." He backhanded the moisture from his mouth. What was he thinking?

He couldn't go back.

Jake would want you to come back.

He tried not to be romanced by the notion. But once he'd thought about Jake, he felt himself being reeled in. He could be a father, for Christ's sake. A _father_.

He'd missed so much of his son's life already, but he didn't have to miss it all. He could be there to watch Jake grow to manhood, be there to watch him fall in love and have children of his own.

"Jesus . . ." He sighed and shook his head, surprised at how compelling those words were, how goddamn appealing.

But there was Mariah to think about. He loved her, loved her as he'd never loved any other woman. He knew that; he'd known it when he left her. He thought he'd forget, thought those feelings would fade into the fabric of his footloose life and be forgotten, but that hadn't happened. Instead, he remembered. Every moment of every day, he remembered. When he touched something soft, he thought of her skin; when he touched something rough, he thought of the overlaundered linsey-woolsey she always wore. When he smelled vanilla or lavender or plain old soap, he thought of her. When he looked into green eyes, he remembered brown.

Not brown.

He smiled at the memory and wondered how in the hell he'd been able to leave her. How had he been so stupid, so incredibly blind?

But he knew the answer. It was the same one that kept him from turning away from the bar and heading back to Lonesome Creek right now. She loved him, he was sure of that, and she'd forgive him if he returned. But could he stay?

That was the killer, the question that kept his butt planted on the barstool. He'd never made an honest commitment in his life. Not one. And this one was for keeps.

If he went back, he could never leave again.

"Shit," he cursed, reaching for the bottle and drawing it toward him. He couldn't imagine such a thing. Couldn't imagine getting a job, living on the farm behind that idiotic picket fence, knowing every day where he'd go to bed and where he'd wake up.

With Mariah.

He groaned at the thought and took another dribbling drink, then slammed the bottle down on the bar.

If he went back, he could never leave again.

Shit.

Chapter Twenty-six

Mariah stared at the box in her lap. Tears stung her eyes and slipped down her cheeks, splashing on the pale ivory of her drawers. She eased the lid back from the box and set it beside her, then peeled back the protective layer of wrinkled white linen.

The gown lay just as she had left it exactly a year ago, folded in perfect lines, the high lace collar startlingly white against the rich burgundy velvet of the bodice. She reached out, brushed the delicate lace with her fingertip. It felt frothy and light and feminine; so unlike everything she'd worn for the past fifteen years. A row of round, mother-of-pearl buttons marched down from the throat to the waist and disappeared into a pleated white satin belt.

Sadness filled her, but it was bittersweet, with a tang of remembered happiness. This had been the last Christmas gift she'd ever given her mother. She remembered choosing it with care, poring over dozens and dozens of catalog pages until she found exactly the right one. A gown with heart.

She pulled the dress gently from its box. The burgundy velvet caught the light and shimmered like a glass of rich wine, spilling in soft waves across her lap.

She shoved the box aside and stood up. Holding the gown up to her, she studied her reflection in the mirror and smiled. The rich burgundy hue contrasted with the milky paleness of her cheeks and set off her brown eyes.

Not brown.

The memory came at her unexpectedly. She stared at herself in the mirror, seeing the glitter of tears in her eyes, but, surprisingly, she didn't feel a drenching wave of sadness.

She felt . . . loss, perhaps. Or a quiet sorrow at what might have been.

"Oh, Matt," she sighed, shaking her head.

He was gone, and he wasn't coming back. For weeks she'd put off thinking about that, realizing the truth of it. But now, standing here in front of the mirror, staring into her own eyes, she couldn't deny it any longer.

He was gone, and he wasn't coming back.

It was strange, really, how the realization made her feel. She should have been crushed, desperate. Two years ago—hell, two months ago—she would have been. But somehow, sometime, in the past weeks she'd grown up. It still hurt. She still missed him—she probably always would. But she could live with her past now, and go on. It wasn't like before, with Stephen. Then she'd been sixteen and unable to face reality. Now she was older, wiser, and she was strong enough to survive. She didn't need Mad Dog. She loved him, missed him sometimes so much she ached for him. But she didn't need him.

He'd taught her to say good-bye.

She turned away from the mirror and slipped out of her baggy brown dress. Tossing it aside, she put on the glorious Christmas dress and tied the wide white ribbon around her waist, cinching it tight. The velvet bodice fell in loose, blousy waves over her breasts and tucked into her waist, then cascaded to the floor in undulating sheets of fabric.

She quickly brushed the curly hair away from her face and tied it at her neck with Jake's frayed pink ribbon. She gave her cheeks a quick pinch for color, then hurried down the stairs.

The kitchen was filled with holiday scents—sugar-glazed ham, spiced apple cider, and pecan pie. She walked through the room, glancing quickly at the jams, jellies, pickles, potatoes, vegetables, and breads that sat crowded together in the center of the table.

Clasping her hands together, she strolled to the parlor to wait for Jake. The small room was wreathed in flickering light and draped in evergreen. In the corner, on a red-cloth covered table, sat the small Christmas tree, its boughs weighted down with spun-glass angels, gilded apples, glazed cherries, sugar plums, and twinkling with candlelight. Behind it, the window rippled with reflections.

"Hi, Mariah."

She turned and saw Jake standing in the doorway. He was wearing a pair of Rass's old dress trousers, altered to fit him, and a stark white button-up shirt with black suspenders. A poorly knotted necktie hung at an odd angle from his collar. His coppery hair was slicked back from his forehead, and lay curled in an uncontrollable flip beneath his ears.

Her heart squeezed at the sight of him. He looked so handsome and grown-up and uncertain, standing there, awaiting her approval, with the tiny razor nicks on his cheeks.

"You look handsome."

He beamed at her. "So do you."

He walked up to her, smiling. She looped her arm through his and drew him close. Wordlessly they crossed the room and stared out the window, waiting. Always waiting.

Mariah felt him lean slightly toward her, and she understood. They were doing everything right this year, trying hard, but the ghosts of Christmases past were all around them, clustered in every room, lingering in every activity. This was the first Christmas without parents for both of them, and everything they did hurt.

Mariah stared through the glass, seeing but not seeing the glowing circlets of light cast against the pane by the tree's candles. Outside, the farm was a series of shadowy shapes, without form or substance. Moonlight streamed through the leafless limbs of a hundred skeletal apple trees, turning the snowy landscape into a powdery lake of crushed diamonds. The world was cold and still.

"He isn't coming back." Mariah said the words softly, wishing she could take away the hurt they'd cause.

Jake sighed. "Yeah, I know that."

"I'm glad you're here, Jake," she said quietly, feeling a tiny catch in her heart.

He cleared his throat. "Yeah, me, too."

The moment started to spiral into a familiar, quiet sadness, but Mariah refused to let it. She forced a smile and cleared her throat. "Well, how about we eat some of that fabulous Christmas supper?"

He turned to her, slowly pulling his arm away from her. "I have a present for you first."

She glanced at the tree. "You do?"

"It's not there. Come on." He led her through the well-lit house and onto the darkened porch. Beyond, the world was a midnight blue smear of shapes and forms, all of it limned by the golden-white light of a full winter moon.

He took her arm and led her down the creaking steps. She stepped carefully into the crusty, ankle-deep snow. The cold air stung her lungs and brought tears to her eyes. Her breath clouded the frosty air for a magical moment, then disappeared.

"Do you notice anything different?"

Mariah heard the hesitant pride in his voice and she smiled, glancing around the farm. "Well, the barn is still standing, the bunkhouse looks the same, the woodpile's just as high, the—" She gasped. "Oh, my God, Jake . . ."

"I took it down."

She took a cautious step forward, her gaze riveted to the end of the walkway. The picket fence was gone. That whole corner of the property was wide open. An unbroken, pristine layer of snow rolled from the house, over the road, and into forever. There was nothing to stop it.

She stared at the empty space where the fence had

been and felt a dizzying mix of emotions. Fear, exhilaration, relief.

Jake looked up at her, his cheeks pink from the cold. "I didn't want you to look at it every day."

At his simple words, so caring and understanding, Mariah felt an emotion unlike any she'd ever known. Deep and drenching, it consumed her, filled her with an impossible, light-headed warmth. "I never even thought about taking it down," she said quietly, wondering why she hadn't.

"I thought maybe if it wasn't there . . ."

She gazed down at him, seeing hope and fear in his green eyes. For a split second, she saw herself as he must see her. A thirty-four-year-old spinster who ached for a man who didn't love her and couldn't leave her own farm. And she was ashamed. Tears filled her eyes. She brushed a wayward lock of hair from his forehead; her fingers lingered lovingly at his temple. "What did you think?" she asked in a halting, throaty voice.

He swallowed nervously. "I thought maybe . . . if it wasn't there, you could someday walk past it."

Walk past it. The unexpected words lodged in her heart. She lifted her chin and stared at the snowy emptiness that stretched beyond her farm and melted into the foothills in the distance. There was no fence there anymore; no fence to stop her, no latch to lift, no gate to push open. Nothing to remind her every day of her irrational, stupid fear.

She tried to imagine leaving the farm. Fear spilled through her, icy cold and threatening. Sweat broke out on her forehead, itched against her scalp. But it was a different kind of fear, softer, without the suffocating, debilitating sense of panic.

"Maybe I could." She said the words quietly, unaware that she'd even been about to speak.

The thought filled her with an incredible sense of hope. For the first time in fifteen years, she really believed it was possible. Not easy, perhaps, but possible. The world didn't scare her as much anymore.

If she practiced diligently, took a few baby steps forward every day, and truly let herself believe, maybe she could do it. A smile tugged at her mouth. "Maybe . . ."

Jake turned to her. "I love you, Mariah. Merry Christmas."

She turned to him, gazed down at him through the stinging curtain of her tears. Pulling him into her arms, she gave him a fierce, loving hug. "I love you, too, Jake. Merry Christmas."

Mad Dog saw the farm in the distance and stopped. The boxy farmhouse sat like a perfect tooth in the center of endless snow-covered fields. Dozens of skeletal apple trees fanned out from the house, their bare limbs draped in elegant white.

For the first time since he left, he felt warm. A smile curved his lips. He was home.

Then the smile slid slowly downward. Something was wrong. He glanced around, cataloging the orchard, the house, the barn. Everything looked the same, but something felt . . . different.

The fence was gone.

He smiled again, feeling a surge of pride for Mariah. She'd done it. Jesus Christ, she'd taken down the white picket fence. He could see the repetitive depressions in the snow where the slats had been. It was the best welcome he could have imagined.

He reslung his bag over his back and strolled toward the house. There was a spring in his step that had been missing for weeks. Excitement thudded with every beat of his heart. He couldn't wait to see his family again, couldn't wait to be welcomed back into their loving arms.

"Mad Dog?"

He grinned and glanced up. Jake stood beside the bunkhouse, carrying a load of firewood. "Hiya, kid. I told you I'd be back."

Jake's mouth dropped open. The firewood slid from his arms and thumped into the snow at his feet. "Might be back," he muttered, staring at Mad Dog through huge, round eyes. "You said you *might* be back."

He started to make a flip comeback, then changed his mind. He'd come a long way to tell Jake something. He didn't want to ruin the moment by being his normal, careless self. "I missed you."

"You did?" Jake's voice was a breath of wonder.

He smiled. "Yeah. It surprised me, too." He dropped his bag and waved Jake over. "Come here."

Jake moved cautiously forward, crunching quietly through the snow. About a foot away, he stopped.

Mad Dog felt a moment's disappointment. He pushed it away. He wanted to reach out and squeeze his son's shoulder, wanted it so damn bad, he hurt inside. But he didn't do a thing, didn't move. He wanted to take this thing slow, wanted to make everything right so it would last.

Jake looked painfully young and vulnerable right now, standing there, his arms at his sides, his face scrunched against the bright winter sun. Mad Dog knew how his son felt, remembered waiting for his own father's return with an aching sense of desperation.

"I'm sorry, Jake," he said quietly, feeling a sharp stab of regret. The words were so small, nothing really, and yet they were all he had to offer. That, and a lifetime of commitment and love to back them up.

Jake didn't say anything.

"I shouldn't have left you. It just happened so damned fast—not that that's an excuse—but I didn't know what to do. I was scared shitless of the responsibility."

Jake took a hesitant step forward. "What changed your mind?"

"You're my son." Mad Dog's throat squeezed up at the simple words. "You can't imagine how it makes me feel to say that, Jake. Once I started thinking about it, about you, I couldn't stay away." He looked away. "God, I've missed so much of your life . . . I don't want to miss any more."

Jake made a sobbing, choked sound and launched himself forward. Mad Dog grabbed his son, held him in a fierce, desperate hug.

"I missed you, Mad Dog," Jake said, clinging to his father's neck.

Mad Dog drew back slowly, stared down into Jake's teary eyes. "I don't suppose you'd want to call me dad?"

Jake gave him a watery, quivering smile. "I've waited for that all my life."

"I wish I'd known, Jake," he said softly, realizing for the first time that it was true. He wished he'd known about his son a long time ago. He liked to believe he would have changed, would have stayed.

"Me, too, Dad."

Dad. At the quietly spoken word, Mad Dog felt something in his heart swell almost painfully. He swallowed hard, fighting a surge of raw emotion. "I'd best go see Mariah," he said in a thick voice. "You know, sweep her off her feet and make this family official."

Jake winced. "Mariah's . . . changed."

He grinned. "I can see that by the missing fence. Jesus, I've missed her."

Jake chewed on his lower lip. "I'll just stay here and wait. . . ."

Mad Dog laughed. "Probably a good a idea, Jake. Last time I surprised her, she coldcocked me with the butt of a shotgun."

"I wouldn't rule it out this time."

Mad Dog grinned at Jake's joke. Tossing his bag toward the bunkhouse, he looked up at the house. An idiotic smile curved his mouth.

God, he couldn't wait to see her, to taste her. Ever since he left, his arms had felt empty and lifeless. He needed Mariah to fill them and make him feel complete.

He tousled Jake's hair. "Seeya in a minute, kid. I got some courtin' to do."

"Good luck, Dad."

"I won't need luck. I've got love." Still grinning, Mad Dog raced across the snowy yard and bounded up the sagging porch steps. He turned the knob quietly and went inside.

The house welcomed him in the way it always had, with warmth and comfort and quiet. He heard the crackling sputter of a fire in the sitting room, and the hissing pop of cooking bacon.

He closed the door gently and moved toward the kitchen.

Mariah was in the corner, kneeling in front of the icebox. It took him a moment to notice that she wasn't wearing brown. Her hair was drawn back in a loosely woven braid that brushed the floor behind her, its tail caught up in a frayed pink ribbon. Her dress was pale blue, sprigging with tiny yellow flowers.

She stood up and turned around.

He leaned casually against the doorframe and crossed his arms, smiling at her. "Hiya, darlin'."

"Matt . . ." she breathed. The yellow crockery bowl in her hands crashed to the floor and shattered.

"I'm back."

She stared at him, her mouth parted, her cheeks brightened with spots of color. For a second, her gaze was liquid and warm and welcoming. Then she stiffened. Her face hardened into that austere, disapproving pinch he knew so well. "No, you're not."

"Huh?"

"Good comeback, Matt." She dried her hands on a soggy dish towel and stepped backwards. "I said, you're not back. You're here. There's a difference."

He frowned. "I'm back."

She tried to smile, but her eyes were cold and wary, untrusting. "That's wonderful for Jake. He's missed you. The bunkhouse will be ready on Saturday, as usual. Until then, you may use your bedroll."

She's mad, that's all. You can handle a riled-up woman. Mad Dog gave her his best sexy grin and moved toward her, looping his thumbs through the fraying waistband of his Levi's. "How 'bout you, darlin', did you miss me?"

"I missed you," she said tightly, "for a while."

He halted, stunned. "And you *stopped*?"

She smiled. "And I grew up." Her eyes met his, and this time there was no wariness in her gaze, no coldness. Only a solemn honesty. "You changed me, Matt. First by coming into my life, and then by leaving it. I've learned I can take care of myself."

Mad Dog felt off balance, unsure of himself. He'd thought she'd throw herself at him and smother him with kisses until he couldn't breathe. He'd envisioned it just that way a thousand times, imagined their hot, wet, hard reunion. It had never once occurred to him that there wouldn't be a reunion at all.

The thought made him feel queasy, lost. He sighed, ran a hand through his shoulder-length hair. He couldn't have come this far only to lose the only woman he'd ever loved. Ever would love.

He licked his dry lips and looked at her. This time there was no cocky grin, no sexy smile. There was just pain and honesty and hope. "I want to change your life again," he said softly, "by staying."

She flinched. "Then stay in the bunkhouse."

"You don't understand."

"No, *you* don't understand. You . . . ." Her voice cracked. Tears filled her eyes and she looked away. "You broke my heart. . . . I don't want you anymore."

Mad Dog felt her pain. Regret and shame coiled

around his heart, squeezing until it hurt to breathe. He dug deep in his pocket for the cheap tin ring he'd bought in Albuquerque. He pulled it out, dusted it off, and wished to hell it were gold. "I love you, Mariah, and I want to marry you. I want you and Jake and me to be a real, honest-to-God family."

She didn't look at him or the ring. "Ha."

"I . . . I stopped off at the *Lonesome Creek Ledger* and got a writing job."

She gasped and looked at him. "You got a job?"

He smiled. "Writin' articles twice a week. I figure that'll help us pay some bills and still give me time to manage the orchard."

She clasped her hands and looked away again. "Oh."

He felt a moment's weakness, a hesitation on her part. "Marry me."

She closed her eyes and breathed heavily, then slowly opened them and looked at him. "No. I can't trust you to stay."

"Tell me you don't love me, Mariah. Tell me that and I'll leave right now. Otherwise, I'll stay here a hundred years, proposing to you every morning—until you *do* trust me."

Mariah. A shiver of longing moved through Mariah at the way he said her name, so softly, gently. Memories besieged her, drew her reluctantly back into the way she used to feel about him.

Sweet Lord, she'd missed him.

She clutched the sink and forced herself not to move, but the heat of his gaze, the warmth of his smile, burned through her, made her feel liquid and rubbery inside.

"Oh, God, Matt." She sighed, feeling the sting of tears. She couldn't lie and tell him she didn't love him. The words would be impossible to form. She loved him as much as her own life, needed him as desperately as she needed air to breathe.

He moved toward her, came within a hairsbreadth of touching her, but he didn't. He just stared down at her, gazing at her through painfully honest eyes. "Have I ever lied to you, Mariah?"

"N-No."

He touched her chin, a feather-stroke of a caress that set off a tremble in her stomach. "I'll stay," he whispered, and she saw the moisture in his eyes.

She looked up at him, into the quiet desperation in his eyes, the lingering sadness in his look, and she was lost. She couldn't turn him away, couldn't say she didn't love him. Not if he broke her heart a hundred times, a thousand. The days of protecting herself were long over. She was stronger now, strong enough to reach for what she wanted. Strong enough to let herself believe in him, in herself, in love.

She gave him a fragile, loving smile and started to cry. "Oh, Matt," she breathed, opening her arms to him, "what took you so long?"

Author's Note

Sometimes a writer stumbles across a book that's difficult, perhaps even painful, to write. This was just such a book for me. So I'd like to take this occasion to thank some very special people.

My brother, Kent, and my sister, Laura, who helped me through the sadness and help me still.

Benjamin and Tucker, who make every day a miracle.

And my "other" family, the Hannahs and the Shields, who have faced so much tragedy this year with courage and hope.

Anna, Sharon and Burt ... this one's for you.

THE THINGS WE DO FOR LOVE $5.00 REBATE

Buy one copy of
THE THINGS WE DO FOR LOVE
by Kristin Hannah and receive a
$5.00 rebate!

Name: _____

Address: _____

City: _____

State or Canadian Province: _____ Zip: _____

Country: _____

Consumer: To receive your $5.00 rebate, simply purchase a copy of THE THINGS WE DO FOR LOVE, by Kristin Hannah, and send this completed form with the original, dated cash register receipt for the book to: Ballantine Books, Marketing Department, 1745 Broadway, New York, NY 10019. Offer ends on August 15th, 2004, and coupon with store receipt must be received by that date. Limit one coupon per customer. Not valid with any other offers. Multiple requests, mechanical reproductions, or facsimiles will not be honored. Reproduction, sale, or purchase of this coupon is prohibited. 18 U.S.C. Section 1341 and other mail fraud statutes apply to all redemptions. Ballantine Books reserves the right to reject any proofs or forms not deemed genuine. Offer valid in the United States and Canada (excluding the province of Quebec). Please allow 6-8 weeks for delivery.

MAIL-IN OFFER/MANUFACTURER'S COUPON EXPIRES: 8/15/04

*Subscribe to the new Pillow Talk
e-newsletter—and receive all these
fabulous online features directly in
your e-mail inbox:*

♥ Exclusive essays and other features by major romance
writers like Linda Howard, Kristin Hannah,
Julie Garwood, and Suzanne Brockmann

♥ Exciting behind-the-scenes news from
our romance editors

♥ Special offers, including contests to win signed
romance books and other prizes

♥ Author tour information, and monthly announce-
ments about the newest books on sale

♥ A Pillow Talk readers forum, featuring feedback
from romance fans...like you!

Two easy ways to subscribe:
Go to **www.ballantinebooks.com/PillowTalk**
or send a blank e-mail to
join-PillowTalk@list.randomhouse.com.

Pillow Talk—
the romance e-newsletter brought to you by
Ballantine Books